Live the
fairy tale!

Hugs,

ACKNOWLEDGEMENT

A special thanks goes out to Carolyn Williams, Donna Jeffrey, Franca Pelaccia, Vickie Marise, Mary Barone, Kelly Mueller, Janice Leyh, and Elise Rome. You each made this book wonderful in your own special ways. Finally, my thanks to Count Patrice de Vogüé, owner of Vaux-le-Vicomte, who personally took the time to answer my research questions about his beautiful 17th c. château.

DEDICATION

Please see the back of the book once you finish it! This important dedication contains a **SPOILER**.

Undone

A Fiery Tale

LILA DIPASQUA

Copyright © 2012 Lila DiPasqua

Copyedited by Linda Ingmanson

Cover design by
Hot DAMN DESIGNS
www.hotdamndesigns.com

ISBN: 978-0-9880350-1-0 (trade pbk.)
ISBN: 978-0-9880350-0-3 (e-book)

A HISTORICAL TIDBIT

The court of Louis XIV was as decadent as it was opulent. It was a time of high culture and corruption. Of elegance and excesses. The pursuit of sinful pleasures was a pastime. Sex, an art form. Louis was a lusty king. He and his courtiers were connoisseurs of the carnal arts.

It was during this wicked time period that Charles Perrault, the creator of *The Tales of Mother Goose*, first began writing down fairy tales—the folklore that had been passed on verbally for generations. It wasn't long before fairy tales became a highly fashionable topic of discussion in the renowned salons of Paris.

Female authors also tried their hand at this wonderful new genre. It was Charlotte-Rose de Claumont de La Force's 17th century fairy tale, *Persinette*, that would later inspire the Brothers Grimm to write *Rapunzel*.

Perhaps, just perhaps Mademoiselle de La Force was inspired by hearing stories about characters such as these…

Happy Reading!

Lila

Once upon a time, there was a woman who was shut away in a tower. It was said she'd been there for years. Rumored to be a prisoner of her own making. No one knew much about the mysterious beauty. Or the secrets she guarded. It was certain she'd live out her days cloistered. Yet one day, out of the forest, they say her prince appeared. One look at the lovely enchantress, and he was enthralled. Upon hearing her ethereal voice, he was undone… What happened next, you ask? Well, he scaled the tower and rescued the beauty, of course… Was that the end? No, my dearlings, that was only the beginning.

And what was to follow was the stuff of fairy tales…

CHAPTER ONE

1660
Just before midnight…

Sexual excess was known to alleviate tension. An evening of unbridled lust had a soothing effect on the mind as well as the body. But as Simon Boulenger struggled to maintain his grip on the window ledge—sharp stone cutting into his fingers—he felt anything but relaxed.

Muscles in his upper body corded as he scraped his boots against the stone wall, searching for a foothold. The full moon's silvery light illuminated his predicament.

His feet were too far from the ground below to simply let go and drop.

He grabbed hold of the closest tree branch. Satisfied with its sturdiness, he began his descent, branches and leaves brushing and scraping him along the way until he reached the lowest limb and dropped to the ground.

Definitely too bright a night for an amorous encounter with the beautiful wife of a high-ranking politician of the Republic of Genoa.

Brushing the dirt off his shirt, he slipped into the shadows where the stable boy waited with Simon's horse.

He'd paid the grimy mite to give a warning of two quick whistles at his mistress's window should Marco de Franco return inconveniently early, which he had. Simon's circumspection was born of necessity. Though the Republic of Genoa was a good distance from Spain, he always took precautions. The Genoese's loyalties were with the Spanish. And there were those who would pay handsomely for the capture of the man the Spanish called *El Demonio Negro*—the Black Demon.

The boy handed him the reins.

"*Bravo. Grazie,*" he said, as fluent in the language as any Italian in his employ.

Dropping more coins into the boy's dirty hand, he rode off, a slight smile tugging at the corners of his mouth. If Marco de Franco were to learn that his lovely wife had spent the last few hours in the throes of passion with the son of a French peasant, it would send the pompous fool reeling. It wasn't that de Franco cared if Francesca entertained lovers, for he was preoccupied with the pursuit of power and his own extensive extramarital affairs. But to learn she'd engaged in a carnal encounter with a lowly commoner would be too much for his arrogant sensibilities to digest.

As he negotiated the next bend in the road, Simon caught sight of his carriage in the distance. Moonlight glinted off its roof. His men were there waiting for him, just as he'd ordered. He slowed his horse, his smile disappearing.

The brief sojourn in the Republic of Genoa was over.

Time to face France.

And what awaited him there was far more perilous than a nocturnal liaison with a highborn lady.

He drew in a fortifying breath, and let it out slowly, mindful that he was still too far from his two men for them to notice.

After many months at sea, he'd returned to France three weeks ago to pay the Crown's share of his recent captured prizes from Spanish ships—never imagining what he'd find. Now those images haunted him. Guilt and anger were a constant clash inside him. And assuaging his torment with women and drink in Genoa had proven futile.

Reaching the carriage, Simon dismounted.

Paul took the reins from him. "Good evening, Captain," the young man said.

There was nothing bloody well good about this evening any longer. "Let us be on our way," he ordered, though it was the very last thing he wanted.

Inside the moving carriage, Simon's mood only darkened by the moment. *Merde...* They'd dangled his dream in front of him.

Then betrayed him.

He'd come a long way from the orphan rescued from starvation in the streets of a French fishing village. He was now the commander of a fleet of privateer ships for France, dressed and spoke like an aristocrat, and was at last wealthy.

But he was still not a noble. Or an official officer in the King's Navy.

His lifelong dream to elevate himself from his station of birth and obtain a respectable place in society was dead.

As dead as Thomas...

Tightening his jaw, he glanced out the window and watched as the darkened trees threaded past. He'd been a colossal fool. And now he was caught in a treacherous trap. How the hell was he to get out of this? He wanted out. He *had* to get out. But how do you stop dancing with the devil once you've sold him your soul?

The carriage stopped dead with a sharp lurch, Simon's shoulder bumping against the window frame. Instinctively, his hand shot to the hilt of his sword.

He jumped from its plush interior, sword drawn, battle-ready.

"I'm sorry, Captain." Paul leaped down. "It is one of the wheels. We will fix it quickly, sir, and be on our way." The young man raced around to the other side of the carriage to join the driver and the broken wheel.

The delay grated on Simon's already thin patience, his frustration churning inside him.

Before he could utter the profanity burning up his throat, a blow to his chest shot the air from his lungs and knocked him off his feet. The back of his head slammed against the ground, dazing him. He squeezed his eyes shut. His sword, still clutched in his hand, lay with him on the packed dirt.

As he drew air back into his lungs, awareness seeped into his senses. There was a body on top of him. Not just any body, but a soft one, with ripe breasts pressed to his chest—the unmistakable body of a full-grown woman.

She gasped near his ear and struggled to an upright position. He could feel the firmness of her thighs on either side of his hips, her hands shoving at his chest, and her lower body squirming against his groin.

Steadying himself against the pain at the back of his skull, he opened his eyes. She stilled. Her gray garb and shoulder-length headdress covered her entirely, leaving her face her only visible feature.

And it was *exquisite*.

The moon's silver light caressed her soft-looking skin, but it was her eyes that drew him. Although the night forbade him the ability to detect their true color, they were light, bright, and spectacular to behold. Her dark brows were delicately arched. Her cheekbones beautifully pronounced. And her mouth—*Dieu*. A hot current rushed through his veins as he stared at that lush mouth. Just the right fullness.

The kind of mouth sure to offer a man untold carnal bliss.

Her lips were parted. The sound of her quickened breaths burned in his ears. Inflaming him further.

Every bedazzling detail of her face and the erotic press of her lower body against his own seared into his senses.

Transfixed, he sat up slowly, his cock straining against his breeches. The heated reaction she effortlessly elicited from him was astounding. So was being suddenly knocked off his feet by a beautiful woman in an unattractive garb in the middle of the night.

Her eyes widened. She squirmed again and made to flee. The friction shot a bolt of sensations along his prick that reverberated all the way up his spine. He gripped her arms, stilling her, barely catching the groan that surged up his throat.

"Let go!" she demanded, threads of panic and anger in her tone.

He didn't want her to leave so soon, but he didn't wish to scare her, and so he slackened his grasp, knowing full well she was going to bolt.

Shoving hard at his chest, she bounded to her feet.

"Wait! What is your name?" The words tumbled from his mouth. But she ran through an open iron gate and disappeared behind a stone wall.

Reeling, Simon rose and walked to the gate, ignoring the astonished looks of his men who he noticed were now standing near the horses. He'd no idea how much they'd witnessed. Nor did he care.

Paul rushed toward him. "Captain? Is everything all right?"

Simon scanned the shadowy grounds for any sign of her. "Yes." *No.* She'd vanished. Yet she'd left him burning.

Utterly seduced.

He could see little. The umbrage of the trees hid much from view. What lunacy was this? How could such a bizarre encounter have stirred his blood this way?

Studying the stone barrier that ran parallel to the road as far as he could see, he wondered why she'd been out all alone at this hour of the night, and what such a captivating woman was doing hidden behind such a formidable wall.

"It is a convent, sir."

He turned to Paul. "Pardon?"

"A convent." He picked up Simon's sword and brought it to him. "The wheel can be fixed easily. We'll be on our way shortly."

The carriage was the furthest thing from his mind as he stood at the threshold of the convent grounds, scanning all visible windows and openings of the stony structure.

Ah, hell. He sheathed his sword. "Wait here."

*****

Heart pounding, Angelica pushed open the wooden door she'd left unlocked and rushed inside. With fumbling fingers, she secured the latch, then raced down the dimly lit corridors, causing each torchère she passed to flicker and dance.

Reaching the chapel, she halted abruptly.

It was empty.

She offered an instant prayer of thanks.

Not only had she made it back in time for the Third Vigil, but she'd escaped whatever might have befallen her at the hands of the man she'd just encountered outside.

The hour was late. The road was deserted. And men who wandered about at this time of night were best avoided.

Racing to return to the convent before she was expected in the chapel, she'd emerged from the thicket and hadn't seen the stranger, shrouded in shadow, until it was too late. She felt as though she'd collided with the stone wall that surrounded the convent instead of a man. Her chest still hurt.

She couldn't afford to be as careless as she'd been this night. She was always guarded. Always careful. Rarely did she leave the convent. For years, she'd embraced a cloistered existence in exchange for security.

However, tonight, unable to turn her back on a family in need, she'd let her conscience win out over her caution.

And run right into danger.

She placed her hand over her agitated heart, willing it to calm. She was safe now.

In a decade, *he* had still not found her. Nor would he ever.

As long as she remained within these protective walls, she was safe.

*****

Simon entered the convent through a partially open window.

Stealthily, he made his way down long corridors, each identical with torchères that offered little light and less warmth. There was no sign of life in the dismal labyrinth.

Turning another corner, he heard a faint noise in the distance.

A voice? No. It's singing. And it was incredibly beautiful. Compelling.

He moved toward it, then paused before a set of ornately carved wooden doors and listened. The singing had stopped.

He pulled open a door wide enough to spy a woman, standing all alone, her back to him, wearing the same gray garb as the moonlit angel he'd met outside.

Was it her?

The chapel was rich with mosaics adorning the walls and floor—a sharp contrast to the austere corridors outside. He slipped inside, finding himself in the shadows of the back corner.

Then it happened. A soft, haunting melody came from the woman, slowly rising, the crescendo building until it filled the chapel, her magnificent voice hitting him full measure with its power and enchantment. A performance unlike any he'd ever witnessed. For a moment, he was lost in it, all that had been weighing on his conscience and soul receding.

The chapel doors slammed open, startling him.

An older woman stood in the entrance, her expression grim. She marched toward the one whose voice had enthralled him.

His gaze shot back to the songbird. She'd turned to face the intruder.

Good Lord, it *was* her—the beauty in the moonlight. As breathtaking as he'd first thought her to be.

"Well, this is a surprise," the old nun said, her tone caustic. "You are actually early for the Hours for once."

"Indeed, I am, *Madre*." The beauty's silky voice rippled through him.

"I'm glad you heeded my words. I'll not tolerate you dashing in at the last moment any longer. Now, go take your place. The others will be here shortly."

"As you will," she responded, her manner regardful.

"Wait." The Mother Superior pulled a twig from the younger woman's garment. "What is this on your clothes?"

The moonlight beauty looked down at her garb. Small leaves and twigs had adhered to its coarse material. Smudges of dirt griming the fabric.

"Where have you been? I demand the truth!"

"Madre," his songbird responded calmly, in contrast to the near shrill of the other woman. "There was a matter that required my attention outside the convent, and I—"

"*Outside the convent?* At this hour? Against *the rules?*"

"Yes, it was a rather important, *urgent*, matter that—"

"How dare you sneak out! You may have been a favorite of the former Madre, but she is gone now. And I will curb your willful ways. You have your own disobedience to blame for *this*." She raised her arm.

It was then that Simon noticed the old nun held a dark walking stick. His stomach dropped.

The beauty's hand shot out. "Madre, allow me to explain—" she tried to reason.

But the words fell on deaf ears. The stick came down. He tore out of the shadows.

The beauty cried out when it slammed into her open palm, but somehow she managed to curl her fingers around it.

The Mother Superior gave a vicious yank on the cane, causing the beauty to lose her grip. And then her footing.

"Stop!" he yelled just as the next blow struck her with brutal force, knocking her to the floor. Hard.

Simon snatched the stick out of the nun's meaty hand, ignoring the old woman's gasp. He snapped the cane in two, then whipped the pieces across the room before turning his attention to the motionless beauty at his feet.

"Wh-Who are you?" the Mother Superior stammered, clearly astonished by his presence. "You…You are not permitted here!"

Sinking to his knee, Simon gently lifted the unconscious woman off the cold floor and rose. Her head lolled against his shoulder, giving him full view of her elegant profile.

Already an ugly welt was forming on her lovely cheek. Seeing the senseless injury ignited his ire. She felt warm and right in his arms. *Dieu.* Who was this woman whose face was as stunning as her voice?

"What are you doing?" the nun asked. "Put her down!"

Furious, he spun around to face the older woman. Fearful, she took a step back, then turned on her heels and ran from the chapel.

"Intruder!" she screamed. "Intruder! Ring the bells!"

This was bloody perfect. He'd never done a rash thing in his entire life. And now he was standing in a convent, holding an injured woman he didn't know. What the hell was he going to do with her?

As Simon took a step toward the door, three women dressed in similar bland garb appeared in the doorway. Upon seeing him, they shrieked, turned, and fled. He held in the expletives that resonated in his head. *Merde. Could this get any worse?*

A fourth woman appeared in the doorway then. Only she didn't run away. Instead, she raced straight to him. Her eyes were watery, and there were tear streaks on her cheeks, evidence that she'd been crying. Simon sensed that she'd somehow witnessed what had just transpired.

"She is injured. Where are you taking her, *signore*?" she asked.

The hell if he knew!

She grabbed his arm. "You must go," she said. "The men from the town will be here shortly, once they hear the bells."

The bells began to chime. Loudly.

Resonating.

Simon muttered a curse. He had no one to blame but himself and his prick for this outrageous disaster. His gaze returned to the beauty in his arms. He wanted to get her out of the convent, but to steal her away seemed as wrong as it seemed right.

"I will show you a quick way out," the woman continued, "but you must take me with you too."

"*What?* No!" He wasn't about to leave this convent with two women.

"Please, I must go with you…" Fresh tears welled from her dark eyes. "She is the only family I have."

The bells continued to toll. He couldn't stand here and argue the matter.

"Quickly, lead the way," he barked over the pealing bells. He'd allow her to come along for now and decide what to do with the two women later.

She turned and ran out of the chapel and into the corridor, with Simon on her heels.

"Bring her back here!" the Mother Superior screamed from the other end of the long hallway. "Gabriella! Stop! Do you hear me? By all that is holy, you will pay for what you are doing!"

The Mother Superior's words only hastened Gabriella's steps. She didn't even offer a backward glance and led him down more darkened corridors before she stopped at one of the wooden doors and opened it for him. He preceded her into the room.

Gabriella darted across the room to a shelf and removed a ring of keys from behind a clay jar, then rushed to the other door in the drab chamber. Her hands were quaking, and Simon worried she was too discomposed to open the lock. But she managed to slip the iron key into the keyhole and unlock it.

The door swung open. The moon's silver light flooded the room.

Wasting no time, they ran out the door.

The bells echoed in the darkened skies. Simon immediately spotted his carriage at the gate and headed straight for it. Paul hastened to open the carriage door at his approach.

Stepping into the carriage, Simon first laid the young woman gently across one of the seats. Then poked his head out and saw both Paul and Gabriella staring back at him. "Well, what are you waiting for?" he said to Paul.

The young man immediately jumped back up beside the driver.

Simon's gaze locked onto Gabriella. As she stood before him in her drab gray garb, he couldn't miss the silent plea in her eyes.

He sighed and extended a hand. "Get in." He yanked her up.

The carriage was on its way, full speed, Simon issuing orders out the window to his men.

The driver guided the carriage off the road, into the woods. Concealed by the foliage and trees, they waited. The men from the town would expect the intruder to be riding away from the convent in the opposite direction, yet Simon was headed straight for the town's waterfront, where his ship was in dock.

The sound of men on horseback grew increasingly loud until they finally thundered past.

When he was confident they were out of harm's way, Simon ordered the carriage to proceed, and then turned his attention to the moonlight beauty lying on the seat. Down on one knee, he moved his hands carefully over her.

"Wh-What are you doing, signore?" Gabriella asked, a little leery.

"I am checking for any bleeding or broken bones." Her body was soft and warm beneath his touch. He did his best to concentrate on her injuries, laboring to ignore the appeal of her form, which despite the layers of her shapeless clothing, his experienced hands could easily discern.

Mentally he chastised himself. These were the very sorts of thoughts that had landed him in this mess in the first place.

Carefully, he turned her face and saw the bruise and swelling on her cheek. A fresh wave of fury crested over him. He pulled off her headdress and tossed it aside. Chestnut-colored tresses spilled out— a mass of long, soft curls. He was suddenly seized with the urge to play with the silky locks, to try to awaken her by lightly teasing her with those luscious curls against her ivory skin.

Dieu, enough.

Simon turned to the other female, who watched him warily. Her features were pleasing in their own right.

"Your name is Gabriella?" He kept his voice gentle, having noted she was the type of woman who could spout tears with little provocation.

"Yes... Gabriella Santino." For all her previous heroics, her response was timid, and she spoke with eyes downcast.

"And this is your sister?"

"N-no, she is my dearest friend. No two sisters could love each other more."

"I see. What is her name?"

"Angelica."

"*Angelica*," he repeated, her name caressing his tongue as he looked back at the woman who lay motionless on the seat.

"Signore, though Angelica and I have not taken our vows and are not nuns, we aren't from distinguished families either. We...we haven't any money to pay you." Gabriella's voice was sad and small, and Simon understood well that her simple sentences carried with them years of hardship. However, this was good news for him. Nobles were known to secure their daughters in convents for safekeeping until marriage. He could relax a little knowing he couldn't be accused of abducting highborn ladies. He'd been incredibly foolish but fortunate this night.

"Is this sort of maltreatment commonplace in your convent?"

The young woman's eyes filled with tears. "No. Madre Paola is very strict, and, well, unkind, but she has never done anything like this before. Angelica should never have disobeyed her... I heard she sneaked out for our convent's apothecary, Sister Celeste, to help a child from the town, to deliver the purgatives he needed."

"And for that she received *this*? Helping a child is not permitted?"

"Well, no, I mean yes, but... Madre Paola has imposed many rules. It was different when Madre Caterina was the Mother Superior, God rest her. We had more freedom then." Her bottom lip trembled. "I-I've never seen Madre Paola so angry. If you had not been there..." She sobbed softly into her hands.

Sighing, Simon labored to maintain his patience, not wanting to vent his fatigue and frustration on the emotional woman. "If the convent is a terrible place, why didn't you leave?"

Gabriella sniffled, wiping away her tears with a swipe of her hand. "We've nowhere else to go."

The carriage came to a halt.

Simon got out and turned to assist Gabriella by holding out his hand.

She remained seated. "I cannot thank you enough for helping her, signore..." She paused and added, "I'm afraid I don't know your name."

"Simon de Villette." The lie—the noble-sounding name—rolled off his tongue and soured his insides. Yet maintaining anonymity outside of France was necessary for his survival. Better that she think him a noble and a naval officer, for there were those who made little distinction between privateer and pirate. The last thing he wanted was to have her in hysterics believing that she was in the presence of outlaws. "That is my ship, and we are ready to set sail." He gestured toward the sea vessel.

Wide-eyed, Gabriella stared past him at his docked ship. "You are going to help my friend, aren't you? Wh-What are you going to do with us, signore?"

Leave them and walk away. But his conscience balked. He couldn't bring himself to simply abandon them, vulnerable and alone. And in the middle of the night. Especially with one of the women injured.

"If you wish, you may return with us to France. I will obtain medical attention for your friend, and I will assist you both whatever way I can. You have my word." He held out his hand again and waited while Gabriella contemplated his offer. "I must insist on a speedy decision. I have no desire to confront any irate townspeople."

It was bad enough he was returning to France tonight without adding to it the complication of having two women in tow, one of whom stirred in him, with inexplicable intensity, a carnal hunger that he was forced to suppress. She was most definitely an innocent. Not the sort of woman he bedded. He wasn't going to add defiling virgins to his long list of sins.

With but a slight hesitation, Gabriella entrusted her hand to his, murmured her acceptance and renewed gratitude. He helped her down.

Given the hour, the dock area was deserted, yet there was much activity on deck. Simon ignored the curious looks from his crew as he carried an unconscious woman onto his ship, while another woman followed behind.

Both in religious clothing.

How ludicrous was this situation? He definitely needed sleep. He was not himself at all.

He wasn't going to allow the women to become a problem. He had enough problems already. He'd see that they were reunited with some long-forgotten cousin or friend, offer them some funds to aid them. And be done with it.

Besides, a beautiful woman had never caused him grief in the past. Or problems.

Why should this one be any different?

CHAPTER TWO

Angelica moaned softly. A terrible ache pounded inside her skull.

Little by little, the darkness dissolved until she could detect rays of light. Objects took on recognizable shapes, yet nothing looked familiar. No resemblance to any room she'd ever seen at the convent. The chamber she was in was decorated with colors of light green and gold. A costly green velvet chair sat before the hearth across from the foot of the bed. The furnishings were too fine. Too ornate.

Where am I?

She moved her gaze to the right. Sunlight cascaded from the window. With a groan, she shut her eyes tightly and turned away from the assailing light. The sudden movement sent a stabbing pain directly to her temples.

She remained still, eyes closed, until the pain subsided. Thoughts came to her slowly, scrambled, as she attempted to recall her last memories. The chapel. Madre. The horrible incident with the stick...

Without moving her head, she opened her eyes once more.

A woman sat near the bed, chin down and fast asleep. A woman she didn't recognize. A woman not in gray, the required dress at the convent. The silver-haired woman's modest clothing was a distinct contrast to the richness of the room.

Unease seeped into her system; her pulse quickened.

The woman beside her stirred, and her eyes fluttered open. She looked straight at Angelica and came to her feet.

"Dieu, you're awake!" she exclaimed and rushed from the room.

Angelica's heart jumped to her throat.

Had the woman just spoken *French*? Though she hadn't spoken the language in years, she'd understood every word.

Dear God. Where was she!

*****

Exhausted, Simon strode toward the dining hall of the Château Arles.

Located by the sea, the isolated château belonged to the recently retired Commodore of the King's Navy—Robert d'Arles. Simon had spent much of his youth here with Robert, when they weren't at sea, at war.

It was an ideal place for Simon to rendezvous with his ships.

Robert had returned from Paris during Simon's brief trip to the Republic of Genoa and was waiting to break fast with him. Normally, Simon would be delighted to spend time with the man who'd saved his life, had raised him as his own and taught him everything he knew about ships and battle.

But not today.

Today there was something he needed to say to Robert. It was a conversation he never thought he'd have. The words he had to voice to his mentor weighed heavily on him.

Dieu, everything was in shambles. Even his good judgment was askew. Last night's events further emphasized that. Never had he pursued a beautiful woman without first giving cautious consideration beforehand to any possible reprisals. He'd always prided himself on his self-control, on his acumen. Yet, last eve he'd done something completely impetuous and chased a pretty face into a *convent*.

Thank God, the two women weren't from noble families.

Having sailed the short distance back to France, his ship had arrived well before dawn. He'd carried the beauty, still trapped in slumber, to one of the second-floor bedchambers and managed to coax her friend to retire to a separate chamber for rest.

He could still feel the heated effects of having Angelica's soft, sweet form against him, desire still humming in his veins. In fact, each time he gazed upon the captivating face that had provoked his uncharacteristic behavior, raw lust licked up his spine. His physical reactions to her were confounding in the extreme.

Anxious to speak to the moonlight angel, he'd given orders to inform him the moment she awoke. No doubt she'd be pleased to be out of that convent. For good.

Yet he forced himself to stop short of imagining the various ways she might demonstrate her appreciation.

Simon entered the dining hall with her divine singing echoing in his mind.

"Ah, Simon, there you are!" Robert d'Arles—Marquis de Névelon, Comte de Sorbon—rose from the table with the assistance of a cane.

The sight was jarring.

A splinter of wood that had fragmented during a cannon attack had pierced Robert's leg, fracturing it. It seemed inconceivable that his life at sea was over. A life Robert so greatly adored. At fifty-five, his strong physique sculpted by his physical lifestyle was evident even in the finery of his silk, olive-green doublet and breeches. Simon had always seen Robert as invincible. A high-ranking naval officer. An Aristo whose conquests on the sea and in the boudoir were legendary.

"I wasn't certain you'd join me this morning. I heard you brought two women back with you. What's the matter, my boy? Are you finding one at a time is not enough these days?" Simon could readily see the physical misery Robert's leg was causing him reflecting in his gray eyes, despite his smile.

Robert was a proud man. Simon purposely schooled his features to show indifference to his condition and forced a smile in return. "I'll have to double my efforts if I'm to hope for a chance of matching your multitude of comely ladies by the time I reach your age," he teased, hoping his answer was enough to put an end to the topic. A discussion about who the women were and how they came to be here was the last thing Simon wanted at the moment.

Robert chuckled as they sat down at the table. "You've done exceedingly well in your own right—not just with the ladies but at sea as well. You do me proud."

It was a great compliment coming from the greatest man Simon had ever known. He was about to respond when the servants entered with the morning meal. Robert continued the moment they were alone again, not allowing him a reply.

"I understand that your ships have been highly successful. As usual." His tone was once again full of pride. "Fouquet must have been quite pleased to see the sum."

Simon swallowed—the food having just turned bitter in his mouth. Simply hearing Fouquet's name soured his insides and rioted with his conscience.

"Why shouldn't he be pleased? I'm certain Nicolas Fouquet could use the money to construct an addition to his enormous new château. Isn't Vaux-le-Vicomte grander than Fontainebleau—the king's finest palace?" He couldn't hold back the venom in his tone.

Robert stopped eating. "Careful, now. To suggest—even remotely—that the Superintendent of Finance is misappropriating funds from the treasury is a dangerous accusation to make. Do not make powerful foes, Simon. Let the king deal with Fouquet. You must stay focused on your goal. It's only a matter of time before you receive the recognition you deserve from our king. Then Louis will at last ennoble you and allow you to become an officer in his navy—just as we have always wanted."

Robert's words stabbed straight into the core of Simon's being. Though he had no choice, Simon hated telling the man to whom he owed his every success, who had championed Simon at every turn, sharing in his dream of betterment—that it was all dead.

The dream was done.

Everything they'd hoped for would never come to pass.

"Robert, it is time to stop dreaming and accept reality; our king is weak. And completely uninterested in his own kingdom," he said in restrained, even tones, wrestling to keep his ire in check. "He's left the realm vulnerable to the corruption that now infests it— namely Fouquet and the First Minister Cardinal Mazarin, who both battle for his power. Louis is not going to change. Nor is he going to recognize anything I do. Or have ever done."

Robert shoved his plate aside. "Nonsense. With your naval successes and the wealth you've earned for the Crown, it will only be a matter of time—"

"It will *not* be a matter of time."

"It will! I believe in our king. He is an intelligent man. He is young—true. But he *will* come around, and he will take the reins from Fouquet and Mazarin, and be the king he was meant to be."

"Dear God, Robert, how can you say that? Louis had his coronation at fifteen. He's now almost twenty-two, and still he doesn't rule, letting others run his country for him—preferring to spend his time with his mistress and on his ridiculous ballets."

Robert sat back, looking incredulous. "What in the world has gotten into you? I've never heard you speak this way. Becoming ennobled and an officer in the King's Navy has always been your dream. Why this change of heart? Why *now*? You are so close to attaining all that you've worked for. What has happened?"

Grim, his heart heavy, Simon shook his head. "Thomas Jaures is dead. He was captured by the Spanish. My men found his body dumped on the French border. All evidence shows that he wasn't executed but rather tortured to death. Gilbert and Daniel have yet to be found."

Robert frowned. "I had no idea."

"Without Thomas, it will prove most difficult to continue as in the past. To infiltrate with another spy of Thomas's caliber will take much time…" *A friend like Thomas can never be replaced.* His brutal, senseless death would never be forgotten. "Fouquet's demands for more captured silver from the Spanish are unceasing and ever growing. Mazarin is unconcerned with what Fouquet does with the Crown's money so long as there is enough to fund his war and expand the realm. And the king simply doesn't care about anything but dancing and fucking. I've had enough." He felt disgust down to the very marrow of his being. Everything he'd done for his country and king, everything he'd worked for was now tainted.

In blood.

"Listen to me." Robert grasped Simon's wrist and gave it a squeeze to punctuate his words. "I know Thomas was your friend and a good man, but you cannot allow his death to cloud your thinking. We are at war with Spain. Men die. This is simply battle fatigue you're experiencing. Nothing more."

"This is not battle fatigue. *Dieu.* Don't you see the corpses scattered around? I returned three weeks ago not only to learn of

Thomas's gruesome death, but also to find that our villages and country roads now resemble battlefields. Only there are no dead soldiers upon the ground. Just the lifeless bodies of innocent men, women, and children—dead of starvation. Driven by his infinite greed, Fouquet is literally taxing our people *to death* and using the funds from the Crown Treasury as his personal wealth!" Outrage yanked Simon to his feet. He began to pace, trying to settle his agitation, fighting back the urge to slam his fist into the wall.

After months at sea, he'd returned to see his dream replaced by a nightmare.

"You have no proof he steals," Robert countered.

That stopped him dead in his tracks. "*Proof?* The proof is that obscene palace he's building, right under Louis's nose!" *Jésus-Christ.* The riches he'd put into Fouquet's hands had helped create this monster!

How it fucking goaded him.

That he'd helped Fouquet succeed in his ambitions, enabling him to wreak such misery on the lower class, that he'd allowed himself and his men to be used as pawns—including Thomas, Gilbert, and Daniel—in Fouquet's schemes had been eating away at his very vitals every waking moment for the last three weeks.

"Though I'd heard Fouquet was building a new abode for himself some time ago," Simon continued, "I'd never seen Vaux-le-Vicomte before. Upon my return, I was ordered to deliver the Crown's share of our recent captured silver directly to his new château. *Merde.* I've never seen anything like it. Gilded ceilings. Gold-woven rugs—opulence both inside and out—while decomposing bodies line the route to his ostentatious castle!"

So many wasted lives... Simon felt sick inside. And responsible. "Our peasants have never before been in such a desperate state." In all the carnage he'd been a party to during their war with Spain, nothing—absolutely nothing—had been more horrific than the devastation he'd witnessed since his return. Infants cold in death at their mothers' breasts. The rotting flesh of countless forsaken souls. People of his own class.

It wasn't all that long ago that he was just like them—helplessly impoverished.

"Simon, the peasants have always experienced hardships."

"Hardships, yes. Decimation of this magnitude, *never.*"

Robert was born into nobility and privilege. He was a good man—in fact, there were few like him in his class—but he didn't nor could he truly understand what it was like to be destitute—hopelessly trapped in poverty.

Always at the mercy of the upper class.

All Simon had ever wanted was never again to be vulnerable to the upper class the way commoners were. It was the reason he'd pursued social status long after he'd attained wealth, for wealth alone wasn't enough to safeguard him. However, while chasing his ambitions, he hadn't intended to impose suffering on those who had already suffered enough.

He should have heeded the niggling doubts he'd had about Fouquet since his appointment as Finance Minister. He should have seen the signs of corruption sooner. Now he could practically trip over the glaring evidence of it.

"Those poor souls are at the mercy of a Superintendent of Finance whose excesses are without conscience or limit, and whose actions go completely unchecked. And I"—Simon jabbed his finger into his chest—"have helped that serpent slither to the top."

"All you have done is what was expected of you—your duty."

Simon set his palms down on the table and looked Robert in the eye. "I've ordered men into battle and had them die in a war that is about nothing but profit for Fouquet and Mazarin. I want no part of Fouquet's nefarious plans of grandeur. I've been chasing a fool's dream. I want no part of any of this anymore."

How could he have been so foolish as to believe that hard work and dedication could ever earn him an elevated position from men such as these?

"Giving up will not make it better for the lower class, I assure you," Robert said. "Without the money you contribute to the Treasury, Fouquet will make it worse for them. For as long as Fouquet and Mazarin maintain their powerful posts, you must continue. Fouquet will not allow you to simply walk away."

Simon slammed his fist down on the table, unable able to stem the fury that boiled in his blood. "*I know.* The accomplishments I believed would have elevated me from commoner and afforded me an officer's commission are the very deeds that hold me bound to him now."

The older man held up his hand. "Enough," he said with finality. "This talk is mad and suicidal. I'll continue my efforts to bend the king's ear. In the meantime, rise above this. Remain focused on the prize you seek. You have earned it! For the love of God, don't do anything to defy Fouquet. You will be arrested and executed for treason—and likely your men as well. Think of them…"

Simon sat back down, feeling weary. "I do think of them, Robert. They have fought, risked their lives, *died*—and for what?"

"For France. For the people. For honor."

"*Honor?* Where is there honor in any of this?"

"There is honor in fighting for your country! And we have fought hard and true during this war! There is honor in *you*, in having the courage to reach beyond what life handed you at birth. Look at where you came from, and look at where you are now. The son of a fisherman is today a privateer commander of fourteen ships, seven of which are rented warships belonging to the king himself! And if that were not enough, do not forget the island."

The island. His island. Oh no, he hadn't forgotten *that*. It was the place he longed for…and hadn't seen for two years.

Years ago, he'd sailed to New Spain to attack Spanish ships and ports for profit for France—just as he'd been ordered. It was there, among the many islands of the West Indies, some controlled by European colonists, others independent pirate kingdoms, that Simon found the island he'd named Marguerite.

It was now home for him, his men, and their families. Solidly fortified. Independently theirs.

"Once I have news about my missing men, I intend to return to the island for a while. Louis's ships will remain, but my own will follow me back to Marguerite."

He needed time away from France and war. He needed time to plan and think. He didn't believe that Robert could sway their king. Moreover, he refused to be an instrument in Fouquet's quest for personal gain any longer. No matter what Robert said, Simon couldn't turn a blind eye to what was happening to his people, nor could he ignore the self-condemnation that tormented him.

What Robert didn't know was that Simon had established new spies, not in Spain—where he'd placed Thomas, Gilbert, and Daniel—but as servants in Fouquet's own domain. Spies who had already begun to provide information about Fouquet's dealings—in commerce and trade, as well as personal matters.

Though it meant the death of a dream he'd craved for so long, he *was* going to get out of Fouquet's clutches—but he'd have to be focused. And at the moment, he was far too enraged to concentrate. Or to lead himself and his men out of this perilous tangled web— *alive*.

"Perhaps a rest is best for now," Robert ceded reluctantly. "But do not make it lengthy. You must make sure you continue to meet Fouquet's demands."

Wishing to change the subject, Simon asked, "Why don't you return with me to Marguerite? There is sun, warm breezes, and attractive women to while away the time with."

His comment drew a soft laugh from Robert. "I serve you better if I stay in France, particularly in Paris, with the king. I plan to return there tomorrow."

"So soon?"

"Now that I am retired, I have been reacquainting myself with old friends…" Robert's smile faded. "At first I missed the sea, Simon. *Dieu*, I missed it so…but now I realize that I miss something else more."

"What is that?"

"A home. A wife. Children."

Simon was shocked. "Regrets? *You*, Robert?" Over the years, he'd witnessed countless mistresses fill Robert's leisure time. He'd always been completely contented with his bachelorhood.

Robert's smile was rueful. "I wonder from time to time what my life would have been like had I chosen to marry."

"It's not too late."

"Perhaps…" Then he added, "Perhaps it is something that you should consider."

"Marriage?" He led a dangerous existence. And given what he was planning to do, it was in greater peril than usual. "That is the very last thing on my mind."

"And what if one day you long for it?"

"Then and only then shall I give it a second thought."

"Your pardon, my lord," the old servant Henri said from the entrance of the dining hall. "Captain, the young lady is awake."

CHAPTER THREE

The unknown woman reentered the chamber.

The pain in Angelica's head was excruciating. Nausea roiled her stomach. But she battled through it, determined to learn where she was and how she'd arrived there.

This was like a bad dream. She used to be plagued by them years ago.

But none had ever been like *this*.

The woman smiled. "Good morning, Signorina Angelica." This time, she spoke in Italian, her tone gentle and no doubt meant to be soothing. But it didn't soothe her in the least.

She clutched her forehead, willing the pounding to stop.

Forced to keep her voice low, knowing her throbbing head would worsen otherwise, she closed her eyes and demanded quietly, "Who are you? How do you know me?"

"My name is Marta. Gabriella told me your name."

At hearing her friend's name, she snapped her eyes open. "*Gabriella?* Where is she? What is this place?" Anxiety, dizziness, and pain all attacked her, torturing her with equal fervor. Reasoning had never been so challenging. The thought of rising from the bed was daunting.

"Where is Madre Paola? The Sisters?"

"Gabriella is fine and sleeping in another room."

"*Where am I?*" she asked more forcefully.

"The captain will be here shortly to answer all of your questions."

Shock and confusion tore through her mind. "Captain? What captain?"

"You may leave us, Marta." A rich male voice came from the entrance of the bedchamber.

Dropping her hand from her forehead, Angelica darted her gaze toward the sound. Filling the doorway with his tall, sculpted form was the most striking man she'd ever seen... He had dark hair and riveting light-colored eyes—the light blue doublet he wore a perfect match.

A slight smile on his lips, he approached, moving with confidence and a masculine grace that exuded authority, and stopped at the foot of her bed.

Marta gave a quick curtsy and left, quietly closing the door behind her.

Oh God, she had no idea where she was, who *he* was. One thing was certain: she'd never seen this dark-haired stranger before. He wasn't the sort of man someone would forget.

Stay calm!

She struggled up to a sitting position. A fresh wave of dizziness hit her squarely between the eyes. Briefly, she squeezed them shut and forced it back, needing to keep her wits sharp.

"I am pleased you're awake. How do you feel?" He spoke in perfect Italian.

She ignored his question, for she had a few of her own. "Who are you? Where am I?" How many times did she have to ask these questions before someone provided answers? If this was indeed a dream, she truly wished to wake up now.

"I can understand your distress. But there is no reason for alarm, I assure you. My name is Simon de Villette. You are in a château in the south of France."

Her blood froze. *No...* She couldn't have heard correctly. He hadn't said... "*France?*" The word tumbled from her lips, barely a whisper.

"Yes. You were injured, and I brought you here onboard one of my ships. I had a physician summoned for you. I'm told he even speaks some Italian," he said.

Motionless, she simply stared at him in horrified astonishment. Then she looked around the chamber, reeling under the enormity of the situation.

Dear God... This can't be real. For the first time in ten years, she was no longer within the sanctuary of the convent. Or within the safe borders of the Republic of Genoa. She was back in France. The very place her nightmares had begun. She was at risk. In danger. Vulnerable.

Judging from the clothes he wore and the lavish surroundings, this man was no doubt a French noble. For that reason alone he couldn't be trusted. Did Madre Paola have something to do with this? Could she have learned her identity? *No. That's impossible!*

And why on earth had he brought Gabriella here too?

"I was in a *convent*. How did you do this?" she demanded a little too fiercely. The pain made her flinch.

"I was on my way to my ship when we *met* outside the convent," he said, still with a smile on his handsome face. "You make quite a first impression."

He was the man outside? Heat rushed to her cheeks as the memory of her body on top of his flooded her distressed mind. "You followed me into the convent? Why?"

At that, he gave a soft chuckle and shook his head. "If truth be told, I'm not at all certain. It isn't every day a man is knocked off his feet by a woman. Literally," he gently teased. "After our rather unorthodox meeting, you had me most intrigued. I wanted to speak to you. Perhaps it was fate that I was at the right place at the right time to be of service to you," he stated, looking rather pleased with himself.

Service? If by "service" he meant bringing her to France, then his "service" had placed her in great peril. "How dare you!"

His smile died. "*Pardon?*"

"You had no right to take me from the convent... I demand you return my friend and me at once!"

He looked completely stunned.

"Signorina," he said, crossing his arms, "you were knocked unconscious, sustained welts to your head and a rather large bruise to your cheek, and *you wish to return?*"

She touched her aching cheek. She knew he was wondering if her injury was affecting her mind, but she didn't care what he thought. She had to leave France. Immediately. Think. Think. *Think!*

He seemed genuine in his belief that he'd somehow aided her. She was fairly certain he was in no way tied to the man in her past. Yet she wasn't about to trust him. Or anyone. Somehow, she had to convince him to return her to the convent. Without explanation. *Now.*

"You don't understand... What you have done is...very wrong. We must return straightaway." Before *he* found out she was in France.

She scanned the room for her missing headdress and shoes, but the quick movements of her head only made her feel worse, forcing her to stop and rest her forehead in her palm.

By the time she finally looked up again, she found him sitting patiently in the chair Marta had occupied, quietly studying her. Although the pose was casual, his scrutiny was not. She felt as though he could read her every thought—know her every secret. Adding to her distress was his closeness. She could detect the appealing scent of his soap, making her feel further flustered.

"What is your full name, Angelica?" Hearing her name from his lips sent an odd tingle down her spine.

She could lie. She could select any name to tell him. She could barely focus with this horrible throbbing in her head, much less invent any believable stories for this tall, dark stranger.

"Angelica?" Leaning forward, he slipped his fingers beneath her chin. She froze. His unexpected touch was gentle and warm as he held her face and her complete attention. "It is just your name," he said, clearly reading her reluctance. "Surely, you can share it."

No, she couldn't. Nor was she about to.

*****

Simon gazed at his moonlight angel. *Jésus-Christ*, she had the sweetest face and the most beautiful moss-green eyes he'd ever seen. In fact, from the moment they'd first touched upon him at the doorway, he felt it down to his groin. Just like last eve, his unruly cock was fully alert to her presence. And eager to please.

He couldn't believe how powerfully attracted he was to this woman.

She remained silent, much to his regret, intent on remaining a mystery.

She was as perplexing as she was bedazzling. Even with the bruise on her cheek, dressed in that unflattering gray garb, she was dangerously alluring, possessing the kind of beauty that could bring a man to his knees. It didn't help that her adorably curly chestnut-colored hair, was sensuously tousled, as if she'd spent some time at carnal play.

If he'd been intrigued by her before, he was doubly so now. He wanted to know everything. He supposed he could ask her friend, but he wanted to learn the information from Angelica directly.

In truth, he wanted more than just information about her.

He wanted to know the taste of her lips, her skin. Her speaking voice was so silky smooth and just as entrancing as her singing had been. He wanted to know the sultry sounds she'd make in the throes of passion. *Dieu*. He wanted to fuck her so badly—a woman whom he considered untouchable.

Reluctantly, he drew his hand away, keeping his expression mild, giving no indication of the havoc she was wreaking on his libido. She'd been through an ordeal and was understandably disquieted. Confident that in due time he'd gain the answers to the questions he had about her, he didn't see any reason to press her now.

"Why have you brought my friend here?" she asked, breaking her silence.

He sat back before he spoke, needing some space between him and his moonlight temptress. "Gabriella assisted me when you were injured and insisted I bring her with me also. She is well and safe. You are safe here too. I know this is overwhelming, waking up in a strange place, but I am not your adversary. Let us be friends. I gave Gabriella my word that I would assist you both in whatever capacity you need."

She looked down at her hands. He took the opportunity to admire her profile. She had the softest skin. He itched to touch her once more.

"I know you don't understand, but we must return to the convent," she said. "Transportation there is the only assistance we require."

Back to *that*. "You are correct. I don't understand."

"It is our home."

Did she know how beguiling her eyes were? "Then it's a miserable one."

"It's been my home for ten years."

Mentally, he groaned. Hidden in a convent for that much of her life made her more innocent than he could comfortably accept. Though his eager cock didn't take exception to the news, his conscience was another matter. He still had a few scraps of honor left. No matter how desirable she was, he was not going to prey on her virtue.

"Why have you been there so long?"

He watched her give careful consideration to whether or not she should answer him.

"My parents are dead," she said at last. "I've been part of the orphanage in the convent ever since."

"Orphanage? An orphanage is for children. You are not a child." His eyes dipped briefly to her breasts, the curves of which were visible despite her attempts to hide them with the bed linen and that drab garment she wore.

"I help the Sisters with the children there."

"I see," he said, feeling frustrated by the situation he'd created for himself. "I'd be pleased to return you and Gabriella to any family member or friend you wish. However, I won't return you to your convent and put you at risk for more abuse." The thought was abhorrent to him. And the last thing he wanted was to be a party to more suffering.

She opened her mouth, ready to object. A knock at the door stopped her.

"Enter," he ordered.

Henri stepped in. "Captain, the physician is here. Shall I send him up?"

"Yes, and bring something for the mademoiselle to eat."

The servant gave a curt bow and left. Simon moved toward the door.

"Wait!" she called out.

He stopped and turned toward her.

"You have no right to decide where I or Gabriella should live. If you are willing to deliver us anywhere, then the convent is no more of an inconvenience to you."

He could make no sense of it. She appeared to be an intelligent woman. Why wasn't she elated to be out of that deplorable convent? Why the hell would she wish to return to a place that would subject her to such ill treatment?

The light rap at the door drew his attention. Simon opened it and allowed the physician in. Although smaller in stature, he was of a similar age and coloring to Simon. They exchanged polite greetings.

"*Mademoiselle.*" The physician smiled at his comely patient and moved toward Angelica before Simon could make introductions. "*You're awake. Excellent. I am Bernard Toussaint, a physician.*" The French words tumbled from his mouth.

Her eyes darted from Toussaint to Simon.

Simon instantly read the uncertainty in her eyes as ignorance of the language. "*Sir, the young lady doesn't speak French. In Italian, please,*" he told the physician in his native tongue.

"Ah, yes. Of course. Signorina, I can speak Italian. How are you feeling?"

She turned those expressive eyes to Simon once more as he watched her bite her bottom lip, looking unsure and completely engaging. Oh, how he wanted to do the very same thing to that pretty bottom lip. She was driving him mad with the simplest, most innocent act. And he was beginning to resent this untamable effect she had on him.

"I have a horrible headache," she replied.

"That is understandable." The physician was grinning at her like a besotted fool. "I've been told you have a rather nasty bump on your head. If I may, I'd like to look at it."

Simon knew he should leave, but his boots were fixed to the floor, and he hadn't the ability to move them.

She lowered her head to allow Toussaint to examine her.

The physician carefully began to move her hair, touching her head gently with his fingertips. Simon placed his hands on his hips and looked away, trying not to think about how silky her gorgeous tresses had felt between his fingers. Or how much he wanted to dive his hands into those soft, loose curls, tilt her head back with a sensual tug, and feast on that perfect mouth of hers.

"Well, it would appear that you are a fortunate woman," Toussaint said. "I don't believe your injuries are serious." The physician eased her down onto her back. She lay stiffly, watching Toussaint warily. Her hands still clutched the bed linens to her chest.

From Simon's vantage point, he could easily appreciate her form with the discerning eye of a libertine. Against his will, his mind flitted through the various ways in which he could coax the stiffness from her body. The various ways to make her warm and yielding—just for him.

"I would advise you to stay abed a few days. I shall leave you some headache powders to help with your pain." Toussaint's gaze lingered on Angelica's face, more of a perusal of her fine features than an assessment of injury.

Simon strode over to the door and snatched it open. "Thank you." He didn't miss Toussaint's look of surprise at the abrupt dismissal.

"Yes...well, you're quite welcome." Turning to Angelica, the physician picked up her hand and pressed a kiss to her knuckle. "It was my pleasure."

*****

Alone at last in her chamber, Angelica took in a fortifying breath. She was going to have to flee from France. Having escaped these borders before, she knew she could do it again. She was accustomed to overcoming challenges. She hadn't survived this long without that skill. Securing Simon de Villette's help would make things easier. However, with or without the stranger's assistance, she would gather Gabriella and leave the realm for good. She could not—would not—remain here.

It was far too dangerous.

Men like Nicolas Fouquet didn't change, no matter how many years passed.

Nicolas Fouquet did not forgive.

Or forget.

CHAPTER FOUR

Domenico Dragani leaned over toward his friend Armand Rancourt seated comfortably in the velvet chair next to him in the library of Château Arles.

"Armand?"

"Yes?"

"Did he"—Domenico indicated Simon with a motion of his chin —"just say *convent*? *Two* women?"

Seated behind the large ebony desk, Simon tightened his jaw. "Yes, that is exactly what I said. Convent. Two women." *Merde*. He felt like a complete imbecile telling two of his top commanders and closest friends about the guests he'd brought with him from the Republic of Genoa. But he could hardly hide the women indefinitely.

Domenico sat back. His lips twitched, his sorry attempt to hold in his mirth. "Ah…Simon? Have you run out of women that you now pluck them out of *convents*?"

"I think we'll move on to more pressing topics." Simon took a drink from his goblet of brandy and set it down on the desk.

Domenico leaned toward him. "Do they have warts and whiskers?" He grinned.

Simon frowned.

"What possible difference could any of this make?" Armand questioned their Italian friend, Armand's blond hair and light eyes a sharp contrast to Domenico's darker coloring. "Just as Simon mentioned—we have more important things to concern ourselves with. Fouquet. Thomas's death. The fate of Gilbert and Daniel. And the imminent arrival of our ships. Or have you forgotten about those, Domenico?"

"Of course not. But, Armand—a *convent*. Women with warts and whiskers." Domenico shuddered in mock horror.

"Excuse me…" Gabriella interrupted from the doorway, looking nervous and unsure.

The old servant, Henri, reached the door in a great rush. "Your pardon, Captain. I will return the mademoiselle to her chambers straightaway."

Simon waved Henri away. "Gabriella, come." He rose, momentarily surprised to see her out of her religious garb and dressed in a pale blue gown. He'd ordered that a chest of women's clothing, captured from one of the Spanish ships, be offered to the two women. From the way Gabriella kept smoothing her hand over the skirt of the gown, he could tell she very much liked the garment made for aristocracy. One of the servants had clearly helped her dress. Her auburn hair was arranged in a fashionable coiffure of ringlets.

What would Angelica look like in such finery? His blood warmed at the mere thought.

Gabriella stepped forward. "I-I'm sorry to disturb you. I would like to see Angelica."

"She is asleep at the moment," Simon said. "She was awake earlier and was seen by a physician. He advises that with some rest, she will be well in a few days. If you wish, you may see her when she awakens."

She brightened. "I would like that very much. I cannot thank you enough for your kindness."

Simon brushed off the comment. He could hardly look at his action as a good deed when his conduct had been initially motivated more by a disreputable inclination than a gallant one. "Allow me to introduce you to two of my commanders. Gabriella Santino, this is Armand Rancourt." Armand gave her a nod and a bow. "And this is Domenico Dragani."

Domenico approached with a smile, took her hand, and pressed a kiss to her knuckle. "It is a pleasure to meet you." He gave her a sweeping bow.

Gabriella blushed and beamed. Simon shook his head, amused.

Armand leaned toward Simon and asked sotto voce, "Does she speak French?"

Simon had asked her that very question onboard the ship. "No."

Turning to Domenico, Armand inquired in French, "Do you detect any warts? Or whiskers?"

Domenico smiled. "Not a one," he responded in kind, his look indicating approval of her feminine qualities.

"Domenico, why don't you show Gabriella the gardens?" Simon suggested, noting her instant pleasure over the prospect.

Needing no further encouragement, Domenico tucked Gabriella's hand in the crook of his arm and left the room, boasting about his knowledge of the botanicals on the château's grounds.

Gabriella looked pleased to be out of the convent and content to keep it that way. If only Simon could understand why her friend felt such a compulsion to return.

*****

"Angelica… Where is my little Angelica?"

She was six and giggled as her father called out to her from the grand foyer of their country estate, his voice drifting up the stairwell to her small ears. Quickly, she dashed down the stairs, her small shoes tapping on each step in her rapid descent.

"Papa!" She jumped into the outstretched arms of the man she loved the most and looked into his adoring eyes, then at her mother who stood by smiling as she watched their loving exchange. Her long, dark curls flounced about as he spun her around. And around. She squealed happily, hugging his neck with fierce affection; his laughter filled her world with joy. Her surroundings blurred. Objects became indistinguishable. And the laughter suddenly changed then from gaiety to harshness. Cruelly taunting her.

Her world stopped revolving at once.

Laughing down at her was the face of another man her mother had called husband, yet Angelica could only call him "Evil" in the quiet of her fourteen-year-old mind.

Angelica jolted awake to find herself sitting up in bed, her heart pounding. Her head balked at the sudden movement, punishing her promptly with a sharp pain.

Pressing her fingers to her temples, she tried to knead away the ache. She hadn't had a nightmare like that in years. No doubt it had occurred because she was in France. *Near Fouquet.*

She suppressed a shudder.

Her stepfather came from one of the most distinguished, powerful parliamentary families in the realm. Fouquet had influence. And authority over her. If he ever found her, she'd be at his mercy.

And he had none.

Never again would she allow herself to be in his clutches. Cunning, manipulative, ambitious, Fouquet had had different faces, one for her and her late mother and another for everyone else. Most had no idea of his malicious nature. For so long his malevolent conduct had been limited to savage words, mostly directed at her poor mother, but shortly after her mother's death, one horrible night, his wickedness had progressed beyond the lash of a vicious tongue.

On that night, she saw what the future held for her. And ran.

She'd been away from France a very long time. She'd no idea how many friends her stepfather had or how far-reaching those friendships were.

She had to return to her safe haven.

She knew she could convince Madre Paola to take both her and Gabriella back. Madre Paola's bad temperament was the lesser of the two evils—by far. In the last six months since Madre Paola had become the new Mother Superior, Angelica had had no serious conflicts with her. As long as she abided by the rules, she'd avoid further discord. And she was going to swear never to break the rules again. How she missed the former Mother Superior, dear, kind Madre Caterina—her tender face. Her gentle ways. Her death had drastically altered Angelica's world.

Or so she'd thought until yesterday.

Yesterday, her world had turned completely upside-down. All because of one man.

Simon de Villette.

The servant had called him *Captain*. That meant he had to be an officer in the King's Navy—as only nobles were granted such commissions in the realm's official navy. He certainly had a commanding presence.

Not to mention the bluest eyes she'd ever seen.

She tossed the covers off, dismayed by her thoughts. *Who cares what color his eyes are?* Or that he was handsome. None of that mattered.

The only thing that mattered was getting out of France.

Simon de Villette not only could but *should* return her and Gabriella safely to Genoa. Though her sweet friend had always been easily discomposed, she had to have been significantly overwrought over Angelica's condition for her to have aided Simon the way she had. She hated having caused Gabriella such distress. She was anxious to find her, reassure her she was all right. That everything was going to be fine.

And return with her to the only real home Gabriella had ever known.

Carefully, she sat up and swung her legs over the side of the bed, the ache in her head a manageable discomfort. Her equilibrium passed a second test when she stood on her own two feet. Pleased, she let out a sigh.

She was going to speak to the man responsible for bringing her to France—determined to leave its borders forever before the next sunset.

Just then something yellow on the bed caught her eye—a brocade gown, garnished with gold ribbon and lace. It was beautiful, reminding her of a gown she'd owned long ago. Reaching out to touch the rich fabric, she stopped short.

That way of life is over. A life she wanted no part of, for it came at a terrible price. Her life now belonged elsewhere.

Smoothing her hand down the coarse fabric of her gray garb, she turned away. A search of the chamber yielded neither her wimple nor veil, but at least her shoes were there. She slipped them on, brushed her fingers through her hair, and walked out the door.

*****

Angelica reached the great foyer on the main floor without encountering a single soul.

All the doors were closed except one, the partially open portal offering a glimpse of what lay inside.

The compelling sight urged her forward.

She opened the door wider and stared in awe. From floor to ceiling, from wall to wall, shelf upon shelf of glorious *books*.

Entering the library, she gazed in appreciation at the extensive collection, while the ornately carved hearth and costly furnishings failed to impress. Gently, she ran her fingertips across the spines of the leather-bound volumes as she walked along, her eyes taking in as much as she could. Oh, how she loved to read.

Having access to a library such as this would be absolute heaven.

One of the books caught her attention. She stopped. Pulling the small brown leather volume from the shelf, she read the cover and smiled, caressing her fingertips over the imprinted gold title.

"What are you doing here?" The male voice shattered the silence.

She jumped. The book dropped from her hands onto the floor with a *thump*. Whirling around, she was startled to see Simon de Villette standing in the doorway, a frown on his handsome face, his devastating blue eyes pinning her to the spot.

CHAPTER FIVE

Simon approached her slowly, his brow slightly furrowed.

Unable to stop herself, Angelica took in his male beauty. He, not the books, now dominated the room. How was it possible that he looked even better than before?

A few wayward strands of his dark hair played against his lashes, but it was his mouth that captured her attention.

Such an appealing mouth…

She looked away, horrified by the workings of her mind. It had to be her headache that was distorting her thinking.

He stopped before her, towering over her.

The bookshelves against her back kept her fixed in place. She was keenly aware of the limited space between their bodies, his proximity causing her body to warm.

"I asked you a question." His voice was quiet but firm.

Gazing up at him, she tried to clear her head by taking in a deep breath, but it only served to draw in his wonderful scent. She couldn't quite describe it, but it was tantalizing in the extreme.

What was the matter with her? She shouldn't be reacting to him this way. She'd chosen a cloistered existence, or rather, it had chosen her. Nonetheless, she'd accepted her future long ago.

"You should not be wandering about alone." He spoke softly, his voice deep and rich in her ears. It reverberated through her belly with wicked appeal. Lightly, he stroked his knuckles along her bruised cheek. "You should be in bed. You are still injured."

She closed her eyes briefly. *Get hold of yourself.* This was the second time he'd touched her. Instead of drawing back, as she would have expected, she found herself wanting to draw near. It was a stunning reaction. As stunning as the tiny tingles that sped up her spine at his caress.

"My malady has much improved," she said, hoping she didn't sound as discomposed as she felt.

He lowered his arm and his gaze.

It took two wild heartbeats before she realized he was staring at something on the floor. She forced her gaze down, her insides still quivering with the residual pleasure of his small caress. The book she had dropped lay on the woven rug.

He was staring at her again, one dark eyebrow slightly cocked, before he retrieved the fallen item.

"You—I'm afraid that you startled me, and the book—I dropped it..." *Definitely not your most eloquent response, Angelica.* She turned her gaze away to a safer sight than the far too attractive Simon de Villette.

"You can read this?" he asked.

Her eyes darted back to his. The book was in French. She wasn't about to divulge that she could indeed read every word in the book of love sonnets. In fact, she was gripped with the most powerful urge to devour each and every beautifully romantic line.

She quashed the silly yearning.

"No. It's written in French, is it not? I couldn't possibly..." His penetrating gaze made her uneasy. She wished she could read his thoughts behind those disarming light-colored eyes.

"But you *can* read, Angelica." Yet again he managed to unbalance her by the way he spoke her name. It was astonishing what it did to her insides every time he said it.

He'd done nothing but show kindness toward her. His manner was gentle, attentive. His words spoke of concern for her welfare. Yet she was forced to stoop to deceit. She simply couldn't lower her guard. Not for a moment. Not with a single soul. Keeping her secrets had kept her safe. And she wasn't about to break with precedent.

Besides, this man *was* dangerous. No one had ever inspired these physical responses from her before. The sooner she left France, the better.

"I learned to read at the convent," she lied. *Again.* "I teach there...the children in the orphanage..." At least that was the truth, albeit clumsily told.

He placed the book back on the shelf. "Why?"

"*Why?*" She knitted her brow in confusion.

"Yes. Of what use is it to teach the children of commoners?" Despite his words, she had the distinct feeling he was not expressing his personal view of literacy and the lower class. He was trying to draw information from her.

She chose her next words carefully. "At the convent, we believe everyone should have the opportunity of an education, noble or peasant. Male or female."

"*Your pardon, Captain.*" The French phrase came from the doorway.

Relief washed over her when she saw the old male servant standing at the threshold of the library.

"*Your meal awaits you in the dining hall, sir.*"

Simon gave a nod. "*Merci, Henri.*" He turned to her. "Have you eaten?"

"No..."

He smiled. "Good. Then you will join me this evening for supper." He tossed out phrases to Henri in French, ordering him to set another place in the dining hall.

Though she'd wanted to speak to him, the thought of dining alone with him was daunting. She seemed to be completely out of sorts in his presence at the moment, struggling to get her mind and mouth to work together.

"Perhaps Gabriella would like to join us?" she said with a polite smile. If he would summon her friend, she was certain she could get through the meal and convince him to return them to the convent.

"She has already eaten. We are the last to dine this evening." Amusement flickered in his eyes. "Are you nervous to be alone with me, Angelica?"

"No." Her smile remained frozen on her face. "Of course not." He didn't frighten her. Though her reactions to his physical appeal were another matter altogether.

"Do you find my company unpleasant? Would you rather dine alone?"

"Unpleasant? No, absolutely not," she quickly assured, wishing at the moment he were old, potbellied, and missing some teeth. "I would be pleased to dine with you, if you consider this suitable attire." She touched her garb.

A slow, gorgeous, knee-weakening smile formed on his appealing face. He leaned in, and in her ear softly he said, "You are beautiful just as you are."

His unexpected words astounded her. As did the look in his eyes when he pulled back. He actually looked...sincere. No one had offered her a compliment, not for a very long time. And certainly not about how she looked. She touched her plain garment once more, so different from his costly attire. He was being far too kind.

He placed her hand in the crook of his arm. "Let us proceed. This will be an excellent opportunity to learn more about each other."

Oh God...

*****

Simon downed some of the burgundy in his goblet as he marveled at Angelica's elegant profile, her lovely face illuminated by an orange hue from the candlelight. She was seated immediately to his left in the dining hall. He was permitted but a glimpse of her pretty eyes before she forced her gaze down, her posture as stiff as the long wooden table before him.

She was driving him to distraction. He was so hard, he was practically ready to crawl out of his skin. She had the most incredible effect on his libido. He still couldn't believe she'd managed to erode his good reasoning and had provoked him into a rare moment of recklessness.

And he was never reckless. Not ever.

Being alone in her company was like playing with fire. But he couldn't draw away. Not yet. Not until he demystified this mystifying woman.

One thing he was certain of was that she was a little fraud. He'd noted her body's response to his touch in the library. He knew she felt the mutual carnal heat between them. There might be a compelling reason this sweet enchantress wanted to return to the convent, but neither a religious calling nor a deep devotion to a cloistered existence were it.

However, that didn't negate that she was still a virgin. And he wasn't about to let himself forget it—no matter how good his every rakish instinct told him it would be between them. He wanted to believe that years of carnage and chasing ambitious dreams hadn't stripped away all decency in him. Whatever it took, he'd resist. He didn't claim maidenheads. And he wasn't about to start with hers.

The women he bedded were experienced in the carnal arts. Enjoyed sex that was recreational. Raw lust with no emotional involvement was his preference.

He was going to draw out her secrets, shatter her mystique, and break this peculiar libidinous hold she had on him once and for all. All it would require was a bit of patience and finesse.

How difficult could it be?

Shifting in his chair, trying to ease the discomfort of his arousal, Simon picked up his spoon. Neither of them had touched the poached-egg soup before them.

"Does the soup not appeal to you, Angelica?"

"Yes… It smells delicious." Her manner was pleasant, despite her obvious unease. She was clearly unaccustomed to being alone with a man. He admired her bravado, fully appreciating how unsettling this entire experience was for her.

He covered her hand with his. She started at the touch. "Easy." He was pleased she didn't pull away from him, more than he'd ever admit, and gave her hand a gentle squeeze to reassure her. "It is but a meal. Try to relax. Pretend we are old friends." He smiled. "I would be very pleased if you would call me Simon."

She took a deep breath and let it out. "Very well…*Simon*."

Reluctantly, he removed his hand. The urge to trail his palm inside her sleeve and lightly up her arm was far too strong. "Let us eat." He tasted his soup, encouraging her to do the same.

She tried the broth. "Your home is lovely," she said, initiating some polite conversation, her alluring mouth capturing his attention.

He was starved for a taste of that mouth. "This is not my home. It belongs to a friend of mine."

"Oh? Where is your home?"

"The sea, mostly." His answer was purposely vague.

"No wife, then? Or children?" she inquired before returning her attention to her soup.

Her response was adorably artless. He waited until finally her gaze was drawn back to him.

"No wife and no children." There it was. A flicker in those eyes indicated that his answer pleased her. She was treading on dangerous territory. He wanted nothing more than to charm his way under her skirts and into her drawers. *Beautiful green-eyed angel, don't play a game you can't afford to lose, for I would surely claim more than a kiss from a curious virgin as my prize.*

"Have you always loved the sea?"

He drank some burgundy and shrugged. "It is where my responsibilities lie." Tamping down the rancor that subject stirred, he turned matters on her just as the roasted duck was brought in. "I notice you did not don the gown provided for you. Was it not your size?"

"I don't know. I didn't try it on."

He leaned in and poured some burgundy into her goblet. "Any particular reason for that?"

"I didn't believe it was suitable attire for me."

"Really?" Unable to stop himself, his eyes drifted quickly over her form, trying to imagine her in finery. "I think the attire would suit you beautifully."

He saw her visibly stiffen. He noted she didn't take compliments as other women did. Could she truly not know how lovely she was? Even dressed like *that*.

"Gabriella was quite pleased with her dress," he added.

"She was?"

"Indeed. In fact, she seems content to be out of the convent."

She shook her head; the candlelight played on her silky locks. "The convent is our home. We've been there since we were young girls. We've no family, no friends outside of it. We must return."

"Surely there's someone…"

"No one," she stated firmly. "You must take us back."

"How can you honestly believe that you belong in that mausoleum?"

She frowned. "It is not a mausoleum. A mausoleum is a tomb that houses the dead."

"Exactly. It is as warm and inviting as a tomb. How alive can you feel living there? Do you not want more out of your life than to spend it cloistered?"

Angelica felt his words strike their intended mark. It stirred her ire. This man was a perfect stranger. He knew nothing of her or her predicament. Who was he to make such comments? "Believe it or not, we serve a purpose there. There are the children that I teach..."

"There are children you can teach outside of the convent."

"Yes, but they are not as needy. I am *not* interested in tutoring anyone from the upper class." To her horror, the disdain in her voice rang clear, even to her own ears.

His chuckle made her flinch. "You've had unpleasant experiences with the upper class?" He was smiling, but her face burned, embarrassed and appalled by her own ungracious utterance.

"Forgive me, I meant no insult. It is just...rather...I apologize." *Perfect, Angelica. He's a noble. And you've just insulted his class—a man whose aid you are trying to secure.* Over the years, she'd become a master at controlling her words and masking her emotions. Once again she blamed her headache for her blunder and unprecedented poor manners.

He chuckled again. "There is no need for embarrassment. There are very few saints among nobles."

Relieved he was not insulted, she relaxed a little, until she saw him reach out. He slipped his fingers under her chin. Sensations spiked from his touch. And quivered over every nerve ending in her body.

She went stock-still, caught in those blue eyes.

"Angelica, I can make no sense of it. I fear I can't fathom how it's right to hide a perfect flower in a place where the sun never shines and no one may gaze upon it to admire its beauty—left to simply wither away. There is far more you're not telling me than just your name."

She pulled away from him, breaking contact, and tried to ignore the tantalizing tingles that remained in the wake of his touch. "Please, do not mock me." She wasn't a "perfect flower." In fact, she was far from perfect. He had no idea the extent.

His brows shot up. "Mock you? I am not mocking you. You don't belong locked away in that place. Why are you hiding in that convent? What are you afraid of?"

She flinched. "I am not hiding, and I am not afraid. The convent is where I should be. Though I thank you for your concern, I don't believe I need to justify my choices in life to you or anyone else. Sir, I don't ask *you* why you choose to spend your days amidst battle and bloodshed."

She struck a nerve. She saw it for the barest instant flash in his eyes.

"Some choices, once made, demands commitment," he responded tightly. "Would your choice in life be one that would have pleased your parents?"

The subject of her parents hit close to the heart. Mortified, she felt tears well in her eyes and blinked them back. Tears were a pitiful waste of time. She didn't cry. Hadn't cried in years.

Collecting herself quickly, she countered, "I pray they would understand that I have done my best under the circumstances." She rose. "I request that you kindly see to our return to the convent tomorrow. Now if you will please excuse me, I would like to lie down." Without waiting for a response, she turned to leave.

He was on his feet in an instant. "Angelica...wait." He caught her arm. "I'm sorry. I didn't mean to upset you. Are you in some sort of trouble? Perhaps I can help." Stepping close, he cupped her face in his strong hands, his action taking her by surprise. "Why don't you tell me who you are."

His sensuous blue eyes gazed back at her, unwavering. There was what appeared to be sincerity in his expression and words.

"Go on, Angelica," he softly urged. "Tell me the secrets you guard." His thumb lightly caressed her uninjured cheek. No one had ever touched her the way he did.

The temptation to confess the whole of her situation surged inside her. She swallowed down the words.

"I can't..." she forced out.

She couldn't trust a complete stranger, despite the longing he inspired.

He leaned in. "Yes, you can," he whispered near her ear. "Trust me..." He slipped his arms around her waist, pulling her against his muscled form. A warmth instantly infused her body, his masculine strength so decadent and delicious. For the first time ever, she felt...feminine. For the first time in years she was leaning on someone, when she hadn't allowed herself to show any weakness or vulnerability before.

She should have been shocked and pushed away, but instead she moved her hands to his waist, laid her cheek against his shoulder. Surrendering herself to his embrace—not realizing until this very moment how much she'd craved this type of contact.

"Tell me your secrets," he said. "Having to carry them is a terrible burden, to be sure."

More than she'd ever admit. But she kept her silence, basking in the quiet, soul-quenching moment.

"Tell me... Allow me to chase away your woes. You need only to reveal them to me."

Oh, if only he could. He almost made her believe that the impossible was possible. Almost.

In the circle of his arms, little by little she became sensitive to the feel of her breasts pressed against his solid chest. To the escalating heat coiling through her system. And mounting by the moment. She felt his heart's rhythm increase, accelerating her own.

"*Angelica...*"

She looked up into his eyes. Something in the way he gazed at her made her insides flutter. His perfect mouth was only inches away. He lowered his head. She held her breath in anticipation, expectant.

He stopped short.

Looking away, he took a deep breath and let it out slowly. Then he grasped her wrists, pulled her hands off his waist, and eased her arms down to her sides.

He stepped back, breaking the tantalizing contact, and bellowed for Henri. The boom of his voice made her jump.

She placed her hand over her racing heart. The heat still coursing through her hadn't dissipated in the least once he'd stepped away.

His body rigid, he issued a curt order to Henri to escort her back to her chamber, then murmured good night to her, and strode out of the dining hall.

*****

When Simon entered the library, he went straight to the brandy, poured himself a goblet, and downed the amber liquid. His body was tense. Aroused. Agitated in the extreme. What the hell was he doing? His thoughts should be on Thomas. His men. Not on this woman. He was becoming drawn into her game of mystery. And he couldn't allow it.

The evening had been a fiasco. He'd learned nothing. It only made matters worse that she'd pressed herself against him with the most perfect pressure over the engorged head of his cock and stared up at him with open curiosity.

Jésus-Christ. The urge to seduce her into indulging in the stunning desire that burned between them was so powerful, he'd all but run from the room.

And he'd never run from anyone.

He couldn't even trust himself to kiss those lush lips just once without surely deflowering her. What the fuck was the matter with him? What about her virginal ways could have possibly ignited his desire to this extent?

She was a problem he needed to rectify. He couldn't allow her to wield such power over him. He had enough people exerting their power to his detriment. Whatever game she was playing, he couldn't permit himself to be drawn into it. He'd no idea what to make of her secrets. Of her. And he shouldn't care to involve himself when his life was already far too involved.

He raked a hand through his hair, then slammed the goblet down on the wooden desk with a resounding clunk.

Tomorrow, he'd have a conversation with Gabriella and learn all that he wished to know about the green-eyed sorceress. Her friend would tell him what Angelica would not. Once he learned her secrets, her magic would be ineffective.

Dieu. What was he going to do with them if they didn't provide him with a destination—other than that horrible convent?

CHAPTER SIX

"Captain!" Henri approached Simon the next morning the moment he returned to Château Arles. Yet another night Simon hadn't slept. After tossing and turning in his bed for hours, he'd given up on sleep and gone down to briefly check on his ships, then to Robert's stable. A long ride had improved his disposition somewhat this morning. It had cleared his head of his moonlight beauty. Though this perilous situation he was in with Fouquet still hung like a noose around his neck.

"Monsieur le Marquis wishes to see you. His things are packed, and he is ready to leave."

Simon swore under his breath. He'd meant to join Robert early this morning, well before his departure.

"Wait, Captain. There is more," his loyal servant advised. "The king's ships have just arrived. And the two missing men... They've been found."

The words hit Simon in the gut. "Gilbert and Daniel? Are they...*alive*?"

"Yes, Captain. They were found at the French border and brought here while you were out. They are weak but alive."

Relief flooded through him. "Where are they now?"

"I had them placed in separate chambers, near yours."

"And where are my commanders from the king's ships?"

"All seven await you in the dining hall. Monsieur Armand has been reviewing the ledgers of each newly returned ship."

Simon nodded, his mind racing. The king's warships had finally returned.

And Gilbert and Daniel had been found alive.

Would they be able to tell him what had happened to Thomas? How much did the Spaniards know? *Jésus-Christ*, he hoped the two men knew the answers to the questions that had plagued him since Thomas was found dead. He needed to speak to them, and he needed to speak to his seven commanders, who were awaiting further orders.

But first there was Robert. Robert always came first.

And then he would have his talk with Gilbert and Daniel.

*****

Though thin and weak, Gilbert quaked with fury, his eyes alight with vengeance. "Captain, I ask permission to work the cannons on the ship that strikes at *La Estrella Blanca*," he said. His voice quavered with emotion.

Daniel had asked the very same thing. In much the same way.

For the last two hours, Simon had questioned the men separately about their capture and escape, what they had learned and revealed while in the Spanish prison—and the specifics of what had happened to Thomas.

Simon rose. "Rest now. Rebuild your strength."

Stopping outside the chamber, Simon rubbed his eyes with his index finger and thumb, wishing he could erase the images of Thomas's torturous death from his mind's eye.

In graphic detail, each man had recounted how the Spanish had killed Thomas. Slowly. Before them. Instead of breaking their wills, the horrific act had strengthened their resolve to maintain their silence long enough to escape. They had reached the French border by stealing horses and food along the way.

However, the most astounding news was that Thomas had provided the two men with one last bit of information before their capture.

Thomas had learned that a Spanish ship was due to reach Spain by the end of the month, with a cargo that promised to be heavy with precious metal.

La Estrella Blanca.

In his insurgent frame of mind, striking at the Spanish ship was the last thing Simon wanted to do. The notion of handing over more riches to Fouquet made him sick.

But how could he *not* strike at the Spanish ship? Thomas had lost his life to provide them with this information. Furthermore, Simon hated to admit it, but he had to capture its rich cargo in case his warships failed to earn enough for the Crown.

Thomas's death wasn't just a terrible personal loss to Simon. It was also a devastating blow to their operations.

He'd have to meet with his commanders and assign the ships' new positions blindly, without the usual insight gained by his spies—Thomas, Daniel, and Gilbert. Simon would have to rely on his instincts and judgment.

And lately, neither was reliable.

Providing results—weakening the Spanish *financially*—was not negotiable to Fouquet. They had to maintain their indispensability in his eyes or face the dire consequences. It wasn't above Fouquet to fabricate allegations of treason to remove Simon's warships from him. For Simon to die was one thing, but to have his men die because they'd followed him in his quest for promotion was another matter altogether.

It was as though a thick, black cloud had descended upon him. Everything looked dark—and he longed for the balmy breezes and serenity his island would offer. Returning there was an absolute necessity.

By rotating his ships, he gave each crew an opportunity to return to the island for mental and physical rest, away from the carnage. Simon, however, had been away from home far too long.

He needed respite. *Merde*, he needed sleep. There were many lives in his hands. He *had* to regain his focus before he could take on a man like Fouquet.

*****

"Are you certain you want to do this?" Gabriella asked. Standing at the top of the stairs, Angelica looked down at the foyer below, then back at her friend. "Do you really want to return to the convent, knowing how angry Madre Paola will be at us?"

The prospect of seeing Madre Paola didn't unnerve Angelica.

The thought of seeing Simon again, however, did.

Her behavior last night demonstrated how important it was for her to hasten her departure.

She'd *wanted* him to kiss her.

He was a complete stranger, yet he had a potent effect on her that unsettled her. These unrelenting physical yearnings he inspired seemed only to escalate with their every encounter. And were out of the question. In fact, any romantic involvement of any kind with any man was completely unthinkable.

"We must go. We cannot stay." Angelica pushed aside the pang of regret she felt at the thought of leaving.

The excitement Simon stirred, the exhilaration of his gentle touch, weren't things she wanted to think about. She'd accepted the future that lay before her, safe and sure, in a convent in the Republic of Genoa. And she would want nothing more out of life.

Leaving was the right thing to do. What other choice was there—for either her or Gabriella? The longer Angelica stayed, the greater the risk of being discovered.

Taking Gabriella's hands, Angelica gave them a reassuring squeeze. "We will speak to Sister Teresa. She will smooth matters with Madre Paola."

Angelica was grateful that she'd easily located Gabriella in the upstairs hall. With Gabriella dressed in a rich purple gown, her auburn hair arranged in pretty ringlets, Angelica almost hadn't recognized her. One look into Gabriella's eyes, and she could see how much she liked wearing such a costly gown.

"Gabriella, we cannot live here. These men are part of the King's Navy. They have duties, responsibilities at sea."

She'd overheard Marta speaking with another servant in French. Ships had arrived. As the captain of the fleet, Simon was dining with his commanders. Several commanders, in fact. She wasn't easily impressed, but everything about this man was impressive.

The men's meal would be over by now. Before his ships set sail, she was determined that she and Gabriella were placed on one set for the Republic of Genoa.

Downcast, Gabriella nodded. "I've liked it here. The people have been so nice...the captain...and the man I told you about, Domenico. They've even given us gowns." Gabriella smoothed her hand over the sleeve. "Is the dress not grand, Angelica? Did you not get yours?" She eyed Angelica's convent garb.

Angelica forced her feet forward, down the steps. "I'm not interested in the gown," she said, wishing it was entirely true. "We're not going to need them at the convent." Having enjoyed the luxury of a bath and freshly laundered clothes mere hours ago, she added, "My convent garments suit me just fine."

She would leave the realm for good this time. Once she was back in the convent, her inappropriate thoughts about fleet commander Simon de Villette would cease, and with them, her uncharacteristic behavior. She was sure of it.

*****

Simon looked down the long table at his top-ranking men, his expression tightly guarded, his emotions firmly in check as they had been for the entire day.

Five of the seven ships had been successful in capturing prizes. The Crown's share of Spanish silver would be delivered within the next few days.

Simon wanted nothing more than to refuse his portion, but to do so would alert his men to the fact that something was amiss. He couldn't let them know he wanted to abandon everything he'd worked for. If a leader wasn't committed, those who followed him wouldn't be either. It would lower the morale of the men and unravel their operations.

Putting everyone at risk.

They were going to maintain their value to Fouquet until Simon found the opportune time to strike, to topple Fouquet from his powerful post. The mission was beyond dangerous.

But Fouquet couldn't be allowed to continue as he did.

Each man was given information only on a need-to-know basis. Nothing more. Even his spies in Fouquet's home knew only that they were to report Fouquet's dealings.

In dispassionate tones, Simon advised his commanders of Thomas's death.

"Bastards," growled a few of the men.

"What of Fouquet?" one of his commanders asked. "I've heard murmurs about him dipping his hand in deeper than is his due."

Simon glanced at Robert. Out of affection and respect for the retired commodore, Simon had asked him to sit in on the meeting before he departed for Paris. The seasoned leader's expression gave nothing away.

Though Simon couldn't very well hide the glaring reality of Fouquet's malpractices, he wasn't about to discuss the Superintendent of Finance's excesses now.

"I will deal with Fouquet," Simon stated. "Your job is to meet your objectives. You have each been assigned new positions and missions to be carried out against Spanish ships and ports. Regardless of what has happened or what is happening, we have a duty. We do this for our king. And Thomas."

"Captain, I'll strike at the Spanish any way you deem fit—in Thomas's memory!" said one of his men.

The rest concurred.

Another raised a goblet. "Let us drink. To Thomas, may he rest in peace, and to the captain, whose wisdom has led us to riches we had not conceived possible, and whose cunning will lead us to victory over our enemies."

Simon forced a smile. Forced himself to join them in drink.

Their greatest enemies weren't foreign but domestic—the unholy trio of Fouquet, Mazarin, and the king. Mazarin had been the one who'd chosen Fouquet for the position of Superintendent of Finance. Fouquet was Mazarin's man, and in the eyes of their young king, the First Minister Cardinal Mazarin was never wrong.

Simon intended to show them all just how wrong a choice Fouquet had been.

While the men ranted about the Spanish and the French government, Robert leaned in.

"Well done, Simon," he murmured in his ear. "I take my leave now and return to Paris." Robert rose with the help of his cane and squeezed his shoulder. "*Dieu vous garde.*" He made his way to the doors that led to a private passageway and his chambers.

Watching him leave, Simon was struck with the unshakeable feeling that the next time he'd see Robert, Simon's life would be changed.

And not for the better.

*****

As Angelica and Gabriella neared the doors of the dining hall, heated voices rose from within the room.

"*The Spaniards will pay for what they have done to our men. They will pay in blood!*" The sheer venom in the man's tone made Angelica stop dead in her tracks.

Gabriella bumped into her. "Angelica?"

Angelica quickly silenced her by pressing a finger over her lips.

The next words were muffled, the tone sharp and furious, until distinct French phrases rushed up at her.

"*...We'll show them what happens when they cross one of our own, Captain. They will see what the Black Demon is capable of... Slit every last one of their worthless throats!*"

Her blood froze, chilled by the ominous words.

"*Captain, if they thought the Black Demon and his men were cold-hearted pirates before, wait until they see what hell we shall unloose upon them now.*"

She recoiled. *Dear God...* Simon de Villette was involved with *pirates.*

He was the leader of these men. *He* was the *Black Demon?* No, it couldn't be. He was an officer in the royal navy. *Wasn't he?* A sick feeling slid down into her stomach as she realized he'd never actually told her he was in the King's Navy.

Oh why? He'd been so...incredible. His touch, his words, his actions, he'd shown her the concern and consideration she hadn't realized she'd lacked in her life.

The image of his attractive face, those gorgeous eyes, his beguiling smile, appeared in her mind. As did the memory of his strong arms around her. Fool. Fool. *Fool!* He was a fraud. A lie. Too good to be true. She tamped down the ridiculous sense of loss.

They were in the company of criminals.

They had to get away. *Now.* Angelica squeezed her friend's hand. "These men are not what they appear. They're pirates!" she said in a sharp whisper.

"*Pirates?*"

"Yes!"

"No, I cannot believe it." Gabriella shook her head. "The captain? *Domenico?*"

"I just *heard* them."

Her friend's eyes widened. "Are you certain? I heard nothing…"

"Yes! Dear God, *yes.*"

Gabriella stepped back, horrified; her leg bumped a chair, causing it to scrape across the floor. The sound resonated in the long corridor. Footsteps immediately followed. The dining hall door was snatched open.

Angelica's stomach dropped.

A large man glared at them from the threshold. Gabriella slapped her hand over her mouth, a sorry attempt to stifle her cry.

Simon stepped around the man and into the hallway. He approached, his dark brows knitted together, his vivid eyes fixed on Angelica. Dressed in a white shirt and black breeches, he had never looked more like an outlaw.

Gabriella began to weep softly into her hands. Though it didn't take much to bring her dear friend to tears, this was no time for histrionics.

Angelica threw her arms around her friend. "There now, Gabriella, you need not cry." With a fixed smile on her lips and her heart in her throat, Angelica turned to Simon as he approached. "Good day, Simon."

"Good day. Is everything all right?" He eyed Gabriella, softly sobbing on her shoulder.

"Yes, of course. Gabriella is so relieved to see me in good health and out of bed, she's been moved to tears. We're both so happy to see each other. Is that not so, Gabriella?" She gave her a small pinch on the arm.

Gabriella jerked up. Angelica looked into her watery eyes and silently commanded her to cease her tears. Gabriella faced Simon with great trepidation.

"Yes, I'm…ha-happy." She offered him a miserable smile.

"*Dieu.*" A dark-haired man walked up behind Simon. "*She doesn't look happy,*" he murmured in French. Then to Gabriella he said in Italian, "Gabriella, your friend is correct. There's no need for tears. We discussed her recovery yesterday, during our walk in the gardens, remember?" Clearly, this was the man Domenico, whom Gabriella had talked about.

At the mention of the walk in the gardens, Gabriella was back to sobbing into her hands. More men began exiting the dining hall, making the corridor feel smaller. They circled like predators. Angelica felt as though she and Gabriella were the prey.

Her smile still frozen on her face, Angelica slid a protective arm around Gabriella's shoulder. "I'm sorry. We seem to have disturbed you. We'll return to our chambers now."

She turned and escorted Gabriella down the hall, praying they couldn't hear her heart thundering.

"Angelica?" She tensed at the sound of her name, every muscle in her body poised for flight. It was Simon.

Leader of sea-bandits.

Hearing her name from him this time didn't have the same tantalizing effect. Swallowing down her terror, she turned to face him. He strode past her and opened the door to the library. "Please, come in."

Angelica lowered her arm and exchanged looks with Gabriella. Her friend's eyes were big and full of fear. Filled with her own dread, Angelica clasped her friend's hand and led her into the room.

Simon and Domenico entered after them.

Simon stopped before her. His size and muscled form had never been more intimidating. She desperately hoped he couldn't read in her eyes the horror she felt inside.

"I don't believe you've met Domenico Dragani. He is a commander of one of my ships," he said.

She exchanged polite greetings with the man; all the while, her mind raced. How were they going to get out of here?

"Are you certain nothing is amiss?" Simon asked.

How could his concern appear so sincere? How could he be so proficient at duplicity? *Because he is a criminal.*

She looked away briefly, needing to break the connection with his gaze, when she noticed a small, blank parchment on the desk.

An idea came to her.

"Actually"—she glanced at both men—"there is something amiss. Gabriella isn't feeling well."

Gabriella gasped. Angelica squeezed her hand to silence her.

"She isn't?" Domenico stepped forward, studying Gabriella closely.

Gabriella looked down at her feet, unable to meet his eyes.

"Yes," Angelica answered for her. "It seems she's been having stomach pains. They come and go." She squeezed her hand harder. Gabriella's attention shot back up to her. Upon making eye contact with her friend, Angelica said, "When the pain hits, it's quite terrible. Even worse than the time she was to go to the village with Madre Paola."

Thankfully, comprehension dawned on Gabriella's face. Clearly, her dear friend remembered the time she'd fabricated a stomach ailment to avoid spending the day with Madre Paola. Unfortunately, afterward, she'd been forced to down considerable amounts of nutmeg oil to combat her "malady."

Gabriella looked unsure for a moment, and Angelica was afraid she might be too frightened to go through with the ruse.

"I-I think the pain is returning…" Gabriella said.

Relieved, Angelica watched her friend begin an impromptu performance, clutching at her stomach with a moan. Then a moan louder still.

"You should sit down," Angelica ordered and grabbed the parchment off the desk.

By the time she returned to her side, Gabriella was not only sitting but doubled over and moaning repeatedly.

"Gabriella… What the devil…?" Domenico dropped to one knee beside her.

Angelica fanned her with the parchment. Gabriella continued to moan as if in dire pain.

Angelica forced herself to meet Simon's gaze. "She needs a physician. I've never seen her quite like this."

"Simon." Domenico looked concerned as he slipped an arm around Gabriella. "I think it's wise. Perhaps we can get a physician from one of the ships—"

"No!" Angelica blurted out. "I mean...Bernard Toussaint was so skilled and so kind. Gabriella would highly benefit from his competence and gentle manner." They needed Toussaint, not one of *their* physicians.

Gabriella wailed out.

"My friend is very sensitive," Angelica added, squeezing Gabriella's shoulder, fearing her performance was a tad overmuch. With her other hand, she surreptitiously concealed the parchment in her sleeve.

Simon frowned. Gabriella's moans grew softer. Angelica held her breath.

"Domenico, carry her upstairs. I'll order a man to ride to the town to find Bernard Toussaint."

Angelica almost collapsed from relief.

Domenico swept Gabriella up in his arms and stalked out of the room. Angelica turned to follow.

"Angelica?" Simon caught her arm.

She jumped back from the contact, and saw the immediate surprise on his face. She mentally chastised herself. *Relax! You will give yourself away.*

"I'm sorry. I'm afraid I'm somewhat jittery." She rubbed her arm, willing away the feel of his fingers. "I'm worried about Gabriella."

"Yes, of course. However, you're quite flushed. Is your head hurting again?"

She wanted to scream at him to stop acting as though he was decent. She was all too aware of the sword against his left hip. Thoughts of what the cutthroat was capable of doing with it, had done with it, tortured her aching brain.

"I'm fine. I must get upstairs. Gabriella needs me."

*****

In Gabriella's chamber, Gabriella lay on her side in the middle of the bed with her arms wrapped tightly around her legs, moaning with dramatic persuasion.

Domenico leaned over to feel her forehead for fever. "Water..." she rasped at him.

He turned around, scanning the room for a water pitcher. There was none to be found.

"I'll be back shortly with some water." He turned on a heel and left with purposeful strides.

As soon as Domenico was gone, Gabriella sat bolt upright. Angelica ran to the hearth and selected a piece of kindling that had burnt only halfway. She used it on the small parchment she'd stolen from the library and quickly scribed a note to Toussaint.

"We're going to need assistance to get out here, and out of the realm. We've no money. No transportation to go back home," Angelica said, returning to the bed. They were going to have to trust someone. And trusting strangers was the last thing she was comfortable doing. "Our choices are rather slim. I have written a note to the physician asking for help. I think we can meet him outside the servants' entrance once everyone is asleep. I will slip him the note—"

"I will give the note to him," Gabriella stated. Her eyes no longer held any fear. "It is my fault we are in this terrible predicament. I helped Simon de Villette take you out of the convent. I am not asking you, Angelica. I'm demanding it! I will give the note to the physician."

Seeing a determination in her friend she'd never seen before, she didn't argue with her and handed the note over. Tucking it into her sleeve, Gabriella lay on the bed once more.

As soon as they heard footsteps approach, she began the second act of her performance. In the next agonizing hour and a half, Domenico paced about the room while Angelica held Gabriella's hand as her moaning friend continued her seemingly tireless act of intermittent attacks. Finally, the door opened and the physician entered with Simon.

"Signorina, it is so good to see you," Toussaint said in his usual friendly manner, "but you should be in bed, resting."

Angelica rose. "I'm feeling much better, really. You have my deepest gratitude, for your talents in medicine afforded me a speedy recovery. I pray that you will be equally effective in treating my friend."

Bernard Toussaint approached the bed. Gabriella moaned softly. "Of course. If I may be permitted some privacy to allow me to examine the young woman…"

Outside in the hallway, Angelica's heart pounded away the moments as she waited with Simon and Domenico. Domenico's continued pacing only made her more nervous.

With Gabriella alone with the physician, she could further explain the predicament they were in.

Domenico stopped abruptly. "I can't understand what could be the matter with her. She was perfectly fine yesterday in the gardens," he said, scrubbing a hand over his face. "I can't stand the wait any longer." Domenico threw open the door to reveal Toussaint standing near the bed, holding the folded parchment.

Angelica's heart dropped to her stomach.

Domenico entered and snatched the note from Toussaint's hand. Reading its contents quickly, he glanced at a panic-stricken Gabriella and then at Angelica. He walked over and handed the note to Simon. "I believe you should read this."

Her limbs went numb.

Simon's gaze moved over her words. His jaw tightened. "*Merde*," he muttered, then crunched the parchment in his fist. Without a word, he grasped her wrist and stalked down the hall, with Angelica all but running to keep up with his long strides.

He pulled her into her chamber and slammed the door shut behind him. Yanking her arm free from his grasp, she ran to the middle of the room and turned to face him. He'd removed his sword, yet he was still very much a threat.

She clenched her fists. Whatever he was about to do, she would not surrender without a fight.

CHAPTER SEVEN

"So, mademoiselle, you speak French," Simon said in his native tongue, no longer intending to speak to her in any other language. "Do enlighten me on everything else you're keeping from me. And do not attempt to lie, pretending you don't understand me when I hold in my hand the proof that you do."

He threw the crumpled parchment into the fireplace. *Fuck.* This predicament was entirely his fault. A moment of carnal fog outside a convent had resulted in this situation.

A situation that had just turned very serious.

He'd failed to learn anything about her. He'd erred in his assumptions concerning her—*she speaks French*—and as a result of his mistakes, she'd overheard his conversation with his men.

The last thing he wanted was to have her entangled in his circumstances.

Now she was caught in the web.

"Monsieur, I've told you all you need to know about me."

She momentarily unbalanced him by speaking for the first time in his language of birth. Each perfect word sounded heavenly.

This was no daughter of a peasant who'd been tutored in a convent. Her manner of speaking and conduct were too refined. Her education had been obtained in France, or perhaps from French tutors in the Republic of Genoa. In short, her family was, at least at one time, notable. What happened? Why had they left her in a convent for so long? She was certainly of marriageable age.

Were they *all* dead?

"You are mistaken, mademoiselle. You have much to tell me. However, first allow me to tell you about me." By the note she had written and the look in her eyes, narrow, accusatory, and full of disdain, he knew she condemned him as a scourge on society. A pirate. It bothered him that she thought so little of him. And he had no idea why it mattered what she thought.

"My name is Simon Boulenger. I am, in fact, the captain of a fleet of privateer ships for France. It is my...*duty*"—he forced the word off his tongue—"to attack Spanish ships and forward proceeds to the Crown. And for your information, Toussaint works for me."

She flinched, but her gaze remained locked on his. He found himself admiring her courage. Under the circumstances, any other woman would have succumbed to tears by now.

"I don't require any explanations or details about you. All I'm interested in is returning to the convent."

He crossed his arms. "I don't think you understand. Matters have just become very *complicated*. You've been made privy to...sensitive information. As a result, I can't risk the lives of my men to take you anywhere now."

She paled. "You can't be serious! We are to be *prisoners*?"

"You will be treated no different than you have been."

"Except we are not permitted to leave!"

"That is correct. I'm sorry."

"*Why?* What possible harm could Gabriella and I cause you?"

"I don't know. I don't know how long you were listening, the extent of what you heard. I don't know who you are. Or who you know. These are dangerous times. There are enemies everywhere, including in the Republic of Genoa. I cannot take *any* risks. This is not a permanent situation. It's only until...certain matters are attended to."

Until his situation with Fouquet was rectified.

Until Fouquet was ruined.

"I heard nothing, really..."

Raising his brow, he gave her a skeptical look.

"Very little, I swear! And any personal information about me is irrelevant, I assure you."

He approached her. She stiffened, her fists still at her sides. Once again he found himself tantalized by her proximity. The sweet, fresh scent drifting from her chestnut tresses seductively swirled through his system. His hungry cock hardened by the second.

Simon gazed at her upturned face. For the first time, he noticed an adorable freckle on her earlobe and another on her neck. He had to fight back the urge to press his lips to her soft skin. *Dieu.* He wanted to coax her into his arms and onto the bed, to turn the fiery look in her eyes into carnal hunger. If she had any idea how badly he wanted to sink himself inside her, knowing she would be deliciously tight and hot, she'd bolt for the door.

He couldn't believe he was lusting after a virgin in convent garb.

A woman who, at the moment, clearly despised him.

He'd never been hated by a woman. And he didn't like being hated by this one.

"It is your game of secrecy that makes me mistrust you as much as you mistrust me," he said.

"You cannot do this. I demand you take us home! You have no right to hold us here against our will!"

"We won't be staying here. We will be sailing for the West Indies in a few days."

Her mouth fell open. She stepped back. There was horror in her eyes, a crack in her brave façade.

"No! We will not go with you!" she countered. "You wear finery and have influential friends"—she indicated the chamber with a sweep of her arm—"but you are not the noble or officer you pretended to be. You are not part of the King's Navy. You are clearly deceitful and no doubt corrupt. I want no part of whatever criminal endeavor you are embarking on!"

Her words gored him to the core.

Furious, he stepped forward. She took another step back, bumping into the tall bedpost at the foot of her bed with a gasp.

"*You* accuse *me* of deceit? Of hiding who I am? You hide more than you reveal! Who the hell are you to judge me?" *Merde.* The day had been long. He was both physically and emotionally depleted. And he was sick and tired of this game. It was no longer intriguing. He wanted answers. Needed answers. "I'm tired of this nonsense. I demand to know who you are, and what truths you conceal. *Right now!*"

She glared at him, her body rigid. In a low voice simmering with ire, she said, "I have told you *all* you will ever know about me."

He was stunned. He was accustomed to compliance to his every order. *Always.* How was it that he could command hundreds of men, yet he couldn't get this one woman to tell him her full name?

*****

Angelica saw his eyes darken and braced herself. She'd faced a man who was pure evil when she was younger. Weaker. She would *not* break her silence. She knew the hell that awaited her if she did.

"Is that so, mademoiselle? Well then, let me tell you this. I know you are running away from something or someone." The accuracy of his words sent a streak of cold terror down her spine.

"I know something more about you," he said. "You don't wish to embrace a life of religious devotion. Or a cloistered existence. You speak of needing to return—but never of *wanting* to return. You say it is where you belong, but you have never said that you *wish* to belong there. Last night you showed me that at least part of you wants more out of life than what you get living in that convent." He cupped her cheek in his warm, strong palm.

Her senses jumped to life, startling her. Her hand flew to his forearm, intending to push him away, to break contact with his evocative touch. He covered her hand with his other, trapping it there. Beneath her fingers, through the fabric of his shirt, she was all too aware of his hard muscles and the appealing heat of his skin.

"Angelica…" he murmured, the seductive quality of his voice so naturally a part of him. It shimmered over her nerve endings. And quickened her heart. "You may despise me, but I am still the man who came to your rescue in that chapel. The man whose arms you were in last night. And last night, you very much wanted me to kiss you." He leaned toward her ear, his soft, dark hair lightly brushing her cheek. "Admit it," he whispered.

Briefly, she closed her eyes and swallowed. She would cut out her own tongue before admitting to *that*. To the kiss she'd craved. To the desire to feel his perfect lips against hers.

"A life cloistered in a convent is not what you wholeheartedly want. It limits and denies, and it demands a chaste existence. Do you really want to live out your entire life never having known what it's like to make love?"

Make love...

His words rippled through her body, down to her feminine core.

He lifted his head, his vibrant blue eyes gazing into hers once more. "Don't you wish to know the pleasure of being kissed...caressed..." He stroked his thumb across her bottom lip, sending sensations lancing to the tips of her breasts. She lost her breath. "Don't you want to know how incredible sex can feel? Being taken to ecstasy and back. Do you not want to experience that? That exquisite feeling of being locked in this most intimate joining, your body yearning, until the rushing release...until the *ultimate fulfillment?*"

Never had she heard someone speak so boldly. Never before had she felt the impulses that now rioted inside her. Nor did she ever think the act between men and women could sound so appealing.

She looked away, desperate to break the allure, needing to quash the physical urges he incited and the desire for things she knew were impossible in her life. But he curled his fingers beneath her chin and turned her face back to his.

"*Chère...*" The unexpected endearment undermined her resolve. "Tell me you don't want to live in that convent. Tell me the truth."

It took a moment to locate her voice. "No. I do wish it." Her words sounded pathetic. Weak.

He dipped his head, his mouth so close to her own. "I don't believe you." His breath mingled with hers, warming her lips. "Sex can be sheer rapture. Something no one should forgo. The greater the attraction of the two people involved, the more intense the encounter. If I were your lover, I would taste every part of your sweet form...starting at your ankles...kissing you lightly up the inside of your legs..." His provocative statement practically buckling her knees. "Or perhaps, we would simply begin with your inviting lips." He lowered his head.

At the first touch of his mouth, he sent a hot rush streaming through her body, leaving her toes tingling. His kiss a decadent attack on her starved senses. Her long-dormant body was suddenly awash with desire she'd never imagined.

Overwhelmed, she fisted his shirt against his chest.

Pulling her away from the bedpost, he wrapped his arms around her tightly, and pushed his tongue past her lips, possessing her mouth with a thrilling thrust. She moaned. He kissed her with dizzying intensity, his tongue giving hers swirling caresses. Her heart hammered. Every inch of her quaked. This was like nothing she'd ever known. His taste was inebriating. The texture and heat of his mouth made her ravenous for more.

He stopped abruptly, pulling away.

She snapped opened her eyes, panting. Bereft. A tormenting need pulsed within her.

He was holding her at arm's length, his expression unreadable, his emotions masked. Yet his accelerated breathing was not so easy to conceal. He'd been no less affected than she by the brief heated kiss.

Dear God, what was she doing? She'd only been out from the convent for a short time. How could her conduct have deteriorated to this level? Just because he had immense appeal and charismatic comportment? So what? *Because when he touches you, he makes you feel like a woman. He makes you feel alive...* She silenced the small voice inside her. None of that mattered!

After living ten years in a convent, accepting its way of life, she shouldn't have landed herself in such a situation with any man. Much less a man some called the Black Demon.

A man who had deceived her and was now refusing to set them free.

Simon Boulenger had his own secrets to guard. And she wanted no part of them or any of this. She had enough to deal with.

Placing his hands on his hips, he released a sharp breath. "*Dieu*, we are playing with fire."

Fire. What an appropriate word. She felt as though she was burning.

"This is not going to go any further," he said.

She gave a nod, all too happy to agree, instantly squelching the disappointment inside.

"This game of intrigue ends tonight, Angelica. I am going to ask you for the final time, and I expect the entire truth—"

Holding up a shaky hand, she halted his words. "Do not ask. I've told you all that I am willing to say."

A man who touched a woman the way he did wasn't the sort of man who inflicted physical harm on one, of that she was certain now. However, for a moment, from the fury in his eyes, she thought he'd reached his limit of patience with her. She was convinced he would rage at her, hurl vicious words.

Instead, he turned and walked out.

*****

Simon stalked toward Gabriella's chamber.

He was putting an end to the fascination he had with this green-eyed woman, permanently. Women had always been a pleasant diversion from the enormous demands and responsibilities placed on him, not a complete distraction.

And not one of them had ever driven him mad.

His sac was painfully full. His cock was stiff as a spike. And worse, the sweet taste of her mouth was consuming him. He was sorely tempted to turn around, satisfy her curiosity, sate his desire.

And end this sexual torment.

He couldn't believe that a few sexual words and a kiss with a virgin could be so erotic.

She was drawing away what little focus he had, at the most dangerous time of his life. The time to reassert control was long overdue.

He would know Angelica's secrets once and for all.

The door to Gabriella's bedchamber opened. Domenico emerged with a string of curses. "Women! Who can understand the female mind?" He strode toward Simon.

Ignoring Domenico's comment, Simon didn't break his stride.

"Gabriella is very upset," Domenico advised as Simon walked past.

"Tell me something I don't know."

"I tried to calm her down. I told her we were not pirates."

"Good." Simon's voice was bland.

"Then I kissed her."

That halted his steps. Simon turned. "And how was that received?"

"She weeps harder now."

Simon grunted. His mood was too foul to be amused over Domenico's rebuffed advances.

"Damned unmanning situation," Domenico muttered to himself. "One moment she's receptive, the next she wails! I've no idea if she's insulted. Or elated."

At the moment, he didn't care a whit about Domenico's amorous difficulties. "I want a watch placed on the women here in the hall. They're to be kept apart until the departure." He wanted no more plotting between the two. "Find Paul. He can sit for the first watch."

*****

Simon found Gabriella standing near the window, staring into the night.

When she turned her red-rimmed eyes toward him, they changed from dispirited to wary in an instant.

He schooled his features into a pleasant smile, and closed the door softly. Walking to the table in the middle of the room, he motioned to one of the chairs. "Please be seated, Gabriella. I merely wish to speak with you." He could see she was skittish.

Reluctantly, she walked over to him and sat on the chair he held out. Making his way around the table, he seated himself across from her.

"Wh-Where is Angelica? What have you done to her? I want to see her." Tears threatened to spill down her cheeks.

"There is no need to be afraid. Angelica is fine, I assure you." He kept his tone gentle, not wishing to have the overly emotional woman in hysterics, knowing she'd be no good to him then. "Tell me, have you and Angelica been treated well here?"

"Y-Yes."

"Well then, if my intentions toward either of you were malevolent, would I be so obliging? Did I not help Angelica at the convent? Attend to her well-being and yours? Did I not give you new gowns?"

"Yes... You've been kind."

"Has Domenico not been kind, attentive, and maybe even a little...taken with you?"

She blushed. The threat of tears, thankfully, had disappeared. "He's been very nice." Her tone and manner were a clear indication of her budding romantic interest in his commander.

Simon found himself, for the first time, a little envious of Domenico. His conscience wasn't burdened as Simon's was, and he didn't carry the weight of leadership on his shoulders. Domenico followed his orders, and his own personal desires, unencumbered. He was free to pursue Gabriella if he wished. He could offer as much or as little as he wanted.

Simon's life was a mess, and thanks to his involvement with Fouquet, corrupted. All he was prepared to offer any woman was a night of casual diversions. Angelica was desirable and definitely worth having, but his soul was blackened enough without compounding his misdeeds by taking her virginity just to satisfy his own selfish wants.

"Is it true what Domenico says? You are not pirates?"

"No, we are not."

She gave him a slight smile.

Encouraged by her reaction, he continued. "We are returning home in a few days. Have you heard of the West Indies?"

"Yes. I've heard."

"I would like you and Angelica to come with us. The weather there is mild. The island of Marguerite is quite beautiful. You will stay with us as our guests for a while. I know Domenico would like it very much if you would come. What say you?"

She blushed again. "I think I would like that."

"Excellent. Now then, Gabriella, you've told me a little about the convent. Can you tell me a little more?"

"All right."

"I know that within the convent there is an orphanage. Were you a part of the orphanage, Gabriella?"

"Yes."

"How long have you been at the convent?"

"Since I was a small child. Fever claimed both my parents' lives. The good Sisters at the convent provided me with a home."

"I'm sorry for your loss. It was undoubtedly a difficult time for a young girl."

She gave him a sad shrug.

"What about Angelica? When did she enter the convent?"

"Ten years ago, when she was fourteen and I was thirteen."

"Did you receive schooling there?"

"Yes. Madre Caterina, God rest her soul, insisted we learn to read and write."

"And Angelica learned to read and write there as well?"

"No. She already knew how when she came to us. She would often help the younger girls."

"Really?"

Gabriella brightened. "Angelica is a wonderful teacher. You should see her work with the children. They adore her. And her singing."

His head was suddenly filled with the haunting song she had sung that night in the chapel. It was a sound he hadn't been able to forget.

"Madre Caterina used to say that Angelica would make a truly wonderful nun one day."

Simon fought back his sudden urge to oppose the notion vehemently. "Oh? Why do you say that?"

"Why, she's kind, always selfless, always giving an encouraging word to all at the convent. Angelica is very bright too. She is the most intelligent person I know. Why, she will look at something and see it seven different ways that wouldn't even occur to me."

He held back a smile at Gabriella's praise of her friend. "What about Angelica's parents? What do you know about them?"

Gabriella lowered her eyes. "Not much. I know that Angelica adored them and that her father died first, followed by her mother sometime later."

"What else?"

"That is all."

Simon raised his eyebrows. "*All?* What were their names? What is Angelica's full name?" His questions rushed out quick and sharp, fatigue threatening his patience.

"I-I do not know…"

Her words yanked him to his feet, his chair scraping backwards against the wooden floor. Gabriella started, her eyes growing wide.

"Do you expect me to believe that you don't know the identity of a female whom you claim to be as close to as a *sister?*" he asked, incredulous. "You know nothing of her family, who they were, what they were?"

She shook her head. "N-No, I do not."

He pressed his palms down on the table between them. "You. Lie."

She burst into tears. "I do not lie! I-I asked her once, years ago. It caused her such obvious pain and upset that I never asked again." Tears continued to spill freely down her cheeks. "I would never cause her the slightest suffering. Whatever happened sometime in the first years of her life was obviously very difficult. It matters not to me or anyone else at the convent what her name is."

He couldn't believe this! "Do you know where she was born? Where she lived before coming to the convent? How she came to learn French?"

"No. No. No! She arrived during the night, ten years ago. I-I was completely unaware that she understood your language."

"It wasn't taught in the convent?"

"No. Never."

Simon hung his head, holding in the profanity bellowing in his brain. He'd been certain Gabriella knew all of Angelica's secrets.

The entire conversation might as well not have taken place. Nothing was gained. He still had more questions than answers. All he'd done was upset Gabriella.

She was back to sobbing audibly, abrading his sleep-deprived, agitated nerves.

CHAPTER EIGHT

The day of departure had arrived. The morning sun shone, but its warm rays didn't soothe Angelica.

Not when anger roared inside her.

Though she hadn't seen Simon since their kiss, at the moment, nothing would give her more satisfaction than to drown him in the very sea that surrounded her.

She looked across at the two men rowing their small boat toward the large ships. They were grinning at her. Self-conscious, she folded her arms over her chest, trying her best to shield the top curves of her breasts showing above the neckline of her fitted taffeta gown.

Ignoring their soft chuckles, she looked away, searching the people on the shore and the other tenders for Gabriella.

She was furious with Simon and his self-imposed authority over her and Gabriella. He'd kept them apart for two days and was too occupied to speak to her, no matter how many times she demanded it. She was livid about being forced to embark on this voyage and angry with herself for having failed to find a way of escape. She hated that Simon had introduced her to his luscious kiss—and that it had had such a potent effect on her.

And she hated that she was wearing the gown fit for an Aristo.

A breeze blew across her bare shoulders—a blatant reminder of her mode of dress. She couldn't believe she was out in public without her convent garb. It might have been drab and dull, but it made her feel connected to the one place that had kept her safe, alive and hidden. Wearing the familiar loose-fitted garment gave her a sense of comfort. Without it, she felt naked—in more ways than one.

Simon had no right to have it destroyed.

She still seethed over how Marta had tricked her into giving up her clothes last night for laundering and had returned this morning with the rich blue dress and underthings she now wore.

"The captain says that since you're no longer in a convent, there's no need for you to dress that way," Marta had advised. Once again Angelica had demanded to see him, intending to vent her outrage, but as before, he refused, advising through his servants that he was too busy with the imminent departure to attend to her dress dilemma.

Dress dilemma!

It wasn't a trivial matter. The convent garb was a reminder of her future. And after his kiss, she needed all the reminding she could get. For the last two days, she hadn't been able to take her mind off it or his seductive words.

Slowly he was stripping away pieces of her comfortable existence. Gone were her freedom, her peace of mind, and now her convent clothes. She felt unnerved, desperate to hold on to something familiar. And he wasn't letting her.

In all these years, she hadn't worn a color other than gray. Dressed in a gown that molded to her body, she hadn't recognized the image staring back at her in the mirror that morning. Nor had she taken much notice of how much her body had changed since the last time she'd worn a gown this fine—and *fine* wasn't strong enough to describe the luxurious feel of the fabric against her skin.

She blamed Simon for this too. She didn't want to miss the things he was showing her when she finally returned to the convent.

Nearing the large ship, she spotted Gabriella on one of the tenders. She looked well. *Thank God…* At the moment, there were only two things Angelica was grateful for: first, she was leaving France. And second, having been told that she'd be reunited with her friend on board the ship, she was grateful she'd have Gabriella with her.

The idea of being on the same ship as Simon for weeks was unnerving without her.

They reached the first ship, and a rope ladder was tossed down from the deck above. The men in the tender held their small boat as still as possible as it bobbed alongside the much larger sea vessel. Angelica grabbed the ropes and looked up to see two men waiting for her on deck. From their vantage point, they could easily look down her gown. She gritted her teeth, trying to banish the thoughts of inflicting extensive bodily harm on their leader, and slipped her foot onto the rope ladder. She began her ascent.

When she reached the top, the two men on board helped her over. With her feet securely on deck, she spotted Gabriella's tender again. Sitting beside Domenico, Gabriella waved to her with a large smile.

Before she could wave back, one of the men on deck began pulling the rope ladder up.

"What are you doing?" Angelica asked. "The ladder is still needed."

"Excuse me, mademoiselle?" She turned to the tall blond man addressing her. "My name is Mathieu Godeau. I am second in command here. Is there a problem?"

"Yes, my friend is coming on board, and this man is taking away the ladder."

"I'm sorry. You're mistaken. She is being placed on another ship."

"What? No. You're wrong. Gabriella is to be on this ship. I was advised by—" Her next word was going to be *Marta*. Marta. The same woman who'd lied to her on behalf of her master about laundering her garment. How could she be so foolish?

"*By?*" Godeau pressed.

"Never mind."

"As you wish. If you will please follow Denis to your cabin…"

A dark-haired, burly man approached her.

"No, I will not. Where is your captain? I wish to speak to him."

"He has not come aboard yet. If you will follow Denis—"

"No. I shall wait for the captain here."

"I'm afraid that is out of the question. I'll tell him of your displeasure the moment he boards." He nodded to the man beside her.

The brute Denis clasped her arm in his iron grip and started toward her cabin. She tried to pull free without success. Laughter erupted from the men on deck.

Denis easily hauled her below to a small cabin and shoved her unceremoniously inside, despite her protests. She stumbled back and almost landed on the wooden floor.

It was then she heard the distinct, devastating sound of the lock turning into place.

Rushing to the door, she tried the latch.

No! She pounded on the door as hard and as fast as her heart hammered. He couldn't... He wouldn't! She wasn't going to be locked up like this!

Her stepfather's control over her mother had been stifling. Fouquet's heavy-handed manner had eventually eroded her mother's spirit until she became merely an empty shell. Seeing it unfold before her eyes had shattered Angelica's heart. She loved her mother dearly. But she was nothing like her. Had sworn to herself that she was *never* going to be like her. And what was happening now was frighteningly familiar.

*****

"C-Captain?" Paul interrupted Simon as he spoke with his ship's commander on deck. France had just disappeared from the horizon. "The woman, Captain, the one in the carpenter's cabin... She is *quite* upset. She can be heard all the way to the galley. She has been carrying on for some time now... I believe that she is...well...throwing the furniture against the door."

"*Dieu*, is the door locked?"

"Yes, Captain, just as you ordered."

"I gave no such order."

"Denis was under the impression you had. He placed her in there."

Simon swore and stalked toward the carpenter's cabin with young Paul right behind him.

Preparing for the voyage had required Simon's undivided attention. And therefore, he'd purposely avoided Angelica. He'd refused to be interrupted from the final meetings with his commanders, or distracted from the important communiqués he had to write to his spies in Fouquet's household—communiqués that would be surreptitiously delivered along with the proceeds from the five warships.

Merde. This was the last thing he wanted to deal with. The capture of *La Estrella Blanca* was imminent. He couldn't have his mind clouded with lust at a time like this.

The moment he went belowdecks, he could hear the commotion coming from her cabin. Loud, devastating thuds from a heavy object bashing against the door. What was she using? A chair? The table?

Dieu, the bed?

He understood now why Paul had felt compelled to report her behavior.

Simon reached the door. Paul stopped well back. "D-Do you wish me to assist, Captain?"

Another loud slam crashed against the door.

"Is that you?" Angelica shouted. "Are you there?" She gave the door a lesser blow, perhaps with her fist.

Simon glanced at Paul. The younger man shifted his weight from one foot to the other, looking as though he wanted to bolt rather than deal with this one irate woman.

Simon cleared his throat. "Yes," he said.

"I knew you were unsavory, but I never knew that you were a coward too! Do you hear me? You are a worthless COWARD!" Her words seem to resonate through the entire ship.

Paul's mouth fell agape, then closed, then opened once more.

She smashed another object against the abused door.

Paul jumped. "Wh-What do you wish to do, Captain?" he whispered.

"Come in here and face me, *coward!* Or are you afraid?"

Knowing she was looking to provoke him, Simon forced himself to draw in a deep breath and exhale slowly before he spoke. "Paul."

"Captain?"

"Go."

The young man obeyed immediately, disappearing into the galley.

"Why send him away?" She kicked the door. "Don't you need others to do your dirty work for you? Are you certain you have the courage to come in here *alone*?" Wood splintered against the door with the intensity of a thunderclap.

Jésus-Christ. He seized the door handle. "That's enough! You've done enough damage—"

"No! *You* have done the damage! Open this door!" She struck the door and gave a cry as if in pain.

His anger drained away the moment he realized she'd injured herself.

He unlocked the door and snatched it open.

She stood in the middle of the cabin, holding her hand. Her head was down and her hair, arranged in a cascade of dark curls, was mussed. But it was her gown, and not the chaotic condition of the room, that froze his breath in his throat.

Deep blue, trimmed with pale yellow ribbons, it accentuated her female attributes in the most mouthwatering way—her body clearly defined before him for the first time. His cock hardened.

Her breasts rose and fell rapidly with her quickened breaths, the creamy skin above the bodice holding him transfixed. The temptation to run his fingers along the delicate scoop of the décolletage was overwhelming. He wanted to pull the strand of pale yellow ribbon resting so temptingly between those pretty breasts and stroke the silky skin that beckoned and beguiled him.

For a reckless moment, he considered finishing what they had started two days ago. If he'd had any idea she'd be this sexually inciting in finery, he'd never have taken the horrible gray garment away. What was he thinking? Was he looking to punish himself in new, excruciating ways?

Her head snapped up. She stepped forward. The sting of her palm against his cheek instantly cleared the fog of lust. Not exactly the type of greeting he generally received from a woman.

He caught her wrists just in time to avoid another blow. Clearly, she was back to fully despising him.

Simon twisted her easily around and held her securely, restricting her fight. "Easy. Allow me to explain..."

"How dare you lock me in here! You've no authority over Gabriella and me!" Her soft bottom squirmed vigorously as she tried to break free of his hold. "I'll not be governed by you. Let go of me." She kicked him in the shin. His grunt of pain did little to appease her. She yanked her arm free. Twisting her upper body, she landed another open palm to his cheek.

He swore. "Enough, Angelica! Calm down." He turned her around to face him just as she jerked away from him. His boot caught on the leg of an overturned broken chair. They tumbled down, landing on the bed that had been shoved to the middle of the cabin.

Grasping her wrists, he pressed them against the mattress and eased his body over hers, his weight muting her thrashing. *Dieu.* She wouldn't stop writhing, trying to twist out of his grasp, and the friction against his engorged cock was making his blood pump faster. Hotter.

"You're a liar! Overbearing, insufferable, and cold-hearted! You've no regard for others. You care nothing about the suffering you inflict!"

"*Enough.*" Simon squeezed her wrists to punctuate his command, her accusations bothering him more than she could ever know.

She stopped abruptly, panting, her cheeks pink. "You've taken my clothes, my friend, my freedom." Between ragged breaths, she tossed at him, "You said we would be treated as before, yet you forced me to stay in my chambers and now lock me in this cabin. I won't stand for this. I won't let you treat me this way."

He saw the hint of emotional pain in her eyes he'd never detected before.

Damn it. It hadn't been his intention to cause her such distress.

He eased himself off her slightly; his body immediately balked. The pressure in his prick was immense, his cock rioting for release.

Clamoring for her.

She turned her face away, her mouth all but brushing his thumb, her warm, rapid breaths caressing his hand. "You are proficient at duplicity. I cannot believe I thought, even for a moment, you to be an honorable man."

Those words cut deep.

He was unable to muster a defense. There was no honor to him. He owned no honorable name. Or position. And now he was forced to put her through this voyage because of his predicament, his choices in life.

He released her wrists and turned her face to his.

"Angelica..." He wanted...*what?* Her body? More? Her understanding? Her trust? He terminated his thoughts, unwilling to delve further. "I'm sorry, *chère*. You were not supposed to be locked in here. As for the rest, they were done out of necessity."

"*Necessity?* What have you done with Gabriella?"

"Gabriella is fine. No harm will come to her. She's been placed on one of the other ships, commanded by Domenico. She went quite willingly. No one forced her. Her destination is the same as ours. You will see her on the island."

He saw the mistrust in her eyes, and hated it.

"Why did you have Marta lie? She told me Gabriella was going to be on this ship."

"She did not lie. It was a last-minute change to allow you both as much comfort as possible during the voyage. On the other ship, Gabriella will have her own cabin. Domenico will take care of her." Domenico had approached him last eve and requested that Gabriella be placed on his ship. Knowing how agreeable Gabriella would find the idea, Simon had consented.

"Why are we on this voyage? What are you up to?"

The subject of Fouquet was multilayered, politically sensitive, and not something he wanted to, nor was free to discuss with her, no matter how much or how little she'd overheard. "We're returning home for some rest. We've been at war for some time. The island is a very pleasant place. Perhaps you and Gabriella will decide to make it your home."

"The convent is my only home. You had no right to take my clothes!"

"Angelica, how long could you have continued to wear the same garment? Besides, as the voyage lengthens, the weather will become considerably warmer. You will be more comfortable in lighter clothing." Remembering how she took a compliment, he refrained from telling her how ravishing she looked in the gown.

He hoped that by ridding her of the convent clothes, perhaps, in time, she would shed her secrets as well. He still couldn't believe that not even Gabriella was privy to them.

"I know you don't trust me, but I tell you this," he said. "I ran to your aid that night because I couldn't stand to see you hurt." There was the slightest softening in her eyes. It pleased him more than he could have imagined. "If I was willing to do that, then why would I harm you or Gabriella? You are safe. There is nothing to be afraid of. You can tell me who you are and what the secrecy is about." *Merde.* He couldn't let go of his desire to know.

She stared at him, unsure. He rejoiced at it. At least part of her wanted to trust in him.

He caressed her cheek. "Tell me," he urged. "Trust me..."

Her eyes hardened. She pushed his hand away. "I should trust you when you don't trust me?"

He hung his head and sighed. Her ear with that adorable little freckle was so temptingly close to his mouth.

He lifted his head. "I suppose we are at an impasse until one of us relents."

"It will not be me." She tried to sit up; her face, especially those sweet lips, were now closer to his. He hadn't been able to stop thinking about her delicious mouth for two days and nights. Her gaze dropped to his mouth. She ran her pink tongue along her lush bottom lip.

Dieu, that looked too much like an invitation.

Before he could stop himself, he slipped his fingers into her hair and brushed his mouth against hers. It was a catastrophic error. He knew it. His mind screamed it. The small sampling was his undoing.

He lowered her back down and swooped in for a deeper kiss, his tongue possessing her mouth on her gasp.

She grasped his shoulders, but to his delight, didn't push him away. Instead, she rewarded him with a soft, sensuous moan that made his prick pulse. She tasted so good. He couldn't get enough, sucking and stroking her tongue, their mouths locking and relocking. His kiss was hot and hungry as he unleashed all the pent-up desire he had for her.

Already her breaths were erratic, exciting his own. He couldn't moderate himself. He didn't care. Not when he was dying to sate himself with his moonlight angel. His world was filled with war and corruption. Beautiful, decent, and brave, she was like air and light in the stifling darkness. And he was helplessly drawn to her.

Cupping her breast, he grazed his thumb over her hardened nipple, teasing it, pinching it though the cloth of her gown. He had her pressing to him, arching hard, coaxing mews from her with every tender tug. His siren was on a bed, burning for him. For all that was wrong in his life, this felt so right.

With his mind no longer ruling his body, he plucked at the ribbon on her décolletage, his practiced fingers making quick work of the silk ribbons that laced her bodice, tugging and pulling at the neckline until

he'd freed her soft breasts. He took all of two wild heartbeats to take in the sight before him—her breasts just as gorgeous as he'd imagined them to be.

"Beautiful…" he murmured, driving an arm beneath her back, arching her to him. He sucked a sensitive tip into his greedy mouth. She drove her fingers into his hair, her soft cry sending a delicious hard throb through his cock. His sac was tight and full. His prick never felt so thick and heavy; he was so hard, he felt light-headed. Turning to her other breast, he lavished upon it equal attention. *You are mine…*

He grabbed her skirts and began pulling them up, dying to get at her sweet sex. Needing to possess her. Or lose his fucking mind.

Suddenly, he heard a jarring word escape her mouth. Loud and clear. Simon's head shot up. He felt as though he'd been torn out of the most incredible dream, his mind numbed by carnal fever, his body hot and tense.

"*No?*" He repeated the word, hoping he'd heard wrong.

She pushed at him. Her eyes were filled with tears. "Stop."

Stop. That word was worse.

His entire body was in revolt, demanding her. He wanted to howl in frustration. Closing his eyes, he drew a deep breath into his lungs and released it slowly, trying to master this feral desire, his heart still pounding. She trembled beneath him. *Merde.* He felt shaky too. He'd never experienced anything so intense. In the heat of the moment had he actually thought she was *his? Jésus-Christ*, had he said it out loud?

He sat up. Shaken, she quickly covered herself—concealing her sweet breasts from his view—and tried to scramble off the bed. He caught her arm, keeping her beside him. Thankfully, she didn't pull away. But she wouldn't look at him.

He scrubbed a hand down his face. *Dieu*, this was a novel situation. Normally given carte blanche during sex, *no* and *stop* weren't words he normally heard in bed. Then again, he'd never almost taken a woman who was a virgin.

He tried to clear his heated mind, trying to find words for the delicate circumstance.

Angelica's heart thundered. She couldn't believe it had happened again. Only this time, she'd let him do so much more. This time, it was even more heated and consuming.

It terrified her to the core.

She felt so exposed, not just physically but emotionally.

How did this man have the power to do this to her? He'd all but completely unraveled her.

He'd left her breasts feeling heavy, achy, all because of the sensations he'd created, sensations that had streaked downward to her sex, which now felt slick and empty, needing to be filled.

"Angelica, look at me." His gentle tone only unnerved her more.

She couldn't look at him. Not when she was so rattled. Not when she could feel the sting of tears in her eyes.

"There is nothing to be embarrassed or ashamed about. You're very beautiful. Desirable. We are attracted to each other. These things happen. But you were right to stop."

These things happen? Oh yes. Of course. They happened every day. She had a penchant for indulging in carnal activity with every man who broke into her convent and whisked her away.

Briefly, she closed her eyes.

No one had ever incited these heated cravings before. She didn't want Simon to affect her like this. She didn't want him to tell her she was beautiful and desirable. Most of all, she didn't want him to make her feel as though she were both. She wanted her life back. Safe and familiar. Emptiness and all.

"Please go," she said softly, keeping her eyes averted, despising her show of cowardliness.

He stood. "I won't lock the door. However, you must stay in your cabin for a short time still. It is for your own safety." The timbre of his voice told her he was as unsettled as she was.

He walked out and quietly closed the door behind him.

She placed her forehead in her palm and squeezed her knees together. The ache between her legs was unbearable. She wasn't supposed to know any of this. A man's touch. Passion. Nor did she want to know this sense of longing that lingered in his wake. She didn't want to think about Simon. Or wonder why he would be so affected. She didn't want to feel any of the things he made her feel. It only hurt to want for more when more was impossible.

She wished he'd never shown her just how wrong the image she'd carried with her about this act between a man and woman had been.

On a cold autumn night, her stepfather had destroyed her world and her future. She thought she'd buried her past and would never have to deal with it again. But a French privateer with seductive blue eyes and a magic touch had entered her life and effortlessly shaken the foundations of her carefully guarded world, more than he could ever know.

CHAPTER NINE

"Good morning, mademoiselle, I'm sorry this is so late. You must be famished," Suzette apologized cheerfully as she carried in the morning meal. Pretty, blonde, and nineteen, she was friendly and broke the monotony of Angelica's solitude each time she brought her food.

Angelica shook her head. "It's all right. I'm not that hungry."

Suzette set her tray down on the table in front of Angelica. "Are you all right, mademoiselle?"

No, she was not all right. Thoughts of Simon had kept her up most of the night. She'd spent hours trying to vanquish the memory of their amorous encounter.

Before she could offer a polite response, there was a knock at the door. Suzette opened it. Two large men entered, carrying a wooden trunk.

"Place it near her bed," Suzette told them.

They mutely obeyed and left.

Angelica stood. A trunk overflowing with dresses, shoes, and undergarments had been delivered to her cabin yesterday. The last thing she needed was more of the same. "What is this?"

Suzette smiled. "This trunk was supposed to be brought to your cabin with the trunk of dresses." She pulled back the lid, revealing the incredible contents. "They are from the captain. They're books, mademoiselle."

Angelica approached, stunned. There were *so* many books. The trunk was completely full. "They're all for...*me?*" she asked, incredulous.

"Yes. All the books are yours."

Her heart danced.

She moved closer. On the top, she noticed a familiar brown leather volume, realizing that it was the very book she'd pulled from the shelf in the library the night she and Simon had dined together. The book of sonnets.

He'd remembered?

She couldn't stop herself from picking it up, enjoying the feel of it in her hands, yearning to read it.

"They're a gift, mademoiselle. The captain hopes they will help combat the tedium."

She was speechless.

She couldn't remember the last time she'd been offered a gift as wonderful as this. He had thought of her. He'd given her *books*. The book of love sonnets.

He is also a man who is forcing you to go with him on a voyage to the West Indies and remain there for an indefinite amount of time, she forced herself to remember, needing to steel her resolve and to settle the fluttering inside her stomach. It was dangerous to entertain soft feelings where he was concerned.

Her past limited what she could have in the future. Her secrets were dark and layered and best kept confined to the hole they'd made in her heart. She had to resist the strength of his appeal, and return to the convent where the events of years ago did not penetrate its stone walls.

Realizing Suzette was watching her, Angelica reluctantly placed the book back in the trunk.

"Please offer my thanks to…the captain." *Coward. You haven't the courage to face him and thank him in person.* After what had happened yesterday, she'd no idea how she would face him again.

"Of course, mademoiselle. Come, eat. Marta asked me to bring you plenty of the cheese she says you're fond of." Angelica returned to the table and sat down. "She likes you." Suzette placed the bread before her. "I think the captain likes you too."

Angelica's face warmed. "I'm sure you're mistaken," she quickly denied, not in the least bit comfortable with this subject.

"It's not a bad thing. The captain is quite handsome."

She'd have to be completely blind not to have noticed that.

Suzette cut her a piece of cheese. "On our island, Marguerite, everyone has great affection for him and holds the captain in high esteem. He's brought many families to Marguerite, at first only the crewmen's families, then later, anyone who was in dire straits. He gave them employ in the fields. He gave us an opportunity to survive rather than to die in France."

She had no idea he'd impacted so many lives.

"I think you will like the island very much. It has all the comforts of France without the starvation or any terrible Aristos. In the village where I grew up, we never even had a schoolmaster. Yet on the island, we have a school, thanks to the captain."

"A school?" she marveled. He'd never said a word.

"Yes. The captain was taught to read and write when he was young, and he wishes it for others."

A knot formed in her throat. She was discovering a side of him she'd never known, and yet somehow this same man had earned himself the name the Black Demon. He was up to something. Something that required extreme precautions. Just how sinister, she didn't know. Nor seemingly did Suzette and Marta, for she'd asked for the details of Simon's plans. Yet, he was also a man whose touch could inflame her senses. He was perplexing.

He is exciting, whispered her heart.

Pouring a goblet of wine for Angelica, Suzette added, "I only wish I had learned to read."

Angelica leaped at the opportunity. "If you wish to learn, I could teach you." The voyage was long, and spending time teaching Suzette would be a pleasant way to fill the hours and feel useful.

"Really, mademoiselle?"

"Yes, of course; but you must call me Angelica."

"Oh, how wonderful, Angelica! In turn, perhaps I can make you some more dresses. There are some fine fabrics onboard. The captain has given his permission to use them. I'm quite good with a needle. I can make a dress fit for an *Aristo*!"

The last thing Angelica wanted was more dresses suitable for the upper class. However, Suzette's face shone with the prospect of sewing them for her, and she didn't have the heart to deny her.

"That sounds lovely." She smiled.

Sweet Suzette looked ecstatic. "Perhaps I can return later this afternoon for my first lesson?"

"Yes. Absolutely."

Still smiling, Suzette walked to the door. "Oh, I almost forgot. The rule is that women are not permitted on deck unless permission is granted. In fact, we're to restrict ourselves to our sleeping quarters and the galley."

That suited her just fine. She preferred to avoid Simon for the time being.

The moment Suzette left her cabin, Angelica moved to the trunk of books and pulled out the book of love sonnets.

Walking back to the table with it, she was still amazed by his unexpected gesture and the things she'd learned about this complex man.

The urge to devour the contents of the volume was oh so compelling. Perhaps she shouldn't. What was the point of reading romantic poetry? She placed the book on the table.

It stared back at her, beckoning her.

She glanced around the cabin. There was nothing else to do. Perhaps she could read another book. But this one was out of the trunk already. What harm if she, say, thumbed through it a little?

Snatching it up off the table, she sat down and opened it to the first page.

A knock at the door startled her. Quickly, she rose and placed the book behind her back. "Yes?"

Simon entered the cabin and closed the door. Her heart missed a beat.

He gave her one of his knee-weakening smiles. "Good morning."

He wore tanned breeches, a loose white shirt, and black boots. Tall, darkly handsome, with strength, intelligence, and devilish charm. Heaven help her. Did the man have to be utterly irresistible? *You need to respond. He's waiting for a reply.*

"Good morning," she managed to force out.

Simon took in the sight of her in the rich green gown. It was a perfect match for her sensual eyes. Green was his favorite color, and on her, it was breathtaking. She made a perfect vision. A sweet torture. Already he was hard.

He exhaled slowly, certain that she would derive some measure of satisfaction if she only knew the amount of physical discomfort and mental anguish she caused him. When he wasn't punishing himself with guilt over his role with Fouquet, he was in the throes of sexual fantasy with visions of her naked in his bed. Yesterday's heated incident had only stoked the fire hotter. It had only made him more enthralled by her. *Dieu*, it was a terrible idea to come to her cabin, yet here he was.

"Is there something you wanted?" she asked.

That wasn't the question to ask him this morning. Not after a wretched night alone in his cabin. His entire body roared, *I want you!*

"I came to see how you fared after your first night onboard." He stopped short of mentioning what happened between them yesterday. She looked as though it was the last subject she wanted to discuss.

He'd considered apologizing, but it felt hypocritical. He didn't think he could say he was sorry he'd touched or kissed her and mean it.

"I'm fine. Thank you." Her manner was stiff, and she had that look in her eyes that challenged him every time. The look that told him she was fortifying the wall she'd built around herself. Steeling her determination to maintain her secrets. Didn't she know he'd spent years weakening others' defenses? The more she tried to arm herself against him, the more he wanted to bring down the barrier she'd erected. How he wished he could simply let go of his obsession with her and to know more about her.

Though her distance was indeed the wisest thing to keep, he disliked it as much as the present tension and awkwardness between them.

Noticing the open trunk of books, he remarked pleasantly, "I see you've received the books."

"Yes, it was kind of you to provide them. Thank you, Simon."

"You're welcome. All I request in return is that you keep this to yourself."

Her delicate brows drew together. "Oh?"

"It is an act that is completely out of my 'overbearing, insufferable, and cold-hearted' character. I'll surely be tossed out of the pirates' league if this gets out."

She looked down and fought back a smile. He was pleased that he'd amused her. Perhaps this meant she didn't see him as a cutthroat. How he saw himself, however, was an entirely different matter.

He approached her. She gazed up at him, still trying to maintain a straight face. "Then I shall have to report you and win myself freedom from your hold."

The look of mischief in her eyes delighted him. The wall was crumbling a little.

He sat down on the edge of the table. "Why, Angelica, you wound me. You would have another take my place? Someone who would not be known for his book-giving ways?" His jesting wasn't without a personal price. He didn't let on just how sensitive this subject was for him, especially when he was no better than a pirate-for-hire rather than a naval officer. It led to thoughts of his dealings with Fouquet and of his many personal failings there.

Her shoulders relaxed. She shook her head. "You are incorrigible." More of the wall crumbled away—though she still refused him the pleasure of seeing a full smile.

"I am. It's entirely in keeping with the pirate code." Unable to stop himself, he brushed back an errant curl from her cheek.

She took a small step back, away from his touch. He fought the urge to reach out and pull her to him. Now that he knew how delicious her soft skin tasted, he couldn't seem to remove the memory from his mind. What he wouldn't give to have her just once.

"I wanted to apologize for my actions yesterday," she said in a more serious tone. "The things I said...the broken furniture...and...uhm...well, I don't normally behave that way."

Simon knew she was talking about more than just her words and some broken furniture. "*Chère*, there were things that happened yesterday that could be discussed or forgotten. Which do you prefer?"

"Forgotten."

"Done." The disappointment he felt from her answer surprised him. It was then he realized she'd had her hands behind her back the entire time. His curiosity was piqued. "Angelica, do you have something behind your back?"

"*Hmm?*"

He stood and reached around her, forcing himself not to look down at the neckline of her gown. She stiffened. His mouth was so close to her bare shoulder. At her proximity, his greedy cock gave a hungry throb.

His fingers touched upon a book. Reluctantly, she let it go.

He straightened and looked at the book of love sonnets in his hand. It was his turn to hold back a smile. "Do you have a fondness for this particular book?"

"No. I mean…" She gave him one of her pretty blushes. "I haven't read it. I couldn't say."

"But you wish to read it, don't you?"

"I…don't know. It was on top of the pile. I simply picked it up…" She looked adorably flustered, and he knew she was lying.

He shook his head, feigning dismay. "Perhaps it was a mistake to add this book to the lot," he said. "No doubt, you prefer religious literature—as you're used to at the convent—over these romantic verses. No?"

She looked longingly at the book in his hand before she returned his gaze. "I…suppose."

"Then I won't offend you by leaving this book here." He turned as if to leave with it in hand.

"Wait!"

He smiled to himself and turned to face her, the smile purposefully removed, his brow cocked inquisitively.

"It doesn't offend me," she said.

"*Oh?*"

"What I mean to say is, perhaps I'll read it and let you know if it offends me or not."

He made his way back to her. "Angelica, why don't you just admit you like this book and very much want to read it?" He held it up before her.

She stared at it silently. Finally, she said, "I'd like to read it."

He grinned. "There, that wasn't so difficult. You may have your book back." He extended it to her. At last, she gave him the smile he'd wanted as she reached for the book. Abruptly, he pulled it away. "When you tell me your name."

The look of surprise on her face quickly turned to anger. "Keep your book." She marched over to the trunk and slammed the lid shut. "And take these with you too. I'll not be baited. I'll not tell you a thing. My personal affairs are personal."

Dieu, if he was going to be at the receiving end of that amount of fire from her, he most certainly preferred it to be in bed.

He walked over to her, lifted her hand, and placed the book on her palm. "I'm not going to take any of the books away. They are yours. Enjoy them."

"Thank you," she murmured and pulled the book to her bosom. How he envied the leather volume.

"You cannot blame me for trying to learn more about you."

"Why not leave matters be?"

"I can't. I've never met a woman quite like you."

"Please," she scoffed.

"I find it most intriguing that you seem quite unaware of your own charms. It leaves me to wonder if it is genuine or merely part of your game. Any man would tell you that you look spectacular in that gown. You move about as though you were born into the upper circle of society, yet you show no interest in its trappings or in perhaps returning there. You leave me to my own imaginings. Sadly, I'm left to guess. Are you perhaps a princess from a faraway land, banished by your enemies to live out your days in the convent?" She looked away. He slipped his fingers beneath her chin and turned her face back to his. "Maybe you are no mortal woman at all. Are you an angel in truth? You certainly have the face and voice of one."

"Your suggestions are absurd."

"Then tell me the truth, *chère*."

"No."

"Because you cannot or because you will not?"

"I will not."

"Then I will have to try harder. However, make no mistake. I will learn your secrets. Do you think a lamb can outwit a fox?"

She removed his hand from her face. "I may be unfamiliar with foxes, but I do know that sheep bite."

He burst out laughing. "I'll consider myself duly warned." He crossed his arms over his chest, cocked his head, and studied her for a moment. "Tell me, doesn't it fatigue you? Keeping yourself closed off the way you do? Not allowing anyone to get close enough to truly know you? Not even your best friend?"

"You spoke to Gabriella about me?"

"Yes. Do you keep the truth from her because you feel she cannot be trusted?"

"No. I trust Gabriella."

"No, you don't. You don't trust anyone. You keep everyone at a distance. You have forgotten how to live, *chère*. You're merely existing. And there is nothing worse than to live your life only half alive." He'd known it growing up. The lower class struggled to exist. They never really lived.

He couldn't tell if his words hit the mark. The wall was erected so tall and solid. She merely held his gaze for a moment before she said, "What about you, Simon? Do *you* live? Are you whom I should emulate in my life?"

Simon walked calmly to the door despite the visceral surge of bitterness that welled inside him—his usual reaction to any subject connected to the choices he'd made in his naval career and with Fouquet.

"Don't concern yourself with my life. You should contemplate your own. Look at those around you and see how they strive to improve theirs, Angelica. They want so much more out of life, whereas you want so much less."

He opened the door and walked out.

*****

Standing on deck, Simon focused his gaze on the Spanish ships on the horizon. Recklessly, he toyed with the thought of defying Fouquet's demands for more riches, to pull back and let the ships pass—*to hell with Fouquet and his hold on them*—but then Thomas came to mind, decimating his insurgent thoughts.

"Hold her steady," Simon ordered his commander.

"Yes, Captain."

As always, the information gathered by Thomas had been reliable. After two weeks at sea, *La Estrella Blanca* was in view—as were the two galleons Thomas had advised would be escorting her for protection.

The Spanish ship wasn't part of the biannual convoys arriving from New Spain. *La Estrella Blanca* was an additional treasure ship. Thomas had been shrewd enough to learn its secret date of arrival, privy to only a small circle of high-ranking, trusted individuals. There was the very real possibility that all three ships were laden with silver. In short, this was a large capture before them.

With Simon's ships outnumbering theirs six to three, he felt confident of a victory.

More wealth for Fouquet. Just the thought tortured his jaundiced soul. How many prizes had he captured for the Crown already?

Too many.

Too many good men under his command had perished. Too vivid were his memories of their dying screams rising from their mutilated bodies, limbs shot away by cannons, bodies torn open by swords or impaled by the large splinters of wood torn off from the ship's masts by the cannon blasts. Too many bodies lay within the dark cold ocean depths.

For what? A country that was dying—decay prevalent in each of its social classes? For a king who spent his time on vice rather than on his kingdom and its people?

Simon's men knew the risks involved with each potential capture, yet they risked everything because they believed in him. If they only knew that he didn't believe in himself anymore. His self-confidence had been, until recently, steadfast in every challenge he encountered. Unfaltering in every endeavor he undertook. Never in his entire adult life had he vacillated, even for an instant, from his intended target.

Or from his dream of promotion to the upper class and a respected officer's commission in the realm's official navy—rather than the mere supplement he and his ships were now.

Abandoning that dream was a small price to pay for his involvement with Fouquet.

For the part Simon had played in the suffering and deaths that had occurred.

What he was forced to do now felt so wrong. This valuable capture would only aid in Fouquet's success as Superintendent of Finance, giving him more power and prestige.

Simon clenched his teeth to keep from growling out loud.

The deck was prepared for battle.

The men were in place.

The cannons were ready. They awaited his order to begin firing.

The usual stillness settled on them. The last moments of serenity before the chaos.

During the dwindling minutes of peace, before the blood and gore began, his mind drifted to Angelica. Normally, he didn't permit women on board his ships when the business of ship battles and capture were at hand. However, with *La Estrella Blanca* and its escort outnumbered two to one, he knew there was very little risk to them. *La Estrella Blanca* would go down.

If only it would be as easy to bring down Nicolas Fouquet.

How would Angelica react when the cannons began to blast?

What would she think of the things he'd done in the name of the king, in order to climb the social ladder that had placed him at the bottom at birth? Or of the extent of the destruction and devastation he'd caused?

Why should he care what she thought of him?

It grated on his frayed nerves that throughout each day he was aware of her, down below in her cabin. He hadn't set eyes on her since the second day of the voyage, and yet here she was in his thoughts. At the worst possible time.

*****

Another roar of the cannons rocked the ship, sending shock waves of mortal terror through Angelica. She'd lost track of how many rounds had been fired at them and how many had been fired at the enemy. Suzette and Marta sat with her on the edge of the bed in her cabin, waiting for the battle—that had begun an eternity ago—to end.

Another round of guns erupted. Petrified, Suzette squeezed her hand painfully.

Three more blasts in quick succession reverberated around them, their terrifying booms leaving Angelica's ears ringing in the aftermath. Suzette shrieked and covered her ears, but the sound was drowned out by more cannon fire.

"Battle is part of war," Marta had explained only moments before the calamity began. She had looked relatively calm until the thunder of the cannons commenced.

Angelica's heart hammered wildly. Concern for Simon and Gabriella consumed her; thoughts of their welfare tormented her with each blast she heard.

The men moved rapidly on the deck above. Images of carnage filled her mind. And sickened her stomach. She thought of Simon up there. Was he hurt? Dying? Dead? She wanted him to be safe, to survive, unharmed.

Another round of fire shook the vessel. Wood splintered, then crashed onto the deck above. Her heart dropped to her stomach; she tensed with fright. Once all this was over, once she could see with her own eyes that Simon and Gabriella were safe and uninjured, she would kill him herself for putting them through this.

The battle raged on, round after round, making the ship tremble, shaking Angelica's flagging courage. She shut her eyes and covered her ears, just like Marta and Suzette. Engulfed in the hellish noise, she lost all sense of time. All she could do was pray that they would come out of this alive, that the ships would withstand all that the enemy could fire at them.

There were two more quick blasts in the distance, then a sudden round of cheers on deck.

"It's over!" Suzette exclaimed. Jumping to her feet, she clasped her hands together. "Please God, let Paul be safe." Angelica knew Suzette had a *tendre* for the shy young man, always trying to engage him in conversation.

Marta made the sign of the cross, relief etched on her face.

Angelica wished she felt as tranquil as Marta looked. Were Simon and Gabriella all right? She wasn't about to wait for someone to stroll belowdecks hours from now with the answer. She needed to know. Now.

The quiet on deck was as chilling as the battle.

*****

"Captain?" the commander inquired, awaiting Simon's command.

The crew stood by for the final order: the order to send the fireship. The small vessel would finish off *La Estrella Blanca* by setting her ablaze.

Outnumbered and outgunned, the three Spanish ships had had little chance of escaping their fate. While the other two Spanish ships, already stripped of their cargo, were burning, grappling irons had been tossed onto *La Estrella Blanca*.

Climbing onto the rigging, the men had leaped across once the ships were close together. The fighting continued with guns and swords until they'd finally subdued the Spaniards.

Simon looked at the bounty of silver from *La Estrella Blanca* now resting on the deck of his ship, then cast a glance at the misbegotten Spanish vessel. His stomach fisted. To give the order meant certain death for its crew—a fate already shared by their comrades on the other two burning ships. Yet more wasted lives for profit.

It was what he was supposed to do. What was expected of him.

You have no choice here.

To spare the enemy was treason. He and all who served under him would be labeled pirates by France, punishable by death. He wasn't afraid to die. Death was a part of his reality—he could be killed or captured at any time. However, his men were another matter altogether. He wouldn't sacrifice their lives just to demonstrate his outrage at Fouquet and Louis.

He clenched his jaw and gave the commander the nod to begin the sinking of *La Estrella Blanca*.

The grappling hooks were removed in haste, and *La Estrella Blanca* was set free.

It didn't take long before the vessel was on fire. The few men still alive on the unfortunate ship jumped into the sea to escape the lapping flames, trading one type of death for another.

The angry flames burned before Simon's eyes.

Thomas, I pray I give you sufficient honor this day. Rest in peace knowing your wife and child shall want for nothing for as long as I live. Simon turned away with a heavy heart then winced. His shoulder was injured, a minor thing that had been caused by a flying piece of wood from the broken mast. So absorbed in battle, in shouting orders, his eyes stinging from the smoke, he'd barely felt it when it happened. He'd simply yanked the piece out and carried on. His shirt was soiled by gunpowder and his own blood.

Simon looked down at his hands. They were slick with the blood of others. He wiped them on his breeches, but it didn't remove the sickening sight from his mind.

Fallen men were being gathered for medical assessment. The rest stood around the captured silver prize. Expected to show the men how pleased he was at a successful capture, he readied himself for a convincing performance and approached his purser and commander, mindful of the blood and debris covering the deck. The silver was inventoried before the entire crew, with the ship's purser dutifully recording the amount of precious metal captured. The repeated cheers from his men as well as the echoed jubilation from his other ships thankfully drowned out the haunting cries from the men of *La Estrella Blanca* and its sister ships.

Just then a flash of pale blue skirts caught the corner of his eye. He looked up. His stomach dropped when he saw Angelica on deck staring at the burning ships, at the devastation around her. Torn sails, pieces of wood, and bodies littered the deck and the sea.

Dieu. The very last thing he wanted was for her to see *this*.

CHAPTER TEN

Simon watched as Angelica turned toward him, her hand clutching the rail, ignoring Marta and Suzette, who were trying to urge her back belowdecks. She looked pale and overwhelmed by the battle she'd heard and the aftermath she saw. The horror in her eyes as she took in the gruesome scene was unmistakable.

It took a moment to find his voice. He murmured to his commander to continue, then approached her. The self-loathing he'd been feeling wasn't nearly as bad as having her see what he was capable of.

Forced to step around some of the injured lying on the deck, and Toussaint, who was busy examining them, he finally reached his green-eyed beauty.

"I'm sorry, Captain. But the mademoiselle is worried about her friend," Marta said.

Angelica stepped closer to him. "You're injured."

"It's nothing," he said. "My ships are fine." He nodded toward Domenico's ship nearby. "Gabriella is fine."

She glanced toward the ship. The sun's rays on her chestnut tresses created lovely reddish highlights in her hair. For an instant, he was overcome with the urge to pull her near, bury his face in those soft, curly locks, and envelop himself in her, shutting out the horrific scene he'd witnessed more times in his life than he could count.

But he was never more mindful of his blood-soiled hands.

It was absurd, completely ludicrous, actually, but he wanted her to understand, even when he couldn't accept his own actions.

And he was completely at a loss as to why the opinion of this one woman should mean anything to him at all.

She turned to face him. "So this is what the Black Demon does, then. Those men…must they die?"

No, this isn't all I did or have done. I convinced my closest friend to join my cause—resulting in his slow, tortured death. "This is war. Return to your cabin, Angelica. This is no place for a woman." She was only causing him more agony.

And he condemned himself enough.

"Three cheers for the captain!" one crewmember shouted. It was followed immediately by three boisterous cheers.

He turned away from her and walked toward his crew; he heard Marta and Suzette behind him, coaxing her from the rail back to the stairs that led belowdecks.

"*Simon Boulenger, le Démon Noir, ruler of the seas!*" shouted another crewmember. Resounding approval rang out.

He schooled his features, forcing a smile, feigning a gladness he didn't feel.

One way or another, he'd just captured his last silver treasure. To that he swore.

*****

Simon sat bolt upright and muttered an oath.

He swung his legs over the side of the bed and dropped his head in his hands waiting for his heart and breathing to calm.

Another bloody nightmare involving Thomas.

Reaching for the brandy decanter he kept in his cabin, he downed several gulps, seeking the amber liquid's numbing appeal. It had taken him far too long to fall asleep, only to be torn out of it all too soon. There was no point staying in his cabin only to toss and turn in bed. He stood.

Yanking on his breeches, then his boots, he ignored the pain in his shoulder where Toussaint had stitched his wound.

One of his men had lost an arm in the battle, others their lives. Soon he would be given the list of casualties from all six ships.

Merde, at least they had a bounty of silver for Fouquet and France! Won't that be comforting to the women on the island who were waiting for their husbands to return, men whose bodies were now at the bottom of the sea in a watery grave.

Snatching a clean shirt off the chair, he clutched it in his fist and marched out of his cabin.

He stopped abruptly the moment he saw Angelica exit her cabin. She looked surprised. Good Lord, not her. Not now. He needed solitude to master his vexation, and his lungs burned for fresh air. He didn't want to discuss today. Or anything at the moment.

Her eyes took in his bare chest.

Just having those gorgeous eyes move over his body was already making his cock hard. *Jésus-Christ.* He didn't need this type of frustration on top of everything else.

"You shouldn't be out here at this hour," he snapped.

"I couldn't sleep. I was going to see if Suzette was awake."

"She's helping Toussaint attend to the injured. Go back to your cabin." He started for the deck.

"Simon?"

He sighed and turned around.

"Are you all right?" she asked, softly.

Dieu, what was he doing? He might be battling his personal demons, but she'd just seen her first glimpse of the horrors of war. *You don't need to be a colossal ass when she's only showing concern.*

He walked up to her. "I am fine. Are you all right?"

"Yes." Her manner was tightly guarded. He couldn't read much into the one word.

"The rest of the voyage should be without incident." Every fiber of his being wanted nothing more than to pull her into her cabin, take this beautiful, untaught female, and initiate her into sexual pleasures. He knew the experience would be nothing short of mind-melting with her. By God, he wanted to fuck her so badly, it hurt. "Return to your cabin, *chère.*"

Once on deck, he murmured to the men who greeted him and walked over to the starboard side. Gripping the ship's rail, he breathed in the sea air and let it out slowly. The half-crescent moon cast its silver light. He looked out at the dark sea and took in the tiny stars that punctured the blackened sky.

There was the distinct rustling of skirts behind him. He didn't turn around, hoping he was mistaken. Then Angelica stood next to him.

He swore under his breath. "Did you not hear my order?"

"I am not one of your men. I don't take orders."

He turned to face her and rested his hip against the rail. "On my ships and on the island, every man, woman, and child obeys me. I am in charge. Keeping order is paramount."

"Yes, I've noticed you take your responsibilities very seriously."

"What is that supposed to mean?"

She pulled the shirt out of his hand and touched it lightly to his shoulder. It was then he noticed he was bleeding. She gently blotted the blood, her ministrations taking him by surprise. For a moment, he forgot everything else, luxuriating in her tender touch.

She stopped and looked him in the eye. "You perform your duty, but it is not what you want to do."

Her insight shocked him. He glanced around to make certain no one had overheard her words.

"That's absurd. I work for my king and my country. It is an honor. I do it willingly, and I am committed to it."

"Perhaps once you were, but how things began and how they are now are very different. You must carry on with what is expected of you, but inside you wish to cease." She took his hand and placed his shirt in it. "You have no stomach for battle any longer. Admit it."

No one other than Robert knew of his true feelings about wanting to walk away. Even his men didn't know of his ill intentions toward Fouquet. The fact that she couldn't have overheard this in the conversation he'd had with Robert, for she'd been unconscious then, meant she sensed his feelings of displeasure. Impossible. He was not so plain about his emotions.

Was she guessing? Was she attempting to draw out *his* secrets?

Keeping his tone even, giving nothing away, he said, "No man ever has the stomach for battle. To ever develop a tolerance for it would be very bad indeed."

Angelica drank in the masculine perfection before her. Strong shoulders, a muscled chest, and an abdomen so beautifully sculpted she had an enormous desire to reach out and run her fingers over every gorgeous dip and ripple. To draw near. To feel his touch again, for his touch always felt so wonderful.

He was courageous, capable, and had undoubtedly encountered his share of obstacles in his life, meeting each challenge, hiding from nothing. How she admired that.

She'd questioned his decency and honor. Today proved that this man was no cutthroat. Not once had he boasted about the victory or the killing related to it. Despite his attempts to mask his emotions, she could tell he derived no pleasure from war and the carnage.

There was a profound unrest in him that resonated inside her, one she understood. It was a feeling that had blossomed in her since she'd met him. A desire for change.

She wanted to know more about this man, to learn all the facets that made him who he was. Yet how could she learn anything when every time she was in his presence, she was helplessly drawn into the sultry heat that sizzled between them? When she was forced to pull away, to fight against something she wanted to give in to but was afraid to.

"Something is causing you great distress, Simon, whether you wish to admit it or not." She turned to leave, recognizing that the flare of arousal was becoming hotter the longer she remained. That warming from the inside out, her nipples pressing hard inside her chemise, eager for his attention, and that familiar ache between her legs—all conspiring against her. Not trusting these physical impulses he alone inspired, frightened by how strong they were and what they beckoned her to do, she thought it best to return to the safety of her cabin.

He pulled her back. Placing his hands on either side of her on the wooden rail, he had her hemmed in.

"Oh, there is something that is causing me great distress. You."

His body, though not actually touching hers, practically surrounded her, her anxiousness to leave clashing further with the temptation to remain. "*Me?*"

"Yes, *you*. I may be upset because I lost men today, but you cause me distress."

"How so?"

He leaned in and tilted his head, his mouth all but touching hers. "Because I want you." His warm breath caressed her lips. A thrill rippled through her. "I want to take you to your cabin and strip off your gown. I want to take you, hard and fast, then again, slow and deep. I want to make you come for me, over and over until we're both sated."

"Oh..." *Oh? What sort of answer is that?*

"In this world, bliss is difficult to find. I've learned that you must seize it in whatever form it takes, for you never know when or if it will be offered again. It would be sheer bliss being inside you, *chère.* But I can't take you below and indulge in that bliss, can I, Angelica?"

Her pulse raced, and her every nerve ending hummed with desire. Speechless, she was alarmed and inflamed by his words. *He's waiting for an answer.* What was the answer? "No?"

"No." He straightened. "Return to your cabin, Angelica. You don't want me to escort you there—unless you are willing to partake in some sexual excess."

She remained fixed to her spot, staring up into his light blue eyes, not wanting to leave, yet afraid to stay. Finally, she drew in a ragged breath and let it out slowly.

She couldn't do this.

As much as her heart and body screamed yes, a dark voice reminded her of her past and roared, *NO.* Forcing one shaky limb before the other, she walked away.

CHAPTER ELEVEN

A clap of thunder exploded.

Angelica jumped.

The heavy seas rolled the ship, the tempest sending huge waves crashing against the hull.

Clutching the bed linens, she sat on the edge of her bed, trying her best not to topple off. Tense, she battled back dread. There had been other storms over the last several weeks of the lengthy voyage. But nothing like this.

Taking a deep breath, she then let it out slowly, willing herself to remain calm. But disturbing thoughts of the sea vessel's ability to withstand the storm's abuse ate away at her confidence.

Trying to distract herself, she thought about the pleasant afternoons she'd spent with Suzette, teaching her to read. Evenings in the galley with Marta and the ship's two Italian cooks, brothers Lucio and Nicolo, whose lively fiddle music equaled their fine culinary skills.

The ship surged sharply. The menacing roar from the angry skies assailed her ears.

She moved to the floor before she fell there. Bracing her back against the bed, she drew her knees up and wrapped her arms around her legs. The ship groaned and creaked. Her thoughts ran to the man who had brought her on this voyage.

She'd barely seen Simon in weeks.

She was permitted to be on deck at midday. Each day, she found her gaze roaming away from the sea to the deck, searching him out.

Occasionally, they would pass each other. He would offer her a pleasant greeting—wreak havoc with her pulse—and go on his way.

Thunder boomed, followed by another violent surge of the ship as the storm continued to howl and enrage the sea.

Pushing back the panic, she refused to think about perishing. Not when the undeniable truth was that she hadn't truly lived. Not really. She hadn't just been hiding from her stepfather.

She'd been hiding from life. Simon was right. It was true.

Though this storm was one experience she could have done without, she wasn't as certain that she wanted to forgo the ones she'd had with him.

She'd shut so much out of her life. Dwindled her existence and experiences down to barely anything.

She wanted more. Deserved more. And she knew exactly what she wanted more of.

Simon.

His words echoed in her mind: *"In this world, bliss is difficult to find...you should seize it in whatever form it takes, for in life you can never know when or if it will be offered again..."*

She was being offered an opportunity for a bit of true bliss. And for once, she didn't want to deny herself. Simon made her feel alive. He made her body feel things she'd never thought possible. Whenever he was near, he made her feel like a woman—desirable, whole—despite the scars deep inside. She loved it when he touched her, and trusted in his touch.

She tightened her arms around her legs.

Could she, for once, push away her past and give herself over to the desire that burned between them? She was determined to try. But she wasn't naïve. Simon wasn't likely to propose marriage afterward. After what her stepfather had done to her, marriage was out of the question, but some *bliss* was attainable.

All she had to do was surrender to it.

*****

Simon walked toward his cabin. He had been through many such storms. They were common in the West Indies at this time of year. It had finally begun to subside. Now he looked forward to some rest.

His eyes were drawn to Angelica's cabin door. She couldn't have slept through the storm. Was she frightened? Crying? She was the only female he knew who restrained her flow of tears in any way.

He stopped in front of her door and pressed his ear to it. Silence. Was she hurt? Perhaps she had fallen and was injured.

He wrenched open the door, stepped inside, and closed it behind him.

Seated at the edge of the bed, she quickly rose.

He took in the vision she made. The gown she wore fit her body so tantalizingly, its pale color a contrast to her dark hair and those bewitching eyes. His blood warmed.

"You have news, Simon?" she asked, sounding anxious.

"News?"

"Yes, about the ship. Its condition. If the ship is badly damaged, please tell me. I wish the truth." She lifted her chin, trying to appear brave.

The fact that she was determined to put a brave face forward when others facing the possibility of death would not have possessed sufficient courage to do so raised his opinion of her yet another notch.

"The ship is fine. She has been through worse storms."

"What about—"

"—all the ships are fine."

She stepped closer and smiled. Though his hair was wet and his sea-drenched clothes were cold and stuck to his body, his blood was now coursing white-hot.

"The storm is subsiding. There is no need for alarm."

"Thank you. It was kind of you to come to my cabin and inform me of this, to spare me further concern."

He gave her a curt nod. *Leave now*, his inner voice warned. And he was going to heed it.

As he turned to go, he heard, "Simon?"

She approached and stopped before him, her body now too close for his sanity.

She bit her bottom lip as though she was searching for her next words. There was something different about her tonight.

"Simon, how does a woman ask a man to kiss her?"

He felt as if cold water had just splashed him in the face. "*What? What man do you think to ask?*" he demanded, seized by an unnerving sense of possessiveness.

"You." Her one word dissolved his ire and tightened his groin. "Do I give you leave? Or...am I to kiss you first?"

He blinked. This couldn't be real. This was one of his many erotic dreams of her. It would only escalate from here, and he would wake up alone. His cock rock-hard.

She raised her hand and covered her breast. "Will you...touch me and kiss me here again?"

Christ. If her words weren't enough, seeing her touch herself was too much. He grasped her wrist and pulled her hand away from her breast, unable to muster words while she beguiled him so.

"You cannot ask me to kiss you and touch you and expect me to stop there." How much will did she think he possessed?

"Then don't stop."

His brows shot up. "Do you know what you are asking? What you are giving me leave to do?"

She looked back at the bed. His gaze followed hers, his mind filling with the image of her lying naked under him, taking every hard inch of his cock inside. He quashed the groan that surged in his throat.

Capturing her face between his palms, he forced her to look at him. "What you are suggesting will impact on the rest of your life."

"I was hoping it would," she said softly. "You're right about what you have said. Everything you have said. I don't want to just exist. I want to live. Feel alive. I want to know the pleasure you described. I want you to do to me what you did the first day of the voyage. And more."

Good God. He closed his eyes and rested his forehead against hers. "Angelica... I want you too much. I'm no saint..." *She's offering herself to you! Practically begging for it.* What was he waiting for?

"Just one time, Simon. Just tonight... Show me what the release, the 'ultimate fulfillment' feels like...please..."

That was the prettiest plea he'd ever heard. He hauled her up against him, and had her mouth in an instant, crushing it with savage intensity. Somewhere in the back of his mind, he knew he should stop, but as she laced her arms around his neck and returned his heated kiss, all his objections burned away.

Just once was all she wanted. Just once was all he needed to end his sexual suffering. But he was going to make sure she participated in this debauchery so that she couldn't condemn him in the morning.

"Open your bodice," he murmured. "Offer me those gorgeous breasts."

He drew back to look at her, her hands sliding from around his neck down to his chest. She glanced at the neckline of her gown and paused. He feared she was vacillating. And he wasn't about to let her stop now.

He brushed his mouth over the sensitive spot below her ear and lightly bit her earlobe, adorable freckle and all, enjoying her little gasp. Cupping her breast, he pinched her excited nipple through her clothing. For his efforts, she rewarded him with a delicious little mew. He held the sensitive tip firmly, letting the pressure build into inflaming throbs.

"Open your bodice, *chère*. Let me give you what you want," he said in her ear, releasing her nipple, then lightly pinching the other. She whimpered. "You like that, don't you? You want more, no?"

Her quickened breaths warmed his ear. "Yes…"

He released the tip and stroked his thumb across it. He felt her little shiver of excitement all the way down to the end of his cock.

"Will…Will you do what you did the last time, Simon?"

"Oh yes."

"You said that…this act between men and women is pleasurable in the extreme. You'll show me…everything?"

"Open your bodice." His voice was gruff with impatience. "I will give you what you're looking for."

He watched as she tried to unfasten her clothing. Garnished with bows of ribbon down the front, the bodice posed a challenge for her nervous fingers.

His patience snapped. He pulled her up against him, captured her lush mouth, penetrating it with his tongue. His eager cock twitched with anticipation. She gave his tongue a long, luscious suck, her actions sending heat through him like a bolt of lightning, inciting him further when he was already in a state that required no encouragement.

He stripped away her clothing, coaxing her along with hot whispers and caresses. He told her how much he wanted her, how good it was going to feel being inside her, how hard he was going to make her come.

When he was done, he paused to devour the sight before him. She had the sweetest, most edible form he'd ever seen. Beautiful breasts that rose and fell with her rapid breaths. Gorgeous curves. The softest skin. Eyes shut, she tried to shield her body from his view, but he caught her wrists and held them apart, looking his fill. Tonight, she was all his. And she was definitely worth the wait.

"You are every bit as beautiful as I envisioned," he said.

Her eyes snapped open. The small smile adorning her lips told him that his comment pleased her.

Cradling her breast in his palm, he dipped his head and sucked her nipple into his hungry mouth. She thrust her fingers in his hair, instantly frenzied by the erotic sensations.

He pressed her down on the bed, still drawing on her breast, enticing sharp, shallow pants from her. He wouldn't relent until he had her writhing. Until she panted out his name. She was so damned desirable. Every untaught movement and uncontrolled sound she made drove him wild. Turning to her other breast, he swirled his tongue around the pretty peak before giving it the tiniest bite. Her cry of pleasure lanced into his groin, milking a dollop of pre-come from his cock.

Simon yanked off his shirt and tossed it onto the floor.

This time, he wasn't going to be denied. There was no way he could stop. Not even if the bloody ship was sinking. He'd be the one to introduce her to carnal delights. That incredible thought pulsated through every nerve ending in his body. The gift she was giving him moved him.

She wrapped her arms around his neck and pressed her mouth to his. Urgency pounded in his blood. Yet he forced himself to slow down, noting she was squeezing her thighs together.

Intent on spiking her hunger, he grazed a hand over her smooth belly, then cupped her sex. They both groaned. She was so slick, her curls already wet with her juices. His cock seeped more spunk. With the heel of his hand he applying direct pressure over her clit, relishing her mewl. "Spread your legs for me. I can make you feel so much more." He kissed her neck and slipped a single finger between the wet folds of her sex. "Trust me..." Lightly, he delivered a stroke over her clit so swollen with need. This time, she jerked back before losing her breath, stunned by the sharp, carnal sensation.

"I trust you," she said between pants.

He smiled against her skin. He couldn't explain why, but it gave him such joy to hear those words from her. He delivered another measured stroke to her clit. She shuddered and tightened her arms around him. "That feels good, doesn't it?"

He felt her nod and her legs slacken. She was so adorably sweet and incredibly alluring in her fiery state. He couldn't wait to sink his length into her and give her long, deep, luscious strokes until she came on his cock.

He eased her legs apart with his knee, his hand massaging her sex all the while, fingering her with finesse, his mouth muffling the sensual sounds she made. Arching to him hard, she was quickly reaching the precipice to her release. A release he refused to give her this way. She was going to reach orgasm with him inside her.

Removing his hand from her wet sex, he was up on his knees in an instant, opening his breeches in record haste, finally freeing his cock from its restraints. He stroked his slick fingers along his length. He'd never been so hard, his cock feeling heavy as lead.

She gave an impatient squirm, the pretty crinkle in her brow telling him she didn't like the loss of his hand on her excited sex. Leaning over her, he pressed a palm down on the mattress above her shoulder, and lightly fingered her with his other hand. Purposely avoiding her clit. Keeping her keen and craving more. "Beautiful Angelica, I am going to give you the release you seek. But I'm not going to let you come with my hand. You're going to come with my cock." The very idea of her wet heat clasped around him tightly made his heart pound harder. "You want to come for me. You want a release right now, don't you." It was more of a statement than a question, given her quickened breaths. Her wet little cunt. And those mouthwatering nipples of hers that were straining for him, begging to be sucked once more.

She gave him a nod, her cheeks pink. *Dieu*, she looked so good. Better than any fantasy he had of her.

He lowered himself on her. His weight on his elbows, he finally had his moonlight temptress right where he wanted her. "Tell me you don't want me to stop." He stroked his cock down along her dewy folds, coating it with her cream for easy penetration. It took everything he had not to thrust into her all at once. "Tell me," he said, stroking himself back up to her needy clit, purposely making her moan. "Angelica, say it." He had to hear her voice the words one more time. "If I am going to take your virginity, I'm going to need you to say it." He wedged his cock at her entrance. A groan surged up his throat. *Jésus-Christ*, the most magnificent hot silk was gripping the tip of his prick.

"Don't stop..." she said breathlessly.

That simple phrase nearly unraveled him before he reined in his hunger and pressed into her enticing wet core slowly.

"*Simon!*"

His senses reveled. He groaned long and hard. She was soft, and so incredibly snug, the head of his cock was actually pulsing under the exquisite pressure.

She squirmed sharply, causing his prick to penetrate suddenly, faster than he intended. He gripped her hips to still her. The friction that shot along the sensitive underside of his cock was mind-melting. He held himself immobile, his body shaking with effort. His length was dipped halfway into splendor.

"Easy. Allow me to be gentle," he forced out, barely able to command his voice as he dragged air in and out of his lungs. All he wanted to do was sink in. Balls-deep. But he couldn't forget she was a virgin. If it weren't for that, he'd be riding her into oblivion right now. "I'll make it good for you, I swear. Our bodies were meant to join this way. *Just relax...*" He tunneled deeper, her perfect sheath drawing him in. He withdrew a little, then sank his whole length into her with a final deep, easy glide. Her low cry of shock and pleasure reverberated through him. He clenched his teeth. She was clasped so tightly around him, he thought he'd go mad.

In the haze of blinding passion, one thought suddenly pierced through his heated mind: *there had been no barrier...*

Blood roared in his ears. His body rioted for more. He was long past the point of no return, and began driving into her repeatedly with deep, solid thrusts, unable to stop, fiercely fighting back his release so he could continue to bask in the tight confines of her slick walls. In the sublime squeeze of her sex. And the stunning sensations coursing along his cock.

Their chests heaved together. Their breaths mingled, wild and erratic. Somewhere in the distance, through the blinding pleasure he heard her cry out as she climaxed.

Her inner muscles contracted around his thrusting shaft, clenching and releasing. The sensation—pure ecstasy. His control snapped. His orgasm came thundering down on him. Abruptly, he reared. Burying his face in her hair, he came with brutal intensity, his body shuddering from the sheer force of his release as he spent himself in a glorious, draining rush onto the sheets.

His limbs were heavy. His body was sluggish. But his mind raced, the mental fog dissipating in the wake of burning questions.

How was it possible that she was not a virgin? How could it be? She'd been with another man? Other *men*? No, he was mistaken. Somehow, he was wrong.

He rolled off her and onto his back. Keenly aware of her warm body next to his, he stared at the ceiling with his one arm resting on his forehead and his other hand on his chest, waiting for his heart and breathing to calm, knowing that his pulse now raced for an entirely new reason having nothing to do with his devastating orgasm.

He knew his instincts were not sharp of late. He knew he had been wrong in his assumptions about her thus far... But *this*? He couldn't be wrong about her innocence. Could he? She wouldn't have given him her body and not this information. Would she? Questions whirled in his head. He didn't know what to believe. He wasn't sure of anything right now except the need to know the truth.

But he didn't want to look.

Slowly, he sat up. Gripping the base of his cock, he saw a mixture of semen and her own juices. No blood. His stomach clenched.

He forced himself to stand and face her.

She sat up, her long, dark curly hair hanging so beautifully covering most of her torso. She smiled at him, but her smile faded when she noticed the look on his face. He gazed down at her silky thighs and then to the sheet below her. More semen.

No blood.

The missing evidence of her virginity tore through him. All this time he'd kept himself from her, enduring weeks of agony, fighting against the staggering attraction between them, because of her innocence. And she wasn't?

How the hell had she fooled him? *Twice!*

Did she think he wouldn't realize she wasn't a virgin? Was this the way she'd wanted him to learn of it all along?

Why wouldn't she tell him? She'd finally said she trusted him. *Dieu.* What a fool! People said a lot of things in bed they didn't mean. Heartfelt declarations didn't mix with casual sex. She had, after all, asked for just one night. Nothing more. *Jésus-Christ.* She was a woman from a *convent.* It occurred to him then that the night they'd met, she'd been out of the convent. And *she* had never told him why. Had she sneaked out to see another man? Was he the reason she wanted to return so badly?

The entire situation was almost laughable if it wasn't so gut-wrenching.

"Simon…?"

He felt duped. Lied to. And he loathed the fact that any of this should matter to him at all. Fury scorched through his veins. He had to leave. *Now.*

He yanked at his breeches, closing them with quick, angry tugs, and left the room, slamming the door shut with the intensity of a thunderclap.

CHAPTER TWELVE

He knew.

Angelica had seen it in his eyes. He'd discovered that she wasn't a virgin. And he was furious with her. Heaven knew what he was thinking.

Fully dressed and sitting at the table near her trunk of beloved books, she impatiently swiped the tears from her cheeks. She hadn't allowed herself to cry for years. She hated to cry. It made her feel pathetic and weak, and she was neither.

She'd survived rape. She'd escaped her stepfather's clutches and successfully eluded him for ten years. It had taken strength and courage to do both. And it had taken courage to give herself over to the desire she felt for Simon. How she wished he could know this.

But she didn't know how to tell him.

The only real courage she lacked was voicing the ugly truth.

She'd never told a single soul about the events of the night that had left her tainted and dishonored and changed her life forever.

It had to be almost morning. The sea was gentle, its rocking of the vessel slight.

She knew she'd have to face him sooner or later.

But what would she say?

At least a half dozen times over the last excruciating hours, she'd intended to seek him out and explain. To tell him what her stepfather had done to her. But she'd faltered every time. How did one voice such shame? What were the right words to say so he wouldn't look at her as demeaned? With pity? Or worse—repugnance?

She rose from the table and felt a twinge of tenderness between her legs. Proof that things were very different this morning.

She didn't regret what she'd done last night with Simon.

She'd needed his touch and the way he'd made her feel. And he had touched her in places she would never have let any other man touch her. He'd helped her to overcome her fear of this act, and had replaced the foul image she'd had with a glorious memory she'd quietly cherish the rest of her days.

Ten years ago, her maid Audrey had told her that a man could be fooled into believing her virtue was still intact but had never told her how one would execute such deceit. How was it possible to tell? Angelica had been young and had fled before ever learning the answer. At the convent, the answer no longer mattered. She knew she'd been disgraced. Sullied. No man would ever want her. And she would never want a man to touch her.

Until she met Simon.

A beautiful experience with a beautiful man had been tainted because of her past. Hadn't her past caused her enough suffering already?

An urgent knock startled her. "Yes?"

Suzette entered in a terrible hurry.

"We are home!" she exclaimed. Rushing to her, she gave Angelica a hug.

"Home?" She pulled away, surprised.

"Yes!" Suzette beamed. "Marguerite. The island. We've arrived!"

Last eve, she'd seized a moment for herself, something special to hold on to—with a man like none she'd ever known. But now, having tasted heaven, she wanted more.

With him.

It was an unrealistic longing. Simon wasn't likely to want to have anything more to do with her. She had no explanation to offer to fix matters between them. And to tell him the truth, to allow him to know her repulsive secret, wasn't something she could bring herself to do.

"We will be on land shortly," Suzette said, so full of enthusiasm.

What was to become of her now? For so long, her life had been laid out. She was going to live out her days in the convent, safe from the world that had devastated her—from a stepfather who had destroyed everything, and stripped her of her innocence.

The convent was no longer a part of her future. She simply couldn't return there now that she felt so different.

But what would replace it?

Suzette squeezed her hand. "A new beginning lies on the horizon. You'll see! Things will look different on our beautiful island."

Things looked very different now.

*****

Their tender reached the shore.

Angelica was helped out of the boat by Paul and Lucio. Crowds of people pressed past her—people of all ages in presentable clothing of varying degrees of quality and expense.

This was not at all what she'd expected.

She couldn't believe the number of people on the beach.

Cheers went up as each tender containing the men from the ships touched the shore. Gestures of affection ranging from a pat on the back to heartwarming embraces were all around her.

In the excited crowd, she was pushed and shoved along until Lucio grabbed hold of her arm. "This way," he said, leading her out of the mass.

"Is this island part of France?" she asked over the din.

"No, mademoiselle. The French government gave up on the islands here. Lots of problems. Pirates, Caribs, civil wars. They wanted no part of it any longer. The islands were sold to their governors."

"Pirates and Caribs?"

Lucio smiled. "No need to worry. We know how to combat the local pirates. Or anyone else interested in Marguerite. We are heavily fortified. The captain made sure of it. A fortress wall surrounds the island up to the cliffs. The cliffs are treacherous and impossible to scale without being detected or killed. You need not fear."

"So this island belongs to…?"

"The captain and all of us. There are many islands here. Many have come to claim them—the pirates, the Spanish… That is the way here. You fight. You take. The island is yours."

He escorted her up to the road where open, empty carriages were parked in a row and assisted her into one before excusing himself and returning to the crowd. Little by little, the carriages filled with the people from the ships.

Angelica caught sight of Gabriella and Domenico just as they reached the shore. A cheer immediately rose up from the enthusiastic crowd at Domenico's arrival. Smiles were on both his and Gabriella's faces as he escorted her through the throng.

Within a short time, Gabriella was seated beside her, and they were locked in an enthusiastic hug.

"I've missed you, Angelica!"

Angelica squeezed her eyes shut, grateful to be with her dear friend again. Not only did Gabriella mean the world to her, but her presence at the moment was ever so comforting.

A man cleared his throat. She was so overwhelmed to have Gabriella near, she'd completely forgotten that Domenico sat across from them in the carriage.

"I'm sorry." Angelica apologized to him with tears in her eyes. She hated how emotional she was today. "Good day, Domenico."

"Good day, Angelica." He smiled and then reached over and took Gabriella's hand. "Are you going to tell her, my darling?"

"Of course!" Gabriella grinned. "Angelica, I have wonderful news. Domenico and I are getting married!" The couple stared back at her, their faces clearly aglow over the prospect.

"Oh! How wonderful!" She hugged Gabriella. "Congratulations to both of you." Her good wishes came from the heart.

Clearly, this voyage had changed them both. Gabriella had found happiness, and Angelica had discovered how much she had been missing in her life.

The crowd suddenly whipped into a frenzy of cheers and shouts, a roar far greater than before.

Angelica's gaze darted back to the shoreline.

Simon stepped out of one of the tenders. The wind caressed his hair and pressed his shirt to his strong chest. He looked absolutely beautiful. She tamped down the emotions that welled inside her.

She was not like Gabriella. Gabriella was free to love and accept love in return. Gabriella had nothing to hide and wasn't forced to hold back in any way.

The people on the beach, hysterical with joy, pressed in on Simon. Hands from every direction reached out to him. A smile was upon his lips, and his dark head turned this way and that, trying to acknowledge as many people as he could as he made his way through the crowd.

Awed by his reception, all Angelica could do was stare.

A woman with a little girl of about seven years of age caught Angelica's eye as they stood holding hands, apart from the commotion. Simon finally exited the large group and walked straight to them.

Stopping before them, he bent his head and spoke to the woman. Suddenly, she lowered her head and wept into her trembling hand. Not tears of joy. Simon pulled her into his arms, allowing her to bury her face in his chest. He held her while she wept.

"Who is that woman with the captain?" Angelica heard Gabriella ask Domenico the very same question that was in her mind. Domenico stepped down from the carriage, no longer smiling.

"That is Marie Jaures and her daughter, Monique. Her husband, Thomas, was killed. He died a hero. Thomas and Simon were good friends. He consoles her for her loss. There are others about to learn of their husbands' deaths. As commander of one of the ships, I must go offer my condolences. I will speak to Simon and advise him of our marriage plans, and tell him that you have gone with Angelica to his home. He'll not mind if you stay there until our wedding. The old priest, Père Crotteau, however, will most definitely voice his disapproval if I keep you in my home with me until we are wed. Although, if he's not willing to forgo the practice of posting the banns to allow us to marry sooner, I may threaten it." He smiled.

Gabriella blushed. She leaned down and kissed him. Angelica tried to ignore the tug at her heart. Domenico gave orders to the driver and left.

Simon continued to hold Marie Jaures, speaking to her in her ear, her sorrow heart-wrenching. He reached down and tenderly stroked Monique's head while the child wept into her mother's skirt. A knot formed in Angelica's throat.

He was a man with compassion. Perhaps she should tell him about her past. Perhaps she should try.

*****

"This is lovely!" Gabriella voiced Angelica's sentiments.

Angelica approached the large bed in the middle of the room on the second floor of Simon's home and gently stroked the diaphanous white drapery that surrounded it. Noticing double doors, she walked over, opened them, and stepped out onto the small balcony, staring out at the lush tropics and distant sea.

Gabriella stopped beside her. "Have you ever seen any sight more spectacular?"

Yes, she thought, the sight of Simon's smile and the way he looked at her with desire in his eyes. She had to stop this. Now.

"Mademoiselle?" Assunta, the housekeeper, addressed Gabriella. "If you will follow me, I'll show you to your room next door."

"I'd like to stay here awhile with my friend. I can show myself to my room later. *Merci.*" Gabriella astounded Angelica by speaking to the housekeeper entirely in French.

Assunta nodded. "As you wish," she said.

Gabriella turned to her and smiled. "Domenico has been teaching me French on the voyage. What do you think?"

"I think you are full of wonderful surprises today, Gabriella."

The moment Assunta closed the door, Gabriella spun around with her arms open wide. "I am so happy, I fear I'll burst!"

Angelica couldn't help but smile.

Gabriella grabbed her hands, pulled her into the room and down with her onto the edge of the bed. Her private area came in quick contact with the mattress. She felt an instant twinge of tenderness.

"Angelica, I cannot tell you how wonderful Domenico is." Gabriella flopped onto her back and stared at the ceiling dreamy-eyed. Rolling onto her side, she rested her cheek on her palm. Angelica mimicked her pose.

When they were young, they had often sneaked into each other's beds, lain just like this, and had lengthy conversations. This felt good. And familiar. She wanted to lose herself in Gabriella's story of love, hoping it would help her to stave off the feelings of anxiety. Every minute that passed brought her closer to the inevitable confrontation with Simon. She only hoped it would occur much later, for she still had no idea what she'd say.

The door opened, startling the two women. They sat up.

Simon stood inside the threshold, his light blue eyes unreadable. It didn't matter that he masked his anger. Angelica could sense it just the same. Her stomach tightened.

The time had come.

Angelica could tell Simon hadn't expected to find Gabriella in her room.

"Gabriella," he said tightly. "I understand that congratulations are in order. Domenico tells me of your upcoming nuptials."

"Yes, Captain. Thank you." Gabriella stood. "I wish to offer my condolences for the loss of your friend, Thomas Jaures."

Angelica rose. "Yes, me too, Simon."

He glanced at her briefly. "Thank you." Then he returned his gaze to Gabriella. "Gabriella, I'd like a private word with Angelica."

"Of course." Gabriella gave her a hug. "We shall talk more later," she whispered in her ear, and then left the room.

Simon walked over to a small table and pulled out a chair. He turned it around to face her.

"Sit down."

Angelica straightened her spine. Though she didn't like it when he tried to command her, at the moment, it wasn't her sole reason for not wishing to comply. The hard surface of the chair didn't look comfortable, given the delicate state of her lower region.

"I prefer to stand, thank you."

He lifted an eyebrow. "Sit. Down. Now." Each word was firmly dealt.

Given the look in his eyes and the sound of his tone, she thought it best to bend. She'd bear the soreness.

She walked over and sat.

Her senses were keenly aware of his presence behind her, of his muscled thighs near her back, and of his fingers near her shoulder as his hand rested on the back of her chair. She felt small near his towering form. He was physically overwhelming. Every beautiful part of him was strong, sculpted, and large. She shifted in her chair.

He walked around and lowered himself onto his haunches before her. Resting his elbows on the arms of her chair, he gazed up at her.

Her heart pounded. She fought not to fidget.

"*Dieu*, look at you," he breathed. "You are exquisite to behold."

She kept her hands tightly folded on her lap and forced herself to return his gaze. His closeness and the velvety sound of his voice made her yearn for him on so many disquieting levels.

"Such a beautiful face...masks so much deceit. Tell me, what twisted pleasure have you derived from having me believe you were a virgin?"

She'd known this was coming, but now, in the moment, it felt so much worse than anticipated. His cool manner was far more distressing than if he'd raged at her.

She could feel the wall she'd always hidden behind becoming higher. More solid. She could feel herself slipping into familiar patterns, her old ways of silence. Her throat tightened, choking off words from her heart she wanted to voice, words about what he meant to her, what last night had meant to her.

It was just as well. He wasn't interested in hearing soft sentiment. At the moment, he was *only* interested in the truth about her past.

"No answer, *chère*? What a surprise." He rose and pulled a chair over. He sat down in front of her, his knees on either side of hers. Leaning forward, he rested his elbows on his thighs. "You have fooled me at every turn. Shame on me. Good for you."

His familiar scent, so appealing, enveloped her. She found herself wishing she could erase his discovery of her lost innocence from his memory. He'd never looked at her so dispassionately. Cold anger was the only way to describe it.

"Tell me, did you plan for me to discover your lack of innocence last night, or were you simply hoping I wouldn't realize you were not a virgin?"

"I didn't make any such plan. Nor did I give it perhaps the consideration I should have. I just wanted...to be with you."

"Lovely answer." His voice was bland. "Too bad I no longer have any confidence in your sincerity. I no longer know when you are being true or false. I'd love to know, however, if I have sufficiently amused you with this game you choose to play with me."

"I derive no amusement from any of this."

"You must gain some benefit from it, *chère*. Why else would you do it?"

"It's complicated."

"Really."

He placed his strong hands on the arms of her chair and dragged it closer to him. Surprised, she stiffened.

"I have no problem with anonymous sex, Angelica, since that seems to be your preference. What I do have a problem with, is being made a fool of."

"Simon," she began.

"Before you attempt to tell me that I have withheld information about myself as well, I wish to remind you that you know a good deal more about me than I know about you. Now then, if you have something to tell me—*anything at all*—this would be an *excellent* time to say it."

She looked into his eyes, hating his sarcastic tone. *Tell him*, a voice inside her urged. *Let him know. Perhaps he'll understand.*

He waited. Time stretched.

She swallowed and to tried break the barrier of silence; she tried to select the words to say, but they all sounded sordid. Ugly. Faced with the moment of truth, she came to the defeating realization that she couldn't do it. There was still the chance that whenever he'd look at her, all he'd see was her soiling. And she couldn't stand that. She would rather deal with his anger, for anger fades, but disgust and pity linger on indefinitely.

"I wasn't trying to make a fool of you. I never said I was a virgin. I've told you, all personal information about me is irrelevant. I'm willing to wager that the women you have been with in the past haven't been virgins either. No?"

"What does that have to do with this?"

"If the others were not virgins, then what difference can it make if I wasn't one too? Why must it be important?"

He rose abruptly, startling her. Placing a hand on the arm of her chair and another under her chin, he said, "You are correct. None of this is important." He straightened. "I suppose all that is left to say, mademoiselle, is thank you for the tumble."

*****

Standing in front of the window of his library, Simon stared outside as he braced his hands on the frame. He wrestled to get hold of his fury, resentful of the emotions clashing inside of him. As a matter of pride, he'd refused to ask Angelica about her former lovers.

Since when had he ever cared about any woman's past?

He couldn't believe that on the day he'd had to tell Marie that Thomas was dead, he was wasting a moment's thought on a woman who toyed with him. He'd reviewed every detail of last night, every detail of every conversation they'd ever had, trying to understand how he could have been so mistaken about her, every time.

Was there anything else he'd bloody well missed that he should have noted?

He'd thought of every possible scenario to explain why she had not been a virgin—from rape to whoredom, and everything in between. Each scenario churned his stomach. He had no idea who she was. Where she was born. Or when she'd lost her virginity.

Absolutely nothing!

She'd had him entangled in her game of mystery from the start. And he'd played along, panting after her all the while, devoting far more time and effort to her than he ever had to any other woman.

If all she was willing to offer him was her body for a night—fine. He had gladly accepted it and enjoyed it. The luscious memory conjured in his mind, and sure enough, predictably, he was stiff as a spike.

He was sick of the effect she had on him.

Turning away from the window, he walked over to the decanter of brandy, poured himself some, and drank it down.

Now was the time to move on.

He was glad to be home. Marguerite was special to him. It was his. The only place he could call his own. It was scenic and balmy. And there were women on Marguerite willing to indulge in sex without the mental torment.

He was here for rest and to make key decisions about Fouquet's downfall, not to mention what he was going to do with the rest of his life, if he survived.

Simon poured himself another goblet of brandy.

So fucking Angelica had been even better than he'd anticipated. So she had the sweetest sex he'd ever known—all that snug heat squeezing him so tightly she'd made him throb. He'd wanted Angelica since he'd laid eyes on her. Last night, he'd had her. She wasn't a virgin. So what? He should be rejoicing. He didn't have to add dishonoring innocents to his lengthy list of sins.

What did he care if she lied to him in or out of bed?

He turned and whipped his goblet against the wall. *Merde!*

This was eating him up inside. And he hated it that it bothered him at all. Worse, he loathed the idea that she saw him as a man unworthy of her trust.

"Would it not be better to *drink* the brandy?"

Simon spun around and saw his friend, Jules de Moutier, standing at the entrance of the library, his brow cocked.

Simon shook his head, embarrassed at his display. "Jules." He forced a smile.

"*Dieu*, it's good to see you." Jules approached with a broad grin. The two men of similar age and build exchanged greetings with a manly embrace.

Jules nodded at the mess on the floor. "Does this have to do with Thomas? I saw Armand. He told me the news."

It had to do with everything, including Thomas. His world was a snarled web, and somehow he'd allowed a woman to play him and turn him inside out. "Let us say that I have had better days."

Jules nodded. Then a slight smile tugged at his lips. "What is this I hear about you finding women in a convent and bringing them to the island?"

Simon sat down behind his desk. "Armand doesn't waste any time in filling your ears, does he?"

Jules chuckled. "Is it true Domenico has decided to marry one of them?"

"Yes, it's true. And no, I don't intend to discuss the women today. We will talk tomorrow. You can fill me in on the details of Marguerite and our sugar profits then."

Angelica was the very last subject he wanted to discuss at the moment. He hadn't seen his friend in almost two years. He and Jules had much to catch up on. In his absence, Simon had left the island in Jules's capable hands.

"Absolutely. I must confess, I'm looking forward to the convent story. What about the other woman? Are you keeping her for yourself?"

"Jules..." His exasperation was mounting.

Jules grinned. "That beautiful, eh? Is she the reason you christened the floor with brandy?"

"How is your wife?"

Jules laughed, shaking his head. "Changing the subject, I see. Sabine is absolutely perfect. We have a daughter, Isabelle, born over a year ago. She is a raving beauty, like her mother."

Jules and Sabine had married in France almost two years ago. "Congratulations," he offered sincerely.

"Thank you," Jules said, still grinning. "*Dieu*, Simon, I could not have imagined I would find marriage so agreeable. I'm so happy my feet scarcely touch the ground. It saves me a great deal on my footwear."

Simon laughed, despite himself.

"I tell you it is something you should try."

Simon lifted a brow. "Marriage? Fatherhood? No, thank you. I have no desire for either." First, a good night's sleep, then days of sexual oblivion were all that were on his list.

The delectable memory of Angelica standing naked in front of him whispered through his thoughts. He forced it back, but not before he felt a fresh wave of lust rush straight to his groin and along his prick. He would have uttered every expletive he'd ever learned if Jules hadn't been there. His friend would derive great amusement from Simon's predicament. Women had never wreaked havoc with Simon's mind and body. In fact, he rarely had any thoughts of them once he left their bed.

"And the convent woman? Do you have desire for her?" Jules asked with mischief in his dark eyes.

"I am not going to discuss Angelica."

"Angelica? Lovely name. Different." Jules walked over to him. "I am only trying to leaven the moment. Thomas would have wanted that." He patted his shoulder. "I'm happy you've returned. I am glad to turn the reins back over to you. And I won't press for details about *Angelica*. Yet." The beginnings of another smile tugged at the corners of his mouth. "Welcome back. It has been a long time. You've earned your rest."

Rest. How the hell was he to accomplish that when Fouquet and Thomas tormented his soul, and a little sorceress had blinded and beguiled him and all but reduced him to a single-minded fool?

CHAPTER THIRTEEN

"In nomine Patris, et Filii, et Spiritus Sancti…"

Simon tried to concentrate on the old priest's Latin drone. The church was filled to capacity for Domenico and Gabriella's wedding ceremony.

Angelica stood on Gabriella's left-hand side as one of the two witnesses she'd chosen. And he refused to look at Angelica. *Again.*

Only a short distance from her, he, along with Jules and Armand, were to the right of Domenico.

Simon seldom entered churches. Having seen every kind of suffering imaginable, he'd often question if there were any kind of higher power in all this. As a boy, he'd lost his family, one by one. Orphaned, he'd been left to face a slow, agonizing death—starvation—alone.

For as long as he lived, he'd never forget the hunger pains he'd known within his once malnourished body.

It had been that hunger inside him—a hunger to escape his baseborn existence and attain nobility—that had saved his life. And driven him to the financial success he'd attained. It had been his reason for rising every morning.

And it had taken Thomas's death and the death of all those Fouquet had preyed upon to make him see he couldn't chase his ambitions without paying a price.

Now that his dream to have an elevated station in life was not to be, how did he live his life without it? It would take self-discipline and strength to relinquish the need that had burned inside him most of his life.

He'd had both in great reserve until he met the green-eyed woman standing only a few feet from him. A month ago, he'd weakened so badly that he had forged ahead and done something he'd never been willing to do before—compromise a woman's virtue. But there had been no virtue to compromise, and he was left reeling from the sting of her deceit.

Had he been so desperate to believe she was uncorrupted and true, he'd convinced himself she was something she was not?

"*Dominum Deum Nostrum…*" Père Crotteau began to give the nuptial blessing. Thankfully, the ceremony would be over soon, and Simon could leave.

Trying to keep his eyes focused anywhere other than on Angelica, he looked out at the crowded church. Claudine Renaud gave him a saucy wink, then blew him a kiss. He turned away, irritated. A widow of thirty-two, she was the niece of his island's architect, Xavier Beloit.

Wanting to erase Angelica from his mind and body, he'd made the mistake of visiting Claudine. But, no matter how hard he'd fought it, with every touch of Claudine's body, he felt Angelica's, and worse, he heard those arousing sounds she'd made in the back of her throat that he'd been convinced were completely unpracticed.

He couldn't even muster the desire to kiss Claudine with Angelica's taste still haunting him. Never had he been with a woman without finishing what he started, but he lost all interest and left.

He glanced at Angelica just as the sun broke through a cloud. A streak of sunlight shone through the small windowpanes fifteen feet up directly onto her chestnut hair, giving it a warm glow, making her look divine, as if a finger from heaven pointed down on her alone.

Tightening his jaw, he dragged his gaze back to Père Crotteau.

Since his return, Simon had immersed himself in the daily responsibilities of running the island. However, at night, in his bed, knowing Angelica was under the same roof, he couldn't force away memories of her lush mouth or the glorious feeling of being inside her as she came. *That*, at least, had been genuine. Her passion and the pleasure were real.

How much of her inexperienced behavior in bed had been contrived? There could not have been more than one lover. Could there? *Dieu*, what other secrets did she keep?

Why was she refusing to tell him?

"*Ahhhh...*" The collective sound from the crowd grabbed Simon's attention. He saw Domenico giving his bride a kiss.

The priest finally finished with the ceremony.

Gabriella had wanted to share Angelica's room instead of using her own. At night, he'd often heard the murmur of their voices or the sound of their laughter as he passed Angelica's door.

Tonight, Gabriella would leave and finally go to Domenico's home.

How was he going to find any rest knowing Angelica was alone in her bed?

*****

"He watches you," Sabine de Moutier said in Angelica's ear. She knew Sabine was referring to Simon, seated at the end of the table.

Tables were set up outside near Simon's home overlooking the sea. In the dying light of day, the torches around the perimeter had already been lit.

Jules's lovely wife had organized a group of women to prepare the wedding feast for the newlyweds and had assisted with other details to make the celebration truly special.

Focusing on the slices of roasted duck on her plate, Angelica tried to ignore how gorgeous Simon looked. Nor did she want to notice his hands that were so tanned and had felt so good.

She didn't want to desire him. Or his tender sentiment. But to be immune to the longings she was experiencing. In order to have more with Simon—if he were interested any longer—she'd have to reveal things about herself that she couldn't reveal.

"You're mistaken, Sabine. He's quite occupied at the moment." With the number of females that seemed to always hover around him, he didn't look as though he missed her in the least.

"Them? That is only Claudine Renaud and her friend Antoinette Garnier. Claudine chases Simon. She always has, but she's a terrible woman. He has been avoiding her for many days, Jules tells me."

The fiddlers began to play.

Suzette approached, grinning. "Good evening."

"Why do you look so happy?" Angelica asked, returning her infectious smile.

"I think Paul is going to ask me to dance!"

"He will if he has any good sense at all," said Sabine.

Before Angelica could reply, she heard, "Mademoiselle?"

A young man stood before her. She'd seen him before. He was a member of the crew and not a worker from the cane fields.

"My name is Yves. Would you care to dance?" He held out his hand.

The lively music beckoned her. Losing herself in it would be a delightful, much-needed distraction. She looked at Suzette and Sabine. They nodded, urging her to go.

"Thank you, Yves. That would be very nice."

*****

"Angelica is quite a popular woman," Jules said, walking up with a big grin.

Simon tried to ignore his irritating friend.

"I believe that is her fifth dance in a row."

Seventh, Simon wanted to say.

"And I believe it must be her second with Yves."

Third. But who is counting?

"I don't think the lovely Angelica will be lacking in male company in any way tonight," Toussaint remarked.

Simon clenched his teeth. Watching as Angelica went from Yves to her next dance partner, he didn't need the obvious pointed out to him.

She was smiling, flushed from dancing, her breasts beautifully enhanced by her dropped neckline. The memory of how those same sweet breasts had looked and felt in his hands, filled his mind, and stiffened his unruly cock. He could still taste her delicious, pert nipples on his tongue.

He found himself mourning the loss of the convent garb.

Claudine rubbed her thigh against his, again. He wished she'd chosen to sit elsewhere during the meal. "Wasn't she on your ship, Simon?" she purred annoyingly.

"Yes."

Jules leaned in and murmured in his ear. "You've omitted some delectable details of the voyage, by the way." Simon could hear the smile in Jules's voice. If he didn't have an enormous erection at the moment, he would stand up and toss Jules over the cliff.

"I heard that no one knows much about her, and that you found her in a convent," Claudine said with a laugh. Her friend Antoinette and Jules joined in. Toussaint simply smiled.

Simon glared darkly at Jules. His laughter died.

"I must admit I was a bit jealous when I learned she'd be living in your home, Simon," Claudine added. "But a *convent?*" Her laughter bubbled to the surface once more. "With her limited knowledge of men, I sincerely doubt she could hold your interest, *cher.*"

That was just it. Angelica had held his interest from the moment he'd laid eyes on her.

Against his will, Simon watched the parade of her dance partners. Each man left looking love-struck or lust-struck. She wove her magic on unsuspecting males with devastating proficiency.

When, at long last, Simon saw her step away from the dancing and walk over to the tables, he couldn't stop himself from approaching her.

Standing alone, she reached for a goblet of wine.

"Good evening," he said. "Are you enjoying yourself, *chère?*"

"Yes. Thank you." She looked past his shoulder at the small group he had left. "Are you?"

"Of course." This was the first real conversation he'd had with her since the day they had arrived. "Tell me, you didn't happen to mention your real name to any of the men you danced with, did you? It would bring our game to an end. I won't feel special anymore."

She stiffened. And there was a flare of anger in her eyes. Good. It was only part of what he felt after watching her moving from man to man.

For the life of him, he couldn't understand her. She was compassionate, gentle, and sometimes shy, yet she was also feisty, strong, and brave. She looked like an innocent, yet she was not. In bed, she'd been passionate, yet virginal in manner. It was driving him mad. No matter what he did, no matter how hard he tried, he couldn't quash this damned fixation he had with her.

"I didn't tell them anything, Simon, but there is something I have been meaning to tell you."

"Oh? And what is that?"

She set the goblet down onto the table and stepped close to him. "I wanted to thank *you* for the tumble." She turned to go. He caught her arm and marched into the forest beyond the torches, pulling her with him. "Simon, what are you doing?"

He didn't stop until he reached a small clearing, secluded by trees and shadow.

He released her arm. "I want to know what it is you seek. Are you working up the men because you are looking for a tumble?"

"I am not a whore."

"I never said you were. And I don't think ill of women with, shall we say, a healthy sexual appetite. I consider those women to be among my personal favorites."

"Really? From the looks of it, you have a lot of 'personal favorites.' Tell me, Simon, are you working them up? Are you looking for a tumble?"

Her words pulled a smile from him. "*Chère*, you sound jealous."

Normally, possessive feelings from a woman, such as jealousy, inspired him to turn and walk, but seeing it in her eyes, hearing it in her tone, oddly pleased him. He'd noticed that since he'd pulled her into the secluded spot, her breathing had hastened a little, and he was willing to wager that if he ran his fingers along her smooth neck, he would find her pulse racing. He was affecting her. And it wasn't anger that was causing the quickening in her body, but rather hot sexual excitement, the same scorching heat that was rushing through him.

Dieu. There was no debate about it. The desire between them was an undeniable truth.

After all her toying, he should have had enough of her, but he knew down to his marrow he wasn't even close to sating himself with his moonlight angel.

He *would* break this mind-bending obsession for good. To that end, he was going to make himself available to her. But on his terms.

He wouldn't play by her rules any longer

"Jealous?" Angelica scoffed. "That's ridiculous…"

She was alone with Simon under the stars, in a forest, with the scent of pine and the sounds of music and the ocean in the air. And he had the most seductive look in his eyes. The one she recognized as the usual prelude to her downfall. She tried to ignore how stimulated her senses were, while trying to deny the truth: yes, she was jealous! She hated to see him with other women, or worse, to imagine him giving them the same joy and pleasure he'd given her.

"Is it?" he pressed.

"It is." She turned to leave, needing to distance herself. His hand closed over her shoulder, halting her. With a sudden sweep, he picked her up in his arms and placed her bottom on a fallen log, her legs coming down on either side of it. Before she could pull her leg over and move into a more modest sitting position, he seated himself behind her, and slipped his arms around her. Holding her in place.

Her senses were already tingling, all too aware of the bulge in his breeches pressing against her lower back. He dipped his head, bringing his mouth near her ear.

"Angelica," he murmured. "I'm not with those other women. I'm here with you. I want you. Can you not feel how hard you make me?" How in heaven could she miss that? Just the feel of that delicious part of his male anatomy against her, knowing how masterfully he knew how to use it, made her sex clench. "If you want a man, come to me. Day or night… Let me be your lover."

He cupped her breast. She fisted her skirts. Heat radiated from everywhere his body touched hers. She'd never felt so hot. Her nipples were hard, straining for him, anxious for his touch.

"There are carnal delights yet to explore. The last night of the voyage was but a small sampling. I want you to come to me and only me. Let me be the one to give you pleasure." He gave her nipple the lightest pinch through her gown. She jerked with a gasp. "I have yet to make love to you." He continued to tease the tip of her breast with tender twists and tugs, sending scintillating sensations quivering into her core. Moisture pooled between her legs. She couldn't catch her breath, her breathing now shallower. And sharper.

"We...did that on the ship," she managed to say. But the rest of her words caught in her throat the moment she felt his other hand slip under her skirts, moving steadily up along her inner thigh. She held her breath, waiting. Anticipating. The bud between her legs pulsating in time with her frenzied heart.

"No, *chère*, we did not." He grazed his hot mouth along her neck. "When you offer up your body and nothing else, then it is but an anonymous encounter. Making love is far more intimate, and I know it would be oh so erotic and intense between us."

He cupped her sex. A soft cry surged up her throat.

"*Dieu*... You're not wearing any drawers." He stroked his fingers along her wet cleft, lightly massaging her sex. Her head fell back against his shoulder. She closed her eyes. She knew full well she lacked the will to stop any of this. Not when it was his hands on her. Not when it was his arms around her. His light caresses had her desperate and aching for more.

"The island...is very hot," she tried to explain, barely able to form words. She hadn't expected anyone to learn of her recently acquired practice.

She hadn't expected anything like this. What he was doing to her breast and her sex was melting her mind.

"Always full of surprises, aren't you?" he said, his warm breath tickling her ear. She heard the smile in his tone. "I must say, this one is by far my favorite."

He slid a finger inside her. She whimpered.

"So warm...and soft... and wet.... *Christ*, you have the sweetest cunt." He withdrew his finger, maddeningly circled her needy nub, then slid two fingers back into her slick sex. She arched, desperate for any kind of friction against that very bud between her legs he'd just teased, trying to grind up against his hand.

He chuckled softly. "You want your clit rubbed? This sweet little bud right here..." He gave it a gentle pinch. She practically shot up off the log. He tightened his hold, keeping her in place. "We could take this to another level of intimacy, Angelica, but you are going to have to reveal yourself to me. Not just your body. You are going to have to tell me who you are."

His skillful hand was pumping her, hurling her closer and closer to a powerful release. She tightened around his fingers, so out of control, his thumb occasionally grazing her clit, purposely giving her spikes of heightened sensations. "Your body is hungry for a release, isn't it, Angelica? You want to come for me, don't you?"

She was panting now. Delirious with desire. "Yes! Don't stop..."

"I won't. *Trust me*. I know what you want. And I know how to make it better..." Curling his buried fingers, he stroked over an ultrasensitive spot inside her slick walls.

She thrust back against him with a strangled cry, the sensation stunningly sharp. But he held her fast, not allowing her to escape the fierce pleasure from each stroke he gave that oversensitive spot.

"It feels intense, doesn't it?" He delivered three stronger strokes, snatching a cry from her lungs. She shuddered, the sensations overwhelming. "Just ride through them," he coaxed in her ear. "The release is going to be so strong...Let go, *mon ange*. I have you."

She bit her lip, her orgasm imminent. Straining hard, she dug her fingers into his thighs, barreling toward a shattering release, she could neither contain nor control.

"That's right. I love how strongly you're tightening and quivering around my fingers. You're so close. Come for me," he groaned.

Ecstasy exploded inside her. A cry burst from her lips, her inner muscles clenching and unclenching wildly around his busy fingers, each strong spasm sending waves of pleasure cresting over her.

He didn't stop until the last spasm faded, until she was boneless and slumped against him.

He eased his fingers from her and held her until her breathing calmed, until she found the strength to pull her leaden leg over the fallen tree so that she could face him. She met his gaze. Desire burned in his beautiful light-colored eyes.

Sliding his arms away from her, he leaned his elbows on his thighs and folded his hands. Unable to stop herself, she cupped his face and kissed him, slowly, softly. He returned her kiss but did not reach for her.

Make love... Those words flitted through her mind. From his lips, they held such appeal. Her heart cried out to him, welling with the desire to tell him all, to connect with him on a deeper level.

She silenced the foolish thing. He wouldn't offer to make love to her if he knew the truth about her. How could anyone know about the soiling and not feel disgust. He could never see her as a whole woman the way he did now. How could anyone?

She refused to risk lessening herself in his eyes that way. Her feelings for him ran too deep.

Even though he'd been angry with her, he still wanted her. Maybe her happiness would have to be limited to his touch if not his heart. Would that be so bad? Would it be enough?

She broke the kiss. "Simon, if you want to... If you are interested..."

"Yes, I want to. Yes, I am interested. Are you prepared to reveal yourself? Are you going to tell me who you are?"

Her hands fell away from his face. "Why is this so important to you?"

He sighed and shook his head. "It just is, *mon ange*. It's best you return to the celebration. You will be missed soon."

It was the second time he'd called her *my angel*, and he'd said it so softly, it made her heart ache. "What about you?"

He gave her a rueful smile. "After watching you come, I'm going to need a few minutes." His smile faded. "I want you to come to me, Angelica. I want you, but I'm going to need to know who you are. The door is open and the invitation has been extended. You decide if you are going to accept it or decline it."

*****

Two days later, Simon sat in his library. She hadn't come to him, *still*. For two nights he'd waited, expectant, hopeful. Nothing. *Merde*. Enough. He had work to do.

He picked up the drawings for the new sugar mill and reviewed them. While some of the islands in the West Indies were importing slaves from Africa to work on the cane estates, he wanted nothing to do with slavery. Bringing peasants from France and providing them with shelter and fair wages not only fostered self-dignity but also loyalty and a desire to work and remain.

Since his return, he'd made a thorough inspection of the island's structures. Walls and lookout towers that protected the island from invaders needed attention. There were also construction plans he had in mind that would require further meetings and planning with his architect, Xavier.

He'd hoped by keeping himself occupied, it would take his mind off Angelica. It had not.

There was a knock at the door.

"Enter," he bid.

Jules entered, sporting his usual smile, and closed the door.

"You brought the ledgers," Simon stated, eyeing them in Jules's hand.

"Good morning to you too." Jules handed them to Simon and seated himself comfortably on the opposite side of the desk. "No need to ask how you are. Tell me, what of the beautiful Angelica? How is she?"

Simon purposely engrossed himself in the ledgers before responding, "How would I know?"

"She lives in your home. By the way, is this going to be a permanent arrangement?"

Without looking up from the ledgers, Simon stated, "You can cease your grinning, Jules. I will find a place for her. Until then, she's fine staying where she is." He didn't add that it was killing him to have her there every night.

He was responsible for her, and Domenico wanted his bride all to himself. Simon wasn't about to place Angelica in the shared accommodations where the field workers lived. The other islanders had their own homes. In essence, there was nowhere else for her to go.

There is my bed...

"Ah, such a sacrifice," Jules said with laughter in his voice.

Simon frowned.

"Come now," his friend said, chuckling. "There isn't a soul on this island who doesn't believe you've enjoyed her favors, innocent or not. She was on board your ship for weeks and now is under your roof. She is far too lovely not to tempt any man, much less a man with your reputation."

"I don't give a damn what people think. Have we become so lax here that everyone has time to sit around and speculate about whom I bed?"

"You are a favorite subject of interest here. And you avoid discussing this woman at every turn."

Simon sighed. "*Merde*, Jules. What do you wish to hear?"

He sat back. "For starters, every detail."

"There's nothing to tell."

With mirth in his eyes, Jules rose. "Fine. Have it your way. Don't forget today is the first of the month."

Simon groaned. "I'd completely forgotten."

"I have not. This is one duty I'm more than happy to relinquish to you—mediating disputes between the islanders. I swear, if I had to settle one more dispute regarding chickens, I would drown myself in the sea. All parties concerned will be in attendance in the village square this afternoon at two."

"How many items are on the list to be settled?"

"Thus far, six. It would seem they are eager for your good judgment to settle their differences."

Simon sighed. "How many are about chickens?"

"No doubt all."

"You will be there?"

Jules smiled broadly. "Of course, I wouldn't miss your decisive judgment on the fate of our poultry for anything in the world."

*****

"I'm sorry, Angelica. This is all my fault," Gabriella said, breaking the silence on the carriage ride back home. "I didn't mean to get you into trouble with the old priest. I didn't think Père Crotteau would object so strongly to you singing your mother's song inside the church when no one was around. For Heaven's sake, even horrible Madre Paola would allow it from time to time." Gabriella patted her hand. "But don't worry. Domenico will be there in the village square. I will explain everything. All will be well," she assured.

She wasn't sorry she'd sung. They'd stopped briefly to light a candle for their dear Madre Caterina while the church was empty, and at Gabriella's prompting, Angelica had sung Madre's favorite song. One Angelica's mother had taught her. The old priest flew into a fit and had told her he was going to report her this afternoon at the village square, where trials and disputes were heard. Wagging a gnarled finger at her, he'd warned her to be there to receive whatever punishment her disrespect warranted. True, the song she'd sung in church wasn't religious but a lovely love song instead.

It gave her great comfort to sing it again. She hadn't done so since that night in the chapel with Madre Paola. And Simon.

The man who had inspired her to take risks, to reach for happiness.

This final obstacle to putting her past behind her and revealing her stepfather's sick act was proving to be insurmountable.

She was about to respond to Gabriella when something caught her eye just past Gabriella's shoulder. "Gabriella, is that not the school?"

Gabriella turned and gasped. "That is André Grignon, the schoolmaster. He is *whipping* that child!"

Standing outside the schoolhouse, the schoolmaster viciously lashed a small boy with a switch across his back as the child wailed in agony.

"Stop this carriage!" Angelica shouted to the driver and jumped down the moment it came to an abrupt halt. She ran and snatched the boy to her. Pushing the sobbing child behind her, she turned to confront the schoolmaster, fury burning through her veins.

"What do you think you are doing?" She shook with outrage.

"Stand aside," the tall, thin man ordered. "I discipline the children as I see fit."

"No! This is not discipline! This is brutality. What could he possibly have done to deserve a beating of this magnitude?"

The schoolmaster snorted. "I do not answer to *you*."

"I'm taking him home." She turned to the boy when Grignon grabbed her arm. Instinctively, she swung around and struck him with an open palm across his face. "Don't touch me! I am not one of these helpless children you enjoy mistreating."

Angelica ignored the man as he held his cheek, stunned. She gently picked up the sobbing boy and briskly carried him to the carriage, Gabriella rushing alongside her.

In short order, they found themselves standing in the Moutier home, having learned en route from the young boy, Tristan, that his mother worked in the Moutier's household.

Sabine stepped out into the foyer, wearing a welcoming smile.

Her smile died the instant she saw the crying boy in Angelica's arms and his blood-soaked shirt. Sabine rushed forward, gently lifted the shirt, and saw the open cuts slashed across his back.

"My God, what happened?"

"Grignon did this to him," Angelica explained, still livid.

"Brute!" Sabine's single word was rife with disgust. Calling to a male servant, she ordered him to carry the child upstairs.

"This treatment of children cannot be tolerated," Angelica said.

"Oh, I quite agree!" Sabine looked just as enraged. "First, I must inform Claire about what happened to her son. Then we shall get to the bottom of this. If this is the first time Grignon has done this to a child, it is one time too many. Today is the day disputes are heard in the village square. We'll attend and advise Simon of the schoolmaster's practices. I don't believe Simon or Jules had any idea that Grignon was capable of this!"

Angelica glanced at Gabriella and cleared her throat. "I'm afraid I already have a matter before Simon today. This one involving the schoolmaster will make *two*."

CHAPTER FOURTEEN

Simon sat at a long table in the village square with Jules, Domenico, and Armand. A large crowd had assembled before them. As Domenico called out each item from the list, the concerned parties stepped forward before Simon and took turns arguing the merits of their dispute against the opposing individual.

Simon tried to render judgments that were fair and would set boundaries of conduct for all. By the sixth dispute, he was hard-pressed to stay focused. *Merde*. This was tedious in the extreme. Jules hadn't jested when he'd told him these were mostly about chickens.

Armand diligently recorded every dispute and resolution.

"That was the last one, was it not?" Simon inquired, anxious to put an end to the tiresome task.

Domenico shook his head. "No, I'm afraid. There is one more that was added at the last minute."

Simon sighed. "Domenico, tell me it isn't over any more livestock."

"No, definitely not livestock…"

"I am next, am I not?" Père Crotteau stepped out of the crowd to the middle of the square before the table of four.

"Yes, you are. Proceed," Domenico ordered.

"I have a very serious matter to put before you, Captain. A matter of grievous importance. A conduct that cannot, must not, be tolerated. There is an individual amongst us who has committed a crime against the Church." Gasps and murmurs swept through the crowd.

"*Dieu.*" Simon groaned to himself. This was the last thing he was in the mood to deal with. Could this day get any worse?

He rubbed his tired eyes with his finger and thumb. "Who is this individual?" His voice was flat. "And what is the crime?"

"A woman, Captain. She entered the church and attempted to desecrate the holy house with a sacrilegious act." Cries of astonishment rose anew from the spectators.

With a heavy sigh, Simon asked, "Where is this woman? What is her name?" The prolonging of this monotony irked him.

"Here," a voice called out from the back of the crowd. With another wave of murmurs, necks craned and turned, followed by a collective gasp as Angelica finally broke through the mass to enter the center of the square.

Simon swore under his breath.

Jules leaned into him. "Oh, this is going to be interesting." He grinned.

Domenico poorly suppressed a chuckle.

Simon ignored his friends as he watched Angelica approach and stop beside the old priest. From the top of her glossy brown curls down to the simple cut of her pale yellow gown, she looked stunning. She fixed him with her full attention, her hands folded in front of her, her chin raised.

"I'm the one Père Crotteau accuses."

His insides twisted with a mixture of desire, longing, and vexation. Did she have to cause him grief *all* of the time?

"What have you to say regarding this charge against you?" he demanded. What he really wanted to ask her was, *Where have you been the last two nights?* She was the only woman who'd ever kept him waiting. She was the only woman he'd ever waited for.

"The charge is absurd. I was with her, and I convinced her to do it," Gabriella called out as she stepped into the center and stopped beside her friend. Another round of gasps and murmurs swept through the crowd. "If there is to be a punishment, then it is for me as well!"

"Gabriella!" Domenico exclaimed, no longer sharing Jules's amusement at the scene before them.

"I have no objection to having both women punished," the priest magnanimously offered.

"What did she do?" Simon asked.

"She entered the Holy Church today and she—*sang*," Père Crotteau announced. "And it was *not* a Psalm," he was quick to add.

Simon briefly closed his eyes and held back the expletives bellowing in his head as murmurs rippled through the mass once again. His exasperation made him feel suddenly weary.

Armand leaned toward the three other men at the table. "Did the priest say, *'sang not a Psalm'*?"

"Yes," Jules confirmed, still smiling. "That is what he said."

This was an area Simon wasn't comfortable with, for he lacked the devotion some had. Yet he didn't want to appear unconcerned.

He couldn't believe he was about to settle a religious dispute, of all things.

"Captain," the priest continued. "The sanctity of the church must be maintained. I won't tolerate anything but pious devotion within its walls."

"Père Crotteau is right. She must be punished!" the schoolmaster, André Grignon, exclaimed as he stepped forward to join Angelica, Gabriella, and the priest. "She must learn her place. This morning, this woman came to the school and took one of the children...and then she"—he paused, touching his cheek—"struck me when I tried to stop her!"

A roar erupted from the spectators. Sabine de Moutier stepped out into the center with the others.

"Sabine..." Jules's amusement died the instant he saw his wife standing defiantly with Angelica.

"*Silence,*" Simon commanded the crowd.

"This woman is guilty of nothing but falling victim to two pompous individuals who are under the misguided belief that your reasoning would ever be as absurd as theirs." Sabine leveled her husband and Simon with a stern look.

"*Oh Dieu,*" Jules softly swore.

"Did you do the things these men accuse you of?" Simon ignored Sabine's comment, too vexed at the willful, green-eyed woman before him and her errant ways.

Angelica took a step forward toward him. Her delicate shoulders back, she stood tall and held his gaze. "I did attend church, and I did sing. I sang a song that was taught to me by my mother. It has been a form of prayer to her since her death. As for your schoolmaster, I admit I did take the boy and that I did strike Grignon. In fact, I am hard-pressed at the moment not to strike him again."

Gasps and murmurs swelled in the square again and died down just as quickly. A smile tugged at the corners of Simon's mouth, despite himself, remembering full well the force with which she could deliver a palm to the cheek. Grignon looked positively outraged.

"You see! She freely admits to her evil deeds," Père Crotteau chimed in.

"She has not committed evil deeds! There is nothing evil about Angelica's song," Gabriella argued. She moved to Angelica's side. "If there has ever been a voice truly angelic, then surely it is her voice. Her song is heavenly. Sing to us, Angelica. Sing to these people, and let them judge if there is anything sacrilegious about your song."

"Gabriella!" Angelica exclaimed in a heated whisper.

"What of her act of sacrilege?" the priest demanded.

Domenico leaned into Simon and rasped in his ear, "You are not going to punish my wife. I, on the other hand—"

"Easy, Domenico," Simon stated softly. He didn't feel Angelica deserved to be punished because of her song, yet he couldn't show favoritism here. Fairness as well as impartiality was expected of him. Nor could he offend those who were devout and clung to the Church's rules by making light of the matter.

Simon turned his attention back to the small group before his table. "I find myself rather liking Madame Dragani's suggestion. Angelica will sing us the song she says is a prayer to her mother."

Her eyes widened. "I've never sung before such an audience." There was unease in those moss-green eyes.

"Go on, Angelica. You can do it," Gabriella said.

"What do you hope to prove with this?" Jules murmured.

"Wait and see." Simon found himself anxiously anticipating her song. "Are you curious to hear the song Père Crotteau believes has defiled the sanctity of the church?" Simon asked the people.

The crowd responded with a roar. "*Yes!*"

He'd given her no choice. She looked around at the throng clamoring to hear her song, and then at him. *Why are you doing this?* was clearly etched on her lovely face. He wanted to answer her unspoken question, to tell her to trust him, that it was the only way he could think of to avoid having to punish her yet still appear impartial. But then again, she didn't trust him. Did she? Not with a single meaningful detail about herself?

"*Sing,*" he commanded her.

She looked around again, then back at him and finally took a deep breath. She closed her eyes and paused. Eagerly, he awaited that first heavenly note. She didn't disappoint. She began to sing. Softly at first, then stronger.

The crowd fell silent.

He hadn't forgotten the song. That beautiful, haunting voice pervaded his heavy soul. It was but one of the many multifaceted reasons he was so very drawn to her.

Absorbing every sweet note, he wanted to remain suspended in it. Her voice and that song had a way of vanquishing all else but its melody. And the woman it came from.

When the last note faded, she opened her eyes and scanned the crowd. For a moment, there was only silence.

Lucio and Nicolo were the first to clap vigorously, followed by thunderous applause from the rest of the throng, their cheers and whistles filling the air. The look of astonishment on her face was priceless. Slowly, a brilliant smile formed on her sweet lips. He couldn't hold back his own grin. It was obvious she'd never truly realized until this moment how moving that song was. There was pure joy in her eyes, and in his heart for her.

His beautiful songbird had succeeded in winning over the entire crowd.

Just as he knew she would.

He glanced at Jules, Armand, and Domenico, thoroughly enjoying the stunned looks on their faces.

Simon raised his hand, and the jovial noise dissipated. "I must agree with Madame Dragani. That sounded far too angelic to be wicked. Would you not agree?" he questioned the crowd. They cheered anew.

"This is preposterous!" the priest began to spout, red-faced. "The church is no place for—"

"That song is as close to heaven as some of us here will ever get," Simon interjected. There was applause and some laughter that rippled through the crowd. "The mademoiselle will henceforth refrain from singing her *prayer* in the church, and you, Père Crotteau, will accept her onetime form of spiritual devotion to her mother's memory. We are finished with this matter. Step back," Simon ordered. The old priest complied with a nod, being wise enough to know how far to push.

"Now then, I'll hear about the incident at the schoolhouse next." Simon's gaze was fixed on Angelica. He'd schooled his features into a more purposeful look, though he still reeled with pleasure over her accomplishment.

With regret, he saw her smile die, yet she didn't flinch under the weight of his stare as others did. She never had. Inner strength was something he'd always admired. And she had an abundance of it.

"Today, I observed, while on my way past the schoolhouse, Grignon whipping a child severely," she responded, her tone dripping with disdain and anger.

"That is nonsense. A gross exaggeration of the truth," the schoolmaster argued.

"It is not an exaggeration." She cast Grignon a look of contempt. "The boy was terribly wounded. This man does not teach. He terrifies these children. No child can possibly learn under these conditions. Nor should they be made to."

"You know nothing of what you speak. And you know nothing of teaching," Grignon countered.

"Not true. I have taught children in the past, and they can learn, even difficult passages, when you stir within them the desire to learn," she shot back.

Simon watched as she stood her ground, not allowing Grignon to intimidate her. She spoke with conviction. And she was completely alluring in her temper.

She was completely alluring always.

"Is this true, Grignon? Did you beat this child?" he asked.

"The child was simply disciplined. Discipline is an important part of any child's education."

Simon nodded. "I will see the boy for myself before making a decision on this matter."

"But she is out of control. She needs punishment!" the schoolmaster exclaimed, his eyes scanning about for someone to concur.

Simon frowned. "Grignon, do you dare question my judgment?"

Grignon's brows shot up. "No-No, of course not." He cleared his throat. "I am confident your decision will be just and proper, as always." He forced a weak smile.

"Simon, the boy is here," Sabine announced. She motioned to her servant, who carried the boy to the center of the square next to Sabine.

Sabine lifted the boy's shirt.

Instantly, a soft cry quivered through the crowd. Simon felt his ire grow as he gazed at the child's back.

"Grignon, you call this discipline?" Simon demanded.

"Yes. It is important—"

"It is excessive. And unacceptable!"

Jules let loose a string of expletives. "If I'd had any inkling he was capable of doing something like this," he growled, "I would have broken his skinny neck."

Simon knew if Grignon had done this to other children, their parents would have been afraid to report authority to authority. It was often the way with peasants. Regardless, he had to know for certain. "Have others among you had children suffer something similar to what this boy has suffered at Grignon's hands? I demand a show of hands."

People exchanged uneasy glances. Slowly, some reluctant hands began to rise.

Merde. "Grignon, you are relieved of your duty as schoolmaster."

"*What?*" Grignon paled.

"Furthermore, three months' labor in the fields, without pay, will hopefully give you enough time to consider your ill ways."

"But..."

"Don't speak!" he barked. "Or I'll reconsider my punishment and flog you myself. That is all." Simon stood.

The crowd began to depart.

Simon stepped around the table. "Angelica?"

Standing with Gabriella, Sabine, and their husbands, she turned around. She was smiling, despite the marital discord near her.

"A word with you," he requested.

She approached. He wanted to shake her, to hold her, to lose himself in the sweet oblivion she induced with just one of her kisses.

"Yes?"

"A warning, if you will. In a single morning, you have managed to offend the Church and unsettle our system of schooling. Tell me, do you have any plans for the afternoon?"

"No, I believe I'm done for the day."

"Excellent. I think we need to keep you busy. You have been teaching Suzette to read and have taught children in the past. Would you like the position of schoolmistress?"

A small gasp escaped her. "Oh yes! Yes, I would!"

Angelica felt as though her heart was ready to burst, overjoyed by what she'd just observed—his anger and outrage over the abuse the boy suffered. How many more times did she need to see him demonstrate his compassion for others? With each matter brought before him today, he'd been fair. Considerate. He'd even assisted her with the old priest—and now he was granting her a position that meant the world to her—*schoolmistress*.

Why keep her past a secret from him when it cost her more than it gained? When it was keeping her from more bliss. From more with him. Everything she'd seen today further confirmed in her heart that she should take the risk. He'd shown himself to be worthy of her trust. And she was going to lay her secret bare.

The wall of silence that kept her apart from him was going to be torn down.

"If you like, you may start tomorrow, Angelica."

She couldn't stop smiling. "Thank you!" She threw her arms around his neck and kissed his cheek. "For the position and for making me sing." Each time she sang that song, it gave her great comfort and strength. She stepped back. He looked utterly stunned.

She laughed. "That wasn't very discreet of me, I suppose," she said without apology. She didn't care who was watching. She wasn't going to be afraid. Or hide anymore.

Everything was going to be all right. *He'll understand.*

He smiled back at her. "I'm glad you are so pleased."

"I want to accept your invitation," she blurted out.

He was speechless for a moment, her words astounding him more than her public affection. "*Really...*"

"Yes, Simon, truly. Will you come to my room tonight?" She had the overwhelming urge to kiss that perfect mouth. Never to stop.

"You understand what this means, don't you?"

"Yes."

"You will reveal yourself to me completely, without holding back?"

Old fears rose within her. She quickly said, "Yes," before they could overtake her. "I will, but—"

"But what?"

"I want to be with you first, just like on the ship. One more time. Then I will tell you what you wish to know. I promise."

*****

Simon walked through the front door of his home. The day couldn't have trickled by more slowly. He'd gone through the motions, meetings, and inspections, but all he could think about was Angelica. In his arms. Finally trusting him. His knowing all her secrets.

He climbed the stairs. Each step that brought him closer to her made his heart beat a little faster. By the time he reached Angelica's door, he felt nervous. Incredible. He'd never been nervous with any woman. Not ever.

Entering her room, he found her standing on the small balcony. The breeze caressed her hair and the hem of her pale-colored dressing gown.

Basking in the moon's silver light was his moonlight angel.

Momentarily transfixed, he watched as she inhaled the night air and gazed at the multitude of starry lights. Raw hunger shot through his body. Hardening his cock.

His desire for her was humbling.

He approached, the sound of the distant sea becoming more pronounced.

"That is indeed a beautiful moon," he said.

Startled, she spun around, then smiled. Her smile wasn't as joyful as it had been earlier. It was a little nervous, a little apprehensive.

She threw herself against him, taking him off guard. Twining her arms around his neck, she planted a zealous kiss on his mouth. There was nothing apprehensive about that.

Capturing her face between his hands, he angled her head and took command of the kiss, sliding his tongue past her lips, possessing her mouth. He gave her slow, measured strokes of his tongue, enjoying the sensual sound of her soft moan, and the sweet, hot press of her form against him. For an instant, he wondered if he should shatter her mystique at all. Did he really want this enchantment to end? Would it end?

She ended the kiss, breathless. Big green eyes stared back at him, darkened with desire. Taking his hand, she began to pull him toward the bed. "There was a moon just like that one on the night we met," she said.

He rooted his feet to the floor, halting them from moving any closer to the bed. Yet he couldn't stop his gaze from stroking down the length of her body. A breeze stole its way into the room and swirled her dressing gown, giving him a glimpse of her legs. Beneath the wrap, she had on only a night chemise. The two layers of thin material didn't come close to shielding her from his burning regard.

"You are beautiful. Passionate," he said. "A devastating combination."

She blushed. It was an appealing novelty. The women he normally bedded were not the blushing types. Especially in the boudoir.

"We have matters to discuss before we do *that*." He nodded toward the bed. He couldn't believe he was hesitating, in any way, to take a beautiful woman who was offering herself to him. To take his fantasy angel.

She slipped her arms around his waist, her soft belly pressing against his stone-hard cock. His eager prick twitched hungrily. "Take me first, Simon. I love the way you make me feel... Just one more time before we talk." She pressed her mouth against his neck and trailed hot kisses toward his throat. He closed his eyes. She was moving things along, using the oldest of ploys. And it was working. The crest of his cock was already wet with pre-come. Yet he wasn't going to let her use his body against him. He was here for more than sex. She'd made him promises she was going to keep. He'd never agreed to her suggestion of sex first.

He picked her up and had her on her back on the bed in one fluid movement. He lowered his body on top of hers. Taking her wrists, he slowly raised her arms above her head and pinned them there with one hand. Her eyes widened, but she didn't fight him.

"You are still playing games, and you are trying to distract me with sex."

"No, Simon, I just want—"

"I know what you want. We are not leaving this room until you have told me everything you've promised to tell me." He wanted her to trust him enough to tell him the truth. He wanted to stop obsessing about her. His gaze fell to her sweet breasts, rising and falling with her excited breaths.

God help him, he just plain wanted her.

He couldn't keep chasing after her or tormenting himself with questions about her. Nor did he want to be jealous of phantom lovers he envisioned with her. He had to have answers. Or lose his bloody mind. Maybe then he could return to his old self or at least to some semblance of that person.

Slowly, he opened her dressing gown and untied the silk ribbon at the neckline of her chemise. "We are going to play *my* game, *chère.*"

CHAPTER FIFTEEN

Pushing aside Angelica's clothing, Simon stroked the warm curve of her breast. She gasped and strained a little in his hold. She was so deliciously responsive to him, and he was going to use it to his advantage.

If it didn't kill him first.

"I'm going to ask you your name no more than three times. All you have to do is tell me before the third and final time, and our game of pleasure continues. If you fail to answer by then, we stop. Are you ready to play?"

"*Simon...*"

He shifted his body. "Do you know you have the prettiest nipples?" Holding her gaze, he dipped his head, purposely hovering his mouth over one taut peak. "I especially love them when you're aroused and they are pert like this, begging to be sucked."

He gave her nipple a gentle flick of his tongue, then brushed the contour of his lips over it, drawing a whimper from her. "Shall I suck this pretty pink nipple, Angelica? Do you want that?"

Her breaths were already sharp and shallow. "*Yes!*"

He smiled. "As you wish." He captured her nipple with his mouth, lightly sucking and biting it, making her squirm and strain beneath him, unable to contain the urge. A sweet demand for more. And more was exactly what he was going to give his green-eyed siren. Releasing her nipple from his mouth, he gently pinched and pulled it as he turned his attention to her other breast, and suckled the pebbled peak. The seductive sounds she made swirled though his system, and tightened his sac.

Simon pressed his thigh between her legs, precisely over her clit, applying just enough pressure to make her breath catch. And feed her fever.

"Please..." She arched hard against him. Her voice was but a shaky whisper. She was begging him, and he should derive some satisfaction from it, but instead he was unraveling because of it.

He trailed his mouth up toward the tantalizing column of her neck, nipping and tasting the satiny skin along the way.

"Do you wish me to stop?"

"No."

"Then tell me your name. Say it."

A strangled sound escaped past her lips. "Simon...not like this. Don't do this now... *I want you.*"

He'd heard those three words uttered many times in bed before. Why did they sound so different when they came from her? Why did those three words from her lips send him straight to the edge?

He claimed her mouth to silence her. She parted her lips for him. Unable to resist, he slid his tongue inside.

She returned his kiss, drawing on his tongue, causing his prick to pulse. With a groan, he kissed her harder. Hungrier. She squirmed against his leg, then began rocking her hips against his thigh.

He tore his mouth from hers and quickly stilled her, unable to withstand her provocatively rubbing against him.

Reluctantly, he removed his thigh from between her legs.

"Angelica..." His breaths were as sharp and quick as hers. "You want my cock, don't you? Deep inside...like before..."

She shivered with excitement. "Yes."

"Then tell me your name. And I'll give you what you want." He cupped her breast, stroking her beaded nipple with his thumb.

He could feel her heart racing, her body yielding, and his will to see this mad plan through slipping away from him.

It shouldn't matter who she was or whom she had ever been with. He shouldn't want to erase former lovers from her mind so she'd long only for him, or struggle this hard against an overwhelming need to claim her as his own when exclusivity had never been important to him before.

He bloody well shouldn't want any woman who had this potent effect on his body and mind.

Grabbing the hem of her knee-length chemise, he pushed the fabric up along her thighs, deliberately letting her feel it inching higher and higher up her legs. "This is what you want, isn't it?"

She gave him a quick nod, her cheeks adorably flushed. He cupped her sex, his fingers covering her damp, downy curls. Softly, she moaned. He gritted his teeth, his cock having stiffened to painful proportions. Thoughts of taking her regardless and ending his own suffering were running rampant in his head. He was dangerously close to losing this game of wills and desires. He had to play this out. Quickly.

He couldn't withstand much more.

Knowing she was already close to climax, he was careful not to stroke her clit or increase the pressure of his hand. It took everything he had to resist the lure of her wet sex, battling back the overwhelming urge to plunge his fingers inside that heavenly snug heat.

"*Mon ange*, I am going to ask you one last time—" She thrust her hips up and grazed her clit against his palm. They both groaned. *Damn her.*

Her sex was warm, slick and so inviting...

On the brink of letting go of the façade of control, he pulled his hand away, his cock pulsing stronger, in rhythm with his wild heartbeat.

He took in a ragged breath. "Tell me who you really are. Tell me something about you."

Lifting her head from the bed, she pressed a kiss against the hollow of his throat. "What difference can a name make right now?" she said against his skin.

Her words jarred him.

With a growled oath, he pushed himself off her and sat up.

He raked a hand through his hair, his every muscle taut. Why the hell didn't he just fuck her? She was offering! It was what he would have done with anyone else.

What difference can a name make right now. It made a difference! *Merde.*

She touched his sleeve.

He turned to face her. "The game is over. You win."

Her hand tightened on his arm. "If you leave, I lose." Her eyes were without guile, her tone sincere and soft. "Don't go, Simon. I made you a promise. I will keep it. I will tell you my name."

He turned his body to face her better. "Go on."

She looked at him, then looked away with a sad smile. "I have not said my own name in ten years."

He cupped her cheek and turned her face to his. "Say it now."

She wrapped her arms around his neck. "It would change everything. I don't want anything to change this...for this is perfect bliss." She kissed him, her mouth so soft and sweet.

Breaking the kiss, he pulled her arms from around his neck and held her hands. "Why would it change everything? Who are you? Who do your secrets protect?"

She swallowed as if something was obstructing her throat.

"Perhaps it would be easier if you tell me about your parents?" he suggested. "Was your father a politician in the Republic of Genoa?"

She bit her lip and shook her head.

"Nobility, then?" he asked. His heart pounded in anticipation, not knowing what he was about to learn. She gave him the slightest nod.

His heart lurched. *Jésus-Christ*, he'd stolen a highborn lady from a convent.

He gripped her shoulders. "*Dieu*, enough. Who are you? To which noble family do you belong?"

She paused, struggling with her emotions and her next words. He held his breath.

"My name is...Angelica Marie-Louise de Castel. My father was Étienne Philippe de Castel, and my mother, Louise Fourché. They were the Comte and Comtesse de Beaulieu. I was their only child. I am French."

For an instant, he was frozen. *A French Aristo...* "But your name, Angelica, that is not French." His voice was nothing more than a raspy whisper.

"No. It was a name my father read once in a book, and when I was born, my parents agreed it suited me. It took some convincing of the priest at my christening, though..."

His head was spinning. Frantically, he scoured his memory, trying to recall if Robert had ever mentioned the Comte de Beaulieu before. "Why have you been in the Republic of Genoa for ten years?"

"I ran away from my home."

He released her.

"To be with your lover?" He hated how much the notion bothered him as the image of a young girl full of romantic notions running off with a young man Paul's age flashed in his mind. "You were an heiress, and yet you relinquished everything for him? Did he leave you, abandon you at the convent?"

"No. No." She shook her head.

"Do you miss him?" He was horrified that the question left his mouth and that he would even care to know the answer.

"*Never.*" He could see pain in her eyes. She was vacillating. Part of her wanted to tell him, to reach out beyond the silence that had its hold on her.

Cupping her cheek again, he stared into her distraught eyes. He couldn't stop his next words. "Did he break your heart? Did he make empty promises just to have you?"

She squeezed her eyes shut for a moment before she whispered, "No…"

"My God, Angelica…" He couldn't stand the secrecy of her past a moment longer. "Who is this man whom you gave the gift of your innocence to?"

She jumped back, pushing against his chest, surprising him. "I did not give him anything! He took it from me when he *raped* me."

Her words were like a physical blow; he lost the air from his lungs.

Reeling, he stared at her, willing her to take back the words, to tell him it wasn't so. Rape had been something he'd considered but the last thing he would have ever wanted to hear. It took a moment before he could breathe, before he could speak. Somehow, he forced out a single word. "*Who?*"

Tears glistened in her eyes. She looked away. Ever so softly, she said, "My stepfather."

His stomach clenched.

"My mother was devastated when my father died. Afraid and feeling alone, she was unable to cope and remarried as quickly as she could. My stepfather turned out to be very different than he first appeared. Their marriage lasted a year. My mother died. He'd obtained guardianship over me and control of my estate. One night, when he was well into his cups, he told me I was his and that I should start behaving like the lady of the house. He said that I would have…new duties now…"

Simon wanted to shout for her to stop, uncertain just how many details of the cruelty inflicted on her he could endure before he'd snap and succumb to the fit of rage simmering inside him, growing stronger with each and every hard thud of his heart. How could anyone harm this woman, his moonlight angel? He tried to speak, but he couldn't command his voice, leaving him trapped in mute anguish.

Frozen with fury.

"I fought him. I tried to run. I fell." She wrapped her arms around herself. "We wrestled…" She paused and met his gaze. The sorrowful look in her eyes, knowing the horror she'd endured, devastated him.

She looked down at the bed before she spoke again. "He…pulled up my skirts…and he…" Her voice faded. Simon closed his eyes briefly. She returned her gaze to his, waiting for a response he was unable to give.

"He did not…finish what he started. He passed out, but…by then the damage was done. The servants ran in and pulled him off me. My maid Audrey rushed me upstairs and helped me clean off the"—she looked away—"blood. That night, she and a servant named Renier took me away from that house, and it was decided that we would go to the Republic of Genoa, where my mother had a cousin. The journey was long. We were afraid my stepfather would find us. When we reached San Remo, the streets were very busy. A festival was in progress that day, and I became separated from Audrey and Renier. I searched…I don't know how long… Madre Caterina found me in the crowd and brought me back to the convent, a distance away. I never told her what happened. I never told her about my cousin. I decided to stay and live out my days there…until I met you."

She searched his face for his thoughts or a reaction.

Simon spoke not a word, not trusting himself to speak, not while excruciating images of a fourteen-year-old girl fighting off the perverted advances of a lecher as he overpowered and violated her tore through his mind. He fisted his hand. He was so incensed, his blood practically boiled in his veins. The air in his lungs burned. How he wished he had his sword and the very man who committed this deed before him.

Jésus-Christ. Not only did she have her innocence taken from her. But the man responsible had robbed her birthright as well.

He wanted nothing more than to fucking kill this man. *Slowly.* With as much physical agony as he could mete out.

She watched him, waiting for him to say something. The pain in her eyes gored his heart. "Have you no more questions? Have you nothing to say? Where are your words now? Go on. Say to me your best!" she challenged him, trying to prompt him.

She'd been through such a horrible ordeal.

He was too overcome. And too enraged—at her stepfather. At himself. *Merde.* He was a scoundrel of the highest order.

He'd seduced her, bedded her, when he should never have touched her.

Emotions were tearing him apart, urging him from the room. His grip on his fury, his outrage was slipping. She didn't need to witness the ferocity of his turmoil. It would only cause her more distress to watch him rage. The only thing at the moment he could do for her was to leave.

He stood.

"Simon, say something to me."

Angelica was on her feet in an instant. His body was stiff, and he looked as though he wanted to run from her. *Dear God, no...* This was what she'd feared all along. He was supposed to understand. He was supposed to take her in his arms.

"I demand you say something!"

He stared outside, not looking at her. *He is repulsed. He cannot even bring himself to look at me.* The tears in her eyes blurred her vision. She blinked them back.

Finally he returned his gaze to her. His light blue eyes were void of emotion. He'd schooled his features. He didn't want her to know his true feelings. Was this his way of being kind? By masking his disgust?

She choked back a sob. Nothing in her life had hurt more than his distance and his expressionless face.

"I am...so very sorry you had to endure such a thing," he said. "I'm sorry for any and all distress I have caused you. You were an innocent and we...*I* should not have done to you the things I have done. I had no right to touch you. No right at all."

Oh God, regret too? She stepped back and turned away from him. "Please leave my room." She knew she couldn't hold back the tears any longer.

She heard his footsteps. She heard the door close.

Her heart broke.

*****

FUCK!

In a hut near the mill on the west side of the island, Simon tilted his head back against his chair and closed his eyes, the horrific images of Angelica's attack torturing his mind.

Even though he hadn't slept all night, he was too distraught to feel fatigue.

He'd spent the night trying to wrestle down his rage—the broken chair he'd smashed against the wall proof of his violent mood.

He shoved the drawings of the mill and his accounting ledgers off the desk and onto the floor with a growl. Distracting his agitated mind with work had proved fruitless. He'd made so many blunders at her expense. Certainly, he shouldn't have left her in such a vulnerable state after she'd finally revealed her past to him.

He glanced at the door and rose. It was dawn.

Perhaps he would check to see how she was.

He let out a sharp breath, and set his palms down on the desk. If he spoke to her now or any time soon, he wouldn't be able to stop himself from drawing her into his arms. Given the intense attraction between them, he knew exactly where that would lead.

And he was intent on keeping his rude hands off her.

His gut had told him she was an innocent, yet that hadn't stopped him from unleashing his desire. But...*Dieu*, just because her lecherous stepfather had violated her, was she never to know a man's touch? Never to know how wonderful sex could be?

He shoved himself off the desk and began to pace.

But *he* shouldn't be the man to show her. She was a noble. He was not.

A noble. He'd suspected it. Feared it. Where could this possibly go? His life was complicated and layered. He had nothing to offer her but physical encounters, and she should find that in a marriage bed with her husband. Her *noble* husband. He tamped down the pang of regret that notion caused.

He had to extricate himself from Fouquet's hold—without having every man under his command arrested and executed. There were also the island's financial stability and safety to maintain. In short, people depended on him. He needed a clear head, and yet when Angelica was around, all he wanted was to touch her, take her.

And that was the last thing either of them needed.

There were two things he could do for her.

First, stay away. Second, when he returned to France, hunt down the man who'd taken so much from her.

And make him pay. Dearly.

CHAPTER SIXTEEN

She had not broken.

Although Simon's silence had stabbed her through the heart, she refused to curl up and die.

Angelica walked up to the crowd in the square and glanced around, unable to locate her friends in the throng. The island's springtime celebration was underway. She'd prepared tomorrow's teaching lessons, promising Suzette to return later when the music began—purposely hoping to avoid being ensnared in the games or competitions held during the afternoon for which she was in no mood.

During the last two weeks, she'd completely immersed herself in her teaching position. She'd forgotten just how much satisfaction she derived from teaching children. She adored her students and had taken it upon herself to encourage the girls to attend too. In two short weeks, her little school population had grown by six.

A sudden roar of laughter from the crowd broke through her thoughts. She scanned about again.

Simon would be here soon. Good. For she was going to confront him.

Today.

Though they shared the same roof, since revealing her past to him weeks ago, she'd barely seen him. He spent most of his time on the opposite side of the island and was rarely home.

On the few occasions they'd encountered each other at the door, they had exchanged customary pleasantries, and he'd politely inquired about how she was finding her new position. Although courteous, he'd been brief and eager to part company.

Revealing her secret to him had done exactly what she'd feared it would do. It had driven him away. Didn't he realize what it had taken for her to expose herself to him so completely?

Well, she was *not* going to allow him to avoid her any longer.

She wasn't going to permit him to hide his true feelings behind a pleasant mask. He was repulsed by her past. By her. So be it. But she wanted to hear him say it—to her face.

How could she have been so wrong about him? Why wasn't he able to offer her the acceptance she'd craved from him? Since the night she'd told him the truth, she'd dealt with feelings of betrayal, pain.

She was not going to punish herself or be a victim any longer.

Not to her stepfather. And certainly not to Simon. She'd come out of this experience stronger. She'd even found the courage to tell Gabriella and Suzette everything. They, unlike Simon, had offered her genuine comfort and understanding.

Simon had asked for the truth. Now he had it, and she was going to force him to deal with it. To deal with her. This very day.

Just as old Benjamin stepped up onto the makeshift stage and was about to make an announcement, she heard the gallop of horses approaching. Loud cheers rose from the throng.

Simon, Jules, Armand, and Domenico had arrived.

On his mount, Simon appeared every bit the commander he was. Dressed in a crisp white shirt and black breeches, he looked so good it hurt.

The moment he dismounted, young lads hurried forward for the privilege of attending to his horse.

"Good sirs, welcome!" Old Benjamin said with a theatric flare. "You have arrived just in time for our final competition. *The bachelors' competition!*" His booming voice set the crowd cheering anew, with much more enthusiasm from the females for the newly arrived men.

"I believe, Captain, that you and Monsieur Armand are still bachelors, no?" Benjamin inquired, grinning at the crowd's deafening jubilation.

Angelica watched Simon and Armand smile good-naturedly.

"We are," Simon responded. A distinctly female cheer rose from the mass. Angelica tried to ignore how much their enthusiastic interest bothered her.

"Well, dear ladies, do you not agree that they should enter the final contest?" Again a female cheer emphatically concurred.

Before Simon and Armand could comment, Benjamin pressed on. "The prize for the winner is a kiss from the most comely mademoiselle on the island." Jubilant cheers assailed Angelica's ears. "She was selected by the bachelors, Captain, voted upon just prior to the commencement of the celebration. When asked which fair maiden they would most like to kiss, you will be surprised to know this year's fair mademoiselle is someone who has never been selected before..." Excited murmurs from female hopefuls tore through the group.

Benjamin continued, "Good people, this year's selection is a young woman who is the overwhelming favorite choice among our young men!"

This time, it was the young men's turn to cheer.

Suzette suddenly squeezed Angelica's arm, startling her. "Oh, let it be me. Paul is entered in the contest!" Her eyes sparkled with excitement. "Wouldn't it be wonderful if he won, and I was the selected mademoiselle, Angelica? Just think, a kiss from Paul!"

"Before we announce this fair maiden's name, you must agree to join in the competition, Captain," said Benjamin.

The crowd was whipped into a frenzy. Simon chuckled and held up his hand to silence the overwhelming ovation. "Very well. I agree to join."

Her stomach dropped. If he won, she was not going to watch him kiss another.

Angelica turned, intending to leave the competition and return later, but the crowd around her was large. She was trapped within the enthusiastic mass.

Benjamin's grin was from ear to ear. He spread his arms out wide with great flair. "Excellent! And now, our most popular mademoiselle..." He gave a bow. Then, lifting his head, he darted his eyes back and forth slyly. "Do you wish her name now? Or after the knife-throwing competition is complete?"

"NOW!" the crowd roared.

Benjamin straightened and smoothed his shirt. "Well then, the good people have spoken, and with your permission, Captain, I shall obey."

Simon was still smiling, obviously enjoying Benjamin's antics in engaging the crowd. "Proceed, Benjamin."

"Very well. Our mademoiselle this year is...a very special woman." The people let out a collective groan of frustration. Benjamin quickly continued, realizing he'd tested the limits of their patience. "She is as kind as she is fine... Mademoiselle Angelica."

The air from Angelica's lungs expelled all at once. Her ears began to ring; the roaring crowd around her made but a distant din. She felt herself being pushed forward. Faintly, she heard Suzette's enthusiastic words, "It's you! It's you!"

Somehow, she found herself in front of the wooden stage.

"Come, mademoiselle," Benjamin urged. Stepping down, he took her hand in his calloused one and helped her up onto the stage. "Please sit in the chair of honor!"

Her knees easily gave way as she sat down on the wooden chair adorned with flowers. The crowd before her still carried on with great zeal. Someone placed a ring of flowers on her head.

She met Simon's gaze. He no longer smiled.

"What say you, Monsieur Armand?" Benjamin asked. "Would you like to join in the competition? Would you care for a kiss from the beautiful mademoiselle?"

Simon gave Armand a sharp look.

All traces of the smile he'd been sporting instantly disappeared from Armand's face.

He cleared his throat. "I...um, a kiss from the mademoiselle would be wonderful indeed..." Male hoots filled the air. Armand shifted his weight, avoiding Simon's murderous glare as he waited for the noise to die down. "But I must respectfully decline. My arm has been rather sore..." He rubbed it to underscore his statement.

"As you wish. Without further ado, gentlemen..."

"Wait!" Claudine called out. "Do we not need the mademoiselle's full name? I mean, really, the woman surely must have had parents. Even orphans have more than just a Christian name."

There were a few giggles from the women in the crowd near Claudine. She shot Angelica a glare. Anger prickled Angelica's skin.

"I cannot see why that's relevant," Sabine said in her defense.

"Every year we record the winners of the competitions as well as the chosen mademoiselle," Claudine said. "I'm simply trying to give the woman the opportunity to have her name properly recorded in our feast celebration book. What, Mademoiselle Angelica, is the big mystery about your name?"

A murmur shot through the crowd.

Angelica stood up. "No mystery here. I thank you for your concern. For the record, my name is"—Angelica looked Simon in the eye—"Angelica de Castel, daughter of the late Comte and Comtesse de Beaulieu."

She saw surprise flicker in Simon's eyes. He hadn't expected her to do it.

"*A noble*," tore through the crowd.

"Well, well, what a treat!" said Benjamin enthusiastically. "We've never had a noble take this honor before. Think of the fierce competition to kiss a *lady*."

Male cheers rose up. Angelica gave Simon a satisfied smile and sat down on her throne. Yet, she didn't feel satisfied in the least. Being this close to him caused a sense of longing to crowd in on her anger. She wrestled it back.

"To the targets, sirs!" Benjamin exclaimed.

The people moved from the front of the stage to the opposite side of the square, allowing Angelica a prime view from her chair. Four posts had been driven into the ground, with painted targets affixed to them.

The men began to line up in four rows a distance from the targets.

Simon had yet to move from his spot. Those walking past him wished him good luck, but he remained where he stood with his gaze fixed on her as he murmured his responses. Her heart galloped. She refused to show her unease. They'd both been coaxed into this ridiculous situation. What was he going to do? Win? Or lose on purpose so as to avoid having to kiss her?

"Mademoiselle?"

Angelica tore her gaze from Simon and noticed a tall young man standing before her. A grin slowly spread wide across his face. His gaze swept over her in an open perusal that shocked her.

"My name is Anton, mademoiselle. I'm the man who'll win this contest. And your kiss. I look forward to seeing if there is a difference between the lips of a highborn lady and a common wench. Either way"—his gaze dropped to her breasts, then slowly moved back to her eyes—"I'll have you wanting more." He chuckled and swaggered away.

Oh, perfect. Were matters not bad enough?

When Anton walked by Simon, he said, "Good luck, Captain," with the same arrogant smile and continued on his way.

Simon had heard every word Anton said to her, she was sure of it. He gave her one last look before he turned to join the others for the contest.

Each man was given three knives to toss on each of their three turns at the targets. Each attempt earned points.

With her heart in her throat, she watched the competition. Those with the greatest skill were Simon's crewmen. Seasoned sea-warriors trained to wield weapons with deadly accuracy were easily distinguishable from the rest.

She was going to have to kiss one of them. She wanted to kiss only one specific man among them. The one man in the competition who didn't wish to kiss her.

"Simon has stiff competition," Jules said as he and Sabine stepped up onto the stage. "Anton never loses in knives." Angelica felt ill.

Sabine patted Angelica's shoulder. "Don't worry. Whatever happens, it's only a kiss. Over quickly."

None of this was helping to relax the knots in her stomach.

Simon didn't smile or blow her a kiss as some of the others did. He stared straight ahead, his tall, muscled form turned away from her, never glancing her way, concentrating on the targets. She watched as he hit the center target on his first two turns. A perfect score. He hadn't missed once in all six knives. Did he *want* to win? *Of course he does, you fool.* He didn't want to lose face before his men.

His desire to win was strictly motivated by male pride.

A loud "*ahhhhh*" jolted her from her musings. Anton was on his final turn and had, for the first time, missed the center circle. He picked up his final knife. Undaunted, he smiled at her and kissed the blade. Turning, he tossed it and sank it directly into the center of the target. The people cheered.

"Well done, Anton!" Benjamin applauded. "Captain, you are the last competitor, and your final turn is at hand. Anton has the highest number of points. You'll need no less than a perfect score to beat his outstanding performance."

Perched on the edge of her chair, she couldn't take much more of this, not wanting either to win—for very different reasons. Her heart pounded so hard it resonated inside her ears.

Confidently, Anton looked on.

She squeezed the arms of the chair as Simon tossed the first knife. A perfect hit. The crowd cheered. She breathed again, not realizing she'd been holding her breath.

Simon picked up the second knife and paused, weighing it in his hand for a moment. She bit her lip. With a quick movement of his sculpted arm, the knife sliced through the air and hit the target dead center.

She sighed as the spectators shouted boisterously. *One more.*

Simon picked up the final knife.

Old Benjamin spoke up, loudly proclaiming, "Captain, sink this knife into its mark; then you can focus on a different target. One with ruby lips." Laughter ensued. She glared up at Benjamin. She didn't need his fool-headed comments to grate on her frayed nerves.

Simon gave Benjamin a nod, but his face remained impassive. He turned and positioned his arm. A silence fell upon the square. She felt a bead of sweat trickle down her back.

She couldn't look, yet she was too afraid to turn away. He tossed the knife. She closed her eyes.

Applause and cheers erupted. She snapped her eyes open. There, piercing the center circle was Simon's knife. She was so relieved she felt weak. But her relief was short-lived. She wouldn't have to kiss Anton, but now she would have to face Simon.

The men approached him, including Anton, to offer their congratulations.

"Captain!" Old Benjamin bellowed beside her. "Please, step forward and claim your prize!"

Her heart leaped to her throat. The crowd parted. Jules and Sabine cleared the stage as Simon stepped up onto it. Still seated, she looked up at him.

He extended a hand to her, a slight smile tilting his sensuous mouth. The mass erupted anew. She placed her hand in his and forced her legs to stand.

Looking into the depths of his eyes, she was unsure what to do. If kissing her was something he was forcing himself to do, then she didn't wish the touch of his lips either. *Liar!* cried the foolish voice inside her. The same one that had convinced her to reread the book of love sonnets more times than she should have.

"You do not have to do this," she whispered.

Somehow, he heard her over the loud spectators. His dark brows drew together. "I've just won a contest, and your kiss, *chère*, is my prize. Why would I not claim it?"

"Because we both know how you feel about me."

"Make her swoon, *Captain!*" Shouts from the rambunctious crowd pierced their conversation. She turned to the large group, but Simon slipped his fingers under her chin and turned her face to his.

"How do I feel about you?"

"You are...*repulsed.*" There, she'd said it. And while she looked him directly in the eye.

He looked stunned for a moment before anger flared in the depths of his eyes. "How can you think—"

"A kiss! A kiss!" they chanted, drowning him out. Anxiously, she looked out at the sea of shouting faces.

Once more, he turned her face to his, this time capturing it between his strong hands. "Don't look at them."

"Show her a commoner can kiss as good as any Aristo, Captain!" There was laughter again. She stiffened.

"Ignore them," he said. "Let them fade from your mind. It's just you and me here. No one else. I'm going to kiss you. Show you exactly how I feel about you." He caressed his thumb across her cheek, sending tiny tingles racing down her spine. She watched him lower his mouth, then let her eyes flutter shut.

At the first touch of his lips, exhilaration shot through her system. She braced her hands against his solid chest. His taste, his scent, were a seductive combination. The last vague sounds from the jovial mass of whistles and applause faded into the distance.

She returned his kiss with zeal. Starved for more. Battling with the overwhelming urge to pull his shirt free, slip her hands beneath, and stroke his warm skin.

And those gorgeous ripples on his sculpted abdomen.

He thrust his tongue past her parted lips. Her sex clenched. Her nipples pressed hard against her chemise, just as tantalized and tormented by this heat he alone inspired. There was so much of this magic he created she had still to know...

He broke the kiss abruptly. "*Dieu.* We must stop..." At the loss of his mouth, she snapped her eyes open. Gazing up at him, she fought to catch her breath. The look in his eyes and his accelerated breathing were telling. He was just as affected.

He took a deep breath and let it out slowly before turning to face the exuberant group. They cheered louder. Forming a smile, he took her hand, bowed low over it, and kissed it. "Thank you, mademoiselle," he exclaimed for all to hear. "Benjamin!"

"Yes, Captain." The old fool still grinned.

"Does this celebration have any music?"

"Of course!" Benjamin motioned to the fiddlers.

The instant the music started, the crowd began to disperse toward the lively melody.

Simon helped her down from the stage, then stalked away in the opposite direction, pulling her along with him.

"Simon, what are you doing? Where are we going?"

Without breaking his stride, he said, "We need to talk."

"About what?"

He stopped abruptly and turned to face her. She almost collided into him.

"*About what?*" he repeated. "About how hard you make me with just one kiss. Hell, just seeing you standing there breathing drives me wild. About how I fight to keep myself from you, all the while wanting you day and night. And about the bloody ridiculous notion you have in your head that I could *ever* be repulsed by you." He resumed his brisk pace.

She bit her lip to keep from smiling.

CHAPTER SEVENTEEN

Angelica watched Simon close the schoolhouse door, muffling the merry sounds from the festival outside. His large masculine form made the one-room school feel smaller. And deliciously warmer than usual.

He stalked over to her desk, raking his hand through his hair. "Angelica, I may have been staying away from you, avoiding you, but only because I am trying to do what is right, and that is to keep my desire for you in check. *Jésus-Christ*, when I look at you, the last thing I could ever feel is repulsion." His eyes still reflected the heated effects of their kiss. A warm current rushed through her heart.

He let out a frustrated sigh. "My actions have given you the wrong impression. Forgive me, for I do not know how to be near you and not touch you," he said softly. "You are difficult to resist for any man... For me."

A lump formed in her throat. Tears welled in her eyes.

"The knowledge of your past, I assure you, makes no difference to me. It isn't who you are. It is something that happened to you."

She averted her gaze and quickly swiped away an errant tear. Acceptance. Understanding. Compassion. He was giving her all three, just as she had believed he would. She wanted to throw her arms around him and declare her love for him right there and then. He knew everything, and yet he still saw her as a woman, complete and whole. He hadn't felt disgust. He still desired her. Like a balm, his words soothed the gaping wound she'd had deep in her soul.

"I knew the men would select you...and though I've been trying to restrain my desire for you, I'll be damned if I was going to sit back and allow Anton or any of them to kiss you."

Restrain his desire? That was the last thing she wanted. In fact, she wanted him to give of himself freely. Heart and body.

She clasped her hands before her to keep from reaching out and touching him. He was devastating and distracting, and she needed to think. To decide what exactly to do with this revelation. And the heavenly opportunity it offered.

He fixed her with his regard, his look sincere. "I wish to be clear, so there is no misunderstanding between us. What you told me that night engaged my wrath, but not at you. It was directed at your stepfather, and at myself for my behavior toward you—"

"Stop!" She marched up to him, pointed at her chair, and in her strictest teacher's voice said, "Sit down, Simon."

His brows shot up at her command.

For a moment, she thought he wasn't going to comply, but then, much to her relief, he lowered his strong body onto the chair. There was a touch of amusement in his eyes. Clearly, no one had ever commanded this dominant male before.

"Good. Now you shall listen to me, for there are a few things I wish to tell you. Firstly, you will *never* mention my stepfather again. He'll not be discussed or given any more importance." She tried not to shudder at the mention of the loathsome creature.

Simon looked as though he wanted to debate the matter. But then he ceded with a slight nod of his head.

She pressed on. "Secondly, you were the one who took me from a way of life in which I was barely alive and forced me to acknowledge my past. And I am grateful. I am glad to be unburdened of a secret I carried for far too long. As far as your '*behavior toward me*' is concerned, the physical intimacies we've shared have been more heaven than I expected to know on this side of the stars. You showed me how incredible it can be between a man and a woman."

Between us.

She turned and stepped away. There were more words she wanted to say, some involving soft sentiments he wasn't ready to hear, some involving physical yearnings, words her old self would have shied away from, unable to grasp for such bliss.

But she was different now.

She faced him again. "I have a proposal for you."

He cocked a brow. "A proposal?"

Say it. Just utter the words. She knew exactly what she wanted to say. She would make him a sumptuous offer.

"Yes… If you wish to blame yourself unnecessarily, then I have a way in which you can redeem yourself."

He leaned forward and rested his elbows on the arms of the chair, his curiosity clearly piqued. "Oh? And in what way might I redeem myself?"

She gazed at his handsome face, trying not to be distracted by his sensual, most kissable mouth. If she said it all at once, it would be easiest. It wasn't the sort of thing she voiced every day. "You could…provide more of the kind of carnal pleasures you've already shown me."

He froze. Obviously astounded.

Then shot to his feet. "*Merde!*"

He stalked around the chair, putting it between them. "I've been fighting back my desire for you, and you propose I redeem myself by *becoming your lover?*"

She gave a nod. "On a frequent basis," she added, in case the point was lost on him.

His mouth fell agape before he clamped it shut and began to pace. "Do not do this. Don't expect that I can be the strong one for both of us on *this*…"

She tried not to smile, despite herself. He looked incredibly adorable in his flustered state. She was willing to wager that few people had ever managed to rattle him so.

"I'm a grown woman. I am quite capable of making my own decisions. I don't need you to be a self-appointed protector of my virtue."

He arrested his steps. Jabbing his index finger into his chest, he said, "I have been trying not to complicate your life."

"Good, because what I propose is quite simple."

"It is not simple!" He rested his hands on his hips and let out a breath. In a more rational voice, he said, "Do you understand what it is I do with women? I do not woo them. Or marry them. I am simply there to…"

"Bed them?" she added for him when he hesitated.

"Yes! Sex. For mutual pleasure. I'm not Domenico or Jules. A sexual relationship with me will not result in marriage, for many reasons, *chère*, not the least of which is our different social class."

Thanks to her circumstances, her past, she'd come to believe that the prospect of marriage had been permanently removed from her future. Her days were to have been spent in a convent. Alone. She never imagined meeting a man and falling in love. But now she had.

She wanted a lifetime with him. There was no reason her station of birth, void of any meaning for her, should pose an obstacle.

"What I seek is to grab hold of whatever bliss life offers me. You taught me that." She held back her tender feelings. Given his state, hearing such sentiment would no doubt send him bolting from the schoolhouse. She needed time with him, wanted some uninterrupted special time before she would voice the words that burned inside her.

Her plan was simple. If she claimed his body as her own, perhaps, just perhaps, his heart would follow close behind. He was worth the effort. And the risk to her heart.

Whatever the outcome, she was determined to seize the chance to be with the man she loved. If in the end everything crumbled, she would at the very least have the memory of the time she had with him to cherish.

He sat down on the edge of the desk and quietly studied her with those knee-weakening blue eyes.

Smiling, she walked up to him and caressed his cheek, then rested her palm against it. There was undeniable interest in his eyes, no matter how much he foolishly protested.

She leaned into him. "Don't hold back your desire, Simon. There is no reason to. It is not what either of us wants." She brushed her lips along his jaw, to his neck. Drawing on his warm skin, she gave him a gentle suck, delighting in his soft groan. His heart rate quickened beneath her lips. But the stubborn man pulled back, despite the heated effect she had on him.

Reaching up, he removed her hand from his cheek and held it between his warm palms, lightly caressing it with his thumb.

"I must return to France," he said, his eyes full of regret.

Her stomach dropped. "When?"

"In a few weeks, a month at the most."

"I see." She tried to hide her overwhelming disappointment. And her fear. She'd only have a few weeks to forge something permanent with him.

"I don't know how long I'll be there before I can return."

If he was to leave soon, then she was even more determined not to lose out on this opportunity.

"Simon, you have said a fire burns between us. Why not bask in it until it's completely extinguished. Or until you leave—whichever comes first."

He wouldn't leave unaffected.

Without a word, he hauled her up against him, and crushed his mouth to hers, taking her by surprise. Every nerve ending sparked to life. He drove his tongue into her mouth, muting her moan. Her pulse raced. Liquid heat coursed through her veins. And the bud between her legs began to throb, hard and heavy, along with her heart. She wove her fingers into his soft, cool hair, reveling in the delicious desire rushing through her. His hands gripped her bottom and ground her against the hard bulge in his breeches, applying the most perfect pressure on her sensitive clit. Practically buckled her knees.

"All right," he murmured against her mouth. "If this is what you want, I agree." Her heart leaped with joy. "You're going to let me have at your sweet, snug sex anytime I want." His lips brushed that tantalizing spot under her ear. Her belly fluttered. "And in turn, I'll be your most ardent lover...make you come for me. Hard. And often." He drew on her neck. She lost her breath, a fresh surge of raw hunger swamping her senses. "Agreed?" he asked.

"Yes. Agreed."

"Good." She heard the smile in his tone. He bit her earlobe, tearing another gasp from her throat. "Damn the celebration... I could be inside of you right now..."

Being in his arms was like being caught in a storm, overwhelming and obliterating. She'd completely forgotten about the celebration. He was expected to be there at the formal commencement of the feast.

Reluctantly, she stepped back. Placing a hand on his chest, she fought to reclaim a semblance of rational composure, trying to calm the urgency pounding in her blood. "You should go. They await you."

Simon let out a breath. "Give me a moment." *Jésus-Christ*, her proposition had taken him completely by surprise. He should have refused. But she had made him an offer not even a monk could turn down.

He closed his eyes, trying to shut out the lush vision she made, trying to ignore, with little success, the discomfort of his erection, thick, full.

"Nine hundred ninety-three," he muttered. "Nine hundred eighty-six..."

"What are you doing?"

Keeping his eyes closed, knowing that looking at her would only be counterproductive, he said, "I am counting backwards from one thousand by sevens. And you have made me lose my spot."

"Why?"

He snapped open his eyes. "In case you haven't noticed, *chère*, you have me stiff as a spike. I am trying to combat my rather...*amorous state*."

"Oh..." Her cheeks flushed sweetly. "Nine hundred seventy-nine."

"Pardon?"

"That is your next number." She bit her lip, trying to conceal a smile.

He felt a smile tug at his lips too. They both burst into laughter. Some of the tension left his body.

It gave him such delight to see her laugh.

"If your method is unsuccessful," she said, "you could try reciting the Greek alphabet."

He chuckled. "I'm glad you derive amusement from my miserable state."

She attempted to look contrite. "I'm sorry for your miserable state."

"Oh?" He stood up, sporting a mischievous grin, and slowly advanced on her. "How sorry?"

She took a playful step back. "Very. I shall make it up to you. I promise."

He took another step toward her, caught up in her playfulness. "When?"

She took another step back. "After the feast."

He groaned. That seemed like forever. He advanced. "*How?*"

She backed into the wall. Her smile faded. Her beautiful eyes darkened with desire. "Any way you wish…as long as it includes more kissing."

He stopped in front of her, grinning. "I believe I can live with those conditions," he said, enjoying himself. He ran his finger gingerly over the gentle swell of her breasts, following the contour of her scooped neckline. He heard her breath catch.

His ability to resist her was nominal at best. He didn't have it in him to fight the temptation that was Angelica de Castel anymore. It was too strong. Nothing he did seemed to lessen his need for her or shatter the enchantment.

Clearly, he was on dangerous ground.

She was a noble. For someone of his social standing, she was forbidden fruit. He prayed that this fascination he had with her would eventually diminish.

He had to hold their relationship to sex and sex alone. This inexplicable allurement had to end. No matter how incredible it felt when he was with her, he had no choice but to cling to what was best. What was best was that by the time he returned to France, the flame of their desire would have burned out. And that he would have lost, by that time, all the invading emotions constricting his heart.

It was the only acceptable outcome. For both of them.

His plan was simple. To enjoy each other fully, extensively, with the goal in mind to cool the passion between them that at the moment was scorching hot. In this he couldn't fail. Because there was no future for them. Not for the son of a commoner and the daughter of a count.

"You will make this up to me." He smiled and took hold of her hand. Pressing a kiss to it, he added, "In my chamber later tonight." Still holding her hand, he opened the door and stepped outside. "Let's join the feast." Walking briskly toward the merrymaking, he glanced back at the siren of his fantasies. "Eat quickly."

CHAPTER EIGHTEEN

Some distance away, the rest of the island continued with the celebration, but in the privacy of Simon's chamber, Angelica watched as he closed the door.

They were finally alone.

Anticipation gripped her.

Conscious of her cold fingers, she clasped her hands together, trying to warm them. One hand was warmer than the other. It was the hand he'd held as he led her up the stairs to his room.

She took in a quiet breath and let it out slowly, trying to ignore her pounding heart.

He watched her from the door, his head slightly cocked. Strands of dark hair rested on one perfect ebony brow, creating such dramatic contrast with his light blue eyes. He was far too handsome. Far too confident. And he had a way of drawing her to him, heart, body, and soul.

Dear God, had she set herself up for inevitable heartache? How realistic was it to hope that over the next few weeks he would fully engage his heart? What if he held her at arm's length emotionally the entire month? In all the time she'd known him, he'd offered her little personal information. He was even better at keeping secrets and distance than she had been.

She forced back the doubts. He would be all hers for the next few weeks. It was inevitable that they would grow closer. But would she be able to get close enough to claim his heart?

He smiled and slowly advanced. Her stomach fluttered.

His presence beside her during the feast had made it impossible for her to eat. The occasional brush of his thigh, the heat of his regard, and the intermittent caress of his hand on her arm had kept her senses on alert and her body quivering in anticipation for what would follow the meal.

And now he was looking at her with the same desire that had been in his eyes all evening.

He stopped before her, their bodies all but touching.

With a gentle stroke of his fingers over her shoulder, he picked up one of her cascading tresses. Silently, he studied it as it curled naturally around his finger. Looking into her eyes, he brushed the lock of her hair against his lips.

She shivered.

"Are you cold?" His voice was low and soft in the stillness of the room.

"No." His closeness made her hot from the inside out.

"Are you afraid? Do you think I will devour you?" he gently teased.

She knew he was trying to make her smile, to ease her nerves. It only made her love and want him more.

"No, I'm not afraid," she said with a small smile, "nor do I think you will devour me."

"Good, because I don't devour women until after midnight."

A laugh escaped her. "Then I am safe for a few more hours."

"Precisely." He grinned, releasing her curl.

She glanced over at his bed, noticing the details of his chamber for the first time. It was decorated with wall coverings in various shades of blue, woven rugs on the floor, and a large four-poster bed with deep-blue drapery. It was elegant, serene, and tasteful.

Why was she not surprised? His birth may have been in the common class, but there was nothing common about him. This very chamber was a perfect reflection of him—a man who had achieved success yet wasn't ostentatious. It exemplified what courage and determination could bring.

Inspired by his example, she too was unwilling to accept what fate had offered and was extending her hand to reach for more.

"Would you like me to lie down on the bed?" Mentally she cringed, mortified at her artless words. The nervous excitement, rampant inside her, was as distracting as he was.

His smile was unwavering. "No." He slipped his fingers beneath her chin. "All I want you to do at the moment is to relax. The night is young, *mon ange*. There is no need to rush."

Again he'd called her *my angel*. And it sounded sublime, soothing over her embarrassment.

Taking her hands, he drew her arms around his waist, then circled his arms around her. She pressed herself a little closer, drawn to his wonderful scent and the divine feel of his hard body against hers. She never felt more alive than when she was with him.

"We've done this before," he reminded her. "We will only do that which pleases us both. I wouldn't force you to do anything you don't want to do."

She looked up at him. "I know." *I love you...* "I trust you."

The look on his face told her that her answer pleased him.

"Simon, I want you to treat me no differently in bed than you would any other woman."

He placed a soft stirring kiss at the corner of her mouth. "I've not been able to treat you the same as other women yet." His words and sensuous voice played havoc with her senses.

Gracious God...He was too good at this...

"You didn't eat this evening at the feast. I had Assunta leave early to lay out some food here in my chamber. Are you hungry?"

Food was the last thing on her mind. "No. All I want right now is you..." Threading her fingers through his hair, she pulled his head down.

The moment their mouths met, a rush of arousal flooded her body. She laced her arms around his neck, and deepened her kiss, drawing his tongue into her mouth. His groan thrilled her. She told him with her kiss what she couldn't—wouldn't—say at the moment: how much she needed, wanted, and loved him.

Capturing her face between his palms, he angled her head, slanting his mouth over hers, taking command of the kiss. Heightening her hunger.

"Angelica," he breathed.

She kissed him again. In *this*, she wouldn't hold back in any way.

"To hell with proceeding slowly," he said between shallow breaths. "I'm having you. Right now. Turn around."

Before she could command her legs, he spun her around and wrapped an arm around her waist, his fingers quickly undoing the lacing down her back with expert ease. He slipped his hands inside her loosened bodice and captured her nipples though the cloth of her chemise. She sucked in a sharp breath, his fingers plying the tips with tender tugs and light pinches, sending sensations lancing from her breasts to her core. Her sex answered with a warm gush.

"I have fantasized about this," he murmured near her ear, "about you, here in my chamber...and what I would do to you." His words, his actions made the bud between her legs throb.

As her bodice dropped to the floor, her only coherent thought was that she would have weeks of this sort of pleasure with him.

Turning her back around, he dipped his head and brushed his lips over the material covering her nipple, then drew on it through the cloth. Her knees almost gave way.

She arched to him, driving her hands into his hair. "Simon..." His name came out a mixture of a plea and a moan.

Grasping her wrists, he pulled her arms down to her sides and returned his mouth to hers. "I like your heated enthusiasm." She heard the smile in his tone despite his own advanced state of arousal. "Let's remove these cumbersome clothes."

Between hot kisses, with more determination than skill, she managed to free his shirt from his breeches, while he smoothly stripped away her clothing—his fingers brushing her bare skin, making her breath catch—until he had her down to her chemise.

Finally, she pulled off his shirt and tossed it carelessly behind her. Her gaze was riveted to the male perfection before her.

She moved her hands over the muscled contours of his chest, letting her fingers purposely brush across his nipples. With a groan, he grabbed the hem of her knee-length chemise.

"Wait." Breathless, she stepped back on shaky limbs.

"*Wait?*"

"I want to see you first. All of you." She wouldn't be denied the pleasure of seeing every bit of his exquisite masculine physique this time. He was all hers, and she wanted to see all of him. "That night on the ship…you remained partially dressed," she reminded him.

Despite the intense desire in his eyes, she saw a smile tug at the corners of his mouth.

Without a word, he stepped back and toed off his boots. Completely at ease, he undid his breeches, watching her reaction. She swallowed. Her insides fluttered in anticipation. She'd never had the desire to see a naked man before. Until Simon. She so desperately wanted to see him.

Casually, he stripped off his remaining clothing and stood naked before her, allowing her to look her fill.

His sex snared her attention. Its generous length and girth made her wonder how they could have possibly fit together, but they had, she quickly reminded herself, *oh so incredibly…*

"Come here, Angelica."

He was smiling at her—the devil—having observed her ogling him. She blushed. Tamping down her embarrassment, she forced her legs to move forward.

Slipping one hand through her hair, he pulled her close and gave her a quick, hard kiss. "If you are going to look," he said, "you might as well touch."

Her heart missed a beat. His suggestion was overwhelmingly appealing. And utterly irresistible.

She reached out and carefully wrapped her fingers around his erect shaft. He gripped her hand and squeezed harder than she would have dared. A deep sound of pure pleasure escaped his throat and reverberated inside her.

"*Christ.* I love your hand on my cock," he said, guiding her hand down his length, then back up to the tip. Though he was hard, his skin felt like satin. He loosened his hold, and she repeated the stroke, eliciting another thrilling groan from him. Touching him this way, watching how it affected him, was empowering. Enthralling. Her blood coursed hotter.

"I want to learn all the ways that give you pleasure, Simon." She caressed him with another languid stroke. "Will you show me?"

Briefly closing his eyes, he made a sound—a combination of a laugh and a groan. "Even if it kills me," he promised.

A glistening drop of fluid appeared on the tip. She touched it with her thumb, then spread it with light circular caresses.

He stilled her hand with a sharp groan, then drew in a ragged breath. Softly, he swore. "Does it excite you to see what you're doing to me?"

"Yes," she responded, without embarrassment.

"Are you wet for me, Angelica?"

"I am." She couldn't help it. It's what he did to her.

He smiled. "That's excellent. Because you're going to show me just how wet you are."

Before she could remark, he swept her up in his arms and carried her to the bed. The next thing she knew was the feel of the soft mattress against her back.

He straddled her, pressing his palms on the bed at either side of her shoulders. "It's my turn to look at *you*." Reaching down, he took hold of the hem of her chemise and gently slid it up her thighs. "Let's remove this."

She remained motionless, burning with fever.

He moved her hem a little higher. "I swear, my eyes cannot get enough of you." Those eyes he spoke of reflected the sincerity of his words.

Tamping down her inhibition, she helped him remove her last article of clothing.

With a few easy movements, the garment was on the floor, and he'd rearranged her legs so that he now knelt between her knees.

She bit down on her lip and fought back her instinctive shyness, battling the urge to cover herself with her arms.

He sat back on his heels and let his gaze move down the length of her body. She saw the warming look of appreciation in his eyes. Her discomfort melted away.

"You take my breath away… Every time." Her throat tightened with emotion. "Bend your knees. Let me look at the rest of you."

She went stock-still. She could not possibly have heard correctly. He wasn't actually going to look at her *there*?

He must have noticed the uncertainty in her eyes because he said, "This is what lovers do. They enjoy each other, filling their senses with one another. Touch, taste, sight." He smoothed his warm palms up her thighs. "Let me see you." His voice was like velvet. "Bend your knees for me."

Her entire body flushed warm. His request was as exciting as it was intimidating. She reminded herself that this was what she wanted. To have Simon Boulenger as her lover. To be with him this way.

She closed her eyes and slowly bent her knees. Erotic expectation seized her. Her mental focus was now on her private area, open to his view. She tried not to squirm, unaccustomed to this sort of casual scrutiny, yet braced herself for the thrill of his touch.

His fingers lightly stroked along her inner thighs, moving toward her sex. She fisted the sheets, her feminine flesh feeling overly sensitive and slick with desire.

"*Chérie*, look at me."

Her eyes snapped open. He said *chérie* instead of *chère*. For the first time, he called her '*my darling*.'

The smile on his lips and the soft look in his eyes pulled at her heart.

"Don't be embarrassed." His fingertips brushed against her moist cleft. She gasped. "You are so beautiful here..." His finger gently circled her opening, the soft strokes making her moan. She closed her eyes, instinctively arching to him, trying to draw his fingers inside her. Eluding her, he glided his hand a little higher. She opened her eyes and stilled, barely breathing, his fingers so close to where she ached.

"And this pretty little clit," he said, circling yet barely touching the excited bud. "It's not only perfect, but it also looks completely...delicious." He gave her a light pinch.

She cried out at the sharp pleasure.

Leaning over her, he kissed her, sliding his fingers inside her. She mewed against his mouth and threw her arms around him. Lowering himself onto the bed, he began long even strokes with his practiced hand. The finesse of his touch fueling her frenzy. Driving her wild.

"I want to taste you," he muttered. "But I can't wait to have you any longer."

Wantonly aroused, she had no idea what he was saying. Slowly, he withdrew his fingers. She protested with a whimper. Her sex throbbed with need.

A roguish smile formed on his handsome face. "Perhaps just a small sampling now..." he said and stroked her bottom lip with his finger, applying her essence to it. She jerked, shocked.

Dipping his head, he licked it off. "So sweet...You taste as good as I knew you would."

His weight pinning her to the mattress, he claimed her mouth in a hot, hungry kiss, and lodged the blunt tip of his sex against her opening. She returned his kiss with equal hunger, her pulse racing wildly.

Slowly, steadily he began to push into her. The delicate muscles inside her resisted. She tensed. A sudden wave of anxiety washed over her, a fleeting distant memory of a long-ago event threatening the delicious sexual abandon she felt. She tried to relax, knowing from experience the unpleasant feelings would vanish once Simon was completely inside her. She would then lose herself in the pleasure he created...

He stopped. He was no longer kissing her. No longer pressing into her.

Reluctantly, she opened her eyes.

There was comprehension in the blue eyes staring back at her. With a sinking feeling, she realized that not only had he noticed her sudden apprehension, but, given his knowledge of her past, guessed at the reason behind it too.

He looked concerned, as though he was going to say something on the abhorrent subject. Dear God. She didn't wish to discuss this. *Not now.*

But then he surprised her and smiled. "Let's try something different."

Before she could object to alterations to their intended course of action, he rolled with her in his arms. She found herself lying on top of him.

He pressed a finger to her lips just as she was about to speak up. "Let's make love in a different position tonight."

She jerked back. "There are different positions?" What an appealing concept.

He chuckled. "There are." She opened her mouth. He placed his finger back on her lips. "And yes, before you ask, I'll take you in as many as you want. As for now, I'm dying to be inside you. Sit up. Straddle me. In this position, you dictate the pace."

He would be under her. She'd be in control. A fresh wave of arousal rushed through her. She sat up, the folds of her slick sex inadvertently kissing his hard length. He growled her name, a low, sensual sound that quivered up her spine. Urgency swamped her.

He brought her hand to the base of his shaft. She quickly wrapped her fingers around it.

"It is entirely up to you, how deep, how fast, *chérie*." His voice was strained, his eyes darkened with raw need, his reactions to her inflaming her further.

She positioned him at her opening. He held her hips and urged her down. His thumb gently stroked her clit, creating tiny shocks of pleasure.

She sank down on him, her body opening to him, sheathing him inch by glorious inch. The decadent strokes of his thumb and the feel of him slowly filling her were indescribable bliss. When at last she'd taken his entire length, her head fell back. Oh God. He was so deep. Deeper than before. It felt so good. She felt so full.

It felt incredible.

He rose. Fisting her hair, he gave it a sensual tug, bending her backward over his arm, latching onto her breast hungrily. A cry escaped her throat. She grabbed hold of his strong shoulders and held on. Every sensual pull of his hot mouth, together with the sensation of him buried inside her—the pressure sublime—sent her senses reeling. Spiking her fever. She ground herself against him. "Simon, now!"

He released her and lay back, his blue eyes mirroring the same feral hunger burning through her blood. "All right...*now.*"

Gripping her hips, he guided her initial movements. She quickly learned the rhythm and angle, lost to the pleasure of his thick length stroking her sex. Each rise and fall of her hips driving her into delirium.

Digging her fingers into his chest, she increased the tempo, moving faster, and surer, unable to stop. Completely engulfed in the stunning sensations. A shattering release fast approached. She could feel it coming on. Tiny contractions were already rippling through her core, around his cock.

"Oh, *Christ*, that's perfect," he growled just before he gave her clit another perfect pinch.

Rapture burst inside her, hurling her into ecstasy. She screamed, her orgasm rocking her body, untamable spasms contracting her sex.

He flipped her onto her back. Muffling her with a hard kiss, he drove into her repeatedly, driving her into the mattress with his powerful plunges, sweeping her along with him until another climax slammed into her. She cried out and arched hard against him, riding out her second orgasm while he continued to thrust into her with bedeviling skill. Suddenly, he reared, jerking his cock out, then clutched her tightly and groaned his release against the curve of her shoulder until at last he was spent.

She held him, their breathing slowly returning to normal. Caressing his back, she felt sated and languorous, basking in a wonderful sense of peace in the quiet afterglow.

He lifted his head. His tender smile moved her to one as well. She was so deeply in love with him.

"Have I told you how much I like this proposal of yours? I only pray I haven't redeemed myself just yet," he teased.

She laughed. "Fortunately, I'm unforgiving."

Softly, he chuckled. "I'm pleased to hear it."

Rolling off her, he reached for his shirt and wiped her stomach clean of his semen, and then himself. "Does this offend you?" he asked, tossing his shirt across the room.

She rolled onto her side, propping herself up on her elbow to match his pose. "No. I loved every moment. *Everything.*"

He smiled and tucked her hair behind her ear. "I'm glad my lady is well pleased."

Studying the cherished face before her, she answered, "I would be even more pleased if you tell me we can do this again tonight." She wasn't surprised by her boldness. He always had the ability to draw out a different side of her—a side that acknowledged her wants and needs rather than denied them.

He gave her a purely male grin. "I was thinking more along the lines of doing this all night."

Hiding her smile, she studied her nails on her left hand with mock interest. "I think I could be persuaded to your way of thinking."

He flipped her onto her back; she squeaked with surprise. Pinning her under him, he chuckled. "It would take persuasion, would it?"

She giggled. "Oh yes. Amorous persuasion and extensive homage to my person."

He laughed. She adored the sound of it, rich and deep.

She held back the tender words that surged up her throat. Words she knew she wouldn't utter just yet. "I don't suppose you realize you have been unfair," she said.

"Unfair? How so?"

"I don't know you as well as you know me."

"You know me as intimately as any woman can know a man." Dipping his head, he murmured near her ear, "I've been inside you, remember?" His warm breath tickled her neck, sending tingles rippling through her. "What more do you wish to know?" His lips against her skin, his skillful mouth threatened to scatter her thoughts.

"I wish to know about Marguerite. The woman."

He lifted his head. "*Pardon?*"

She hadn't meant to ask quite so abruptly, but she was dying to know about his past. About him. If he hadn't been distracting her, she would have broached the subject with more finesse. Judging from the look in his eyes, she'd touched upon a sensitive subject.

"Someone in the village told me it was your mother's name—" She arrested her words when he rolled off her. Lying on his side, he propped himself up on his elbow again, suddenly pensive, creating a distance between them even though he was within reach.

She wished she could take back the words, but they were out there now, looming between them. Rolling onto her side, she too propped herself up on her elbow to face him.

"Simon, I didn't mean to upset you. You named the island after her. She must have been very special—"

"She was." He surprised her by answering when he looked as though he would not. "She was the most beautiful woman in our village. As beautiful as this island, with eyes as blue as the sky above it and as warm in spirit as the balmy weather found here."

"When did she...die?" she asked ever so softly.

"When I was eight. In childbirth. My brother, born then, died one week later."

"I'm sorry..."

"You would be the only one in your class who would be. No noble would care in the least about the death of a young peasant woman, a fisherman's wife, or her baby."

She understood the pain behind those words. It shamed her to learn over the years the indifference her class felt toward those born to the common masses. "Your father was a fisherman, then. What was he like?"

His jaw tightened. "Heartless and cold. In his miserable existence, he never showed affection or consideration to his wife or his only son. The happiest times were when my father was out at sea and it was just my mother and I." A rueful smile formed on his mouth. "She was a dreamer. A wonderful storyteller. She couldn't read a word, but she had the greatest imagination. She inspired me to reach for more out of life rather than to follow in my father's footsteps."

He rolled onto his back and stared up at the ceiling. "One day, a year later, after a terrible storm, he didn't return."

She hated the pain he'd suffered as a boy, knowing he'd only given her a glimpse of it. Simon had been all of nine when he was orphaned. She understood, all too well, what it was like to find yourself young, alone, impoverished. "What did you do then?"

He gave a mirthless laugh. "I starved a little more each day until one day I found a man who gave a poor boy a new life." Finally he looked at her and pulled her into his arms. She returned his embrace, resting her cheek on his shoulder, holding him tightly.

"I have never lain in bed with a beautiful woman and discussed my past."

She looked into his eyes. He brushed a soft kiss against her lips. "There is nothing of interest in my family. Peasant begot peasant. No duke, count, marquis. Common. Ordinary."

"Common?" She pushed at his chest and sat up. "Is it common for the son of a fisherman to live in this fashion?" She gestured to his chamber. "It is common to settle for your lot in life. It is not common to have the courage to try to change your destiny."

He studied her quietly before he sat up too. "Destiny can be capricious—not at all within one's control."

"You've created your destiny, Simon, and along the way you have bettered the lives of those around you." He made a sound as though he scoffed at the idea. It shocked her. "These people here adore you. You should have been a fisherman, but instead you are a commander of the king's ships. You have done great things with your life."

"You don't know what I've done in my life. Nothing comes without a price."

"What does that mean?"

"Nothing. Forget it."

"What torments you, Simon?" she asked boldly. Something briefly flickered in his eyes, and then he hid it behind a more carnal gaze.

He pressed her back onto the bed, his warm body covering hers. "Not getting enough of you torments me." He gave her a long, luscious kiss that warmed her blood.

"*Chérie*, whatever time we have together, we will enjoy each other...extensively; yet I won't do anything to complicate our situation. This is an interlude of bliss. It cannot be more. You are a noble."

"Nobility means nothing."

"You are wrong. It means everything. But enough of this." He kissed her again, his tongue giving hers slow, swirling caresses. Gently, he stroked the curve of her breast and murmured, "If your father were alive, he'd have me hanged from the tallest branch for doing what I've done to you in this bed. For touching his noble daughter with my common hands."

"I love what you've done to me in this bed." She would never regret it.

He smiled. "And I love doing it to you, far too much." He gave her neck a love bite. She sucked in a sharp breath. He dipped his head and sucked her tender nipple into his mouth. Closing her eyes, she moaned and wrapped her arms around him.

Time. It was what she needed in order to impress upon him that he was making too much of their different social class.

But was there enough time left?

CHAPTER NINETEEN

Simon entered his home the next morning. He looked up the stairs and smiled. The thought of Angelica up there in his bed quickened his heart.

Hoping she was still fast asleep, he began to climb the stairs. Not wishing to look like a madman taking the stairs two at a time at full speed, he forced himself not to be transparent about his eagerness to see her. Even if he didn't race, his mind did. Ideas of how to wake her ran through his thoughts and thickened his cock.

He couldn't stop his grin.

Reluctantly, he'd left her in deep slumber to attend an early meeting with Jules and some of the other men. However, Simon had found it impossible to concentrate on the mill's construction while memories of last night still hummed through his mind and body. Walking out of the hut on the opposite side of the island, he ignored Jules's knowing grin, as well as the hidden smiles Simon sensed from the others. Smiles they wouldn't dare to show.

He was no stranger to a night of carnal pleasures, but he'd never had a night like last eve.

Never had he known such soul-satisfying sex before.

They'd made love twice on his bed before they rose to dine on the food Assunta had set out for them. Her sweet smiles from across the table had touched him, while her sensual green eyes and enticing pink mouth had beguiled him. He'd barely allowed her to eat her meal when he'd reached his breaking point and had lowered himself to his knees before her chair. He'd pulled open her dressing gown, aroused her to a fiery pitch and, with her legs wrapped around his waist, buried the entire length of his ravenous cock into her sweet sex.

Later, together with him in his tub, adorably shy at the notion of bathing together, she had nonetheless allowed him the pleasure of washing every appealing curve and dip on her body. He'd teased and aroused her until the water had become a cool contrast against their heated bodies. They had barely made it to the bed when she had welcomed him inside her with a tender eagerness that was uniquely hers.

Simon reached the last step.

He should have been exhausted this morning, but instead he felt exhilarated. And he wanted her again.

He strode purposefully toward his chambers.

Last night, he'd told her about his past when he'd always been tightlipped about offering women personal information in bed. It was wrong to do so for many reasons, not the least of which was that it left a false impression—that there was more than just a physical connection. But there was something about her that inspired the desire to confide in her—a level of intimacy that was new to him.

And he was determined to blame his slip and his present eagerness on the knee-buckling desire he had for his moonlight angel.

With a smile, he opened his chamber door.

A garment hit him in the face.

He heard female gasps. Pulling the article off his head, he found Assunta, Marta, and Suzette staring at him, horrified.

Suzette, who stood closest to him, was the first to find her voice and begin apologizing. Marta and Assunta, standing near his bed, quickly followed suit. The three women were speaking at the same time. He'd no idea what they were saying, catching partial phrases here and there.

"...I tossed the dress to Suzette—"

"—trying to clean up..."

Looking around his chamber, he was struck speechless. His bed was empty. Angelica was gone. But her presence filled his room.

In fact, her things were *everywhere*.

Gowns were tossed on his bed, on chairs, on the floor. Undergarments were sprinkled in here and there. Shoes, no pair together, were also scattered all over the rugs. It was as though the entire contents of the trunk he'd ordered moved into his room were at the moment emptied all over it.

"What... Where is Angelica?" he asked, surprised over the condition of his once personal space.

"She left for the schoolhouse, Captain," Suzette answered.

Marta stepped forward. "She was in a great hurry this morning, running a bit late for school. We couldn't find some of her things..."

He looked at Marta, utterly baffled. *Couldn't find her things?* They were all over the room.

Assunta spoke up. "She couldn't locate the matching garments a lady needs, Captain," she explained matter-of-factly.

He blinked. "I see." He had no idea what she was talking about. Scanning his room, he gazed at the chaos before him. Was this some female morning ritual he was simply unaware of?

He stepped farther into his room. His boot caught on something on the floor. Looking down, he recognized it as the chemise she had worn last night.

The last article of clothing he'd removed from her lush form.

Still clutching a garment in one hand, he bent down and picked up the chemise with the other. Memories of her in it, slipping her out of it, filled his mind. He caressed his thumb over the chemise, enjoying the feel of it in his hand once more, when he sensed three pairs of eyes on him.

Simon looked up. The three women stared back at him with curious looks.

He cleared his throat. "You'll have this chamber in order soon, I assume," he said, not wishing it in the least. He couldn't explain why, but he rather liked seeing her personal items tossed about his chamber.

"Of course, Captain," Assunta assured.

"Good." His gaze swept the room once more. Her things, spread out everywhere, inspired warm emotions and renewed his desire to see her. Disappointed, he'd have to wait until midday, when school was finished, to have the opportunity.

"Is there anything else you wish, Captain?" Assunta inquired.

"*Hmmm?*" Had she said, "*wish*"? There were a lot of things he wished at that moment. They all had to do with Angelica, in his arms. An idea suddenly came to him. "Yes, actually, there is. I wish for you to prepare a special lunch." As he gave his instructions, Suzette and Marta smiled. By the time he was finished, they were wearing great big foolish grins.

"Certainly, Captain. I'll see to the preparations immediately," Assunta said, the only one able to maintain a serious expression.

Simon nodded and reluctantly handed Angelica's things to Suzette. He gave his room a last look. Angelica's belongings completely dominated his chamber, yet he left, barely able to contain his own smile.

*****

Simon finally spotted Angelica in front of Madame Blanche's tiny shop with Gabriella and Sabine. He was running late because of Xavier Beloit and his long-winded suggestions about additions he felt were needed around the island.

Simon had gone to the schoolhouse and found it empty. He was about to return home, hoping to find Angelica there, when he caught a glimpse of Gabriella and then Angelica, partially hidden from his view by Sabine as the three women stood closely together talking.

He was certain it was Angelica. He'd know those glossy curls anywhere. He took a step toward the trio just as Sabine moved, allowing him an unobstructed view.

He stopped dead in his tracks. *Dieu*, she looked stunning. Her pink gown made her skin look creamier, her hair all the richer. If tossing her clothing about his room was what it took to look like that, he would gladly have his chamber in disarray.

His heart thundered just to have her in his sight. He took in a deep breath and let it out slowly.

"Captain! Oh, Captain!"

Simon swore under his breath. A female voice behind him called to him. *Perfect. Another delay.*

He turned and was surprised to see Marie Jaures and her young daughter, Monique.

Marie hurried toward him, holding her child's hand. They stopped before him, and Marie smiled. It was the first time Simon had seen her smile since his return, since he gave her the news about Thomas's death. His impatience melted away.

"Captain, I wish to thank you."

"Thank me, Marie? For what?"

"For the school. For encouraging the girls to attend. Monique is a pupil there now."

The child's shy smile easily elicited a grin from him. He crouched down to her eye level.

"Is that so, Monique? Do you attend school now?"

Monique nodded. "Yes, Captain. I am learning to read and do numbers. Mademoiselle Angelica says I am very smart."

He chuckled. "She would most definitely be correct."

"She is very kind. We all like her. She's as beautiful as a queen."

Simon looked over his shoulder at Angelica. "She is indeed," he agreed softly, and stood up.

"Captain," Marie said. "Being part of the school has helped Monique with her grief. And in doing so, it has helped me as well. I cannot believe we have such a wonderful teacher for the children."

He felt tremendous pride over Marie's praise of Angelica.

"It was Angelica's idea to encourage the girls."

"She is an incredible woman. I mean, she is a *noble*. Yet she is so kind and considerate toward us." Marie shook her head. "Whoever heard of a woman born into privilege lowering herself to teach the children of peasants?"

Simon's smile died. He glanced over at Angelica. She was laughing with the women around her. Marie was right. Angelica could be so much more than she was. Her exalted bloodlines held her in esteem in society, apart from the common masses. She could be married to an Aristo and her children, heirs to wealth, title, and power.

"She is indeed extraordinary. Good afternoon, Captain."

Simon murmured a good-bye before he turned on his heel and strode toward Angelica.

The haze from last night had lifted. Ruthlessly, he pushed away pangs of regret. His plan was in sharp focus once more, and he wouldn't allow soft feelings to upend them. She was out of his reach. Not his to keep. She was his mistress. A temporary one. Her life was in France. And he was going to see she was returned all that had been taken from her.

But that was later.

Now, and for the next few weeks, he had to get over the fever known as Angelica de Castel.

*****

Sabine poked Angelica. "He approaches."

Angelica turned around. Her heart flip-flopped. Dressed in a light gray doublet and dark breeches, Simon approached her, his blue eyes shining seductively at her. Just watching him walk toward her made her insides quiver.

She couldn't hold back her smile.

"Good afternoon, ladies." His rich voice tickled down her spine.

Sabine and Gabriella returned his greeting.

Stop staring and smiling. Respond. "Good afternoon," she said, a little too breathless.

She'd spent the morning in class suppressing yawns and secret smiles. Simon had given her little rest last night, but she hadn't minded in the least. Last night had been magic. No sonnet could come close to describing how it had felt to be loved through the night and into the morning by this man. She had more nights like last night to look forward to. To become closer to Simon. There was still plenty of time. Last night had been an excellent start. Most definitely something to build on.

"I have been looking for you, *chérie.*"

"Oh?" God help her, she was smiling up at him again. The fact that Sabine and Gabriella, not to mention anyone in the square, were openly observing them didn't matter a whit at the moment.

"*Mademoiselle la Comtesse!*"

Angelica's head snapped around. *Oh dear God, no.* Rushing toward her was Madame Blanche, waving and grinning.

"Mademoiselle la Comtesse!"

Angelica mentally cringed. Sweet Madame Blanche was the only one who refused to acknowledge Angelica without reference to her station of birth. Last night at the feast, she'd gushed about it. No matter how many times Angelica had asked to be called by her first name, Madame Blanche insisted on *"showing the proper respect to a noble lady."*

Madame Blanche's "respect" was overdone, in her well-meaning way, and it was about to be demonstrated in front of Simon. She hadn't announced her name yesterday to be treated differently. She'd done it only to show Simon that she was strong and unashamed. Now she wished she could roll the name back onto her tongue and swallow it. The last thing she wanted was to have something so meaningless to her as nobility emphasized before Simon when he'd shown such sensitivity on the subject.

Silently, she prayed that today Madame Blanche would approach her and not—the older woman stopped, lowered her head, and sank low—*curtsy*. Mentally, she groaned.

Quickly pulling the woman upright, Angelica squeezed her hands and said, "Good afternoon, Madame."

Madame Blanche clasped her hands before her ample bosom. Heaven help her. Why did the woman have to gaze at her as though she was looking upon a deity?

"Oh, Mademoiselle la Comtesse, how good to see you." She tried to curtsy again, but Angelica quickly secured an arm around Madame Blanche's shoulders, halting her intent.

"So good to see you too. My, what a lovely dress, Madame." Angelica peeked up at Simon.

He watched and smiled, yet she noted, disheartened, that the smile on his lips didn't reflect in his eyes.

"Why, thank you. It's so kind of you to say so. You know, I've made gowns for many important women in France. Women of the aristocracy, just like yourself, wo—"

"Madame Blanche." Angelica abruptly stopped the woman's flow of words and grabbed Gabriella's hand. "Madame Dragani is in need of new gowns. Isn't that so, Gabriella?"

"Ah…yes! Yes, it is." She wanted to kiss her friend for her assistance.

"Madame Dragani?" Madame Blanche looked around as though noticing the others for the first time. "Oh my, forgive my manners." She was quick to greet Simon, Sabine, and Gabriella. "How wonderful, Madame Dragani! Please, come this way. I shall attend to you." The older woman gestured toward her shop.

Angelica and her two friends exchanged knowing nods. She was happy to see them walk away with the dear dressmaker.

Madame Blanche turned. "Oh, Mademoiselle la Comtesse, you must come too. I have set aside my finest fabrics for you." She raised a hand, halting Angelica's response. "Now, I know Suzette has made you lovely gowns. She is indeed talented with a needle, but I would ask for the honor of making you a gown. My gift to you." The woman curtsied low.

Angelica briefly closed her eyes, wishing Madame Blanche wouldn't continue to stand on unwanted ceremony. She felt Simon place his hand at the small of her back. The thrill of his touch made her insides dance. She wanted to be alone with him. She didn't want to discuss gowns, and she certainly didn't want the constant references to her class—a class she'd never really belonged to—in front of Simon. She couldn't leave dear Madame's presence fast enough.

"Madame Blanche, you are too generous, but—"

"Oh, I insist! A lovely gown for our island's exalted citizen," she gushed. "An Aristo!"

Dear God, could the woman not be silent? She felt Simon remove his hand from her back. She stiffened, not wishing to see what was reflected in his eyes. Then he brushed his fingers against the nape of her neck before he rested his warm palm there.

Leaning in, he said softly in her ear, "It is just a gown. Let her make it for you. It will make her very happy."

He was right, of course. Why was she refusing? It was only making matters worse, and Madame Blanche had only good intentions.

Angelica smiled. "I accept your lovely gift. Thank you, Madame."

"Oooh!" She clapped her hands with glee. "Come. I shall take your measurements."

"Not today, Madame." Simon surprised Angelica with his answer. She looked up at him questioningly. Returning her gaze, he said, "Perhaps tomorrow."

Angelica seized the opportunity of escape Simon had just created for her. "Yes! Tomorrow would be better."

Madame Blanche looked slightly disappointed. "Certainly. Tomorrow it is, then. I shall make you the finest gown—"

"You shall make her four fine gowns," Simon interjected.

"*Four?*" Angelica and Blanche asked in chorus.

"Yes. One will be a gift from you, Madame, and the other three, gifts from me. Only the finest fabrics are to be used '*befitting her station of birth.*'"

"Oh, Captain, of course. Until tomorrow!" She curtsied for Angelica one last time before rushing back to her shop.

Angelica turned to Simon, frowning.

"I don't require gowns '*befitting my station of birth.*' I don't desire excesses. Nor do I need pampering. Nobility and its trappings do not hold importance to me."

The last thing Simon wanted was to argue about this now. He simply smiled, indicating a state of cheerfulness he didn't feel. "What if I wish to pamper you for the simple pleasure I would derive from it? I am hardly poor. I can afford to buy you some gowns."

He saw she was about to protest further and cupped her cheek. Drawing his thumb lightly over her lips, he quelled her words. "Angelica, although you would be stunning barefoot, wearing sackcloth, I enjoy seeing you in finery. Allow me to buy them for you. Like Madame Blanche, it would make me happy." But that was not the entire truth. He wanted her to have gowns just as an Aristo would. She would need them when she returned to her proper life.

And there was a part of him that wanted her to have something from him. He couldn't help wondering if she'd think of him years from now. It shouldn't matter whether she did.

He shoved the thoughts away, unsettled by them and the emotions warring inside him. He had to be detached—reminding himself why he'd agreed to her arrangement in the first place. To purge her from his system.

He had to believe what he felt for her was no more than a mere infatuation. Eventually, as with the others, he'd have his fill. Then he could go on with his life. And she could do the same. In France. Within her rightful social circle.

"I shall accept your gift only because it makes you happy," she said, "but there are things I seek that would please me."

He shouldn't ask; the warm look in her eyes gave him pause. "What do you seek?" The words left his mouth nonetheless.

She stepped forward and surprised him when she slipped her arms around his waist—right in the middle of the village for everyone to see. Rising up onto the balls of her feet, she brought her mouth close to his ear and said, "*You.*"

The single word and her display of public affection left him feeling as if warm, sweet nectar had just melted over his insides.

Before he realized it, his arms had encircled her, and his cheek rested against her silky curls. He couldn't bring himself to ask if she meant his body or...more. Either way, he didn't want to know the answer.

Noticing a number of onlookers, remembering himself, his plan, and his lunch arrangement, Simon murmured near her ear. "I have a surprise for you. I've cleared my commitments for the rest of the day, and if you are free, perhaps I can interest you in sharing a picnic with me." *Dieu*, he needed this time with her. Time and overindulgence. That was the remedy for breaking this fever.

She pulled back instantly. Delight danced in her eyes. He fought back the urge to pull her to him again.

"How wonderful. Where?"

Her smile was contagious. "Somewhere special."

"More surprises, Simon?" She took his hand in hers. "If you keep this up, I shall become spoiled and unbearably demanding."

A soft chuckle escaped him. "I have no problem indulging your every carnal whim," he felt constrained to say, forcing himself to keep their involvement within the boundaries that were comfortable for him—sexual in nature only.

He was glad he had the entire afternoon and into the night to spend with her. Most of all, he was grateful for the weeks that still lay ahead before he'd return to face France and Fouquet.

Time would be his greatest ally. It was time to focus on decadent pleasures, to focus on his plan and indulge in this delectable woman.

CHAPTER TWENTY

The sound of rushing water pouring over gray rock mingled with their quickened breaths and soft moans. Lying on a blanket near the natural pool, their lunch now forgotten, his doublet and some of her clothing scattered around them, Simon realized he was a drowning man.

Drowning in the woman under him.

He sat up abruptly, his breathing labored, overwhelmed by the intensity between them. And the foreign, unrelenting emotions overtaking him.

He dragged a hand over his face. *Dieu.* He needed a moment.

His last thought had sent him sitting bolt upright.

The thought that he would not let her go. Ever.

He'd brought Angelica to his favorite spot. He'd ordered that the picnic be set up so that they could enjoy the scenic waterfalls and the pool beneath it, an oasis that was secluded by trees and lush foliage, and she'd been moved by the gesture. A small voice inside him chastised him for the error. He should limit what they shared to his bedroom. But when he'd seen how pleased he'd made her, the small voice had been subdued by the contentment that welled up inside him.

Simon heard her sit up.

"Simon, what is amiss?"

Her chestnut-colored hair was down in long, soft curls. Having coaxed the clothes from her sweet form, he had her down to her chemise. The veil of cloth hid little from his hungry view. However, there was more than physical attraction affecting him.

He beat the emotions back, and glanced toward the waterfalls.

Merde. He wasn't used to feelings like these during sex.

He might have made a lot of mistakes in his quest for betterment, but he would not err here. He couldn't—wouldn't—deny her the life that had been denied to him. He wouldn't let her lose her nobility—and that was the consequence for a noblewoman who married a commoner.

He *would* let her go. He would *not* keep her.

"What is it, Simon?" She forced his face back to hers. "This has to do with nobility…"

He quickly kissed her. Uncomfortable with his emotional turmoil, he didn't want to talk about this now, afraid of what he might say. He used the moment to collect himself, drawing upon years of experience in disguising his true thoughts and feelings to help him.

If he'd learned to hide his emotions, emotions as strong as fear, since he was a boy growing up on warships with Robert, then he could certainly manage to hide *this*, as a man, until, by strength of will, he'd master it.

She broke the kiss and frowned. "Simon, I wish to talk about this."

"Not now." He formed a smile. "There is something I want to do first." He stood and held out his hand.

She remained seated, arms at her sides, staring up at him.

He indicated the environs with a sweep of this other hand. "This is our private Eden. Come, I'll make it worth your while." His right hand still jutted out, waiting for hers.

She folded her arms, not looking inclined to comply.

"I see my Eve requires further encouragement." He pulled off his shirt and tossed it down onto his doublet. The sunshine felt good against his skin.

He bent down, easily picking her up in his arms and, walking toward the water's edge, climbed up onto a rock.

"Simon, what are you doing?"

"Enjoying our private paradise. A little fun and frolic in the sun." He glanced at the inviting water before them.

Her pretty eyes narrowed slightly. "You wouldn't dare…"

He cocked a brow. "Wouldn't I?"

He tossed her into the blue-green water, hearing her yelp of surprise just as she broke the surface. This was exactly what he needed—lighthearted diversions to lift his spirits and sexual indulgence to diminish the enchantment.

It had to work.

Quickly, he stripped away his remaining clothing and jumped in after her, welcoming the water's cool sting against his body.

Just as he resurfaced, she splashed him.

He wiped the water off his face with a swipe of his hand, then reached out and pulled her into his arms.

"Sorry, but you looked as though you needed cooling off," he teased.

"Really?" She was miffed, keeping her hands on his shoulders instead of around him. Surrounded by the turquoise water, her eyes took on a spectacular shade of green. For a moment, he lost himself within their depths. She looked utterly ravishing, with the soaked chemise plastered to her body, her wet hair, and the droplets of water on her skin.

She pulled away from him. Her gaze dropped to his erection below the surface. "I think you are the one in need of cooling off. I hope the water helps." Turning, she began to make her way to the shoreline. "I'll be on the blanket waiting for you, when you are ready to talk."

In a quick movement, he caught her hand and pulled her to him, trapping her in his arms. Dipping his head, he licked a water drop off her shoulder and heard her breath catch.

"I'm sorry, Angelica." The apology had risen from deep inside him. From the pit of that emotional ache he couldn't seem to vanquish. Although, what he was truly apologizing for was what was most defeating, for he found himself in that moment wishing he could give her more than he had to offer. "I don't wish your ire. I brought you here to spend time with you. Just you and I. It's a beautiful day. Why discuss things that cannot be changed? Why not simply enjoy what we have together?"

He felt delighted when she wrapped her arms around his neck. "I give of myself freely and completely to you. Without reservation. But you are holding back from me. And it's because of my station of birth."

Instantly, he sealed his mouth against hers, fearing certain words might escape him. Words he couldn't say nor take back afterwards.

Ending the kiss, he forced himself to look into her mesmerizing eyes once more. "There *is* more I wish to give. Last night was but a small sampling of decadent delights. We've only just begun..." His tone was full of carnal promise. *Much better.*

He claimed her mouth, his kiss languid yet heated. He sensed her fighting the hot impulses building between them. He couldn't let her.

"What about our talk, Simon?" she said between kisses.

"I promise before I leave for France, we will talk," he said. "But not now..." Lifting her, he then slid her sex down along his stiff cock. She softly moaned.

Stubbornly, she pulled back slightly and breathlessly said, "I'm going to hold you to your promise."

"I know. I want to make it up to you for tossing you into the water. Would that be all right, *chérie?*"

"That depends on what you had in mind." Though she sounded suspicious, he saw clear interest reflected in those stunning green eyes.

"I was thinking of paying 'extensive homage to your person.'" He quoted her words from the night before.

She paused as though thinking his proposition over. "I believe that would be satisfactory...*as a start.*"

A laugh escaped him. *Dieu,* she had a way of enticing smiles and laughter from him. "How about if I start by telling you about a dream I had on the ship on our voyage here?"

"You wish to tell me about a dream?" By her tone, he sensed she left out the word *now?*

He continued to smile, unable to help himself. "An erotic dream. About you."

"*Oh.*" It was a breathy sound. "Go on."

He lightly caressed her back under the water. "In my dream, you were here with me, in the water, before the falls, just as you are."

"I see..."

"And I held you just like this, tightly against me, letting you feel how hard you make me."

"What...else?"

"Then I kissed you, like this." He brushed his mouth against her lips, then deepened his kiss. Even though his voice had been soft, his heart pounded. Every fiber of his being clamored for her, for a connection he'd never desired with any other woman. Moving his hand to the back of her head, he kissed her with unbridled hunger, wanting to obliterate everything he was feeling except raw lust.

By the time he lifted his head, they were both breathing hard.

She licked her lips. "What happened next?"

"I'll show you."

He took her hand and led her to a wall of smooth rock, near the waterfalls. What he wanted to do with her had been a long-held fantasy of his. One of many he intended to act out, hoping the hold she had on him would lessen with each one.

He pulled her into an inlet secluded by the large rocks.

Touching the sun-warmed stone, he made certain it wasn't too hot for her back, and then gently pressed her against it.

"Are you comfortable?"

"Yes. Now what happens in your dream?"

He pulled off her wet chemise and tossed it to the side. "I look at you."

Taking a step back, he let his gaze move over her. The water here reached her mid-thigh. He watched in fascination as the splatters of sunlight, reflecting on the glassy water surface, danced on her skin.

"My dream does not do justice to how truly incredible you look in the flesh."

Her blush reached to her sweet breasts.

"Then what happens?"

He stepped forward and leaned his palms against the warm stone near her shoulders. "Then I confess to you how much I have wanted to taste you." She stared at him intently, adorably trying to decipher the full meaning behind his words.

"I ask you, 'Angelica, will you let me taste your pretty sex? Will you let me suck that perfect little clit and make you come with my mouth?'"

Her lips parted. Over the sound of the waterfall, he heard her soft gasp.

"Men…do that to women?" she asked, full of delightful astonishment.

Dieu, she was precious. He found himself thankful to whatever heavenly forces had allowed him to cross her path, allowed him this experience with her.

"Lovers do 'that' to each other." He knelt before her, the water rippling just above his waist. Placing his hands on her hips, he looked up at her. "What say you? I have been dying to taste you for so long."

Her eyes scanned about.

"No one will interrupt us," he reminded her. On the way to their picnic spot, she'd seen the man he'd ordered to remain on the main path to the waterfalls to keep others away.

"I promise, you'll enjoy every moment." He grazed his hands up her thighs. "What is your answer, *chérie*? Will you let me taste you?"

He desperately wanted to be the first man to pleasure her this way. This he could do. It was something he actually had to offer.

Her cheeks were flushed. Her nipples were erect, like two ripe berries begging to be sucked. She bit her lip, then finally gave him a shaky nod. A wave of joy crested over him.

It took him a moment before he could say, "Place your foot here." His voice was husky with desire as he helped her balance her foot up on a rock beside him.

Her fingers dug into the stone. Her breathing was rapid and shallow. And her pink sex was wet. She was as excited as she was anxious over the unknown experience.

He placed his hands back on her hips. With care, he ran his thumbs over her silky, slick folds, opening her further. She stiffened.

"Just relax."

She nodded, yet she looked anything but.

He kissed a warm path along her inner thigh, inching closer and closer to that private place he ached to taste. Then he lowered his mouth onto her. She lurched and cried out at the first stroke of his tongue.

He stopped immediately. She was all but panting. "Are you all right?"

She nodded.

"Do you wish me to stop?"

She shook her head.

"Then you must be still. You don't want to injure your back against the rocks."

She nodded. "Please...continue."

He managed to contain his smile. She was delightfully sweet during carnal play, and he wanted nothing more than to cherish every inch of the delicate pink flesh exposed to him.

He tightened his grip on her hips, anticipating another sudden movement, then stroked his tongue tenderly along her inner lips. She jerked only slightly. He glided his tongue inside her slit, enjoying her soft whimper. He relished the taste of her warmth, her wetness. Her. The rest of the world and its problems disappeared. Nothing existed but this moment and this woman. And he savored both. Taking his time, using his tongue, he gave her a most intimate, erotic kiss—a kiss he wanted her never to forget.

He made his way to her sweet clit, so sensitive and engorged with need, and swirled his tongue around it, teasing her, building her anticipation, until finally he drew it into his mouth. Her sultry moan filled his ears. Steadily, he suckled her, settling into a rhythm that drove her wild. He continued until he had her straining hard against him, until she screamed without reservation as a shattering orgasm shook her. Still he persisted, gently tasting her, waiting for her to finally quiet before reluctantly lifting his mouth.

She collapsed to her knees. Wrapping her arms around him, she buried her face in his neck, her breathing warm and quick. He held her tightly, her luscious taste still on his tongue.

She looked up into his eyes, her cheeks flushed. "I want to taste you."

His cock jerked hungrily at her provocative words, but he shook his head. "After having you come against my mouth, I'm so hard I've got to have you right now." Not to mention that given the insanity inside him, he was afraid he would begin reciting love sonnets within moments of having her delectable mouth on him.

He stood.

She stayed put and reached out, taking hold of his rock-hard cock.

"Angelica," he gently admonished and grasped her wrist, intending to pull her hand away. She brought her mouth closer to him.

"Tell me what to do." She brushed her lips over the tip of his prick. His knees almost gave way.

"Angelica..." Her name escaped his throat in a raspy whisper.

"Tell me how a woman tastes a man, Simon. Is this right?" She gently licked across the engorged head of his erection.

He jerked and groaned. A second swipe of her tongue was all it took to snap his resolve. He leaned back against the rock, not trusting the strength in his legs, not caring that something was jabbing into his spine.

"Take me inside your mouth," he heard himself say, barely recognizing the sound of his strained voice. "No teeth." His hands were on her head, urging her on. "In and out."

His blood thundered as she drew the crest of his cock into the wet heat of her mouth. Then back out. Then in again, a little deeper, and *Dieu*, out. The torture was sublime. Tentative at first, she quickly became bolder, her strokes, licks, and sucks more sure and devastating. Taking more of him in her mouth each time. He closed his eyes. He was dying. There could be no better way to perish. Her novice mouth had him utterly enthralled, the friction unbearable. His body screamed for release, his semen needing to escape, about to spill. Abruptly, he pulled away.

With his heart pounding, his body ravenous for her, he picked her up and placed her onto the flat, smooth stone where he'd tossed her chemise, then laid her back on the wet garment.

Beautifully flushed, she frowned. "Why did you stop? Was I not doing it correctly?"

Standing between her thighs, he bent her knees and leaned over her. "If you did it any better, my heart would stop," he said, his breathing erratic.

She smiled and laced her arms around him. "It's been hours since you have been inside me. I've missed you." *Christ*, the things she said. She pulled him down and drew on his bottom lip before she kissed him.

Taking his cock in hand, he wedged it at her entrance and slowly pushed his hard length into her juicy core, savoring the stunning sensations streaming along his cock, her tight, slick, heat slowly sucking him in. He closed his eyes, but it wasn't possible to shut her out, to concentrate solely on the pleasure. Even without sight, the feel of her, the sounds she made, the taste of her, and the light scent of her soft skin, all made him acutely aware of the woman and not just the act.

He began to move with languid strokes, wanting to prolong the moment, battling back his release and the load of come he was dying to purge. Wishing to suspend time. He was lost in a dream. This was far better than the actual dream he'd had. He was in Eden—with his moonlight angel—lost to the appeal and temptation of his forbidden fruit. And at the moment, he didn't care.

Soon, he had her impatient and yearning. Her fragmented sentences, urging him to hurry, were punctuated by hot, hungry kisses. Quickening his pace, he gripped her bottom, lifting her hips into his every deep, driving thrust.

She cried out her release; the glorious spasms rippling along his thrusting cock sent him over the edge. He withdrew just in the nick of time. Clenching his teeth, he drained his cock outside her body in a pulsating rush that went on and on. Each shuddering eruption pure euphoria.

The sun shone warmly on his back. His muscles were lax. A sense of peace, the likes of which he'd never known, settled over him.

He gazed down into her eyes. Gently, she brushed back a lock of his hair from his forehead and gave him a tender smile. Perhaps he'd postpone his trip back to France, prolong their time together just a little more, and hold on to his moonlight angel just a little longer.

"Angelica," he murmured, her name slipping past his lips, full of emotion that came directly from his heart.

Pounding drums shattered the bliss.

Simon jerked his head up. His stomach dropped.

"What is that?" she asked.

He was already standing, pulling her to her feet. Taking her hand, he began making his way through the water toward the shore, his heart pounding along with the drums.

"They're a warning." He tried to keep the anxiety from his voice. "A ship is on the horizon."

"A ship? What kind of ship?"

"I don't know yet."

They reached the shoreline and their clothing.

"Simon, are we being attacked?"

He grabbed his fallen shirt and tossed it over her head. Knowing his men would be coming for him soon, he began pulling on his breeches.

"I don't know. But if we are, we're prepared. My men are highly trained." His mind raced as he considered the possible identity and intentions of the ship. Hell, there could be more than one. The drums continued to pound. A cold sensation slid down Simon's spine. He had a terrible feeling inside. A feeling he couldn't shake. A feeling that all dreams were over.

Reality had come to call.

CHAPTER TWENTY-ONE

"Seven ships in all, Captain, all bearing our flags," the man at the northeast lookout had advised. Simon had felt some relief. At least they weren't being attacked. But why were all seven of his warships returning? What could it mean? It took hours for his commanders to reach the shore and make their way to Simon's dining room before he knew the answer.

"Captain, the war between France and Spain is over," stated one of the warship commanders. A roar of astonishment swept around the table in Simon's dining room.

His heart missed a beat.

He looked around at all fourteen of his ships' commanders. His shock was mirrored in the faces of half the men around the table as the other half relayed the astounding news from France.

"Over?" Domenico exclaimed.

"Yes, over. The king has signed the peace treaty. But that is not all. Mazarin is dead."

Simon sat upright. "The First Minister? *Dead?*"

Armand shook his head. "Unbelievable. I thought the devil was immortal."

"Fouquet still lives," advised another recently returned commander. "If ever a devil there was, it would be Fouquet."

"What does the king do now?" Jules asked. "Mazarin has ruled for Louis since he was a child and inherited the throne—"

"Who will be the next First Minister?" Simon interjected. Silently, he prayed the next words he heard were not *Nicolas Fouquet.* Mazarin had been no less power-hungry than Fouquet; however,

Fouquet, as far as Simon was concerned, was more ruthless than the widely despised Cardinal Mazarin.

"That is the most incredible thing, Captain," explained the commander. "Louis has announced he will rule France *without* a First Minister of any kind."

A murmur of disbelief erupted.

Simon leaned forward, still grappling with the words that were too unbelievable to accept. "And what of Fouquet? Surely he must have believed that he would have been the natural replacement."

"Captain, he still believes it. Raoul and Vilain have provided invaluable information."

"Go on," Simon said. Raoul and Vilain were the two spies he'd planted as servants within Fouquet's household. And he was eager to hear every detail.

"They inform us that Fouquet thinks the king will grow bored of ruling and hand over the responsibilities to him. Fouquet believes Louis cannot rule the realm without him. He thinks he's indispensable. What makes matters worse is that Fouquet has the support of the majority of the nobles. They call him the true king of France. Those who don't support him are indebted to him financially. He has been quite shrewd."

"Captain," began another. "I have a letter from the former commodore, Robert d'Arles, Marquis de Névelon." He handed Simon the parchment with Robert's family seal on it.

Simon opened and read the note. "The marquis believes that the king grows increasingly displeased with Fouquet and his extravagant ways," he relayed.

Jules shook his head. "And yet Fouquet still thinks he'll be the next First Minister."

The commander nodded. "His ambitions and arrogance seem to have no limits. And his excesses are extreme. It seems every day Fouquet spends funds on his new château, making it more and more opulent. He is quite unconcerned about what Louis thinks of Château Vaux-le-Vicomte."

Simon drained the brandy in his goblet, desperate for the fiery liquid to counter the ache he felt inside. The news was bittersweet. And monumental.

In his note, Robert wanted Simon's immediate return and advised that Fouquet had given up his post as a Member of Parliament at Louis's request. Though he was still the Superintendent of Finance, this left Fouquet vulnerable. Could it be that their young king had truly opened his eyes and seen the threat Fouquet was to his throne? Could he be planning Fouquet's downfall, drawing him out of the security of his parliamentary protection?

Between the war ending, Mazarin's death, and the king's request of Fouquet, Simon reeled. The very idea of peace seemed unreal. The war with Spain had been ongoing since '48, and before that, there had been the Thirty Years War.

Would the peace last? He hoped so. He was sick of war. Yet now that it was over, so was the opportunity to become an officer. To become ennobled. It was no longer a matter of choice—whether he wanted to chase the dream or not. The door to betterment had just slammed shut in his face, leaving Simon trapped on the outside. Leaving him a commoner forevermore.

He knew he couldn't delay his return now. He wouldn't be given the extra time with Angelica he'd hoped for. This was an opportunity to get out from under Fouquet's hold with his life and the lives of his men intact, and even aid in his downfall, but Simon knew he would walk away with a life devoid of recognition for his naval successes.

And without Angelica.

That thought left him feeling cold. And empty.

She waited for him in his chambers. He had to go upstairs and tell her that he had to leave. That she had to go too. The king was beginning to rule. This was the perfect time for her to return and reclaim her estate. And her life.

What choice did he have but to take her back? She deserved to return to the upper class—to all the benefit and privilege that came with it. To all the things he'd never have. France held promise for her, though it held nothing for him. He might have failed to elevate himself, but he wouldn't fail her. She deserved more than he had to offer. She was born into privilege. She deserved a husband who could provide her and her children with a name that carried with it esteem. A name that would grant them the prerogatives that came with it.

He stood, dismissed the men, and walked out of the dining room to the stairs, both his legs and his heart leaden.

*****

Angelica paced.

She'd been advised that the ships were friends, not foes, but that didn't seem to give her ease. Something was happening. She feared Simon would need to leave sooner than expected.

Would she be denied her chance before it had even begun?

The chamber door opened. She turned.

Simon gave her a lopsided smile and closed the door quietly. Her heart leaped to her throat. She hadn't missed the way his eyes flashed regret. *Dear God, no. Not this soon.*

"You have to leave, don't you?" The words rushed past her lips. His smile disappeared.

"Yes." The soft word roared in her ears.

She battled back her devastating disappointment. "When?"

He looked as though it pained him to say, "A few days. A week at most. As soon as the ships are prepared for the voyage back."

She sank down onto the edge of the bed. "I'm sorry that you have to leave so soon." She hoped she didn't sound as shaken as she felt.

"So am I."

He walked over and sat down beside her. Taking one of her cold hands in his, he said, "There are great changes that have occurred in France." Lightly, he caressed her hand with his thumb. "France is finally at peace, and our king has for the first time indicated a desire to rule. These are positive changes. The realm will be a much better place for it."

She remained silent, sensing there was more he wanted to say, yet he seemed to be struggling to find his words. He looked heavy-hearted.

"This affair between us has been…beautiful." He gave her a rueful smile. Her heart pounded. She couldn't shake the feeling she was about to hear something worse than his departure.

His gaze caressed her face. "Dear God, you are so fine. Everything a man could want and more. You deserve the finest life has to offer. You are one of the few nobles who truly belong in the exalted class."

"What are you trying to say, Simon?"

"You don't belong here."

Her heart lurched. "*Pardon?*"

"You must go back."

She jumped to her feet. "Go back, *where?*"

"France."

Horrified, she took a step back. "Surely you jest?"

"I would not jest about this." He cleared his throat. "I'm taking you back to France."

Dear God, he was serious! "*Why?* Why must I leave?"

He rose slowly. "Because you were born to walk among royalty, the aristocracy. Not peasants. This is no place for you."

A laugh erupted from her, void of mirth. "Who are you to decide where I should be and what is best for me!"

He looked down and softly responded, "I am in charge here. I decide who remains and who leaves." He met her gaze, his look determined. "You cannot remain here and teach children of commoners—"

"I refuse to go!"

"Your life is elsewhere. You need to return to the life you were meant to live."

"What about the life I wish to live? I wish to stay here, with my friends, with…*you.*"

He closed his eyes briefly, and shook his head.

She could not believe this! How could she make him understand? "I've told you that my nobility means nothing to me!"

"It should." Maddeningly, he kept his tone soft but firm. "Once you return to France, you'll see all the privileges it grants you. Privileges and honor denied to the rest of us."

"Privileges? Honor? What possible difference can any of that make? By forcing me to return to France, you place me in peril. You know what my stepfather did to me. How can you suggest such a thing?"

"No! He will never touch you again. *This I swear.* I and every man in my command will protect you with our lives. He will relinquish all that is yours, and he will pay for what he has done."

Stricken, she reeled.

"*Mon ange*, don't look at me that way. I will not abandon you there. Before we part company, I will make certain you are safe and that the advantages of your birth have been restored to you. The matter will be handled with discretion, for your sake."

He took a step toward her. She took a step back.

"What then, Simon? After my 'advantages' are restored, do I live out my days alone at Beaulieu?"

"No. Once your wealth is restored, you can"—he looked away—"marry."

"*Marry?* I am not a virgin. What man would want me?"

"Every man in France," he murmured. A little louder he said, "There are men in the noble class who would be willing to overlook the lack of a maidenhead. Especially if a sufficient dowry is provided and"—she saw him swallow and look down—"they see you."

"I will not go back to…that place. I refuse to tell you my stepfather's name!"

He nodded. "I know how upsetting it is for you to discuss him. I don't wish to cause you further distress by demanding his name or any details about him. It isn't necessary. Once in France, it won't be difficult to ascertain the identity of the Lord of Beaulieu."

She felt sick inside. Heartsick. He was adamant and determined to take her with him. Tears stung her eyes. "Don't do this, Simon."

"It's the right thing to do. To keep you here when you could have so much more is purely selfish. I've told you before, anything permanent between us is impossible."

She swiped away an errant tear from her cheek. "Because I'm a *noble*." Her final word dripped with disdain.

"Because if a man in my class were to marry a woman in your class, she would be stripped of her status and made insignificant in society. A commoner. A man should bring the woman he marries honor. Not shame."

"Dear God!" she exclaimed, feeling utterly defeated and completely heartbroken. "I see no shame in it. I cannot understand why you hold nobility in such esteem!"

"It is not just I who hold it in esteem, but society. I've chased it all my life. If I cannot have mine, I will not let you lose yours."

The look in his eyes told her he couldn't be dissuaded. He was taking her back. She thought he had some feelings for her, but his intentions coupled with his words indicated differently.

She was to have had a chance—four weeks with him—to build something permanent, but she didn't get four days. She had to leave the room—*right now*—before she made an utter fool of herself by making declarations of love or crumbling to the floor weeping and pleading.

She started for the door. She had no idea where she was going, but she had to get out of his presence, to collect herself. To think. To harden her heart.

"Angelica." He caught her hand and stepped closer. "Don't go." His blue eyes were suddenly less guarded. As always, his proximity enveloped her senses. Gently, he brushed back a lock of her hair. "Being with you has been better than a dream."

His look of utter mournfulness surprised her and caused a little bit of hope to swell inside. She tried to push it away, afraid to believe in it.

"We should have had more time together," he continued, "but there is still some time left. Bliss like this doesn't come around every day." Cupping her face, he kissed her softly. She closed her eyes, trying to steel her strength, yet still clinging to the contact. "I, for one, am not ready to let go just yet," he murmured against her mouth.

She pulled away, needing to see the confirmation of his words in his eyes. It was there. Hope swelled a little more.

"If you would allow," he said, her face still cradled between his palms, "we could be together for the remainder of our time on the island as well as the entire voyage. It is a total of nearly two months.

More than we agreed upon in our arrangement. What say you? Will you be with me until we reach France, *mon ange*? I've no right to ask, but I find it impossible not to ask just the same."

She should say no and run. Pick up the pieces of her heart and guard them fiercely, but she'd made her proposition knowing it was risky. He was offering more time together. Would it be enough to convince him that they belonged together? That their stations of birth shouldn't separate them?

He was back to kissing her mouth with a tenderness she felt down to her heart. If she backed away now, she would lose for certain. Her only chance was to see it through to the end.

To the end of the voyage, and hope to change his mind.

"Angelica...say you will be with me."

What choice did she have but to give it her all? That way, in her old age, she wouldn't condemn herself for not having tried all that was in her power to have the man she loved.

Was regret not worse than a broken heart?

In his eyes, she could see how much he wanted her to agree, how much this situation was causing him pain, and she decided to see her original plan through to the end.

"I will."

He drew her tightly against him and buried his face in her hair. "Thank God."

"But understand this," she said pulling back. "I will not go back to Beaulieu. Ever."

He kissed her again, with more purpose. "Let's not talk about this now. To hell with France and all those in it," he murmured between kisses. "While we're together, we will make the most of it. Nothing exists but the two of us and this magnificent bliss we create together."

His words couldn't be truer.

The stakes were raised. If she reached the shores of France and he hadn't declared his love, she would lose everything and everyone she'd come to hold dear—never to return to Marguerite again.

She would never see Gabriella again. She would never listen to Suzette's bubbly chatter or watch her try to catch Paul's eye anymore. She would never see any of these people again, never know what became of her students.

She would be forced to endure endless days without any of them. Without Simon.

So much uncertainty lay in her future. Everything weighed upon the voyage back to France.

And how deep Simon's feelings truly were for her.

*****

Simon sat behind the desk of his study, swirling his goblet of brandy. Merriment went on beyond the doors of his study. A party for his commanders who were leaving to return to France. A party was the last thing he was in any mood for.

He reminded himself, for surely the thousandth time, that he was doing the right thing.

His plan didn't involve bettering himself for a change. But bettering others—not only Angelica, but also his own kind—the lower class in France whom he'd wronged by aiding Fouquet's climb to power. *May Fouquet and Angelica's stepfather burn in hell for what they've done.*

But what about him?

Upon his own death, would he join them? Could he ever be forgiven for pursuing his ambitions blindly, to the detriment of so many? Could hell be worse than how he felt at the thought of letting Angelica go?

Jules marched into the study and slammed the door shut behind him. "I must speak to you."

Simon frowned. "Thank you for knocking."

Jules's usual smile was notably absent. "You are making a grave error."

Weary, Simon sighed. "What specifically are you talking about? Don't you agree Domenico should stay behind this time?"

Jules frowned. "Of course, I agree. I'm happy to make this voyage, to command one of the ships returning to France. Sabine agrees with the decision as well."

"I'm delighted to hear your wife approves of my selections. Mind getting to the point?"

"My point is Angelica. Sabine tells me of this insane decision to take her back."

"This is none of your concern. Leave it alone."

"You are my concern. As your friend, I cannot watch you do this and remain silent. I watched you at the feast after the bachelors' competition. I saw you the next morning too. I've never seen you look so happy. Any fool can see how much you love her."

The words sliced through Simon like cold steel, opening the gaping gash inside him a little more.

"You are mad," Simon forced out. "And you are acting as though my intentions toward her are ill. I plan to take her back, restore her estate, her standing, and take revenge on the man who...stole it from her in the first place."

"But it is not what she wants."

"Once she is in France and has reclaimed her rightful place in society, she will feel differently."

"You jest!" Jules shook his head. "Simon, you are the most stubborn... Just because nobility has meant everything to you, does not mean that it means everything to everyone. Forget this nonsense and marry her."

"You have gone mad." Simon quickly tossed back the remainder of the brandy from his goblet and filled it again, desperately wishing it would quell his emotions. Damn Jules. Why was he putting him through this?

"You love her."

Jules's words sent a painful jolt through him. Simon slammed down his goblet on the desk, the liquid sloshing out. "Enough!"

Jules set his palms on Simon's desk and leaned forward. "Look me in the eye and tell me she's no more than a good fuck."

Simon rose to his feet. Through clenched teeth he growled, "I'm warning you."

"She loves you."

Simon shook his head, shutting his heart and ears to those words. "She will gain back all that she has lost, all the advantages of her birth. She will then be able to marry someone of her own social station. *It is the right thing to do*." He fought back the misery, trying to ignore how each word cut into him.

"*Merde!* Ask her. Before you make the decision to give her up, ask her if she loves you."

He couldn't do it. If she told him she loved him, he doubted he would have the strength to walk away. If she said that she did not, it would be too painful to bear.

"Ask her to marry you, and you will see the truth of my words."

"*Jésus-Christ*, Jules. Marry the daughter of a count to the son of a fisherman? Would you have her entire ancestry turn in their graves?"

Jules straightened and let out a frustrated sigh. "You may not be a noble, but you are a rich man. You can provide for her as well as any Aristo."

"Only you and Robert know that I have chased after betterment. That dream is over. I must accept that I'm a commoner and shall remain that way. She deserves better. You of all people should understand, Jules. You were born an Aristo and then you were stripped of it. How did it feel to be *nothing*? Would you have me do that to her? Take away her nobility by marrying her?"

"Yes, I felt worthless once, and it was you who gave me the opportunity to change my life. Then I met Sabine. Now, when I look into her eyes, and I see her love for me, I feel greater than the king. Look into the eyes of your highborn lady and see that she adores you. Allow her to decide which she wishes to lose—you or social standing."

"I will not diminish her in anyway. I do *not* wish to marry her." Another sharp pain wrenched inside him. God help him, he was resolved to reject Jules's words at all cost, especially when Simon knew he couldn't keep her.

"Oh no, you wish it," Jules countered, "and you will wish it with each and every piece of your shattered heart, and on your final day, with your final breath, you will die still in want of it."

"This conversation is over." Simon started toward the door. Jules grabbed his arm.

"You feel unworthy of her because you are carrying Fouquet's sins on your soul. You didn't harm those people; he did. As for Thomas, he took a risk because—"

"—of me!"

"No! Because he wanted more too. He wanted bigger and better things out of life. He wouldn't want you to bear any guilt over his death. If you must have nobility before you will marry Angelica, then go to France and get it. Demand it from the king."

"The war is over, Jules. Haven't you heard?" Simon asked caustically. "There isn't a demand for naval officers at the moment. Besides, I want no part of captures and battle any longer. The realm is at peace, and I will return the warships and provide the king's share of the silver from *La Estrella Blanca*—to Louis *personally*. There are important matters I must speak to him about. While I'm in France, I not only plan to help Angelica but also to destroy Fouquet."

"You are going to destroy *Nicolas Fouquet*? Have you received a blow to the head recently? Couldn't you simply get over your guilt and bargain the island to Louis to gain nobility and perhaps a title?"

"It's time to send the devil to hell so that he can stop imposing it on others. As for Marguerite, France isn't interested in the islands here, and it's a good thing. I wouldn't bargain Marguerite away and place it under royal control. I don't want to see royal governors here ruling these people, creating the civil unrest and other problems that have occurred on the other French islands. That's the last thing these people deserve. They don't need oppressive lords."

Besides, there was no guarantee that Louis would ennoble him, no matter what he did.

"Fine. However, Louis is taking a more active role in his kingdom now. You have a sharp mind, Simon. I've seen you outwit the enemy in battle countless times. Now a new challenge lies before you. Convince the king, obtain your letters of nobility, and claim your prize—a beautiful woman who will bring you joy into your old age."

Dieu, Jules made it sound so simple, yet it was not. Simon couldn't bring himself to claim "the prize." Not *her*. If she knew the extent of what he'd done while he'd chased his ambitions, she'd turn away from him, horrified.

The battle she'd witnessed was but a small sampling.

He was willing to risk everything to unseat Fouquet. He was willing to risk everything to regain Angelica her stolen life and make her stepfather pay, but he wasn't willing to dishonor her by marrying her as a commoner.

"I cannot marry her," he said, each word agony.

"Then you have condemned yourself to a life devoid of any true happiness."

CHAPTER TWENTY-TWO

Simon watched Angelica as she stood on deck gazing out at the sea long after the shores of Marguerite had disappeared from view.

If she had shed a tear, he hadn't seen it. She'd walked through the saddened crowd on the beach, accepting flowers and good-byes from them with composure, grace, and a strength he admired—and drew from, to aid his flagging strength. She'd consoled others with quiet fortitude, and it destroyed him a little further to see her step foot onto the tender, leaving the shores of Marguerite.

Simon walked across the deck and slipped his arms around her waist. "Are you all right?"

She turned in his arms to face him. "As all right as you, it would seem." *Dieu*, he felt miserable, but he hadn't meant for her to see it.

He looked out at the sea, remaining silent.

"Tell me, Simon, do you truly wish for what we have to end?"

"No." He couldn't lie to her. "But it has to." He forced out the words.

"What would you do if I were not a noble?"

He refused to dwell on what-ifs. It was too difficult. "You are, and that is reality."

Regardless of the men working on the deck, she rose up onto the balls of her feet and pressed her warm mouth to his, kissing him softly on the lips. "Reality is what you make it," she said. "This voyage will last several weeks. Within that time, I hope you'll see that our reality is one worth holding on to."

"It is the reality of our situation that makes it impossible to hold on."

She studied him with those extraordinary eyes. "No. It is you alone who make it impossible," she countered. "If by the time we reach the shores of France you haven't changed your mind about this, then the reality is that you—not society's rules—have forced an end to what we have, and what could have been."

She stepped around him and walked toward his cabin.

Simon squeezed the wooden rail with a white-knuckle grip. He had no idea when the precise moment had occurred, when exactly she'd slipped passed his defenses and reached his heart. When had he made himself so vulnerable to her that she had an impact of this magnitude on him?

He turned and marched to his cabin.

Wrenching the door open, he stepped in and slammed it shut. She turned to face him, not appearing surprised to see him in the least. For some reason, this angered him further.

"Do you really wish to become one of the 'undesirables'?" he demanded. "Are you eager to bear children—sired by a man of common birth—that nobles would consider as revolting as a rodent? Do you want to always be at the mercy of your 'betters' and have them treat you and your children as less than human each time you're in their presence? That's the life of a commoner! That is what I, my mother, and everyone in our village endured. Do you want to marry me and have half the Aristos look at you with pity while the rest regard you with disgust?"

She crossed her arms. "Was that a marriage proposal?"

"*What?* No!"

"Good, because it wasn't a very good one, the way you were carrying on about rodents and disgust."

He glared at her. "This is no joking matter."

She walked up to him. "As you can tell, I am not laughing. I don't care what nobles think. Pleasing them does not give me joy. You do. Simon, I love—"

He covered her mouth with his hand in an instant. Closing his eyes, he rested his forehead against hers. "Please, don't. Do not say anything more."

He had to tell her what he'd done. He'd hoped that they could have simply had a few wonderful weeks together, but she had to know before she said any more to him. Perversely, a small part of him wanted her disdain, for it might help him to shore up his resolve and do right by her.

Removing his hand, he kissed her, needing one last kiss from her willing lips before he shattered her image of him. Drawing her against him, feeling her soft form melt into him, he kept his kiss languorous and lush, enjoying the contours of her sweet lips, delighting in her response as she parted them for him, welcoming him into her mouth. But he had to refuse the invitation, knowing the folly in accepting it.

There were things to say. He didn't want to do this, but she was giving him no choice.

He broke the kiss, took a deep breath, and stepped back, away from her. "When you return to France, you'll see bodies on the ground, dead peasants, many of them children less than five years old. Gruesome scenes. Some areas far worse than others. When you see this, know that it was I who helped do that to them. Ah, your eyes widen with surprise. Well, *chérie*, there are things you don't know about me."

He turned away and rested his hands on his hips. "I've spent my life dreaming about being a noble. I've been so intent on attaining position, crawling out of the station of my birth, that I chased after betterment without regard for the consequences of my ambitions. I craved the respect given to nobles and recognition for my naval efforts so fiercely that I closed my eyes to the cost of my quest. That price was paid by the deaths of my men and by the helpless peasants of France.

"Over the years, I became better and better at battle and capture. Countless Spaniards died at my command. The king's share of my captured prizes got a little larger each time. My contributions to the Crown treasury have been substantial. They helped a newly appointed Superintendent of Finance become highly successful, ultimately powerful, and unconscionably corrupt. While my efforts helped to make him stronger, he weakened my own kind, decimating the lower class by taxing them into starvation. I chased a fool's dream with my eyes firmly shut until Thomas's death, until I could no longer deny what I had helped do to people who'd already suffered enough. That is when I gave up chasing after betterment."

He looked down and shook his head. "My quest for betterment cost the life of a good friend, Thomas, who, incidentally, didn't die in battle and glory as his wife was told. He was captured by the Spanish and died a horrible death by torture and dismemberment." He wanted to look at her, but he couldn't.

Instead, he lowered himself onto a chair.

Hearing her approach, he braced himself.

Reluctantly, he met her gaze. She studied him, her brows drawn together. "Are those your darkest secrets, then?"

"Yes."

"I'm glad you told me this. It proves to me just what kind of man you are."

His heart sank. "It does, does it?"

"Yes." She placed her hand under his chin. "I have seen you at your best and at your worst, and even at your very worst, you have behaved honorably." Her eyes softened. "The mere fact that you torture yourself shows you are no monster. It is but one of many factors that distinguishes you from those who are. You are distraught because bad things happened, but you are not in control of everything, even if you wish it. You didn't kill Thomas. You didn't kill the peasants. Others did. As for your men and the Spanish, there was war. You fought. You did what you had to do to survive, just like everyone else. You are punishing yourself because you wanted a better life, and you shouldn't, Simon."

Her words wrapped themselves around his heart when he didn't want them to.

Slipping onto his lap, she circled her arms around him. In his ear, she said, "If you are looking for my acceptance, you have always had it."

He was astounded.

He pushed her away to look into her eyes. "I could have done more to stop what happened to those people. I should have helped them rather than those in power."

"How? You have done more for them than the king, it would seem. The greatest sin in what you have told me is that you didn't get your dream—nobility. Though it makes no difference to me whether you are a noble or not, because it is your heart's desire, I wish it for you. You deserve it. But understand this: you have sought to gain nobility, but you are noble. You don't want to be ordinary, but you never have been. You wish to be exalted, but in the eyes of so many, you are."

He was speechless.

He couldn't believe she hadn't turned away from him. He'd heard similar words from Jules and Robert, but until he heard them from her, they had little effect. Her words seemed to be like a salve to his battered conscience and tormented soul. If this incredible woman could know what he'd done yet still see good in him, perhaps he could forgive himself.

"You are more than man enough for me, just as you are." She captured his mouth in a long, languid kiss.

He was undone by her. He had no idea how to resist the swelling emotions in his heart any more than he could stop the stiffening of his cock near her soft bottom.

"Don't let this end," she whispered, her every kiss growing more urgent. Heated.

Her fingers stroked down his abdomen, the light sensation resonating through his senses. His body was instinctively responding to the arousing effect of the woman he desired. Yet his mind and heart were caught in a whirlwind of thoughts and feelings he was no longer certain how to react to.

"I want more than a few weeks, Simon. Open your heart, and tell me you want more too. Tell me before we reach France."

He needed time to think, to reason this out, but she was already pulling his shirt free, slipping her warm hands beneath it and onto his bare chest.

"Make love to me, Simon."

At least this was familiar territory for him, yet as usual, there were those softer sentiments swirling around inside him that only she inspired.

Holding her in his arms, he stood without breaking the contact of their mouths and carried her to the bed, all the while returning her kisses with heated hunger. He laid her down, then covered her with his body.

She wanted him to open his heart to her. Completely. Could he do it? What if he got rid of Fouquet and got even with her stepfather? Would that be enough to assuage his guilt? What if he did as Jules suggested and made another attempt to gain his nobility—for her? What if he failed again?

She writhed under him impatiently. Lowering his head, he savored the taste of her skin at the swell of her breast. He would never have his fill of her. He didn't want to.

"Simon... Hurry."

He wouldn't do it. "Slow down. Make it last..."

He wanted nothing more.

CHAPTER TWENTY-THREE

France. Southeast of Rouen.

Under the summer sun, horses' hooves thundered as Simon and his party of twenty men rode toward Robert's home, Château Névelon.

It had taken all Simon had to walk off his ship and ride away from Angelica. He'd become so accustomed to her presence, he loathed the thought of being without her.

Affections and passions between them had not cooled over the course of the voyage. In fact, the closer they got to France, the closer they became. He knew every endearing dimple, freckle, every sweet part of her. He knew how to make her smile, and he knew what she wanted from him. Forever.

He'd spent weeks vacillating between what was right and what he wanted until the lines began to blur, until he couldn't deny that what he wanted—*her*—felt so right. However, in the end, he hadn't committed to her as she'd asked. Not out loud, anyway.

Not just yet.

Though, he had decided he was going make a last attempt to gain nobility—to be with her. But first, he needed to speak to Robert to fully understand the new attitude of their twenty-two-year-old king. How much or how little would it take to convince Louis to grant him letters of nobility? He had the wealth of silver from *La Estrella Blanca*, and he had his determination to remove Fouquet from his powerful position. Would Louis be interested in any of this?

Because of so many uncertainties and unknowns, Simon was approaching this guardedly. But with conviction. He had, therefore, not been able to bring himself to tell Angelica how much he wanted her to be a permanent part of his life. Despite her declarations that social status didn't matter, he knew from experience it did.

With a resolve he hadn't known since before Thomas's death, Simon pushed his horse, challenging those who rode with him to keep up.

Whatever it took, Louis would ennoble him so that he could marry Angelica and give her all the honor she deserved. She'd changed him, brought him back to life, and revived his dream. Only this time, he didn't want it for personal gain but solely, strictly for her. She'd enriched his life, and he wanted in turn to enrich hers. Once he had his Letters, he'd tell her how much he loved her and ask her to marry him. Over the final week, it had all but killed him not to say the words he longed to voice. But he would. In time.

Simon had held back the king's seven warships, still at sea, north of Le Havre, while his own four ships were at port in Rouen, replenishing supplies. Immediately thereafter, two of his ships would sail to Robert's Château Arles, in the south of France.

He'd left orders for the four ships, instructions for Angelica's safety, organized two parties of men, obtained horses, and left all before Jules could disembark from the ship he commanded and confront him, forcing answers Simon couldn't yet give.

A smile tugged at the corner of his mouth.

It would seem he had luck on his side today.

*****

Angelica awoke, reached out, and realized Simon was gone.

This was not new. He always rose before her and went on deck.

Sighing, she stretched. Sounds from outside drifted into the cabin, the men moving about blending with the lapping of water against the hull of the ship. A woman's shout pierced through the familiar, followed by children's laughter and nickering horses.

Angelica sat bolt upright. *France.*

She jumped out of bed and dressed at a frantic pace. Once done, she snatched open the cabin door, startling Paul, who was walking past.

"Where is he, Paul?"

"The captain has disembarked."

Her stomach dropped. "Disembarked?" Without saying anything to her? "Where are we?"

"Rouen."

Rouen? Simon had kept her in her cabin for the last two days, making love. They had not only reached France, they'd passed Le Havre at the mouth of the Seine and were not far from Paris. "When will he return?" She couldn't keep the anxiety from her tone.

"I don't know. Perhaps several days. Maybe longer. He has matters to attend to."

"What matters?"

"I'm sorry. I cannot say."

She could feel the slow, hard thuds of her heart.

"Cannot say or will not say?"

The young man shifted his weight, looking uneasy and unsure how to answer.

"Paul, bring me Mathieu Godeau. He's second in command of this ship, is he not? I demand to speak to him."

"No need, Paul, I'm here," Godeau said from behind the younger man. Paul stepped aside, looking relieved as the tall blond man approached. "What can I do for you, mademoiselle?"

"I want to know where your captain has gone."

"The captain has left with a number of men to meet a friend. He gave me this note to give to you."

She opened the note quickly and read the words. Brief. To the point. He was gone for two weeks. She was to stay on board. He would speak to her upon his return.

"What friend is he seeing? For what purpose?" She resented this male wall of silence.

"Mademoiselle, the captain will return soon enough. You can ask him the details of his trip then."

"Is he going to Beaulieu? Before you tell me you cannot say, I assure you, you can. In fact, I insist! I have nowhere to go, so it's quite safe to tell me. Now, is he going to Beaulieu? Yes or no!"

The commander remained quiet.

"Answer me!"

"Yes."

The word hit Angelica like a fist. *How could he?* He knew how she felt about returning there. All her hopes, all the dreams of having a lasting loving bond with him were crushed under the weight of that one ugly word. *Beaulieu.*

"Is there anything else?"

She shook her head. Softly, she closed the door and leaned against it. There was nothing more to ask. She crumpled the note in her hand and let it fall to the floor.

She'd asked him to commit to her before they reached France.

And he had not.

He'd had many opportunities to voice words of love and marriage and forever. Yet he'd uttered none. He was carrying on with his original intentions of returning her to Beaulieu and retreating from her life, even after weeks of indescribable bliss.

Any illusions she may have entertained during the voyage, that he would change his mind and not let her go in the end, shattered. How much clearer could he make it?

He was *not* going to stay with her.

He left knowing how she would interpret his departure, and he hadn't even had the courage to tell her in person that he was leaving the ship. She swiped away a tear off her cheek.

She refused to add to her grief. No matter what was done about her stepfather, she could never, *would never*, step foot in Beaulieu again. Not after what had happened to her there.

Simon might have left orders for her to stay on board, but she didn't take orders from him. It would be unbearable to hear the words of rejection. She wouldn't survive hearing him tell her good-bye. He must have felt assured that she would stay put, obey his instructions. After all, where could she go?

Gripped by grief and anger, she marched up to her chest, holding back the tears she wouldn't shed for him.

She opened the lid.

At the bottom of one of her trunks, she had a simple valise already packed. Though she'd prayed she'd never have to use it, she was prepared, in the event this horrible day would come.

The valise had some necessary items, clothing, and money. She'd saved every bit she'd earned as the schoolmistress. Fortunately, Simon had been generous with her pay. In addition, Gabriella, Sabine, and Suzette had insisted on providing her with a tidy sum collectively.

As she moved around her clothing to locate the valise, she stopped, realizing she was touching the fine gowns Simon had insisted on purchasing for her. Prior to their departure, he'd made certain that all four had been completed. Now she understood the true reason why. It was so she could dress the part when he returned her to her social standing.

The realization was a stab in the heart. It hadn't been a gift after all. Not really.

The dresses would remain behind. She could never bring herself to wear them again. Her fingers touched upon the book of love sonnets. Picking it up, she ran her thumb tenderly over its leather cover. A lump formed in her throat. Before she succumbed to the emotions welling up inside her, she put the book down on the dresses and closed the lid.

She had enough money to make it to her destination. There was one man in the realm she could turn to. He'd been her father's friend and had a château not far from Paris. Although her father had seldom seen his friend, she remembered the fond way he spoke of him. Always with high regard. This man had once been an officer in the King's Navy. Was he still alive? She prayed yes. Would he be in residence? She'd no idea. In fact, she knew little about him.

But her father had trusted him, and she had no choice but to do the same.

She would seek out Robert d'Arles, Marquis de Névelon. She would go to his home, Château Névelon.

*****

Late afternoon, Simon heard hooves approaching. He and his men had just stopped to rest the horses. Watching the bend in the road, he waited for the riders to appear from behind the trees. The riders were many, and with a mission in mind, given the pace.

In a country of desperate people, one never knew what to expect. He placed his hand on the hilt of his sword. His men were immediately on their feet. He heard the collective whisper of their blades being unsheathed.

The first riders came into view. Simon was surprised when he recognized the group.

"Simon!" Jules jumped down from his horse almost before the animal came to a complete stop. "Angelica is gone!"

The words froze Simon's blood.

"What do you mean, gone?" he demanded. "She has nowhere to go!"

"We've searched both ships from top to bottom. She is not on board either. What's worse is that the other two ships have already set sail for Château Arles."

"*What?* Are you suggesting she's on one of those ships?"

Mathieu Godeau stepped forward. "Captain, I fear this is my fault. Your lady demanded to know your whereabouts, and I mentioned the party of men heading to Beaulieu. She paled at the very utterance of the name."

Simon felt sick inside. He'd sent a small party to Beaulieu to learn Angelica's stepfather's name, yet no doubt she thought he was proceeding with his original plan to eventually return her there, instead. *Merde!*

Within moments, Simon was racing back to his ships, intent on catching up with the two already sailing to the south of France. Near Genoa.

She's heading back to the convent...

He prayed he was right.

*****

Nicolas Fouquet stood before his massive desk scowling as he watched Pellisson, his paunchy gray-haired secretary, enter the library in his newly completed palace, Château Vaux-le-Vicomte.

"My lord, you wished to see me?"

"What took you so long? Never mind. I don't care. Take those brown ledgers and see that they're put in the *safe place* in my library at Beaulieu. See to the task personally, Pellisson. I want no mistakes."

"Of course, my lord," his trusted assistant responded. "It shall be done immediately."

"I'll have the black ledgers delivered to the king by Bruno."

"As you wish." Pellisson picked up the brown ledgers off the ebony side table.

Exasperated to the limit, Fouquet sat and slammed his fist down on the desk. "Have I not done an excellent job for France, Pellisson?"

"Absolutely, my lord!"

Fouquet rose to his feet, only mildly appeased by the answer. Walking around his desk, he stopped in front of the window to gaze out at his gardens. This château and its splendor was no less than he deserved. It stood as a testament to his success and skill in finance. Over the years, he had turned the impoverished treasury around and built Louis a financially sound kingdom.

"Yet Louis wishes to review *my* accounting," he growled, still reeling from the sting of such an insult. "Why does he question me at all? After all I have done... He should be indebted to me. The young fool has no idea how to run this country without me."

He turned to Pellisson. "Have I not always made certain that there were enough funds to pay for Mazarin's wars and the king's whims? Have I not done everything Louis and Mazarin have asked of me? And more?"

"Yes, my lord."

"Since Mazarin's death, Louis's demands are unceasing, and he gives the appearance that he does not trust me. It's intolerable!"

He began to pace across the rush mats that warmed the stone floor. For years, he'd worked tirelessly, enduring the demands of his post, enduring Mazarin. He'd shown the nobles—everyone—that he belonged in his exalted position. Without his accomplishments, the treasury would be bankrupt. "I intend to do something to remedy this situation, Pellisson."

Pellisson, holding the brown ledgers, stared at him with rapt attention.

Fouquet halted his steps, eager to share his intended course of action with his loyal servant. "Let Louis review the black ledgers all he wants. If he is looking for ways to flex his newly realized power, to answer the *cries of corruption* from the downtrodden"—Fouquet rolled his eyes—"then I shall serve up the perfect diversion until he forgets his ridiculous idea of ruling France by himself," he stated dryly, wishing that Louis was still engrossed in his ballets rather than affairs of state.

"A diversion, my lord?"

"A scapegoat."

"Who, my lord?"

"Someone who Louis could be made to believe is enough of a threat to him to gain his attention. There's a man who is the perfect choice. He's no more than a peasant who has tried to rise above his rank. He has been useful to us in the past, but now with the realm at peace, he's totally dispensable. No one of any significance would protest the arrest and ultimate execution of Simon Boulenger and his group of rebels, except perhaps the Marquis de Névelon, but that can be dealt with too. We shall serve Boulenger's head to Louis in a most convincing way. We'll dangle our carrot, and when Louis bites, we will have deflected the attention from ourselves. Then the king will stop obsessing with my accounting ledgers. I, of course, will see to Boulenger's capture. Louis will be grateful that his Superintendent of Finance has once again demonstrated his value and indispensability."

Fouquet sat back down behind his impressive ebony-and-gold-inlay desk. "I have the nobles in line, and the king will fall into place too. Since he is easily distracted, perhaps we'll find him a new mistress to occupy his time as well. One way or another, I intend to gain the position as First Minister and rule over France just as Mazarin did. *I've more than earned it.* Besides, it's about time someone capable and *French* rules this nation, don't you think? Everyone was sick of that Italian pig, Mazarin. See to the ledgers, Pellisson. Simon Boulenger's ships are due to arrive soon. Do inform me the moment he returns to France."

CHAPTER TWENTY-FOUR

Tired, dressed in men's clothes and a large hat with a long blue plume, Angelica followed the servant through the grand home of Robert d'Arles.

With each step she took, her stomach balked, still suffering the effects of her trip to the marquis's home. She'd traveled the distance from Simon's ship to Château Névelon on a rickety gravedigger's cart with the putrid smell of rotting flesh emanating from the wooden box it carried. With each new breeze, the stench had assailed her nostrils and oozed down her throat. It had taken considerable effort to hold down the contents of her stomach.

But she couldn't complain.

The gravedigger was the only one she'd come across who seemed trustworthy enough to take her to her destination. During the entire nauseating trip, Angelica had to force herself not to think about the deceased or wonder, given the relaxed rate at which the gravedigger traveled, how much worse the foul odor would get.

Thankfully, the gravedigger hadn't questioned her attire; he had taken her for a lad and not a woman traveling alone. She'd held her tongue for most of the trip, afraid to open her mouth while she fought down the bile. He seemed quite content to speak with little participation on her part, telling her just how many bodies he'd buried during the week, month, year.

Seeing the courtyard ahead, Angelica pushed aside the memory of her trip on the gravedigger's cart. Pushing aside the incessant ache for Simon wasn't so easy.

Dressed in oversized breeches tied at the waist with rope and an oversized doublet wasn't how she had wanted to present herself to her father's friend, but at the moment, her choices were limited, her circumstances dire.

She was relieved to learn from the majordomo that the marquis was very much alive and in residence, and she'd felt hopeful when the head servant returned to advise that the marquis would see her.

Entering the courtyard, the servant announced, "Angelica de Castel of the late Comte de Beaulieu." He bowed and stepped away.

Angelica swiped the hat from her head.

Seated at a stone table was a striking older gentleman with salt-and-pepper hair and broad shoulders. He was staring at her as if he were seeing a ghost.

"Sir, forgive me for this intrusion, and for my mode of dress," she began.

He struggled to rise, waving off the assistance of a servant. He grimaced, then straightened. Standing, he was nearly as tall as Simon, yet he leaned heavily on his cane.

"Come closer," he ordered.

She approached, wondering for the thousandth time what she would do if he cast her out.

His gray eyes scrutinized her face for what seemed an eternity.

"I thought Étienne's only daughter had been dead for some time now. Yet, I see in you a striking resemblance to the late Louise Fourché." His tone was incredulous. "You have her unforgettable eyes. Can it be that you are truly Angelica?"

At the mention of her parents, her losses suddenly felt overwhelming. She'd lost them, and Simon. She was alone. Destitute. Tears threatened to spill. She fought them back, refusing to break. Not now. Not in front of the marquis.

Lifting her chin a notch, she looked him directly in the eyes and said, "I swear, I am who I say I am. I know it is shocking, my sudden appearance, dressed in this fashion… But you were my father's friend. He spoke highly of you… I have nowhere else to go…" Her predicament was truly desperate, for she was placing her trust at the feet of a man of whom she had only a vague recollection.

"*Dieu*, you even have her melodious voice," he said. "I've never turned away from a woman in distress. However, I have a question. Tell me, out of the many fine attributes Louise had, what was the one that Étienne loved so—that first drew him to her on the day they met?"

"Her voice, sir. My mother sang that day, thinking she was alone in the gardens. Throughout the years, she sang to both of us, often at my father's behest."

He smiled then, his eyes shining warmly at her.

"Have I passed your test?"

"You have."

Thank God...

He shook his head in disbelief. "I cannot believe Étienne's daughter lives. Where have you been all these years?"

"In a convent, outside of France. I've been hiding from my stepfather."

The marquis's eyes filled with concern. "Why? What has he done?"

She'd come a long way in a short time, thanks to Simon. He'd taught her to confide in others. "The worst thing a stepfather can do to a young stepdaughter. A shameful act that disgraced her and forced her to flee." She would have never voiced this to the marquis or anyone months ago.

"Good Lord! I'm so sorry." He placed his hand on her shoulder. "You're welcome to stay here, as long as you want. I will protect you as best I can."

Relief washed over her. "Thank you for your kindness. I trust you will keep this information to yourself."

"You have my word," he assured. "Your stepfather has told everyone that you're dead. No doubt he wishes it. You should be aware that there have been changes to his status since you've been gone. He is now the Marquis de Belle-Isle, and, many would argue, the most powerful man in the realm. He's become the Superintendent of Finance."

Her heart dropped to her stomach. The Superintendent of Finance. Dear God. That was the man Simon had spoken of. The man who was corrupt and was causing so much suffering. Of course, it was her stepfather. Who else could be so unconscionable?

She and Simon shared a common enemy, and he would learn of it soon enough. He was, after all, headed to Beaulieu. It would give him yet another reason not to be a part of her life, for to be involved with the stepdaughter of his foe would be foolhardy.

Knowing her stepfather's cruel nature, she could never endanger Simon by doing anything that might cause Fouquet to discover her whereabouts and link her and Simon together. The best and only thing she could do was to stay away from Simon.

It was what he wanted anyway.

Now that she knew how powerful Fouquet had become, her stay in France would have to be very brief. Despite the marquis's kind offer, she had to find some place to go. Some place to live out the rest of her life.

"Forgive me, you must be exhausted. Have you any other clothes?"

"Yes. They're in my valise. I left it with your majordomo, Monsi—"

"Enough formalities. Call me Robert. I have no less than a hundred questions rushing through my mind, yet I can see how weary you are. I'll have a room prepared for you and a meal sent to you. Rest. We can talk this evening."

*****

Simon stood rigid and tense on the deck of the ship captained by Armand while the crew searched it for Angelica.

After ten days, Simon and Jules had managed to catch up with the two ships that were sailing to the south of France. They'd searched the first ship from top to bottom without finding any trace of her.

Armand's ship was his last hope.

As he stood with Jules and Armand, his heart pounded away the time. Four ships were anchored in the water. Four sets of crewman's orders stayed while the search was carried out. The silence was thick and heavy. Not one man uttered a single comment.

While he waited. And waited. Hoping she would appear with one of his men. Safe.

The ship's lieutenant approached.

"Well?" Armand demanded.

Simon knew the words he was about to hear simply by the look on the man's face.

"She's not on board, Commander. Captain, there's no sign that she was ever on board."

Simon's heart plummeted. Hearing the words was far worse than anticipating them. If she wasn't on board his ships, she was in the realm.

Alone.

Fear the likes of which he'd never known clutched him in its vise.

Jules placed a hand on Simon's shoulder. "Simon, we'll find her."

If ever he believed he knew anything at all of hell from his past experiences, then he was mistaken. Nothing felt worse than this hollow sense of loss, this terrifying concern he had for the woman he loved.

He had no idea where she was, how she was, and he had no one to blame but himself for her perilous predicament.

Throughout the voyage, he'd stopped her each time she'd attempted to tell him how she felt about him. He'd withheld his own feelings from her. Then, immediately upon reaching France, he'd left her on the ship to chase down *nobility*. *Dieu!*

He couldn't blame her for leaving him. He'd given her no reason to stay. He'd driven her out of his life and into danger. Because of his stubbornness. Because of his beliefs about social status being important. To hell with social position.

Jésus-Christ. She loved him. Just as he was.

But he hadn't embraced it! Instead, he'd kept her at arm's length. Fucking fool!

In the strongest voice Simon could muster, he ordered all four ships to return with him, wanting to have access to as many men as possible. He would tear France apart looking for her.

And he would exhaust every man until she was found. He *would* find her, and yes, she would be safe. She had to be safe. He'd tell her exactly how he felt about her. If she would still have him, he'd marry her. And spend the rest of his days making it up to her.

*****

Angelica heard the commotion from the top of the staircase—an argument between men. Since her arrival a week ago, she'd found Robert's home to be always peaceful. A sanctuary from the danger that lurked for her outside. She rushed down to see what was amiss.

At the bottom of the stairs, she froze. Caught in her gaze was the one the young girl inside her once called *Evil*. She'd know that light brown hair, that tall, slender build anywhere.

Nicolas Fouquet stood in the entrance hall of Robert's home with another man he called Pellisson. Pellisson's argument with Robert's majordomo ceased the moment the three men noticed her. Cold terror froze her blood and limbs.

"Well, well." Fouquet tossed his cape at the servant's face. His dark, soulless eyes raked over her in lewd assessment, making her feel naked. Violated.

A slimy sense of revulsion slid down her throat to her stomach. Her heart pounded. She prayed somehow he didn't recognize her.

"And here I thought, Pellisson, that the marquis had become a recluse. Yet, it's obvious that he has found a beautiful woman in which—" Fouquet arrested his words as recognition struck.

Her legs almost gave way.

He stepped toward her, all smugness dissipated, replaced by horrified astonishment. She stepped back, the air suddenly becoming thin and difficult to inhale. Years fell away. It was as though she wasn't a grown woman but a girl, feeling trapped and vulnerable. Terrified.

"*You?*" Fouquet's characteristic haughtiness deflated with the single word, his complexion ashen.

"Please, my lord, as I've told you, the marquis is not accepting visitors today," the servant said.

Fouquet gave no sign he heard the servant's words as he continued to stare at her, incredulous.

A voice inside her screamed, *Flee!* Another demanded, *Kill him!* Yet, she remained stock-still, overcome by shock.

"It's not possible... How can it be... What...are you...?" The fragmented words came out of him as small, breathless sounds. Gone was his insolent self-assuredness.

"May I help you, sir?" The bellow came from the former Commodore of the French Navy, startling her. She turned and saw an uncustomary scowl on Robert's face as he stood erect and tall in the doorway of his study. Despite his cane, he looked strong, well-muscled from years of a physical life at sea—a sharp contrast to most soft-bellied nobles half his age.

A formidable adversary.

Fouquet tore his eyes away from her. "What is she doing here?"

"Sir, what I do and who I have in my home is none of your concern. Unlike other nobles, I am not financially indebted to you. Nor do I have any family members you can scandalize to bend my will to yours." Robert's eyes narrowed. "I don't answer to you."

Fouquet stiffened. She saw the flash of fury in his eyes, remembering that volatile temper all too well. He turned to face her. "You will come with me!" He grabbed at her. She jumped back, avoiding physical contact with him.

"You will not touch my future wife!" Robert's voice resonated. She gasped.

Fouquet spun back around to face Robert. "Your *what?*"

"Wife." Robert announced firmly.

Fouquet tossed his head back with a roar of laughter. "Névelon, your injury must be to your head. You cannot marry her without my permission."

"Ah, but you will give your consent, and I shall marry her," Robert interjected. "Then she will no longer be of concern to you."

"Oh? And why would I give my consent for this match? Have you gotten her with child?"

Robert motioned for the servant to leave, ignoring the sting of Fouquet's words. His injury had done more damage than Robert would ever admit. He could never bring himself to tell anyone just how debilitating his condition had become and how it had unmanned him. The servant promptly handed Fouquet's cape to Pellisson and left.

With a finger, Robert indicated to Fouquet to approach. Fouquet's lips twitched with amusement. He sauntered over. As soon as he was within arm's reach, Robert seized a fistful of the man's fine doublet and yanked him close, the brim of Fouquet's hat, with its large purple plume, butting against Robert's forehead.

"You will speak of her with the utmost respect, and you will agree to this match unless you wish to be disgraced by having others learn of your *incestuous tendencies*," he growled. How he hated Fouquet for what he'd done to the beautiful woman who now lived with him. Over the last week, he'd grown increasingly fond of Angelica and accustomed to her company. She filled his lonely days. He admired her strength, her gentle grace, and found himself often wishing he could take away the sadness she tried to hide.

A smirk slowly spread across Fouquet's mouth. "Would you have her scandalized as well?"

It was Robert's turn to smile with malevolence. "Thanks to you, she has nothing left to lose. You, on the other hand, have a great distance to fall."

Fouquet's smile dissolved.

Robert continued, "I've had the papers drawn up. They are on my desk. Your unexpected visit has saved me the trouble of coming to see you. If you are wise, you will sign them. Don't tempt me to bring shame to your *good* name with our newly inspired king."

Robert held Fouquet's gaze with ruthless determination. He knew Fouquet was under heavy scrutiny from Louis of late. It was what Robert was counting on to sway him. He kept his features schooled in an expression that had intimidated men under his command over the years.

"You want her," Fouquet forced out tightly, "you can have her, but Beaulieu is mine."

"An appropriate dowry has been indicated on the papers. For appearance's sake, you will make certain it is provided. Sign the marriage contract. Then get out of my home." Robert released him abruptly.

Fouquet smoothed his clothing and threw Angelica a glare. She returned his gaze, her regard full of loathing for the devil incarnate before them.

Fouquet walked past Robert and hastily signed the parchments on his desk. Robert waited and watched in the doorway. The pain shooting up his leg was virtually unbearable. Standing still was agony. Yet, he forced himself to do it, relying on his naval discipline to disguise his suffering. To show no weakness.

When Fouquet finished, he approached. "I came here today for an entirely different matter, certainly not expecting you to be harboring my long-lost stepdaughter."

"State your business," Robert commanded.

Leaning in, he murmured, "There is a certain man, one you would all but call a son. Simon Boulenger. His ships were spotted in France, but they disappeared as quickly as they came. Do tell him that the Superintendent of Finance wishes a meeting." He smiled.

Robert's mind raced as a deep sense of unease seeped into his marrow. Simon was back in France? Why hadn't he contacted him? What the hell was Fouquet up to?

"Tell him yourself. I haven't seen him for many months." He kept his voice bland.

Overwhelmed, Angelica couldn't hear a word they were saying over her thundering heart. She saw Fouquet lift a brow, step back, and bow to Robert. With an arrogant strut, he walked across the large foyer toward her. A sick memory rose before her eyes, causing her stomach to heave and twist. Quaking, she forced herself not to step back. Nor lunge at his throat.

Fouquet stopped before her, an indulgent smile on his lips. "Daughter, you have caused me concern over the years. Where have you been all this time?"

She wanted to slap the smile from his face. Or perhaps sink a dagger into his black, shriveled heart. Instead, she shot back, "I am certain you have fretted little about me."

"Ah, but you are wrong. I thought you were dead. Imagine my newfound delight to know you are alive and well." A terrifying coldness entered his eyes, despite that wicked smile. That same look that had destroyed her mother and had haunted Angelica many nights. In a low growl, he said, "You will keep silent about our past, and you will encourage the marquis to do the same, unless you wish to become a widow soon after you become a bride. Also, you will go along with whatever explanation I give to people regarding your sudden return." He glanced at Robert. "It would seem that you are getting a husband. The marquis is known for his reputation with women, preferring, no doubt, something more passionate in bed than the corpse your mother was."

Her palm stung. His expression turned to shock. She realized that she'd just cracked her hand across his cheek. Yet she didn't feel enough satisfaction from the deed.

"Do not speak of her with your vile tongue," Angelica hissed out between clenched teeth, shaking with rage.

His cruel eyes narrowed. "*How dare you...*"

"I dare," she tossed out, challenging him, her hands fisted at her sides.

"*Enough!*" Robert bellowed.

Fouquet formed another smile, regaining his composure, showing another of his many false faces. "It would seem she has grown impudent as well as beautiful, Névelon. You'll have your hands full. Enjoy." Fouquet stepped back. "You'll both forgive me if I don't attend the wedding?" His bow was mocking. He spun and snatched his cape from Pellisson. Pellisson quickly followed his master out.

She slumped against the wall. She had no more tears left. She felt only bone-chilling dread. Now her stepfather knew she was alive.

He knew where to find her.

Wasn't it bad enough that she missed Simon terribly—that he came to her each night in her bittersweet dreams, only to wake up to the cruel reality, with years of loneliness and emptiness yawning before her? Did she have to have an encounter with her stepfather too?

She was furious with herself. She should've done more. Said more. Made him somehow pay for all the pain he'd inflicted on her. On her mother. But she'd done nothing but deliver a pathetic slap to his face. It wasn't enough. By simply walking into the room, he'd humiliatingly caused her to regress to a fourteen-year-old girl, forcing her to battle that child's fears.

She squeezed her eyes shut and heard Robert approach. He placed a hand on her shoulder. "I know that was most difficult for you. Are you all right?"

She nodded. Then shook her head.

"I understand. I think you handled yourself well, under the extreme circumstances."

She looked into his concerned eyes. "Robert, what is all this about marriage?"

"Your father was a friend and a good man. I wish to help you as best I can. Protecting you from Fouquet is not easy. He's far too powerful—power he'll exert to your detriment without a husband's protection. Angelica, you cannot run and hide indefinitely. And you need funds to survive. Though I was planning to ask your thoughts on marriage before ever discussing it with him, please know I had your best interest at heart."

Dear God, he was serious about this.

"If you marry me, you'll be financially secure and protected. In the event of my death, you'll have wealth, influence, as well as a widow's independence. You'll be safe from Fouquet."

He caressed her cheek. Her eyes suddenly filled with tears, dipping into a reserve she hadn't known existed. She'd wanted to hear a marriage proposal, but only from Simon. No one else. Not even from this dear, sweet man before her.

"I must confess," he continued, "that my motives are not entirely gallant. I have never married. I made my career my bride. However, I've reached a point in my life that I wish for a wife to share the rest of my days with. Even one who loves another."

She stiffened.

He smiled. "I know the signs of a woman suffering from a broken heart. Whoever he is, he's a fool." He paused, the look on his distinguished face soft. "I'm willing to consent to a *mariage de convenance*, as they say," he added. "I would be honored to have you for a wife. It would certainly make me the envy of every man in the realm. Tell me you will marry me."

CHAPTER TWENTY-FIVE

Under the mantle of night, Simon raced on horseback, maneuvering through the narrow streets of Paris. Jules and Armand fought to keep up. Given the hour, the streets were mostly deserted. Passing darkened homes and shops, the only sounds Simon heard were the clattering of the horses' hooves on the cobblestone road and his thundering heart. Only the king's private guard was permitted to race through the streets, but at the moment, Simon didn't care.

He'd wasted considerable time going back and forth with his ships. Each day, no, each hour that Angelica was alone only increased his anxiety. Sick with worry, he couldn't eat. Sleep came only when he was consumed by fatigue—his fitful slumber plagued by nightmares of her lying lifeless by the side of the road. He had to speak to Robert. Without further delay. Negotiating another turn, he urged his horse onward.

He'd already organized search parties, searching villages, towns, and, more frighteningly, Paris itself—with all of its iniquities. With a population of more than one hundred thousand, thieves and murderers weren't difficult to find in certain areas of the city, especially at night.

He slowed his horse as he approached the Palais-Royale, the new court theater, located near the Louvre. Molière and his troupe had recently moved here after the former theater had been demolished. With any luck, Robert might be attending one of Molière's comedies. Knowing how much Louis enjoyed the theater, it was like

Robert to try to seize opportunities to gain the king's ear. If Robert was here, it would save Simon the trip out to Château Névelon.

He needed to gain any information he could about the late Comte de Beaulieu—any acquaintances he may have had or friends Angelica might have turned to, praying she'd found someone trustworthy to help her.

He dismounted. His every muscle taut, Simon marched to the gilded doors of Richelieu's former Palais and entered. People were enjoying, according to the painted sign, *The School for Husbands*. Laughter echoed in the grand corridor, emanating from within the theater.

Jules caught up to him. "Wait." He grabbed Simon's arm, looking around. "You cannot just charge in there. We haven't had time to attain adequate information about what we're facing in France. Furthermore, you're not in the best frame of mind. Let me go. I'll see if I can spot Robert."

"No!" He yanked his arm free. "I'll go." As Simon took a step, Armand placed a hand on his shoulder.

"Listen to Jules, Simon. You're exhausted. We all are. We should not be hasty in our actions... You've taught us that. We cannot risk—"

"Not hasty? *Jésus-Christ*, Armand! How can you say that when—" Simon's words died in his throat the moment a haunting melody rose from the theater. Though slightly muffled, it was distinct, beautiful. *And familiar.* He couldn't move. His ears strained, eagerly trying to draw in the angelic singer's voice.

By God. Was he so far gone that his ears were playing him false? Simon fisted Jules's doublet. "Do you hear that?"

Jules nodded, his stunned gaze traveling to the closed doors of the theater.

The divine voice swirled around Simon. He was afraid to do anything that would shatter the hope swelling in his heart.

He remained fixed to the spot, the magnificent performance quieting his tumultuous emotions. There could be no other who had the same enchanting voice. No other had this effect on him.

It had to be Angelica.

He charged forward.

"Simon!" Jules exclaimed as both Jules and Armand halted Simon's advance.

He drew his sword. "Stand aside. That is Angelica," he insisted. "I'm going to her. I'll not debate this."

Jules stepped back, pulling Armand with him. "I never argue with a man holding a sword. Good luck."

Simon had never drawn his sword on friends, yet now wasn't the time to reflect on his actions. He sheathed his rapier, pulled open the door, and slipped inside.

Filled to capacity, the theater held hundreds of people. The balconies that ran along the sides all had spectators in them. As the singing continued, Simon edged his way through the crowd, unable to see the stage. By the time he found a spot that offered an unobstructed view, the angelic voice had stopped.

There were a number of actors in colorful costumes, moving about enthusiastically to the music, singing in chorus. He began discounting them one by one until he was left with a woman wearing a purple gown and a hat with large, silver-colored plumes. Her back was to the audience. The others sang around her while she stood in the center, silent and still.

Simon could hear his own breathing, quick and shallow, waiting for the woman to turn around, praying it was her. At the crescendo, the woman with the silver plumes spun around. Spreading her arms, she sang out, filling every ear with the full power of her enchanting voice. *Angelica...*

Simon's knees gave way as he slumped back against the wall he hadn't known was there. An urge to weep with relief almost discomposed him there and then. *She's alive.*

A sudden cheer and vigorous applause exploded around him.

Angelica, smiling, curtsied. The other actors moved aside as Louis stepped onto the stage and kissed her hand.

Knowing Louis's reputation for womanizing, Simon's heart leaped into his throat.

Realizing the performance was over, he made his way through the masses, keeping his head down but his eyes on Angelica. Immersing himself in as much shadow as he could find, he kept to the perimeter of the long room. Fouquet could be here, and until he had up-to-date information from his spies in Fouquet's household, he didn't wish to be spotted by him.

Clenching his teeth, Simon watched as the king helped her down from the stage and kissed her hand again. She curtsied once more and made her way to the doors behind the stage.

Simon reached the doors shortly afterward and walked surreptitiously down a narrow corridor filled with actors retreating into small dressing rooms. It didn't take long for him to spot the hat with the silver plumes in the distance.

Maneuvering his way through the crowd, his eyes never left her.

He saw Angelica stop and exchange a few brief words with a female before she entered one of the rooms and closed the door. Simon pressed forward, her door coming closer and closer. His heart hammered louder and harder.

When at last he reached it, he gave a quick look around. The crowd had diminished significantly. He saw Jules and Armand moving toward him quickly, yet not so fast as to draw attention.

Simon placed his hand on the door latch and paused. He hadn't seen her in far too many tortured weeks.

Jules touched his shoulder. Sotto voce, he said, "Have you found her?"

"Yes. It's Angelica."

Jules smiled. "Go on, Simon, get your lady. We'll watch your back."

Simon took a breath and let it out slowly, then opened the door and stepped inside.

His eyes scanned the small room. A dressing table. A chair. A mirror. Costumes strewn about. But no Angelica.

Panicked, he closed the door and spun around. A rustling sound came from behind the tall dressing screen.

"Is that you, Brigitte?" her unmistakable voice called out. "I told you, I will return for another performance. Perhaps in a fortnight?"

His throat constricted.

"Brigitte, are you playing with me?" she inquired as she stepped out from behind the screen, smoothing her gown.

Angelica's breath froze in her throat. There was Simon, standing before her. His dark hair was tousled, and his heart-melting eyes stared at her intently. Just like the many dreams she'd had of him. When she'd eventually awaken without him.

He'd never looked more beautiful. Her chest tightened as her eyes drank their fill. He stepped forward and pulled her into his arms. His mouth came down on hers. His kiss was lush and tender, as if he wanted to draw all the emptiness and sadness from her.

Her heart soared.

Her soul swelled back to life.

She melted into him, trembling and aching with a need so fierce it shook every fiber of her being.

"Angelica," he murmured. She delighted at the sound of his voice in her ears. "I've been so worried. *Dieu*, I've missed you so…"

This was no dream. His lips, his arms, his words were real. She felt a surge of anguish. She was dangerously close to losing the fragile hold she had on her strength to resist.

He was potent. Addictive.

And she was vulnerable to him.

He'd completely destroy her this time if she allowed him in even a tiny bit. How easy it would be to give herself over to the feelings he stirred.

She couldn't do it. Especially now. *God help her…*

His hands moved down her back, and he pulled her more tightly against him as if he never wanted to let her go.

"Angelica… I found you," he whispered between kisses. "I cannot believe I found you."

He drew back and cupped her face, staring at her with joy on his handsome visage. His face blurred behind her hot tears.

"Don't weep." He kissed each one that slipped down her cheeks. "I never want to make you cry. Everything will be all right. I'll do whatever it takes to make it so." He kissed her again.

She had no idea how she managed it, but she pulled away. "Please, Simon, we cannot—" Words failed her. Her hands were on his strong arms. His body trembled too. She looked around, searching for strength.

He turned her face, forcing her to look into his eyes. They weren't guarded but open, his heart reflecting therein. "You're right. This is not the place for this. Come with me. I know an inn outside of Paris."

She shook her head. Another large tear slipped down her cheek.

"To talk!" he quickly added. "There's much to say that has not been said. Give me the chance to make matters right between us." His blue eyes were soft and pleading.

"I cannot come with you, Simon." She took in a ragged breath. "You must go."

"*Go?* No, I cannot." He pulled her back into his arms, and buried his face in her hair. "I love you. Angelica, I love you…"

She choked on a sob before she swallowed hard, unable to restrain the tears that poured from her eyes. How cruel those words sounded in her ears now—those three words she'd longed to hear from him for so long. He was offering them freely—when she was unable to cherish them.

"It's too late, Simon." She was barely capable of speaking as she tottered under the weight of her pain. "I'm…married."

He staggered back. "*What…?*" It was the barest whisper. In his eyes was the desperate hope that he'd heard incorrectly.

With her heart in her throat, she repeated, "I'm married." She couldn't stand his look of devastation. Devastation she shared. He'd had plenty of chances to tell her this before! Why did he have to do this to her now? Her heart fragmented a little more with every moment she lingered in his presence. "I must go." She tried to bolt, but he grabbed her arm and pulled her to him.

"To whom!"

His look gave her pause. It was dark with the promise of violence. The last thing she wanted was for Simon to go after Robert.

"I'm married, Simon. What difference does it make who my husband is? It is done. You must…go on with your life." Speechless, he stared at her with horrified disbelief. She easily pulled her arm out of his slackening grasp. "I wish you happiness in your life and a woman worthy enough to share it with you." Vision blurred by tears, she rushed from the room, not stopping to acknowledge Jules or Armand, desperate to flee while she still possessed the ability to do so. Leaving Simon for a second, *and final*, time was inexpressible torture.

Simon placed his hands on his hips, dragging his breaths up and down his throat, a cold, almost numbing sensation flooding his body.

Jules and Armand rushed in.

"Simon?" Jules inquired.

The word "married" had stabbed through him, slicing cleanly through the heart. The pain was unmercifully keen. Grabbing a nearby chair, he slammed it against the mirror. The force of the impact shattered it, sending shards of glass spraying out.

"*Dieu!*" Armand exclaimed.

Simon spun around to face his friends. "She's married." He forced the words out from between clenched teeth.

"*Merde.* I'm so sorry," Jules said. "Come, we must leave here. There are too many nobles about, and we don't know who is friend or foe. Armand, go outside. See if Robert is here. If not, we'll go to Névelon straightaway. If Angelica has married an Aristo, then surely Robert would know who this man is. He'll know more about the situation."

Armand gave a nod and ran out.

A silence fell upon the room. Simon was lost in his thoughts, fighting to think clearly through the misery and staggering sense of loss, unable to just walk away. To give her up.

"Jules," he finally spoke up. "I *will* learn this man's name, and I *will* get her back. *This I swear.* Whoever he is, his days with her are numbered."

Armand burst into the room. "Robert is here!" he announced with an urgent whisper. "He'll meet us at the back of the building. He's most anxious to talk to you, Simon."

Within minutes, the three men stood behind the Palais-Royal, shrouded by the night. Rain began to fall. Robert approached on horseback, alone. He stopped before them, not attempting to climb down.

"Simon, where have you been? Fouquet has been to my home looking for you. Until we know exactly what he wants from you, you must stay away from him."

"He can go to hell," Simon growled.

"Be that as it may, we must talk. Come to Névelon. Make certain no one follows you. Use the cellar entrance. I'll see that your usual room is ready, along with rooms for Jules and Armand. Early on the morrow, we'll talk."

Simon nodded. "There is much that I must discuss with you."

*****

The next morning, Simon sat down to break fast with Robert, his eyes raw, his head aching. When he'd entered through the cellar last eve, he'd taken as much wine as he could carry up to his room. And drank it all.

At times, during the long hours of the night, he could swear he smelled her fragrance, proving that either he was going mad or that the copious amounts of wine he'd consumed had taunting powers never before realized.

He slept less than an hour before a somber-faced servant woke him to join the marquis. It had been a hellish night as images of Angelica in another man's arms tortured him.

Their kiss last eve tormented him as well. He'd thought about it all night long, the soft feel of her mouth. And how she'd returned his kiss. She'd welcomed his touch, his embrace. The same intense emotions between them were still there. Of this he was certain. She *did* still love him. She'd married simply out of desperation. No, all was not lost. There was hope. As long as there was love, there was hope. He would hold on to that thought.

He'd heard her say she would return for another performance in a fortnight. If Robert was unable to help him with information about Angelica and her new husband, then he would return to the theater and learn all that he could between now and then. Somehow, he would undo this mess. He wouldn't relent until she was his. First, he had to get her to admit her love for him—win her trust and belief in him again.

Then he would deal with the issue of her husband.

"You look terrible," Robert said.

"Thank you," he retorted dryly, feeling irritable.

"There are matters to discuss, Simon, but first I wish to tell you some good news."

"Oh? I could definitely use some good news."

A large grin appeared on Robert's face. "I have married, and I am most anxious for you to meet her."

Simon's brows shot up. "Married?" *Merde.* Was everyone running to the altar suddenly? He offered what he hoped was a semblance of a pleasant smile. "Congratulations." Despite his own misery, he was truly happy to learn that Robert, a renowned bachelor, a man who for decades had enjoyed the sexual favors of countless beauties, had finally found one he wanted to marry. And had. Simon forced back the envy. "I look forward to meeting this extraordinary woman who has managed to get you to the altar when so many others failed."

Robert continued to smile. "She's a rare beauty. I've asked her to join us. But first, I must tell you that Louis has asked to see Fouquet's accounting ledgers and has handed them over to Jean-Baptiste Colbert for review. You will remember that Colbert worked under Mazarin. He has great skill with accounts and knows of Fouquet's excessive expenditures and outrageous profits."

"Really?" He couldn't have cared less. He wanted to discuss Angelica.

"Since Mazarin's death, I think Louis has finally seen that Fouquet is a threat to his throne. With all his arrogance, Fouquet doesn't see that he's doomed. He reassures himself, no doubt, by the fact that he has more nobles on his side than the young king. But Louis is not a fool. Change is coming, and with our king's new attitude, I believe he will finally recognize your achievements for France, peacetime or not. In the meantime, however, you must be cautious. Fouquet is up to something."

Simon would see what his spies had to say about Fouquet's plans. Until he knew more, he was resourceful enough to avoid him. Right now, he couldn't think about Fouquet, delivering the silver from *La Estrella Blanca* to the king, or even Angelica's stepfather. His priority was Angelica.

"There is something I should tell you about my wife before she arrives," Robert said.

"Oh?"

"She is Fouquet's stepdaughter."

"*What?*"

"I know. It is a shock. But I assure you, there is no affection in her heart for the man, and he is a sensitive subject for her. When he came here looking for you, his presence quite upset her—"

Just then, Jules and Armand entered the room. Robert ended his conversation and invited them to join the meal.

Fouquet's stepdaughter? Who knew he had one? Fouquet's present wife, Marie-Madeleine, had been only fifteen when Fouquet had married her ten years ago. Fouquet was twenty-one years her senior. Robert's wife must be the child of Fouquet's first wife. Yet, Simon knew nothing about her except that she'd died years before Fouquet became Superintendent of Finance.

A servant entered and whispered in Robert's ear. He grinned and nodded.

"Gentlemen, I have been advised that my wife will be here shortly. She apologizes for her delay this morning."

Jules and Armand were instantly on their feet, congratulating him on his marriage.

Despite his shock over the news about Robert's wife, Simon suppressed a smile. Apparently, not even a leg injury of this magnitude could keep Robert from his husbandly duties. The poor woman was no doubt exhausted by his infamous stamina.

Simon was looking forward to meeting the new Marquise de Névelon.

CHAPTER TWENTY-SIX

As Angelica approached the dining room, muffled male voices drifted to her. She'd tarried in her room long enough, hoping that by now all telling signs of her night of tears were no longer apparent.

She couldn't believe Simon had found her last night.

She couldn't forget his words, his kiss, or the fact that they had come far too late.

She could never be with him. Not now. She was married, and though it was a marriage that had never been consummated, she'd nonetheless made a commitment. She could never betray Robert in any way. His kindness and love would not be met with abandonment on her part. Last night, she'd raged, she'd wept, and now she was simply numb.

Stopping at the door, Angelica drew in a breath and let it out slowly.

Being with company was the last thing she wanted, yet Robert was eager for her to meet the men within, stating, with affection in his voice, that he'd taken one of these men under his wing when he was just a boy and practically raised him, educated him. It was important to Robert for her to attend the morning meal, and therefore she had to make an effort to play the role of the cordial hostess. This was a small sacrifice to make for dear Robert.

A round of male laughter erupted just as she opened the door.

"Ah, there you are, my darling." Robert struggled but managed to stand. She offered him a smile.

Her gaze fell upon Simon.

Her heart jumped, lodging in her throat.

Simon turned to her. The smile on his beautiful mouth dissolved the moment their gazes locked. His blue eyes turned from shock to horror.

Dear...God...

She'd spent the night trying to come to terms with the fact that he loved her and she would never see him again.

Now he was here. He knew Robert. Her pulse doubled.

She was trapped within those familiar blue eyes. Eyes that had often gazed at her with tenderness or passion now stared at her with astonishment, heart-shattered. Last eve, that very look had torn her heart asunder.

She couldn't stand to have him stare at her that way. Not again.

"Angelica." Robert's voice snapped her out of her thoughts. "Darling, I asked you if you are all right." Robert's eyes were full of concern.

She clasped her hands tightly and forced a smile. "I'm fine."

She could feel Simon's gaze on her. She fought back the compulsion to run to him, throw her arms around him, never to let go again.

Instead, she forced her shaky limbs forward and approached her husband's three guests, as any lady of the château would. Her mind spun, unsure what to do now. The room was far too warm. The walls were closing in on her. What would Simon do now that he knew the identity of her husband? Would he tell Robert the truth? What would be the point? What good would it do to inform Robert that the man she loved was the very man seated at his table?

"Gentlemen, I'd like to introduce to you my wife..." Robert's tone was full of pride, his voice drifting in and out of her mind as she tried to sort through her whirling thoughts, to decide how best to handle the situation at hand. Jules approached her first. He took her hand. Bowing before her, he placed a light kiss to it.

"*Enchanté.*" Jules's gaze held hers for a moment. He was clearly dumbfounded but thankfully hadn't given her away.

Armand did the same.

"Darling, this is Simon Boulenger, the man I was telling you about. He's the captain of a fleet of privateer ships for France. Very successful. I, of course, taught him everything he knows." Robert chuckled.

Out of the corner of her eye, she saw Simon rise and walk toward her. Unable to meet his gaze, afraid of what it would do to either one of them if they looked into each other's eyes, she stared at his perfect left ear. She forced herself not to think about how many times she'd kissed that ear, focusing instead on keeping her pounding heart from puncturing through her chest.

He stopped before her. His familiar scent surrounded her, devastating her.

He took her hand, a hand she had neglected to offer. Was his hand trembling as well? Or was it only hers? He stiffly bowed and murmured an appropriate greeting.

At the touch of his lips to her knuckle, her pulse surged. Briefly, she closed her eyes. Locking her knees, she tried to steady herself on her wobbly legs.

He released her hand immediately, not dallying a moment longer than was necessary—a painful reminder of the reality of the situation. A new dimension to her pain.

She wasn't his to touch.

Simon stepped away from her.

"Angelica, you look quite pale. Are you certain you are all right?" Robert asked.

Somehow, she found her voice. "I'm just a little tired after last night's performance, Robert."

Robert shook his head in dismay. "I took you to the Palais-Royale thinking you would find it enjoyable. I should have anticipated Louis's roving eye would focus on you." Robert turned to the men in the room and explained, "The king learned that my wife can sing. She has quite an exceptional voice, in fact. I never expected him to insist that my wife return to perform in one of Molière's comedies for him. This is my fault." Robert sat down slowly, wincing, looking very much vexed at himself. "Simon, my leg is quite stiff today. Will you kindly escort my wife back to her chambers so that she may rest?"

"No!" she exclaimed. "I mean to say...I'm quite capable of returning to my chambers alone. Do not put Monsieur Boulenger to the task unnecessarily." She smiled for her husband, though she could scarcely breathe.

"Nonsense. He does not mind. Do you, Simon?"

Simon, beset by grief, faced the greatest challenge in his life as he attempted to remain composed before Robert.

Angelica... His moonlight angel... Fouquet's stepdaughter. Robert's wife.

Dieu... What malevolent force could bring about such a cruel twist of fate? He was in agony, certain his soul had torn the moment he laid eyes on her standing in Robert's dining room.

He could never, not ever, come between Robert and his wife. A dagger through the gullet would be less painful and more welcome than knowing that she was now lost to him forever.

He had never known pain like this—a slicing sensation tearing him apart from the inside in slow, excruciating degrees. Since she'd entered the room, his mind screamed one word repeatedly. *NO! NO! NO-O-O-O!*

"No," he managed to croak out.

With her hand in the crook of his arm, Simon escorted her from the room. Silently, they walked toward the stairs at the opposite side of the large foyer. Though they touched, she was now beyond his grasp.

Lost to him.

"Simon...?"

He didn't respond, keeping his gaze straight ahead. He felt vacant inside, his eyes probably no different than the sightless eyes he'd seen on dead men in battle.

"Please, say something to me. I welcome anything over your silence."

Fouquet was her stepfather. Robert was her husband.

He could find no words to express what he felt.

He stopped at the foot of the stairs. "Madame la Marquise, what is there to say?" He didn't look at her as he offered his words. They began to climb the stairs, his muscles beneath her fingers stiff and tense.

Fouquet... Robert... *Dieu...*

"Simon, please don't." He heard the pain in her voice. He wasn't trying to hurt her. He simply had to get away from her before he completely humiliated himself. In this moment, when he'd lost everything that mattered, pride, albeit a small thing, was all he had left to hold on to.

He stopped at the top of the stairs and removed her hand from his arm. "You've made your choice and a wise one at that. The daughter of a comte should marry a marquis." He gave her a curt bow. "I trust that you are able to make your way from this point without me."

*****

There wasn't enough wine in the entire realm to douse the hell that burned inside him, though Simon made an earnest effort to try. Lying on the bed in his chambers in Robert's home, he swore. Where was the servant with more wine?

The wine he'd consumed thus far had barely taken the edge off the stabbing emotional pain that pierced through every inch of his being.

The day could not have ticked away more slowly. Both the marquis and marquise had retired to their chambers, remaining there until dinner.

Thankfully, Simon's men from the various search parties and the group he'd sent to Beaulieu had arrived that afternoon. He'd locked himself in Robert's study, trying to concentrate on Fouquet and his duty to his men, desperate to divert his attention away from the ache in his heart, and the sizzling rage in his gut. Now at least he had a face to the man who'd committed the foul deeds against Angelica. Fouquet. The man was truly a monster.

Needing information from his spies in Fouquet's château and to inform the men still out searching for Angelica to cease, he had spent his time writing communiqués, sending them out with his most trusted soldiers, refusing all the while to permit Jules or Armand to speak of Angelica.

He was calling in his men, even many of the ones on the seven warships waiting near Le Havre, just in case they would be needed. Fouquet was going to be unseated. *Dieu*, he was going to see to it.

There were few pleasures left for him, but the downfall of Fouquet was definitely going to be sweet.

Eager to drink himself into oblivion, Simon opted to retire to his chamber rather than dine below.

Flashes of childhood memories of Robert's multitude of sexual conquests filled Simon's intoxicated mind, their excited laughter echoing in his ears. Visions of Robert's hands on their heated bodies, Robert's hands on *his* angel, tore through his brain. Simon covered his face and let out a groan into his hands.

There was a rap at his door.

His hands fell away as he lifted his head from the bed. That had to be the servant with more wine. Any numbing substance would do.

He snatched open the door, startling Angelica. His heart jumped.

Beautiful green eyes stared back at him. He tried not to notice the outline of her sweet form in the gown she wore or how soft her hair looked. *Merde!* What was she trying to do to him? Where was the servant with the wine!

"What are you doing here?" he growled, and clenched his fists, fighting the urge to reach out and touch her.

"I must ask you a question."

She had a single question for him? He had a million for her.

"What question?" he demanded through gritted teeth.

"May I come in first?"

He hesitated a moment. Yet his wine-soaked mind didn't alert him to the folly of such an action strongly enough. He stepped aside and permitted her entrance.

"What do you want?"

"I want to ask you if it is your intention to tell Robert about us?"

"There is no us. You're married. There's nothing to tell."

He saw how his cold manner wounded her, and it cut him.

She nodded ruefully. "I wouldn't want to see Robert hurt. He has been so kind…"

"Your devotion to your husband is touching," he replied caustically. "Pray tell, Madame la Marquise, how is it that you came to know Robert?"

"Please don't call me Madame la Marquise."

"Why not? It's your title. It's unthinkable for a commoner to address a noble lady any other way."

"Stop it, Simon! I know you are hurt. I'm hurt too."

"You don't know what I feel."

"Yes, I do. Last night was the first time you were honest about your feelings."

He laughed without mirth and turned away. The wine dulled his mind. He couldn't think of a sharp reply to her statement.

She stepped around to face him. "Robert was my father's friend. He was the only one I had to turn to. Robert offered marriage to protect me. I had no other options. Can you not see that?"

"Protect you from your stepfather, *Nicolas Fouquet*."

"Yes," she said softly. "How long have you known?"

"I found out today. As I've told you before, social standing is *everything*. Robert's elevated birth and status are what shields you from Fouquet. I'm glad he helped you. He has succeeded where I have failed." His insides writhed. He'd lost her to a noble. Not just any noble, but Robert.

"I should have been the one to protect you. I should have been the one to marry you and free you from your stepfather's clutches. *Merde!*" He turned and raked both hands through his hair, then spun around to face her again. "I cannot even free myself from Fouquet's hold!" he bellowed.

She jumped.

Closing his eyes briefly, he let out a heavy sigh, trying to calm down. "Angelica, you are where you should be, in the upper circle of society. Please...for the love of God...leave this room." His voice was hoarse.

Her eyes filled with tears. "Simon—"

He held up a hand. "Don't speak. *Just leave.*"

"I wish none of this had happened. I wish we were still on the island..."

The mention of the island only conjured up bittersweet memories. His control snapped. With two quick steps, he grabbed her arm, surprising her.

Stalking to the door, he wrenched it open.

He strode briskly down the long corridor until he reached her chamber door. Throwing it open, he entered her room with her in tow. His body trembled. His heartache was so keen, it was eroding his sanity.

Knowing that Robert's chamber was the adjoining one, he released her and rasped, "Get to your marriage bed. Go to your highborn husband. There's nothing left to say between us."

"Yes, there is," she insisted softly. "I will live the rest of my life grateful for having known you, for you have taught my heart to love in a way it has never known. I do love you, Simon."

A violent jolt sliced through his turmoil, shaking the ground beneath his feet. He took an involuntary step back, unable to catch his breath. "Don't," he whispered.

He watched a single tear slip down one lovely cheek before she wiped it away. "There is no marriage bed. Robert and I have a *mariage de convenance*. There has been no other man. Only you."

Another catastrophic jolt, her words shattering the fragile hold he had on himself.

Grasping her arms, he whirled her around, pressed her against the door he didn't even remember closing, and crushed his mouth to hers. His kiss was demanding, heated, anguished, and desperate. He tasted tears and wasn't at all certain that they were hers alone.

He groaned. Softly, she whimpered.

His heart roared, *She's mine!*

But his mind and conscience balked.

Self-condemnation rang in his head, growing increasingly louder until he could stand it no longer, forcing him to tear his mouth, with a tortured groan, from the staggering allure of her soft lips. From his beloved.

He pressed his forehead against the door and closed his eyes, breathing hard. The denied fulfillment, not just physical but emotional as well, was excruciating.

He delivered a forceful blow to the door with his fist. "I cannot do this." He drew in a ragged breath, then looked into her eyes.

She looked as sorrowful and defeated as he felt. He cupped her cheeks. "Angelica...I want you. I love you. But you belong to *him*. You have married a man I could *never* betray."

A warm tear slipped down her cheek to his thumb. "I could never betray him either."

He drew her to him tightly. Burying his face in her chestnut hair, he allowed himself a final moment, one last time to hold her in his arms.

It took all the will he possessed to release her, breaking contact with her, with the woman he loved and wanted more than his next breath. Placing his shaky hands on her shoulders, he pulled her from the door, opened it, and walked out.

No less shaken, Angelica closed the door. A flood of tears rained down her face as she slid down the portal, sobbing into her hands.

In the shadows of the adjoining closet, Robert quietly turned and silently reentered his room.

CHAPTER TWENTY-SEVEN

Jules steadied the pail of water in his hands, positioning it just right. With a swift jerk of his wrists, he poured it precisely on Simon's sleeping form sprawled out on the bed, fully dressed.

Simon leaped to his feet, startled, coughing, yet still managing to grab hold of his sword and unsheathe it.

"What the—" Simon growled.

"Go ahead. Pierce me with that sword," Jules barked. "It'll be the only thing you'll have done, other than drink yourself to unconsciousness, in two days!"

Simon sank down onto the edge of his wet bed, his head balking at Jules's loud voice. He dropped his sword onto the floor with a clank and clutched his throbbing skull.

"*Merde*. Get out," he mumbled, his tongue feeling thick and heavy. Water droplets dripped from his hair.

"No, I will not. If you wish it so, you will have to remove me."

Simon slanted him a jaundiced look. "What the hell are you doing? Can you not leave me in peace?"

"Peace? Is that what this is? You're going to end up in an early grave. I'll not sit back and watch you do it. Your men need you, and Robert has been asking about you since yesterday. Wash. For God's sake, change your clothes, and then go see him. I'll not lie for you any longer!"

"*Dieu*, stop yelling." Each loud word knifed his aching brain.

"Go see Robert, Simon. He deserves better from you than this. Or is it your desire that he should learn you are in love with his wife?"

"Of course not!" He growled a little too intensely and was instantly punished with a sharp pain tearing through his head. "*Merde.*" He hissed out through clenched teeth. "I would do anything for him not to learn that," he said more softly. "He's far too happy being married to her. I'll not take that joy from him. I owe him everything." And everything was what he was giving Robert, for Angelica was everything to Simon.

Jules sighed. "I'll see that some food is brought here. Wash and dress quickly. Don't keep the man waiting any longer."

*****

An hour later, Simon stood outside Robert's chamber door.

Having bathed, eaten for the first time in days, and donned clean clothes, he didn't feel much better. His mind was dull. His headache was only slightly less torturous now than in the hour before.

Jules was right, though. Simon couldn't keep imbibing, and he couldn't remain in Robert's home either. He decided he was going to leave today. He didn't want Fouquet to return and find him here, nor could he stay under the same roof as Angelica and watch her be with Robert, the only real father he'd ever known.

It was surprising to learn that Robert hadn't consummated the marriage. He could make no sense of it. Robert had a healthy sexual appetite, never passing on an opportunity to bed any beauty. Much less a beautiful wife. Could his injury be more debilitating than Simon had assumed? Robert would never divulge something so unmanning. He was far too proud.

Whatever the reason for their arrangement, it was undeniable that Robert was happy about his marriage.

Intent on informing Robert of his departure, Simon took a fortifying breath and rapped on Robert's door.

When he entered the chamber, he was unprepared to see Robert lying in his large four-poster bed in the middle of the day. Thick velvet curtains covered the window, shutting out the sunlight. Even from across the room in the dim light, Robert looked gray and frail.

Stunned, Simon walked up to the bed.

"Simon." Robert gave him a feeble smile. "Come, sit with me awhile. I would very much enjoy the company. My wife has spent the last two days reading to me. I sent her away to allow her to rest."

Robert's complexion was even worse close up, and he looked and sounded weak. A disturbing sense of unease twisted in Simon's gut. Never had he seen this great commander look so depleted.

He sat down on the edge of the bed. It sagged with his weight. Robert stiffened and growled through clenched teeth.

"Robert?" Alarmed by the pain he'd just caused, Simon tried to stand back up, but Robert grabbed his wrist and squeezed. The excessive warmth of Robert's hand was startling.

"No, stay," Robert rasped with his eyes closed, taking a few moments before he opened them again.

"So what is this I hear about you depleting my supply of wine? Before you say anything, know that Jules has done his best to cover for you, but my servants are loyal to me."

Simon remained silent. His dull wits still grappled with the fever he felt coming from Robert's hand.

"Only one thing can drive a rational man to such limits," Robert said with a slight smile. "A woman, no? I remember the other night, at the theater, you wanted to discuss something with me. Would it be about this same female who is costing me my best wine?" he gently teased.

"That was nothing." Simon tried to dismiss the subject. Neither of them was in any condition to have this conversation. Besides, Simon was planning to take the secret of his feelings for Angelica to his grave.

"Judging by the copious amount of wine you have consumed over the last few days, I would say that this 'nothing' or rather this woman is very significant to you."

If Simon's mind hadn't been so sluggish, he would have skillfully changed the subject by now. "It doesn't matter. She's married, and she is devoted to her husband." He prayed his answer would appease Robert enough to end the subject. It was making him uneasy when he was already unsettled by Robert's condition.

Robert gave a slight nod. "Simon, I've enjoyed life, lived each moment to the fullest. I've known the thrill of battle as well as the pleasure of many ladies in and out of my bed. Battle and women can be equally exhilarating in different ways." He chuckled softly. "By example, I suppose that when it came to women, I never taught you restraint. When it came to a beautiful woman, I was never good at keeping it in my breeches, married or not, and yet, you show restraint with this woman."

Dieu, why did he want to talk about this? Could he know? Impossible. Angelica would never tell him. Could someone have overheard them?

Simon squeezed Robert's hand and looked into the eyes of the man he loved and respected above all others. "Robert, it is over. She belongs to another. I'll not interfere." Just saying the words was excruciating.

"You have fallen in love, Simon. Don't try to deny it. When I was your age, I believed it to be a dangerous thing. I believed it weakened a man, clouded his mind, and a leader must stay focused. Lust is much easier to deal with…" He smiled. "Now that I look back, I see what a fool I was. Love is rare. It should be treasured and not taken lightly, or for granted."

Simon didn't speak, not trusting his voice. Talking about this and seeing Robert in this state was too much to bear.

Robert tried to shift his body, then growled with agony. Simon's stomach clenched.

"*Merde*, this leg is killing me. Those fools who call themselves physicians cannot seem to do anything to improve the situation. I have chewed tobacco leaves, as they've suggested, smoked tobacco and opium too, but the pain persists."

Simon couldn't leave him now. Not in this condition. "You're as strong as an ox and as stubborn as a mule. This leg injury is nothing compared to other challenges you have encountered at sea, overcoming every one of them." He refused to entertain any thoughts of losing him.

Robert gave him a weary smile.

"Now then," Simon rose off the bed carefully. "I shall leave you to rest. Be quick about your recovery. Do not keep your lady waiting. You have a wife who cares for you."

*****

Three days later, Simon briskly made his way to Robert's chamber, fearful that something would happen to him in his absence from the room.

Though he didn't wish to have Angelica bear the suffering alone, he'd been forced to leave Robert's bedchamber when he was informed that more of his men had arrived and needed to speak to him. He had a small army assembled at hand and had received the most interesting information from his spies in Fouquet's household. But he'd done nothing more than digest it. Right now, his focus was on Robert.

Over the last few days, Robert's fever had wavered from alarmingly high to warm. His two physicians had bled him several times each day. The powerful emetics they'd administered purged his system but had done little to combat the fever.

Angelica stepped out of Robert's room.

"How is he?" Simon asked.

Angelica shook her head. Tears glistened in her eyes. She'd been strong for Robert, showing the extent of her worry only outside his chambers.

They were both overwhelmed with feelings of helplessness, drained emotionally and physically.

Seeing her look as lost as he felt, he wanted to pull her into his arms to comfort her, or perhaps to comfort himself, but he was afraid that if he touched her, he would succumb to total discomposure.

Disregarding the physicians' warnings to stay out of the sick room, they had remained with Robert, cooling his fevered brow with damp cloths, reading to him or just sitting near him. There were rare moments when he was not in so much pain, sleep would mercifully take hold.

It was killing him to watch this strong man diminish before his eyes.

"He isn't doing well at all today. I'm afraid..." Her words died. A few tears escaped down her cheek. He fought back the urge to break down as well. He was devoid of any words that would offer consolation.

She looked up at him and quickly wiped her tears away. "He is awake. He wishes to speak to you."

When Simon entered the room, Robert's two physicians, along with Jules and Armand, stood solemnly around the chamber's perimeter. A few servants softly wept in the far corner. As he approached Robert, Simon's stomach fisted. Robert had writhed in agony most of the night. Except for the dark circles under his sunken eyes, his complexion was colorless, despite his fever.

"Simon," he rasped. "Sit close to me. I must speak with you."

Carefully, Simon sat down on the bed, trying to cause as little movement as was possible. Despite his effort, Robert cried out. Simon closed his eyes, Robert's pain stabbing through him.

With surprising strength, Robert gripped Simon's hand and squeezed. He snapped his eyes open. The display of vigor was more in character with the man he knew.

"Simon, come closer."

Carefully, he leaned forward. Robert covered their clasped hands with his other and ordered the physicians, and servants to leave. Jules and Armand remained.

Once the door was closed, Robert began to speak. "Your men love you, Simon, and that is because of the man you are. They respect you and would do anything for you. I want you to swear to me that you will bring down Fouquet. He cannot be left unchecked any longer. Make him pay for all he has done. Do what you must. Promise me!"

Simon tried to swallow despite the lump in his throat. "I promise to do everything in my power to see it done."

"Angelica... You must swear to protect her."

"I swear."

Robert nodded and released one of his hands from Simon's, his strength waning. "I know, Simon." His voice was soft. "I know that Angelica is your love. No, don't say anything. Just listen well, my son, for that is exactly what you are to me. Only a true son would make the great sacrifice you were willing to make for me. You respected my marriage and therefore respected me. Now I ask this of you before your men as my witnesses: *marry her*. When I am gone, do not waste precious time mourning me. You deserve to be ennobled. You mustn't stop until you gain your Letters from the king. Swear to me you'll gain them and marry Angelica."

"Robert—"

"Swear to me you'll gain them and marry her. Swear it!"

"I swear," he whispered, not trusting his voice.

Robert seemed to relax. "I'm a lucky man. I've had a good and full life." His voice quavered. "You are the son I always wanted...and she is the beautiful, beloved wife I'd wished for in my later years. She has brought warm sunshine into my last days... I have told her that she has been an unexpected miracle in my life. I love you both... It is my wish that all I possess go to both of you. Sorbon will be yours upon my death, but you must have nobility to bear the title. Get it. Marry Angelica. I want my titles to pass to you, my son."

"Robert, please—" He couldn't take much more.

"You were my only family... You have made me proud... Raising you into the man you are today has given me a sense of purpose and fulfillment in my life... Simon...there is no limit to what a man can achieve except the limits he places on himself... You must believe it... Make...Louis listen to you..."

Simon swallowed hard, fighting to hold back the tears he could never shed before the man on the bed.

Something in the corner of the room caught his attention. He turned to see Angelica standing near Jules, looking no less stricken than he felt. He'd no idea when she'd entered the room but sensed that she'd heard much of what Robert had said.

Simon returned his attention to Robert, who was gazing up at the ceiling, a faint smile on his gray face, seemingly unaware of her presence in the room. "Simon...the pain is subsiding..."

Alarmed, Simon squeezed his hand, not ready to let him go. "Robert!"

"Ah, what...I wouldn't give...to see the day...our king ennobles you..." Robert drew in a ragged breath and closed his eyes as the air slowly expelled from his lungs. And his grip gently relaxed in Simon's hand.

"*Dieu...*" he moaned, overtaken with grief. He bent his head, pressing the back of Robert's hand against his forehead as a single tear slipped from his eye onto Robert's wrist.

Angelica rushed to Robert's side. "Robert!" She grabbed his arm.

Simon looked up at her. "He's gone."

Her composure finally broke. "No. *Robert...*" Her knees collapsed to the floor. She sobbed into the mattress, her arms folded around her head.

Simon rose to his feet on shaky limbs. Before he could offer her any comfort, there was a knock at the door. The two physicians walked in.

Simon cleared his throat. "The marquis is dead."

They eyed Angelica weeping on the floor. One physician spoke up. "The marquise is most distraught. I have some sleeping powders..."

"No!" Simon exclaimed. He'd seen their incompetence with Robert. He wasn't about to place Angelica in their hands. "The marquise is distraught because her husband is dead. That is not an illness. Get out. Now! Your duties here are concluded."

Thankfully, they didn't challenge him, and left.

Simon turned to Angelica. He didn't have the heart to pull her from the room. She had every right to remain as long as she needed. He, on the other hand, was choking with the need to flee the chamber. Robert was a man of strength. And he desired it in others. Robert had always demanded it from him. If Simon didn't leave soon, he would most assuredly be in much the same state as Angelica. And this he couldn't do.

He drew in a breath and let it out slowly. Devastated by his monumental loss, he left the room.

CHAPTER TWENTY-EIGHT

The day after Robert's funeral, Simon dressed and left the château while most were still abed.

Pink and purple streaked the horizon of the indigo sky, shadows slowly disappearing with the dawn. Breathing the early morning air into his lungs, his brain, he rode hard across Robert's lands, the horse's hooves pounding the earth beneath him.

Today he'd act upon the information gathered by his spies. After his morning ride, he was leaving for Beaulieu, and he'd ask Angelica to wait for his return on board one of his ships, where she'd be safe. Despite the marriage contract Fouquet had signed relinquishing all authority he had over her, Simon refused to trust a man as dishonorable as Fouquet.

The wind blew against his chest. He urged his horse faster, welcoming the wind's resistance, challenging it.

He planned to bribe or fight his way into Beaulieu and attain the ledgers his spies had advised were hidden there. If Fouquet was hiding them, then they were of importance. Before Simon spoke to Louis, he would need all the damning evidence he could gather against Fouquet.

Dismounting in front of the churchyard, he entered the stone church where the funeral had taken place the day before and walked over to where Robert had been laid to rest. A tall statue of the Holy Virgin and her child watched over the white marble crypt.

The day's first rays shone streams of light through the stained glass windows, creating patches of colors on the floor. A stillness enveloped Simon. Staring at the crypt, his throat tightened. It was difficult to believe Robert was gone.

Simon placed his hand on the hilt of the sword against his left hip and unsheathed the precious item. Robert's sword. A priceless possession bequeathed to him. It felt right in his hand. The very weapon he needed to take on a devil like Fouquet.

He'd fought many battles with Robert. And he was going to fight this one with him as well.

There was no doubt in Simon's mind that Louis had serious concerns about his Superintendent of Finance. Why else was the king having Colbert review Fouquet's ledgers when he'd always been given him carte blanche in how he ran the finances for France?

Those hidden ledgers were key. Every instinct told him so. But would they be enough for Louis to take the final step and act against the powerful Nicolas Fouquet?

Whatever it took, he'd live up to his three promises to Robert.

"I fight this final battle with your sword, Robert. Help me to be faithful to all your wishes."

Bring down Fouquet.

Win letters of nobility.

Marry the woman Simon loved.

A monumental task. He hoped that miracles did indeed come in threes.

*****

As Simon rode back to Château Névelon, a sense of unease settled in his bones. One he couldn't shake. One urging him to ride faster.

When the château came into sight, horror struck him through the heart. In the courtyard in front of Robert's home, his men were engaged in battle with a larger group of unknown combatants. The clank of metal swords clashing rang in his ears. This was not a band of thieves, but well-fed, well-trained men. Cold terror flooded his body.

His sole thought—*Angelica.*

He leaped off his mount and ran, sword in hand, battle-ready, the violent beat of his frantic heart pumping his blood hot and fast.

Wielding his weapon, he dropped each man who dared try to stop him from reaching Angelica inside.

Fighting his way into the château, he gave a final thrust into the belly of the man who'd placed himself between Simon and the stairs. The man dropped his sword to clutch the fatal wound. Blood soaked through his shirt and oozed through his fingers. With a look of horror and surprise in his eyes, he fell to his knees, then collapsed forward.

Bloodied bodies littered the floor of the grand entrance. He and his men were outnumbered two to one. The sounds of their losing battle, each and every cry, echoed in the high ceilings.

Simon raced up the stairs, desperate to locate Angelica.

Midway up, he got caught. With one assailant a few steps above him and another a few steps below, he could neither retreat nor advance. Simon struck a rhythm between the two attackers—thrust and parry back and forth, trying to fight them off.

The man above lunged at him with his blade. Simon jerked to the side. Grabbing his wrist, he yanked him down impaling him on the sword of Simon's other assailant. The man shrieked as the blade sliced through his chest. The downward momentum sent him crashing down onto his comrade, toppling both down the long staircase.

Simon took the rest of the stairs two at a time, shouting Angelica's name. The cries of those skewered still swirling around him.

He slammed open the door to Angelica's private chambers. His blood froze in his veins.

She sat tensely in a chair.

Eight men stood calmly in a row behind her.

Her green eyes were large, looking horrified to see him, almost as though she wanted him to run off rather than have him run in and aid her. As if that was a consideration for him. He'd lay down his life for her.

Nicolas Fouquet appeared quite relaxed, seated calmly to her right in a nearby chair, with a goblet of Robert's favorite burgundy in hand. He looked smug and not the least bit surprised to see him.

Simon squeezed the hilt of Robert's sword, his breathing hard and audible through his flared nostrils.

"Daughter, here he is now." Fouquet smiled. "And you said you knew nothing of his whereabouts...Tsk, tsk."

"*Fouquet*..." Simon's tone was low, full of barely restrained violence, his every muscle poised with murderous intent.

Fouquet lifted a brow. "That is *my lord* to you, beggar born." He lifted his goblet and took a drink. "Daughter, do tell, why do you allow this man in your home now that your husband is dead? Oh, don't think to deny it, my dear. Your mode of dress gives you away, not to mention that one of your servants was good enough to advise us of the marquis's death—before the lad met with an unfortunate accident." Fouquet smiled. Some of his men softly chuckled. He nodded toward Simon. "This man is no better than a barbarian and far beneath your station."

Simon snorted. "Some could say the same of you."

Fouquet lowered his cup from his thin lips, indignation narrowing his eyes. "I come from the most distinguished of parliamentary families," he said. "You, beggar born, are no more than the son of a fishmonger. Common scum."

"Enough!" Angelica rose to her feet. "You've no right to do what you've done here, forcing your way into my home! Having your men attack my guests. How dare you! Monsieur Boulenger and his men are welcome. You are not. Take these animals"—she gestured to the others in the room—"and *get out!*"

He could only imagine how difficult it was for her to have to face her stepfather after what he'd done to her. It churned his stomach with disgust each time Fouquet called her "daughter." Hearing it was far worse than enduring his insults.

Though Simon had always admired her courage, she was making things difficult for him. He wanted Fouquet's attention to remain solely on him, away from her. Yet there she stood, trying to protect him and his men.

Fouquet calmly placed his goblet down on the table that separated him from Angelica. Studying the state of the fingernails on his right hand, he lightly commanded, "Do sit down, Angelica." A man behind her reached out and yanked her down onto the chair by her hair. She cried out and clutched her head.

Simon stepped forward immediately but froze when he saw the gleam of a dagger resting horizontally against her throat—the man who had just forced her to sit, holding it there, perversely gleeful.

A fresh wave of terror slammed into his gut.

"Drop your weapon," Fouquet ordered Simon. His expression was as cold as the metal of Simon's blade.

"Don't do it," she whispered hoarsely, knowing as well as he how untrustworthy Fouquet was.

Though his entire being rioted against his inaction, Simon stood stock-still. He battled back blinding rage, knowing it would cloud his mind. He would be focused when dealing with devil before him.

Fouquet stood and strolled over to Angelica. Her hands were clenched into tight fists on her lap, and her soft breasts rose and fell rapidly with her quickened breaths. Simon could see her accelerated pulse on the side of her neck near the blade against her throat. *Oh, how you'll pay for terrorizing her this way, Fouquet…*

"My stepdaughter is not as intelligent as she is beautiful." Fouquet took the dagger from the man who held it against her delicate throat and squatted down beside her. Immediately, she looked away. Using the flat of the blade against her jaw, Fouquet turned her head to face him. "Drop your weapon, beggar born, or watch what I am capable of doing to her."

She flinched.

Simon pushed back his panic and schooled his features into a smug smile. "You won't do a thing to her. The king likes her too much. I've seen it with my own eyes. He'll not take kindly to you harming a beautiful woman."

Fouquet was unfazed. "I'll tell him you harmed her, beggar born. Who would believe your word over mine?"

Simon laughed mirthlessly. "You cannot be that arrogant. Why would anyone believe I would harm Robert's widow?"

Praying his confidence would unbalance Fouquet, he pushed him a little further. Simon lifted his arm, pointing Robert's bloodstained sword at Fouquet's chest.

The collective whisper of the eight swords being unsheathed filled the silence around him. He heard Angelica gasp. Unaffected, he remained poised and said, "Remove that dagger from her, or you'll meet with the end of this sword."

For an instant, Fouquet's eyes flashed shock. Then his arrogant expression returned. "You're outnumbered eight to one. You'll never succeed."

"The end of my blade is only a short distance from you. Willing to wager with your life?"

"You'll be dead too." Fouquet indicated his men.

"Yes, but I'll take you with me." His tone was firm, full of resolve. The smugness drained from Fouquet's face. *Fucking coward.* The man wouldn't last an hour in battle.

The slight color in Fouquet's cheeks was proof he'd further infuriated him. The man didn't like being bested, especially in front of an audience. All the better. He had more public humiliation in store for him. *Just wait... The key to success in any battle is knowing when the most opportune moment is to strike.*

"I came here for you, beggar born. Not her. Drop your sword, and I'll remove the dagger."

Simon was relieved to hear it. "Not acceptable. Remove the dagger, and then I'll drop my blade."

Fouquet held his gaze. Simon held his breath.

Fouquet tossed the dagger to its owner. Angelica leaped to her feet and placed a safe distance between herself, Fouquet, and the man with the knife. Thankfully, she knew her stepfather well; she didn't run to Simon or do anything to give away the extent of their involvement.

He knew what would happen to him the moment he dropped his sword. His taunts and blatant disrespect wouldn't go unpunished. Wishing to spare her from witnessing it, he said, "This is between you and me, Fouquet. Send her away."

"No," she protested.

"*Send her away.*" Simon could feel her gaze on him. He couldn't bring himself to look at her, unsure he had it in him to keep his feelings for her from entering his eyes. Fouquet would use it against them. He couldn't risk it.

His heart lurched when he realized Fouquet was studying her, suspicion growing in his dark eyes. Simon immediately dropped his sword. The clank it made as it hit the floor snapped Fouquet's attention back to him.

Two large men seized his arms and bent them behind his back.

"Stop that!" Angelica's voice rang out. "Release him!"

Simon shouted in Italian, "Any man here who understands me and is willing to join me will be paid three times what you've been promised."

"What is he saying?" Fouquet spun around, looking for comprehension on anyone's face.

Simon noted that not one man understood him. Without looking at Angelica, he continued. *"Don't do anything to indicate you understand, my love. Whatever happens, find as many of my men who are able to ride as you can and send them to your place of birth. Tell them to find the hidden ledgers there and to take them to the king."* Angelica remained silent.

"Enough!" Fouquet commanded and approached.

Standing before Simon, Fouquet folded his hands behind his back and lifted a brow. "Whatever tricks you think to try, rest assured, I am cleverer than you," he advised.

"Why are you here, Fouquet? What are you after? And who are these men?" He struggled, testing their hold on him.

"My friend, Neuchesne, you remember him, don't you, beggar born? He is the Commander-in-Chief of the King's Navy. You know, the same navy that deems you unfit to serve. Neuchesne was good enough to lend out these men to detain you and your motley crew until the king orders your arrest."

"Arrested for what?" Simon knew his questions were only delaying the inevitable beating coming to him.

"You've been stealing from France, keeping its profits for yourself. You've not paid your due to the Crown treasury for some time. Furthermore, you're a notorious rebel who has hidden behind the Marquis de Névelon for too long, inciting other rebels and amassing an army which you plan to use against our country and our king."

"You're mad!" Simon roared. "And you can never prove any of your lies."

"Oh, I can and I shall. Young Paul has told me everything that I want to know, and thanks to him, I have proof that you hold the prize of your latest capture, refusing to pay it to the Crown."

Cold dread sliced through him. "You have Paul?" Simon had sent for most of his men, but Paul and some of the others had yet to arrive. "He's young... What have you done to him?"

Fouquet shrugged. "He's old enough to sign a confession. Apparently, he is slower than your other men at getting away. Capturing him wasn't difficult, I'm told. And his threshold for pain is quite low..." He chuckled along with the other men.

"Dear God..." He heard Angelica's horrified whisper.

"Where is he? Is he—" Simon stopped abruptly, unable to say "dead." He pulled at his arms, sickened that Fouquet would prey upon innocent Paul.

"Easy." Fouquet smiled. "You'll see him soon enough. I am having a party in a few days, a celebration to end all celebrations at Château Vaux-le-Vicomte. The king will be there along with all the nobles. Everyone of significance. I plan to entertain them in a manner so lavish that they will rave about it for generations. At the end, I will present Louis with a prize. *You.*"

"Me?"

"Yes. We all know how sensitive Louis is about rebel uprisings, after the revolt eight years ago. He's in need of a new diversion. You will be a great help in giving him something to focus his attention on—by being arrested and tried. Just think of the recognition you'll finally receive after all these years. Albeit dubious."

"You are truly mad."

"No, just very clever. The king will be grateful that I was able to purge you from our midst, and he'll rethink his decision of abolishing the position of First Minister. I am, after all, the only viable candidate. Even the nobles would agree."

"You'll not get away with this," Angelica said. "You are not removing him from this house."

"Daughter, he's just a commoner with far too much impudence for his own good. It is time someone taught him some manners." Fouquet snapped his fingers.

A large man walked up to Simon and slammed his meaty fist into his midsection. The air rushed out of his lungs. He collapsed forward, fighting to draw a breath.

"No!" From the corner of his eye, he saw Angelica take a step toward him. Fouquet caught her arm.

Simon's head was pulled back by the hair. A fist slammed into his jaw, causing white sparks to flash in his eyes.

"Stop it!" Angelica cried.

"Daughter, I think you protest too much over this man." Fouquet turned to Simon. "Why is that, peasant dog? Why is she so concerned for your welfare?"

Simon tasted blood in his mouth. "I know this is a novelty to you, Fouquet, but she just might possess human decency."

"I don't think that's it. Look at her."

Simon refused.

"Look at her!" Fouquet commanded him. Simon forced his gaze to meet hers. He saw love as well as pain in her eyes before she looked away.

"Have you touched my stepdaughter, beggar born?"

"No." He hated to deny it, but there was no choice here.

"Has he touched you, daughter? Have you spread your legs for this worthless commoner?"

She looked straight into Fouquet's eyes and said firmly, "No."

Fouquet yanked her to him. "I don't believe you. You are a liar and a whore."

Simon kicked Fouquet's legs out from under him and spit out the blood in his mouth, landing it precisely on Fouquet's cheek. "*Never. Touch. Her. Again.*" Each word was growled in a low, venomous tone.

Fouquet wiped away the bloody spittle from his cheek with his lace handkerchief and rose. His nostrils flared. "Get him out of here!" he barked. They began to drag Simon out.

"No!" Angelica exclaimed. She turned to Fouquet. "You will pay for all you've done. I'll see to it! I have the king's ear."

Fouquet laughed in her face. "Foolish daughter, your peasant lover will be tried and executed, and the king will thank me for it. The beggar born is correct on one score. The king is interested in you and will be even more so once he learns of your husband's death. Go to him," he said, unconcerned, "and he will most assuredly order you to lift your skirts for his royal pleasure."

Angelica ran and stood in front of Simon as he and the two men escorting him reached the door of her chambers. "Where are you taking him?"

"He's going to Vaux-le-Vicomte with his men, where he will be turned over to the king and his private guard. Now, stand aside."

"Stand aside, please," Simon implored her. "Everything will be fine." He saw the reservation in her eyes. Silently, he willed her to listen. Reluctantly, she stepped away.

Fouquet walked around Angelica, keeping his gaze the entire time on Simon. The look in his eyes chilled Simon's blood. His heart thudded. Unsure what he was about to do.

Stopping behind her, Fouquet leaned in. She stiffened.

"Indeed, Angelica. Everything will be just fine. For me," he said in her ear, loud enough for Simon to hear. "If you're willing to spread your legs for an old man and this peasant, then you will accommodate me as well. Your lover will be dead soon enough, and when he is, we shall become *reacquainted* once more." He licked her earlobe with his wet tongue. Simon lunged at Fouquet, despite the men holding him. It took four men to wrestle him to the ground. He hit the floor with a hard, painful thud, Fouquet's laughter burning in his ears.

"Bring him," Fouquet ordered.

"What about the woman?" asked one of the men.

Fouquet stopped at the door. "Leave her. She's harmless. Besides, she'll be busy cleaning. It seems we spilled some blood on the stairs."

The men laughed.

"Daughter, I'll send a carriage for you to bring you to my party. I promise it will be most entertaining."

CHAPTER TWENTY-NINE

The door slammed shut.

It took a moment or two before Simon's eyes adjusted to the darkened cellar at Vaux-le-Vicomte. It was cool, dank, and empty. The château was so massive Fouquet hadn't filled all the cellar storage he had.

They'd kept him apart from his men the entire journey to Vaux and, upon arrival, had taken him directly to be imprisoned in the cellar. Alone.

The trip from Robert's home had taken nearly twice as long as it should have. Fouquet wasn't accustomed to hard travel. The frequent stops he demanded only lengthened the ordeal. But Simon was pleased. It would give his men longer to reach Beaulieu, retrieve the ledgers, and bring them to Louis. He could only pray that Angelica had found enough men to make the trip or that more of the men due to arrive from his ships had reached Névelon in time to aid her. Having to leave her with slain bodies gruesomely sprawled in the château's foyer and courtyard tortured him. Each time he looked at Fouquet strutting about only enraged him more. How he ached to drive Fouquet through with any impaling object he could obtain.

A faint noise in a dark corner of the cellar drew Simon's attention. It was then that he noticed him—a man lying on the stone floor. His breathing was fast. He shook violently.

Simon approached. The man's face was turned away, facing the wall. His clothing was stained with blood. Bruises and cuts marred all of his visible skin, including his trembling hands on his chest. His right eye, the only one Simon could see, was swollen almost completely shut. Simon lowered himself onto one knee and leaned closer to him.

The man turned and met Simon's gaze. Recognition slammed into Simon like a fist in the gut when he realized that this badly beaten soul was Paul.

Paul covered his barely recognizable face with his hand and turned away. "Dear God... No..." His voice was hoarse and no louder than a whisper.

"Paul." Simon placed his hand gently on the younger man's head. His hair was blood-encrusted.

"Ca-Captain...I'm sorry. Please forgive me." He quaked harder, anguished.

"Easy." Simon removed Paul's hand from his face and gave it a gentle squeeze. "There's nothing to apologize for. There is nothing to forgive."

"I was weak," he moaned, refusing to look at Simon. "You are here because I was weak. I wasn't strong like Thomas."

"Paul, look at me." Simon waited for him to collect himself enough to return his gaze. It was bad enough that he'd been tortured, but now he was torturing himself. "You are strong. You've survived a horrible ordeal."

"I tried to endure it... I really tried, Captain. B-but the pain..." Paul's breathing became more labored. "It was...unbearable."

"It's all right, Paul." Simon kept his tone calm, trying to soothe him even though his ire burned white-hot. This was yet another example of the inhumanity of Nicolas Fouquet. No doubt he derived twisted pleasure in confining Simon with Paul, wanting him to witness firsthand the brutality inflicted on the young man. "I don't seek the death of any of my men. A dead man is of no use to anyone. You have endured and survived, and that's what's important."

"I want to make you proud, Captain."

"You do." Simon's words seemed to surprise Paul.

After a moment Paul asked, "Wh-what do we do now?"

"Make Fouquet finally pay for all his sins." Simon could barely contain his wrath, his need for vengeance scorching his soul.

Paul fell silent once more, although his body still trembled. "My injuries, do you think...I may die?"

"No. I order you to banish that thought from your mind. Do you understand me?" Simon's voice was sharp and commanding, determined to cut through the haze in Paul's traumatized mind. Paul nodded, always eager to obey.

There wasn't much he could do to help with Paul's injuries at the moment. There was nothing in the cellar he could use to bathe his wounds.

"Why don't you rest now. You'll need your strength when we get out of here." Simon returned Paul's hand to his chest.

"I never kissed her, Captain."

"Who?"

"Suzette."

Simon smiled, glad to hear the young man speak of anything other than death and torture. "Oh? Why not?"

"Because she is too beautiful to touch."

"Really?" Simon said, still smiling. "What a shame you would deny the lady and yourself the pleasurable experience."

"Oh, I don't intend to deny anything any longer. When we return to the island, I intend to kiss her the moment I see her on the beach. I won't stop kissing her until she swears she'll be mine."

"Good. Hold on to that thought until we get out of this hell."

*****

Simon heard the keys in the door and jumped to his feet.

For nearly two days, he'd paced. He was ready to leap out of his skin. Thankfully, Paul had slept much of the time, except when their meager meals had arrived.

"Captain." Vilain smiled as he entered with three of Simon's men.

"*Merde!* Where the hell have you been? It's been days!" Simon exclaimed to his spy.

"Have you any idea how many guards and guests there are?" Vilain replied genially. "You have me playing the part of a servant here. I have been *serving.*" Vilain's smile grew into a wolfish grin as he added, "Today, I finally got the opportunity to serve the guards a *special* burgundy—in celebration of the king's imminent arrival, of course. They'll be asleep for hours. Raoul has released the others. I will show you to them. But first, these men have arrived with a message for you from the Marquise de Névelon."

Angelica? It was then Simon noticed that the three men with Vilain weren't among the men who had been captured.

"Captain." Anton stepped forward. "Our group along with a number of others arrived at Névelon shortly after you departed. The marquise wishes you to know that she and thirty men ride to Beaulieu. The rest are here, nearly two hundred in addition to the fifty already present."

"Angelica is going to Beaulieu?" Simon was stunned, knowing how she felt about her former home, the very place where such a horrific act had been done to her.

"Yes, Captain. She insisted. She rides with Commander Jules de Moutier and Commander Armand Rancourt. She said that with her in attendance, they will open the doors at Beaulieu without the need of physical force. The additional men have come here to aid you, Captain. Commander Moutier wants you to know that they are planning to take the ledgers from Beaulieu along with your ledgers straight to the king."

For a moment, Simon was speechless. He was moved by her act of bravery once more. Yet, putting herself before Louis, with the king's reputation and interest in her, gave Simon unease. Once again, she was aiding and protecting him. And overstepping him while he was trying to avenge her. He wanted to shake her. Could she not follow a single order he gave her? Yet, deep inside, he didn't want her to be any different. He wouldn't change a thing about her. "The king is not here yet, I take it?"

"No," Vilain answered. "He is expected very soon."

"And Fouquet?" Simon inquired.

"He struts about like a peacock. I believe he's out in the gardens with his guests."

Simon nodded. "Take Paul. Treat his wounds. I intend to pay a visit to Fouquet." The roar of fury was deafening inside him.

"Captain, Commander Moutier asked me to give you this." Anton held out Robert's sword and sheath.

Simon took them, elated by the thought that he would seek justice with Robert's sword after all. Fouquet was about to know some overdue agony firsthand.

*****

"Pellisson! The king will be here soon, and the ice sculptures are horrible," Fouquet barked in the Grand Salon. "Find someone to fix them." The music and gaiety drifting in from the gardens was amplified by the domed ceiling.

"The ice sculptures are the least of your worries today," Simon said, stepping into the room with Anton and two of his other men. At long last, he'd located the serpent that slithered out of the garden.

Fouquet turned around. His ire burned in his eyes. Simon knew that his guests were about. A scene was the last thing Fouquet wanted and the first thing on Simon's list of intentions.

"So, beggar born, you are out of your cage. We will have to remedy that."

Simon's eyes narrowed. Unsheathing Robert's sword, he squeezed the hilt. He was poised and ready, dying to unleash the hatred devouring him.

Fouquet gestured to Pellisson. Pellisson wasted no time summoning the guards. Fouquet looked smug, as though he refused to allow one so beneath him to intimidate him.

Within moments, men from the King's Navy filed in. Thirty in total. Simon recognized the faces as some of the same men who had brought him to Vaux-le-Vicomte.

Simon nodded to Anton. The man let out a quick whistle. Fifty of Simon's men entered from every entrance into the oval room.

The commotion drew some of the Aristos from the gardens into the great hall.

Clearly displeased by the scene before his prestigious guests, Fouquet forced a smile. "A small matter here, my lords and ladies…"

"On the contrary, it is no small matter to steal from your country and king." Simon shouted in order to reach as many ears as he could. More of the French aristocracy entered the Grand Salon.

Outraged, Fouquet barked, "Arrest this criminal. This is the Black Demon!"

The men from the King's Navy stepped forward and formed a circle around Fouquet, Simon, and his three men. The sound of his men's swords being unsheathed mixed with the gasps from the spectators.

Simon braced for battle, his blood rushing through his veins.

"Well, what are you waiting for?" Fouquet demanded.

"You didn't tell us before that this man is the Black Demon," one of them advised.

"What possible difference could that make?" Fouquet looked around, clearly made uneasy by the fact that the realm's upper class was watching.

"It makes all the difference," the man answered. "He has fought and won countless heroic battles for France. His valor is legend." The naval man then finally drew his sword and laid it against his own shoulder, bowing his head to Simon in respect.

Astonished, Simon watched as each man around the circle drew his sword and repeated the gesture to demonstrate esteem for an honored comrade, including the large, meaty man who had earlier delivered Simon blows to the stomach and jaw.

Simon's attention returned to Fouquet, who was ashen.

"Your time for raping the good people of France is over." Simon grabbed one of his men's swords and tossed it at Fouquet's feet. The clank the blade made as it hit the floor filled the silence in the Grand Salon with its ominous challenge. "If you are any kind of man, then show it. Pick up the sword, and show us what you're made of," Simon purposely goaded, knowing it would be difficult for Fouquet to resist, especially with his guests watching.

Fouquet looked around for an ally, but the men whom he'd hired had formed a circle around them, keeping everyone else at bay.

Fouquet's eyes returned to Simon and darkened to black. "You are a worthless peasant dog." He bent and picked up the sword. "And I'll put you in your place."

A smile curved Simon's lips. "We shall see."

Fouquet lunged with his sword.

Simon parried.

His men in the inner circle quickly moved back, allowing the two maximum room as they circled each other. Their blades clashed again. And then again.

Fouquet was on the offensive, while Simon blocked each thrust with little difficulty. It didn't take long for Simon to assess that Fouquet's skill was mediocre at best. Furthermore, Fouquet wasn't built for strength.

Let him tire himself, weaken his arm...

Each lunge from Fouquet incited Simon's ire more, making it almost impossible to fight Fouquet and his own violent urge to finish him here and now. His hunger for revenge was overwhelming. To hell with the king. Why should Louis get the pleasure of deciding Fouquet's fate? Fouquet had to die. Today. *Now!*

Fouquet began to falter, his thrusts no longer as zealous as before.

Simon's heart pumped wildly. His nostrils flared. He was mere moments away from terminating the man once and for all, freeing France from his clutches—avenging Angelica for all that Fouquet had stolen from her.

His body trembled with anticipation. Fouquet's death was near. He could almost taste sweet victory.

The moment was *now*.

Wielding all the strength in his arm, Simon delivered blow after powerful blow, forcing Fouquet back a little farther each time. He saw surprise, then terror in Fouquet's eyes, reveling in it with perverse pleasure.

The crowd parted and backed away as Simon continued his advance, ignoring the gasps and cries from the crowd. Yet they did nothing more as they watched with morbid fascination.

Fouquet backed into the wall. Simon delighted in the startled noise that escaped Fouquet's throat. One last hard downstroke knocked the sword from Fouquet's hand.

The Superintendent of Finance had barely the time to register what had happened when Simon pressed the sharp tip of Robert's sword to his vulnerable throat.

Fouquet's eyes grew large.

"What do you intend to do?" He swallowed, his body pressing against the unyielding wall as Simon's blade broke the skin's surface, causing a small, bloody rivulet to trickle down his neck.

Simon's breaths came hard and fast. "I plan to offer you the same mercy and decency that you have shown others." Simon lowered his voice and added, "Including your own stepdaughter. Prepare to go to hell."

"DROP THAT SWORD THIS INSTANT!" a voice boomed, startling Simon from his murderous rage. He searched out the commanding voice when suddenly the mass in the Grand Salon collectively bowed and curtsied low.

As their heads lowered, Simon saw their twenty-two-year-old king at the entrance. "Do *not* kill that man!" Louis demanded, vexed.

Simon's eyes rolled back over to Fouquet, who was smiling even with a blade to his skinny neck.

"You heard your king, beggar born. Kill me, and you die as well."

No. He wanted Fouquet to die so badly. By his hand. With Robert's sword. Simon's vision darkened.

All he had to do was press his sword little more...

"Simon, don't!" Angelica cried out. "Please!"

Her voice scrambled his malevolent thoughts. His head snapped up. She stood beside Louis, her eyes pleading silently with him.

Dieu, he'd sworn to bring Fouquet down, to make him pay, but to defy the king's order would take away his chance of gaining nobility and marrying Angelica, as he'd promised Robert. As his heart so wished to do. But what if Louis did nothing about the ledgers? What if Fouquet was left to continue, unchecked? Oh, how he wanted to drive the blade through him. To hear him howl in pain. To watch him *die*.

"Please, Simon, put down the sword!" Her plea, in her eyes and in her voice, yanked him from his thoughts once more. He returned his attention to Fouquet, who remained frozen against the wall, barely breathing as he keenly watched Simon's reaction.

Simon swallowed hard and took in a breath, trying desperately to quell his murderous desire. Slowly, he forced his sword arm down. His hand shook visibly.

Fouquet grinned, victorious. "You see, someone like you could never stop someone like me." He leaned closer and said in a low voice, "By the way, nothing in my life was sweeter than sinking into the innocent young flesh of my beautiful stepdaughter." Then he laughed.

The words sent a jolt of violent rage through Simon. He shoved Fouquet back against the wall and thrust. His sword sliced through the unsuspecting flesh of Fouquet's shoulder.

Fouquet recoiled, shocked, filling the room with a blood-curdling shriek. Simon leaned in, knowing that the tip of the sword pressed against bone. Fouquet continued to howl in agony. Simon stopped inches away from his ear.

"The pain you feel is small in comparison to the suffering you have imposed on others. And this is a small payment for what you did to her."

Simon yanked out his sword.

Fouquet slammed his palm against his wound, trying to contain the blood, still wailing between pants.

"Arrest him!" Louis bellowed out.

He stepped away from Fouquet, bracing for the moment the King's Musketeers would seize him.

Someone grabbed him and shoved him back.

Stupefied, he saw two musketeers seize Fouquet's arms.

"*Me?*" Fouquet shrieked, reeling between physical pain and shock.

He was dragged before the king. Louis stood erect and authoritative, in sharp contrast to the genial king everyone knew, who enjoyed merriment and women—all indulgences that were the prerogative of a young monarch. He looked regal dressed in a gold-and-white doublet and breeches with a white hat and large gold plume.

"What have I done?" Fouquet cried out.

Angelica watched her stepfather. For a man who had risen so fast and so high in power, who had never offered anyone in his path compassion or mercy, he'd never looked more pitiful.

Louis lifted his chin. "I placed my trust in you, the Superintendent of Finance," the king began. "I expect honesty from you at all times, and yet you steal from me and France!" A collective gasp swept the room.

Fouquet, who was being held by the two musketeers, paled further. Blood ran down his arm, yet arrogantly, he straightened his spine. "I've shown the highest integrity for my post, Sire!"

"*Do not lie to me!* Let it be known before all here that I have proof of your gross deceit! Your wickedness is scribed in these ledgers." Louis gestured beside him at Simon's ledgers held by Jules and Armand.

"Those are not mine!"

"I'm aware of that. They belong to Monsieur Boulenger."

"*Him?* Sire, he's no more than a scoundrel. Completely untrustworthy."

"Perhaps." Louis tilted his head. "But why, then, do his figures match the figures in your ledgers, *written by your hand?*"

Angelica heard Fouquet's gasp when he saw two musketeers holding the brown ledgers he'd hidden at Beaulieu. His dark eyes darted accusingly at her. The silent word, *You!* burned in his eyes.

She glared back at him with smug contempt. Walking into Beaulieu had been the most difficult thing she'd had to do. Memories had swamped her from the moment she stepped into the château. Painful memories lurked in every room—memories of her mother's sadness that had consumed her during her marriage to Fouquet, and of the night that had changed Angelica's life. The night of her rape. It was in the very library where the rape had occurred that Angelica found the hidden ledgers. She'd carried them out of Beaulieu herself, for they symbolized the future, leaving behind the ghosts of the past, ghosts that had haunted her for too long.

Seeing her stepfather's misdeeds finally catching up to him filled her with such satisfaction. She'd done it for Simon. Yet it aided her in ways she couldn't have imagined.

Her stepfather was finally going to pay for all he'd done.

"Be gone from my sight." Louis waved his hand. Immediately, the musketeers dragged Fouquet out pleading and bleeding. Fouquet's wife broke through the crowd. "No, Sire! Please!" she cried out. The pity Angelica felt for the woman who shared her age didn't touch Louis, for he didn't so much as look her way as two more musketeers stepped forward to escort her, weeping, from the room.

"Monsieur Boulenger, approach!" Louis commanded.

Simon hadn't moved from his spot since the musketeers grabbed Fouquet. The unprecedented events unfolding before him held him immobilized with astonishment, leaving him feeling almost light-headed.

Fouquet arrested. *At last.*

Simon forced his legs to move forward. Stopping before the king, he bowed low.

"Sire."

"Boulenger, have you trouble with your hearing?" Louis was still vexed.

Simon didn't require further explanation. He'd raised the king's ire by defying his command and piercing Fouquet with his sword. He might not have been arrested for it, but that didn't mean that he wouldn't still be punished. His fury had gotten the better of him. His act of public defiance had removed the likelihood of gaining nobility. Whatever punishment Louis would render, it couldn't be worse than having failed Robert and his beloved Angelica.

"No, Sire. I have trouble with the injustices imposed by the Finance Minister on the people of the realm who must have the resources to provide themselves with the basic necessities of life to give them the strength to serve you well."

"And you appoint yourself their defender? Their leader?"

"No, Sire. You alone are their leader. You are their king. And they wish your leadership, desperately."

Louis considered Simon's words for a moment. "I have heard their cries and am aware of their needs and wishes, Boulenger, just as I am aware of yours."

Simon looked up at the king, trying to gauge the meaning behind his words. He then turned to Angelica, whose smile was as brilliant as the sun on a summer's day.

Louis continued, "I've heard about you for some time now. The late Marquis de Névelon very much made it a point of taxing my ears with your many naval and financial successes for France. Back then, I left these matters in the hands of others, believing that they were attending to them justly. That has changed. Now then, Monsieur Boulenger, *kneel before me.*"

Simon's brows shot up. His heart sputtered. For a moment, he was frozen in disbelief. His gaze darted to Angelica. She continued to smile, unshed tears glistening in her eyes.

Simon looked down at Robert's sword still clutched firmly in his hand. He swallowed the lump of emotions that welled up in his throat as he thought of Robert. This was what he had wished for him always.

Slowly, Simon turned the sword until the tip touched the floor and used it to aid him down onto his knee, overwhelmed with the incredulity of the moment. The crowd erupted, equally surprised as they realized what the king was about to do.

"This man is Simon Boulenger, the Black Demon. For his outstanding service to his country, I recognize all of his past accomplishments, and I deem them to have been performed while he was the commodore of a distinct elite fleet of the French navy." A cheer filled the room, echoing in the domed ceiling. Simon turned and saw that a battalion of his men had filled the overcrowded salon. The men from the King's Navy joined in the jubilation. His gaze traveled to Angelica, who continued to beam at him, tears of joy welling forth.

Louis raised his hand, silencing the crowd. He continued, "Furthermore, all of his loyal men are to be recognized as part of the French navy and derive any and all benefits that it brings." Another burst of jubilation erupted. "Now then, Monsieur Colbert, if you will read the document."

Simon's heart lost a beat.

Colbert stepped forward. Stopping before Simon, he unrolled the parchment he held in his hands and began to read.

"By the grace and favor of the most serene, most mighty, and most Christian Majesty, King Louis XIV of France, His Majesty, whom we have praised above, affirms and announces publicly by these Letters Patent that Simon Boulenger, in consideration of his merits and valor, and as a reward for services rendered, be hereby ennobled."

Simon lowered his head and closed his eyes. Ennobled. The word that exalted him in society humbled him. He swallowed hard and gazed up at Angelica. Tears rained down her cheeks now, although she still wore a radiant smile on her lips.

"*...the said Simon Boulenger, and his children to be born in loyal marriage, shall hereby enjoy all honors, immunities, prerogatives, and pre-eminences which are customarily enjoyed by noble gentlemen of noble lines...*"

As Colbert continued to read, Simon wrestled to accept what his ears were telling him. *A dream come true.* One he'd had for so long and had all but given up on. He squeezed the hilt of Robert's sword.

His gaze returned to Angelica. Her lovely cheeks were moist with tears of joy, her smile now hidden behind her trembling fingertips. His chest tightened, so overcome with emotion he could barely register the words Colbert read. Colbert suddenly stopped. Another roar of enthusiastic approval reverberated in the Grand Salon.

Colbert stepped back.

Louis silenced the crowd once more with a lift of his hand.

"Monsieur, since Sorbon has been bequeathed to you by the late Marquis de Névelon, with these Letters Patent, I grant you the title, Comte de Sorbon."

Applause and cheers filled the air.

Louis stepped close to Simon and leaned forward to whisper in his ear. "I have convened a special emergency assembly. Fouquet shall be on trial for his life. I expect a favorable result. Without the proof of the ledgers your men and Madame la Marquise provided me last eve, I could not have proceeded as I have today. I'd grown weary waiting to be rid of this man, acquitting him of his self-enriching role. Therefore, it is with tremendous gratitude that I've bestowed upon you the honors you have received today. However, if you ever disobey me in public or private again... Need I say more to you, sir?"

"No, Sire."

"Good. Your men have delivered your last capture of silver. Very impressive."

"Thank you, Sire."

"Now, I understand that the late Marquis de Névelon's wishes were that you marry Madame la Marquise without delay, at which point both lady and Névelon will be yours. Clearly, he loved you like a son."

"And I loved him as greatly as any son could love a father, Sire."

"Then, we shall respect his dying wishes. Thus, upstairs in chapel, at my request, Père Martineau awaits you and your lady. Valid upon marriage, you will be the next Marquis de Névelon. However, out of respect for the memory of the late commodore, you shall marry discreetly, if your lady is willing." Louis gave Angelica a leering assessment. "She's quite magnificent. I could be persuaded into further generosities if you are willing to share."

"She is absolutely not negotiable, Sire." Simon held his wrath in check, but his voice was firm, his words unequivocal.

Louis lifted a brow. "Really? Pity." He straightened and stood tall and regal. "Monsieur le Comte, rise!" he commanded for all to hear.

Applause thundered in the salon as Simon rose to his feet.

Angelica rushed forward and threw her arms around him, burying her face into his shoulder. Simon looked up at Louis. The king rolled his eyes. With an impatient wave of his hand, he dismissed Angelica's actions and walked away.

Simon wrapped his arms around her and pressed his cheek against her soft hair. Closing his eyes, he inhaled her soft fragrance. The joy of holding her once more swelled his heart until he thought it would burst.

She looked up at him; her green eyes shone tenderly. "I'm so happy for you, Simon."

"None of this could have been possible without you. You make my dreams complete. Angelica, will you marry me?"

She lowered her head and shook it slowly. Simon's heart lurched. She looked up again, this time with a radiant smile. "I have loved you for so long. I thought you would never ask. Yes! Yes, I will marry you."

Simon grinned like a fool in love. He knew it and didn't mind a whit. "This is a day of miracles." He squeezed her tightly.

*****

Forced to remain at Vaux-le-Vicomte for the night, Simon swept into the bedchamber with his wife in his arms. Two servants were turning down the bed. He was instantly vexed. After all these hours, they were still not alone.

Married in the chapel at Vaux-le-Vicomte with the priest, Jules, Armand, and two other men from Simon's crew as witness, they'd been requested to join the king and the rest of the aristocracy present immediately following the ceremony. The party at Vaux-le-Vicomte had continued without their host and hostess.

Simon had remained at Angelica's side throughout the evening's festivities, wary of the king's amorous glances toward her. He couldn't wait to get her out of Louis's sight and into his arms. He'd barely tasted the endless courses, four different soups, pheasants, quails, partridges, salads, pastries with crystallized fruits and preserves. He drank little of the wine that generously flowed.

When finally the meal had ended, Simon managed to have them excused from attending the performance of Molière's comedy, *Les Fâcheux*, in the gardens.

Angelica gave no indication she noticed the two servants in the bedchamber. The moment her feet touched the ground, she had her arms around him, pressing her hot mouth to his throat, softly kissing his neck. Stifling a groan, he heard the servants' soft snickers.

"That will be all," he called out to them, startling Angelica. Her cheeks warmed to pink as she tried to step away from him. He tightened his arm, keeping her against him.

"Yes, my lord," smiled the younger female servant as they both left, giggling.

Angelica smiled up at him lovingly. "Simon Boulenger, Marquis de Névelon, Comte de Sorbon. It sounds wonderful, but I care more for your other newly acquired title. *Husband*."

He returned her smile. "And I, my beloved wife, care to consummate this marriage without further delay." His voice was low and provocative.

Her hands were instantly at his waist, fumbling with the closures on his breeches. "Then hurry."

He stilled her hands by covering them with one warm palm. "Let me," he gently urged and began to undress, removing his doublet and linen shirt, tossing them carelessly to the floor.

He had her rapt attention as he undid his breeches. Her breathing deliciously quickened.

Tilting his head to one side, he studied her, the smallest smile touching upon his mouth. He stopped undressing, cupped her face, and kissed her, savoring the texture and taste of her mouth. It wasn't all that long ago that he believed he'd never know her kiss again.

"Please, Simon," she said, breathless. "I don't want to wait any longer." She stepped back. Her gorgeous eyes were on his erection straining out of his opened breeches, and his sac, heavy with come. She fisted the skirt of her gown with both hands and began pulling up at the voluminous material.

Simon grasped her wrists, stilling her. She looked adorably puzzled and wildly aroused. "No. Not like that. I want to feel you completely naked against me," he managed to say despite his thundering heart.

She looked stricken. "But that will take too long."

"We have the rest of our lives, *chérie*. Turn around," he coaxed while trying to maintain a grip on his own feral need. He trailed kisses along her neck and shoulder, enjoying the soft, satiny skin he'd missed so much, stripping off article after article until he had her completely unclothed.

Then he swept her up in his arms and carried her over to the generous bed. Placing her in the center, he sat on the edge of the mattress and pulled off his boots.

She was up on her knees in an instant, raining kisses on his shoulders and along his neck. He closed his eyes, delighting in her heated enthusiasm, reacquainting himself with her eager impatience in bed that he found both compelling and contagious.

Yanking the remainder of his clothing off at an accelerated rate, he twisted around and pressed her down, kissing her in the frenzied manner she desired, banishing all thoughts of moderation from his mind. They could slow down when they were old and gray. For now, he would let her dictate the pace.

Arching hard against him, she urged him inside her. He needed no further prompting, driving home with one easy thrust.

Home.

She sobbed with pleasure. He groaned out his.

Controlling his thrusts, he plunged as deep and as hard as she wanted, filling her repeatedly, her juices bathing his cock. Between heated kisses and caresses, they exchanged whispers and words of love.

She wrapped her legs tightly around him. "Stay inside me," she panted against his mouth. Her words sent a rush of raw heat shuddering through him. He'd never spent himself inside a woman. And he couldn't wait to spend himself inside his beautiful wife.

His moonlight angel.

He reveled in the feel of her. He reveled in *her* in his arms. And in their love and untamable passion.

She cried out as she climaxed, her inner muscles contracting along his plunging length. His heart hammering, he drove into her with a final heavy thrust, and tossed his head back, roaring her name, gripped by the paralyzing pleasure flooding through him. Pouring everything he had in her.

His breathing coming in hard pants, he closed his eyes and rested his forehead on hers. If he could have smiled, he would have. He had a lifetime ahead of more of the same. Was there a man on this earth more fortunate than he?

He gazed down at her. Pink cheeks, heavy lids, freshly sated, she looked so beautiful.

Still semi-hard inside her, Simon rolled over onto his back, taking Angelica with him. He pulled her down for a kiss, enjoying the simple pleasure of having her sweet mouth against his own.

"It's been so long, Simon." A soft smile played on her lips.

"Too long, *mon ange.*"

"I want to go home. Back to the island," she said. Her words filled him with a sense of contentment as images of their future together flitted through his mind.

He was glad to hear it. He had no intention of remaining in France with Louis's carnal interest keenly focused on her. He planned to take the responsibility that came with his title seriously, but not to Angelica's detriment. Making arrangements to meet his obligations would be addressed later. He didn't want to think about it now. At the moment, he just wanted to hold his wife.

"I want Fouquet's wife to keep the remainder of my estate that wasn't forwarded to her by her husband. She'll need it when he's gone. I won't litigate over it. It was part of my old life. I have a new life with you."

He caressed her back. "Very well. If that is what you wish."

"It is." She pressed her lush mouth to his. What began as a tender kiss quickly turned heated and hungry, his cock stiffening inside her. "Love me, Simon," she murmured.

"I do, *mon ange*." He rolled them over, pinning her to the bed. "I always will."

EPILOGUE

Marguerite Island

France was at peace.

Fouquet was on trial.

And life on the island was very good.

On July 1, 1662, Angelica gave birth to a son, with Simon by her side. He refused to leave until he was certain both his wife and child were not in any danger. They named their son Robert Étienne.

The island celebrated.

Domenico, Jules, and Armand couldn't have been happier for the marquis and marquise, deriving great amusement from the changes in their friend as fatherhood took root. Simon was known to disappear for hours at a time only to be discovered in the nursery. Or as the baby grew, much to Assunta's and Marta's protestations, he was to be found playing with six-month-old Robert, who now had his mother's eyes and his father's hair, on a blanket near their favorite spot at the waterfalls. He would regale his son with fascinating tales about a brave commodore named Robert d'Arles and the adventures that they had shared.

Gabriella was thrilled that Angelica had a son who was a year younger than her own son, Matteo. The parents felt certain that the three children, Isabelle de Moutier—Jules and Sabine's little girl— Matteo, and Robert were destined to become the best of friends. Of course, since Isabelle was slightly older and had her mother's will, joked Jules, she would no doubt set the boys straight should they go astray.

Good fortune shone on the inhabitants of the island.

While businesses prospered, love bloomed for Armand and Marie Jaures.

True to his word, Paul did indeed kiss Suzette the moment he saw her on the beach upon his return and has not stopped demonstrating his well-received affection since.

Angelica's life fell into a blissful pattern, teaching with Gabriella each morning in the new two-room schoolhouse, afternoons with her son, joyful evenings with her small family, and nights of passion in her husband's arms.

*****

Late one night while Angelica slept, Simon watched her with a contented smile. Slowly rising from the bed, taking care not to wake her, he donned his black dressing gown and went to Robert's nursery.

He found the baby awake but not crying. Upon seeing his father peering down at him, Robert squealed with delight. Simon grinned and reached down, slipping his finger in his son's chubby hand. The baby squeezed and gurgled happily.

"Robert, have I told you about angels? No? Well then, listen well, my son." Simon bent down and picked up his little boy, cradling him in his arms.

"Should you happen to find one, and I pray that you do, hold on to her tightly and never let her go, for you can never imagine the blessings that she will bring to your life." Robert pulled the tip of Simon's finger into his mouth and sucked contently. Simon, still smiling, walked over to the window, holding his tiny boy. "She may not be easy to find, Robert. She may be hiding, but look in the moonlight, when the moon is at its fullest. She may appear then… Seek her out." He kissed the baby's head. "The unlimited happiness that she will bring you is most definitely worth the effort."

AUTHOR'S NOTE

King Louis did not get his way.

Nicolas Fouquet was never executed.

Louis had Fouquet arrested for embezzlement of Crown funds on his 23rd birthday (September 5, 1661), perhaps as a present to himself, and not three weeks earlier at Fouquet's elaborate party at Vaux-le-Vicomte (August 17, 1661), as indicated in this story. Louis had wanted to arrest Fouquet at the party, but his mother, Anne of Austria, convinced him to wait. Six thousand guests were in attendance, all of whom were served on gold service and given gifts of jewelry, silks, and horses.

Fouquet, although shrewd in finance, completely misunderstood and misjudged his king. Believing he was indispensable, blinded by his ambition to step into Mazarin's shoes after his death, he never saw his doom on the horizon.

After Mazarin's death, Louis asked Jean-Baptiste Colbert, who had worked for Cardinal Mazarin, to examine Fouquet's accounting. Colbert, who disliked Fouquet, took great pleasure in pointing out the malpractices and falsifications. (Perhaps he also had a little help from a privateer fleet commander and his green-eyed moonlight angel *smiles*.)

Fouquet's trial was one of the most sensational in French history. The trial process lasted three years. In his defense, Fouquet tried to blame Mazarin, stating that he'd been fully aware of and often dictated Fouquet's practices, and that Mazarin also made no distinction between the Crown Treasury and his personal fortune.

This incensed Louis. He didn't want the memory of his beloved godfather maligned or Mazarin's name connected with any of Fouquet's misdeeds.

As the trial dragged on, people became more divided in their opinions of Fouquet. Louis made it no secret that he was willing to accept the death penalty. However, he didn't press this because he was concerned it would make him look fearful of Fouquet to his court.

In the end, on December 20, 1664, the assembly sentenced Fouquet to perpetual exile. Louis intervened and changed the sentence to *perpetual imprisonment*, stating that he wasn't about to let a man who knew so many state secrets go free.

Fouquet was imprisoned in a fortress in Pignerolo on the borders of Piedmont. He remained there for sixteen years until his death in 1680. It wasn't until the last years of Fouquet's life that Louis allowed him visitors.

There are some who believe that Nicolas Fouquet was the actual *"Man in the Iron Mask."* There's enough written about Fouquet and his inner circle—from blackmail to secret societies—to keep conspiracy buffs reeling with all the intrigue.

Simon Boulenger's accomplishments in this book were, in actual fact, the true achievements of two important men in French naval history, Jean Bart and Réné DuGuay-Trouin. Both these men were born commoners and commanded fleets sailing as privateers for France. As a result of their remarkable naval achievements, both men earned themselves officers' commissions in the French navy. Bart was ennobled by Louis and made commodore. DuGuay-Trouin eventually made his way from commander of one of King Louis XIV's rented warships (sailing as a privateer) to vice-admiral in the King's Navy.

All names and places mentioned in this book were born in this author's imagination, except King Louis XIV, Nicolas Fouquet, Louise Fourché (Fouquet's first wife—named here as Angelica's mother), Marie-Madeleine de Castille de Villemareuil (Fouquet's second wife), Paul Pellisson (who remained loyal to Fouquet and was imprisoned in the Bastille for four years), Cardinal Mazarin (the son of a Sicilian fisherman, who rose in power and ruled France for

Louis until he died), Jean-Baptiste Colbert, Fontainebleau Palace, Petit Bourbon, Palais-Royale, and Vaux-le-Vicomte.

The Franco-Spanish war ended with the Treaty of Pyrenees on November 7, 1659. I extended this war by just over a year, bringing the event closer to the date of Cardinal Mazarin's death in early 1661.

Fouquet's controversial grand château, Vaux-le-Vicomte, took eighteen thousand men and a constant supply of funds to complete, and still stands in all of its magnificence southeast of Paris, near Melun.

In fact, it was Vaux-le-Vicomte that inspired Louis to build Versailles.

GLOSSARY

Chère—*Dear one. (French* endearment for a woman, *cher* for a man).

Chérie—Darling or cherished one. (French endearment for a woman, *chéri* for a man).

Comte—Count. (French)

Comtesse—Countess. (French)

Démon Noir—Black Demon (French)

Dieu—*God.* (French)

Dieu vous garde—*God keep you.* (French)

Dominum Deum Nostrum—Our Lord God. (Latin)

Estrella Blanca (la)—*The White Star.* (Spanish)

Hôtel/Château—The upper class and the wealthy bourgeois (middle class) often had a mansion in Paris (*hôtel*) in addition to their palatial country estates (*château*). (French)

In nomine Patris, et Filii, et Spiritus Sancti—In the name of the Father, the Son and the Holy Spirit. (Latin)

Madre—Mother—The title for the Mother Superior of a convent. (Italian)

Ma belle—*My beauty. (French endearment* for a woman)

Mariage de convenance—Marriage of convenience. (French)

Merde—*Shit.* (French)

Mon ange—*My angel. (French endearment)*

Vaux-le-Vicomte—Nicolas Fouquet's infamous country palatial home. Literally translated, "Like the Viscount." It's certainly a home befitting a man of influence.

DEDICATION

Whenever I write a book, I do a lot of research. Pulling a reader into 17th century France, getting every fact and historical detail as accurate as possible is a great labor of love. However, with UNDONE my research went beyond the norm, because in this book my heroine is a rape survivor.

On a warm summer night, when I was twenty-one, I was walking back to my hotel along a very crowded street in San Remo, Italy. I got separated from my friends in the massive crowd, and unfortunately I crossed paths with the wrong guy. One who didn't take "no" for an answer. (By the way, I speak Italian fluently, and "no" is said and spelled the same way in both English and Italian, so there was no miscommunication here). I didn't know him. Had never seen him before he approached me that night. To this day, I don't know why he picked me out of the crowd. He offered me a ride. I refused him. He then grabbed hold of me and tried to drag me into his car. Not a soul walking past helped the *straniera* (foreigner—me) out. Though he was about three to five years older, bigger and stronger, I fought and got away. I was lucky. I suffered only a few bruises. And the scare of my life. There are others who have found themselves in the crosshairs of a predator and have not been as fortunate.

It is no coincidence that UNDONE begins in the Republic of Genoa, where modern day San Remo is located.

Dearest readers, I dedicate this book to all those who have survived rape. You are true heroines/heroes in this author's eyes. Like Angelica, you have an inner strength and resilience no words can describe.

FIERY TALES SERIES

Anthologies
AWAKENED BY A KISS
THE PRINCESS IN HIS BED

Full-length novels
A MIDNIGHT DANCE
UNDONE

Holiday Novella
THE DUKE'S MATCH GIRL

Praise for the Fiery Tales:

"Wickedly passionate . . . [A] sensual treat!"
— Sylvia Day, #1 *New York Times* Bestselling author

"Hot enough to warm the coldest winter night."
— Publishers Weekly

"Sure to delight!"
— Jennifer Ashley, *New York Times* Bestselling author

Thank you for reading UNDONE! If you enjoyed it and would like to know when the next release is out, sign up for my **99¢ New Release Alert** newsletter at www.LilaDiPasqua.com. Also, connect with me on Facebook, Twitter and Goodreads!

Lila DiPasqua is a USA TODAY bestselling author of historical romance with heat. She's been published by Penguin/Berkley, as well as having self-published works. She lives with her husband, three children and two rescue dogs and is a firm believer in the happily-ever-after.

Made in the USA
Charleston, SC
16 July 2015